Lipstick
in
Afghanistan

Lipstick in Afghanistan

ROBERTA GATELY

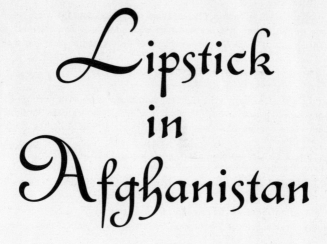

G

GALLERY BOOKS
New York   London   Toronto   Sydney

Gallery Books
A Division of Simon & Schuster, Inc.
1230 Avenue of the Americas
New York, NY 10020

First Gallery Books trade paperback edition November 2010

GALLERY BOOKS and colophon are trademarks of Simon & Schuster, Inc.

For information about special discounts for bulk purchases, please contact Simon & Schuster Special Sales at 1-866-506-1949 or business@simonandschuster.com.

The Simon & Schuster Speakers Bureau can bring authors to your live event. For more information or to book an event contact the Simon & Schuster Speakers Bureau at 1-866-248-3049 or visit our website at www.simonspeakers.com.

Designed by Akasha Archer

Manufactured in the United States of America

1   3   5   7   9   10   8   6   4   2

Library of Congress Cataloging-in-Publication Data

Gately, Roberta.
Lipstick in Afghanistan / Roberta Gately.
p. cm.
1. Nurses—Fiction. 2. Afghan War, 2001—Fiction.
3. Americans—Afghanistan—Fiction. I. Title.
PS3607.A78836L57 2010
813'.6—dc22
2010006735

ISBN 978-1-4391-9138-5
ISBN 978-1-4391-9144-6 (ebook)

In loving memory of my parents, Bob and Mary Gately,
who taught me to dream.

Acknowledgments

Writing a book is a solitary process, but getting it published and into readers' hands is anything but, and I am thankful for the kind assistance of so many.

Infinite gratitude goes first to my agents, Judy Hansen who believed in this project from the start, and to Cynthia Manson who knew just what it needed. They are savvy, insightful, wise women and I count my blessings that they are my agents.

To the incredible team at Simon & Schuster, including Louise Burke, Abby Zidle, Danielle Poiesz, Lisa Litwack, Carole Schwindeller, and Aja Pollock, my eternal gratitude for your enthusiasm, support, and patience for this first-time novelist.

I am indebted to my mentor, Mark Fritz, as well as to my early editorial support, Anna Lvovsky, Steve Saffel, and Ann Pinheiro. To Lauren Kuczala, I can't imagine finishing this up without your keen eye and fervent eraser. A thousand thank-yous.

For my family, Susan Richard, Marianne Pierson, Jim Gately, and my beloved aunt, Doris Barron, who always believed, my thanks. To my countless friends and extended family—your support, understanding, humor, and love have been invaluable. Thank you all.

To the Nursing Department at Boston Medical Center (formerly the Boston City Hospital), and especially Maureen Hilchey-Masters, my gratitude for your support and understanding.

To the U.S. soldiers stationed in Bamiyan in 2002, members of the ODA-963, C-2-19th SFGA and the 345th Psychological Operations Unit, especially Adam Perry, Frank "Doc" Plisko, and Darren

Davila, my thanks for your friendship, your food, your laughter, and your soap.

And finally, to the 42 million refugees who struggle each day to survive, and the selfless aid workers who dedicate themselves to rescuing them, my endless admiration and gratitude for teaching me what really matters in life.

Afghanistan, 2002

"Do you hear it?" The voice was almost a whisper.

Elsa held her breath, and then she heard it too, a faint rustling of footsteps over twigs and leaves. Out of the corner of her eye, she glimpsed several shadowy figures darting through the trees, and when she turned, she saw a glint of sunlight reflecting off the barrel of an assault rifle.

There was no denying it—the Taliban had found them.

Oh, Jesus! she thought. *We'll never escape.*

Elsa knew the Taliban's ruthless hatred; the death and destruction they wrought was undeniable.

Seized by a sickening wave of fear, she wanted to cry or throw up, but there was no time. She tried to catch Parween's eye, but her friend was looking back, intent on finding the source of the sound.

"Run!" someone shouted, and suddenly, the chase was on.

But not for Elsa. Her legs were tangled in the fabric of her all-enveloping *burqa*. She struggled to free herself and finally threw off the covering and ran, her plastic shoes barely touching the ground. She'd never run so fast before, and her heart pounded as she swallowed air in great gulps.

She heard heavy panting.

Was it her own?

Her chest tightened, and a scream rose in her throat, but there was no sound. She couldn't think clearly. She knew only that she didn't want to die there in Afghanistan.

Oh, God, let us make it, she prayed.

Just ahead was a small house, and though unprotected by the walls that surrounded typical Afghani homes, it was their only hope.

If they could reach it in time. But the distance seemed too great and her sprint too slow. Still, she pushed on, her arms pumping wildly.

After what seemed an eternity, Elsa and the others reached the house. She turned and stopped dead in her tracks. A growing sense of panic washed over her.

Parween.

Her eyes swept the horizon, but there was no sign of her friend.

Elsa's throat burned as she tried to catch her breath, and she felt as though her heart would explode in her chest.

She buried her face in her hands.

How had it all gone so wrong? What were they doing here?

What was *she* doing here?

A nurse from Boston in *fucking Afghanistan,* for Christ's sake.

Hot tears stung her eyes. With trembling hands, she tried to wipe them away.

"Oh, God," she whispered. "Where *are* you, Parween?"

PART I

Elsa

Boston, 1994

It was the hopelessness in their eyes that held sixteen-year-old Elsa's attention. The black and white images of starving, big-bellied babies gripped her with horror, but one photo in particular haunted her—a close-up of a skeletal mother holding a shriveled baby while two other gaunt children clung to her frail arms. It felt like they were looking right at Elsa.

She read the caption, which explained that they were refugees who'd escaped a quick death at the hands of rebel tribesmen only to be trapped in a life of misery. They weren't just starving, the story said, they were dying. All four suffered from malaria and dysentery, and without help they would likely be dead in one month's time.

Elsa flipped back to the cover to check the magazine's issue date and her eyes widened.

The magazine was *two* months old.

A strange feeling—a kind of numbness—came over her, and she sat on the floor, her knees bent up, supporting the magazine. She turned the page and held her breath as she read.

> *As the tragedy in Rwanda deepens and the death toll continues to rise, world leaders seem paralyzed, unable to act. It is only the valiant efforts of a few doctors and nurses that are making a difference,*

snatching thousands from death's certain grip. But more relief work-
ers are needed and the UN has issued an urgent plea for help.

Elsa read the words again and then turned the page.

A large picture revealed hundreds of women and children standing in what seemed to be an endless line, waiting for their food
rations. The women, and even the small children, seemed lifeless as
they waited their turn. None of them looked at the camera. It was a
photograph of utter despair.

Elsa sighed and ran her fingers over the picture. She turned to
the next page and found a series of photos, all of corpses—endless
rows of babies and children, entire families, lying in the road or in
fields, clinging to one another in death. Her hand flew to her mouth,
and she closed her eyes.

But when she opened them, the bodies were still there. She
turned back to the first page and read the story again. She lingered
over that first image, the one of the dying mother and her young
children. She wondered where they were, if they'd died or somehow
been rescued. It was hard to believe that people lived like this.

How could she ever complain about her own life again?

She paused at a shiny picture of a nurse cradling a baby. The
nurse seemed to be crying. The caption explained that the baby was
dead and the nurse was looking for his mother.

A nurse, she thought, *doing something that matters.*

Elsa closed the magazine, breathing deeply to calm herself, before
she glanced at her watch. *Four o'clock! Jeez, where did the time go?* She
quickly gathered her remaining books onto her cart and hurried to
the library's front desk.

"Sorry, Miss James, I lost track of time." She needed this job; she
couldn't afford to be fired. "I'll finish these tomorrow."

The old librarian, fidgeting with her hearing aid, smiled up at
Elsa. "What, dear?"

"I'll finish tomorrow," Elsa almost shouted. "And this," she said,
holding out the magazine, "can I keep it? It's two months old."

"You want the magazine?" Miss James confirmed. "That's fine,
dear."

Elsa trudged home along the narrow, crowded streets, the magazine stuffed into her backpack. If she hurried, her mother could still get to work on time. Rushing into the house, she pulled the magazine from her bag and showed the pictures to her mother.

"Oh God, Elsa, why do you look at that stuff? Jesus, it's awful," her mother said, slipping her arms into her old coat.

"But, Mom, I was thinking, I could be a nurse, maybe help someday."

"That's just a wish, don't ya think? Nothin' good ever came from wishing for things you can't have. Look around, honey. We're in the crummiest three-decker in the crummiest part of Dorchester. And with Diana getting sicker, I don't see things getting any better."

"But if we don't wish for more or try for more, things will never change."

"I've worked two jobs since your father died, and every single day, I've wished things would be easier. I just don't want you to be disappointed is all."

But Elsa *was* disappointed. She was always wishing for things she couldn't have—her friend Annie's wild red hair, a nice house, a real family. There was always something else she wanted. God knows, there was a lot to wish for when you lived in Dorchester.

"Learn to be happy with what you've got, Elsa. There's always someone else who's got it worse."

"That's just it—these refugees *have* got it worse. I want to help."

"Well, you can start with Diana. I fed her, but she needs to be changed and put to bed. I'll see you later." With a quick peck on the cheek, her mother left for work, the second shift at the supermarket where she rang up groceries she could barely afford.

Life isn't fair, Elsa thought glumly, *but that doesn't mean you just sit back and accept it.* She shed her coat and moved toward Diana, who sat awkwardly in an oversized high chair. Unable to hold her head up, it bobbed on her spindly neck until Elsa set a pillow behind her.

"There, Diana. Is that better?" she cooed.

Diana, the four-year-old daughter of Elsa's older sister, Janice, was hopelessly disabled, or so the doctors said. It took all of Elsa and her mother's efforts just to feed and take care of Diana. Janice was never home, and her brother, Tommy, the oldest of the three, only came home long enough to swipe money from either his mother or Elsa.

It hadn't always been that way. Though money had always been tight, they'd been a family once, and when Diana was born, she'd brought smiles and laughter into the house, at least for a while. Those were the good days, when even Annie, Elsa's only close friend, still came around.

Annie had lived with her Polish grandmother in another dingy three-decker on the next corner. It was Annie who'd sat with Elsa when she'd fed, changed, and babysat Diana, and it was Annie who'd poked through Janice's bureau drawers one afternoon until she discovered an old tube of lipstick called "Misty Mauve." At Elsa's urging, Annie had opened it and swiped it across her lips. Though the color was hopelessly outdated, they'd taken turns applying it.

Annie, her red hair straining against the elastic that held it back, had peered into the mirror and declared that it was a bad color for her. "With my hair, I need something brown. This is awful."

Elsa, small and narrow, had always wished for hair like Annie's, something that would set her apart. When it was her turn, she'd stood in front of the mirror and swiped the waxy mauve over her mouth. She'd pressed her lips together to spread the stain and peered at her reflection, suddenly boasting violet-colored lips. Against her brown hair, the color had been perfect. She'd turned to Annie.

"Well, what do you think?"

Annie had looked at her friend admiringly.

"You look beautiful, Elsa. You should wear lipstick all the time."

Elsa had looked in the mirror and smiled again. The face that stared back at her was pretty—*really* pretty—she had to admit. She'd grinned at her reflection as though she were seeing herself for the first time—shiny hair, creamy skin, upturned nose, and full violet lips. The very act of applying the lipstick—the gentle stroke of color, the pressing of her lips to spread it evenly, and finally, the gaze into the mirror—fascinated her.

This lipstick is amazing, Elsa had thought. It didn't just put color on her lips, it put an unmistakable glow in her green eyes and made her feel, if only for an instant, as though she were *somebody,* like one of those important women in the fancy magazines. Women who mattered wore lipstick. She smiled at her reflection again.

"Jeez, Elsa," Annie had declared. "You were made for lipstick."

I am, Elsa had thought. *I really am.*

The memory of that afternoon still made her smile, and though Annie had long since moved away, Elsa's love of lipstick was the same. A swipe of bold plum or soft pink was enough to raise her spirits, and in Dorchester, that was a necessity.

Lipstick was magic.

2

By the time Elsa was seventeen, she was buried in responsibilities, and of those responsibilities—work, school, and Diana—it was Diana who took the lion's share of Elsa's time. Diana, always sick, required constant attention so she didn't choke or slide from her seat.

Just feeding her took hours, nudging little spoonfuls of pureed meat or vegetables into her mouth and urging her to swallow. Changing and cleaning her became more difficult with each passing day; though her mind hadn't grown, her body had. She was heavy and stiff and difficult to hold. Their little apartment was crammed with the special equipment and food Diana needed just to survive. Janice hadn't been back in months, so it was up to Elsa and her mother.

Margaret often muttered that she just couldn't imagine what it would be like in ten or twenty years. And Elsa, who took over the responsibility when she arrived home from school, felt a growing resentment toward the sister and brother who'd deserted her.

Finally, an overwhelmed Margaret, with Elsa at her side, approached Diana's doctors.

"We need help," Margaret pleaded. "It's only me and Elsa taking care of her. We just can't do it anymore."

The doctors nodded and made the arrangements to place Diana

in a special home. "St. John's," they said, "is a good nursing home. And the state will cover the costs, so you won't have to worry about that, Mrs. Murphy."

"What about Diana's mother? Does she know about this?" one young doctor inquired.

"We don't know where she is. I'm Diana's guardian." Margaret hung her head, ashamed of Janice's failings. Mother and daughter left the clinic in silence, and as they waited for the bus, Margaret finally spoke.

"It's a good decision," she said hopefully, as if trying to convince herself. "It's the only thing we could do."

And while Elsa knew her mother was right, she couldn't escape her gnawing guilt.

When the day came and went, Elsa found she couldn't just let Diana go. So twice a week, she boarded a train and then a bus, and made the long trip to visit her niece at St. John's.

"Hello, Diana," she said each time, her teenager's voice all but singing when she spied the little girl in her tiny wheelchair. She leaned over to stroke Diana's cheek and plant a kiss, but Diana didn't move. Elsa hoisted her out of the chair and sat holding her tight, but there was no response, not a smile or even a blink, nothing to indicate Diana was in there.

Elsa watched as the nurses and therapists massaged Diana's tight little muscles and bent and stretched her extremities to keep them limber so that they wouldn't become distorted, as Elsa had seen with some of the other children.

One afternoon, as Elsa sat next to Diana, the young girl stiffened and fell into a seizure. Her eyes rolled back in her head, blood and spittle dripped from her mouth, a stain of urine spread out around her, and she fell to the floor in a writhing heap. Jumping up, Elsa ran into the hallway.

"Help!" she screamed. "It's Diana, help! Hurry, please!" She was quickly surrounded by the nurses, who pushed her aside to enter the room.

Someone called an ambulance and the paramedics arrived to

take over. They bundled Diana onto a gurney and lifted her into the ambulance, motioning for Elsa to sit in the front. The wail of the siren echoed in Elsa's head as the ambulance snaked through the crowded Boston streets. She struggled to hear what was going on in the back, where Diana lay, but the screaming siren blocked out all other sound.

When the ambulance screeched to a halt in front of the Boston City Hospital, Elsa fled from the front seat. "I want to see Diana," she said. But her soft words were lost in the urgency that surrounded her and instead she was ushered to a dingy waiting area where the smell of vomit hung in the air. She sat on the edge of an orange plastic chair, chewing her nails and picking at a loose thread on her coat.

Tears pooled in the corners of her eyes and streamed down her cheeks, mixing with the snot that ran from her nose. She drew a sleeve across her face. The door to the hallway squeaked as it opened, and her mother appeared beside her.

"Oh, Jesus, Mary, and Joseph," Margaret sniffled. "They called me from St. John's. What happened?"

"Oh, Ma," Elsa cried, reaching for Margaret. Through her tears, Elsa recounted the afternoon's events. "I don't know where Diana is. They just left me here." Her sobs started anew.

Margaret sighed, gathered herself, and held Elsa close. They sat together in silence, the room already feeling like a little tomb. There was nothing to say. They'd put Diana in a home, and this was what had come of it.

A bespectacled young doctor, fidgeting with a metal clipboard, entered the little room ahead of a portly nurse, who was busily tucking her brown hair behind her ears. They took seats on either side of Margaret and Elsa. The doctor removed his eyeglasses, wiping them clean as he spoke.

"I am sorry to give you the news, Mrs. Murphy," he said, speaking gently to Margaret. "But your daughter has died. We did everything we could, but we just couldn't save her."

He paused, and Elsa gulped back her sobs. The nurse put an arm around her as the doctor continued.

"I've seen her records," he said, holding the clipboard up for emphasis. "This was a very long time coming, I'm afraid." He stood to go and tried awkwardly to offer some reassurance. "She's not suffering anymore. Nevertheless, I am sorry for your loss," he said as he moved toward the door.

The nurse stayed, her ample body spilling over the seat and onto Elsa's chair. She held out some tissues.

"Can I call anyone for you?" she asked quietly. Margaret shook her head no. The nurse paused, then spoke again. "My name's Maureen, and if you have any questions later, please come back to see me or give me a call." She rubbed Elsa's back and she looked right into her eyes. "I lost my little sister when I was about your age. I know how you feel."

"But—" Elsa started to explain that Diana wasn't her sister, but she decided to let it go. Instead, she looked at the floor, her tears falling onto the front of her coat.

"Do you want to see her before you leave?" the nurse asked.

"Diana? We can see her?" Elsa sat up straight and wiped her nose.

"Of course you can. Sometimes it helps to say good-bye."

"Please, yes. I want to see her." Elsa sniffled and stood, eager to escape the mustiness of the old room.

Margaret sighed and looked at the floor.

"Not me, thank you," she said. "I've had enough of these places to last a lifetime. Go on. I'll wait here for you."

Maureen led Elsa down a brightly lit hallway to the room where Diana lay. A nurse scurried about, clearing the equipment, switching off the monitors and pumps. The floor was littered with empty syringes, rubber tubes, streams of paper, and discarded latex gloves. In the midst of the clutter stood a gleaming steel stretcher. Diana looked so tiny and so . . . so *comfortable.* Gone was the pain of her brittle bones and tight muscles, and her mouth seemed fixed in a slight smile.

Elsa took her hand and stroked Diana's forehead. She seemed so peaceful that Elsa turned to Maureen.

"Are you sure she's . . . ?"

Maureen nodded. "We're sure."

Tears streamed down Elsa's face.

"Diana, you know we'll always love you." She leaned over and kissed Diana's cheek, then turned and started for the door.

"Thank you," she said in a whisper to Maureen as Maureen hugged her.

They walked back down the hall to the waiting room.

"Are ya ready then?" Margaret asked as they entered the room. "Come on, let's go home."

Maureen took Margaret's hand and gave Elsa's shoulder a squeeze.

"Call me if you need to talk," she said again. She handed her card to Elsa, who tucked it into her pocket before Margaret could snatch it away. They walked to the exit and stepped into the crisp fall air.

On the way home, Margaret said over and over that Diana's death was for the best, that it was God's will. Elsa suspected that she was trying to convince herself.

Life went back to normal, but Elsa was more lonely than ever. Even her twice-weekly visits to St. John's were gone now. She wanted to talk with someone, but Margaret had never been much for conversation, and Elsa's duties at home and school kept her from making close friends. Her shoulders sagged with the weight of everything, and one night she bundled herself into her coat and headed out into the cold night for a walk. She pulled her coat tighter and shoved her hands deep into her pockets, where her fingers curled around a small card. She pulled it out. *Maureen Hill, RN* was inscribed there along with the telephone number of Boston City's emergency room. Elsa fingered the raised letters, tucked it back into her pocket, and turned for home.

The following day, she turned up at the ER registration desk and asked for Maureen. The clerk smiled.

"Who can I say wants her?" she asked.

"Elsa Murphy," she answered. The clerk disappeared, and after a few uncomfortable minutes she returned with a smiling Maureen. Her brown hair was pulled back in a tight bun and she pushed the stray tendrils away from her face as she neared the desk. As she got closer, Elsa noticed the tiny freckles that sprinkled Maureen's pale skin. It was hard to guess her age but she was old, Elsa thought—at least forty.

"Oh, Elsa, come on in. I'm so glad to see you." Her voice was warm and soft, like a gentle touch. She guided Elsa to the staff lounge, where she pulled up two chairs so they could sit.

"How are you, honey?" She said it in such a soothing way that Elsa started to reply, but her stomach knotted up and she began to cry. A soft whimper rapidly turned to gasping sobs.

In fits and starts, she sobbed out her story. She told Maureen all about Diana and Janice and her mother.

"Poor Diana never had a chance in this family," she finished.

"Honey, you did the best you could for Diana. She was a very sick little girl. I've seen patients like her before, and you and your mom keeping her at home as long as you did was an act of great love."

Maureen leaned forward and spoke softly.

"My own sister was born when I was fifteen years old. I remember how excited I was that a baby was coming—until she was born and we saw how deformed she was. I was heartbroken. She never even came home with us. She died in the hospital without ever sleeping in her fancy new crib or wearing the clothes we bought her." She touched Elsa's hand.

"When she died, I knew I'd be a nurse. So, you see, I do know how sad it can be and I know it's much worse for you than it was for me. You knew Diana; she was a part of your life for a long time. She was lucky to have had you and your mom to love her." Maureen smiled and squeezed Elsa's hand.

Elsa sniffled.

"I'm not so sure that Diana was lucky to have us. We're nothing special. No one's ever graduated from high school in my family, and I don't even have any real friends."

She sniffled again and wiped her nose.

"I don't want to live in Dorchester forever. I want to *be somebody*. I want to go to school and, well, just get out there and *do* something. When I really start feeling sorry for myself, I think about how much worse it could be." She paused and then told Maureen about the magazine article and its terrible photographs. "Have you seen those stories? It's just awful. *Those* people need help. It makes me ashamed to be so selfish."

"Oh, honey," Maureen said as she folded Elsa into her arms. "You're not selfish. It's human nature to want something better for yourself. You know, I went to nursing school so I could help those poor babies who never go home, and here I am in the ER. The best thing you could do is watch out for yourself and make something of yourself. Then you'll be able to help people all you want."

It was almost as though Maureen had read her mind.

"Do you think *I* could be a nurse? I used to watch the nurses at St. John's, and it seemed like, well, maybe as a nurse I could make a difference. It seems like nurses do things that *matter*. I couldn't help Diana and I can't help the refugees, but as a nurse, I *could* help. I know I could." As she said it, her tears stopped and her sadness lifted a little.

"I'm glad to hear that," Maureen said. "God knows we need more nurses. If you'd like, you can bring in a list of your high school courses and we can make sure you're taking the right ones for a nursing career. We can start looking at scholarship applications, too."

Maureen's kindness made Elsa feel weepy again.

"Thank you," she whispered.

Elsa returned the next day, and Maureen helped her to choose the courses she'd need for nursing school.

Over the next few months, Elsa found herself in the ER several times a week hoping to just be around Maureen, whose encouragement helped Elsa forget her own misery. After a while, the reception clerk even knew her by name. "Have a seat, Elsa. I'll page Maureen," she'd say. When it seemed clear that Elsa would continue to be a frequent visitor, Maureen arranged for her to volunteer at the hospital, running errands and helping the patients and visitors.

Elsa felt alive in the emergency room, where everything was a matter of life and death. There in the ER, her own sadness seemed swallowed up and somehow faded. She *mattered* there—at least to Maureen, who always made Elsa feel needed.

She still worked at the library and even increased her hours so that she could help out with the bills that plagued her mother. Margaret continued to work from dawn till dusk and had little time left over for Elsa, who turned to her books and studies in earnest.

With her newfound resolve, Elsa kept on top of her grades more than ever. As graduation approached, Maureen wrote letters of recommendation and said she wasn't surprised when Elsa was accepted to Boston College's nursing program on a full scholarship.

She was going to be a nurse. Even Margaret smiled at the news.

"A *nurse*," she said. "My own daughter, a nurse."

$\mathcal{F}$or Elsa, four years of school passed quickly, and in the spring of 2000 she graduated from Boston College. Almost immediately the nursing boards loomed, and she passed the rigid test with flying colors. She was pronounced an RN—a registered nurse—at last. And with Maureen's help, she was hired in Boston City's ER. She celebrated her new position with a fresh supply of lipsticks—soft pinks and muted beiges, quiet, wholesome colors, fitting for a nurse.

Finally able to contribute a real salary to her small household, Elsa wanted her mother to retire. Maybe they could even buy a cozy house somewhere nearby. Anywhere but Dorchester.

But Margaret frowned at the offer.

"Oh, Elsa, you're a good girl, but I'd go batty if I was home every day. No, honey, I'll keep working, but a new couch would be nice, or maybe a TV that actually works." Margaret smiled. "You know, for a kid who never had a break, you turned out all right. I'm really proud of you." She leaned over and gave Elsa a quick peck on the cheek. "I love you, Elsa."

Her mother had never been much for affection, and her words caught Elsa off guard. But Margaret was up from her chair and out the door before Elsa could respond and say that she loved her, too.

* * *

A week later, Margaret didn't appear for her morning coffee. Certain that she had overslept, Elsa went into her mother's bedroom and found her still in bed with the covers pulled up high to her neck and her eyes closed.

"C'mon, Ma, your coffee's getting cold."

She moved closer and saw that Margaret wasn't breathing and had a bluish cast to her skin. Panicking, Elsa threw off the covers and tried to breathe for her mother, but it was too late. Her mother's skin was ice-cold.

Elsa cradled her mother's limp form and wept.

"Oh, Mama, why now?"

But there was only silence in the tiny apartment.

Elsa, a few neighbors, and Maureen attended the funeral services. Annie, with a small baby in tow, showed up toward the end but left after giving Elsa a quick embrace.

Elsa was on her own.

She was grateful when Maureen asked her if she wanted company, but right then she needed to be alone. She went home and climbed the narrow staircase past the yellowed, flaking wallpaper and inhaled the familiar scent of grease and stale cigarettes. The Murphy apartment was hers now, and its emptiness echoed her life.

She was alone.

And though it had been the way she'd lived, more or less, for all of her life, it wasn't enough. She didn't want to end up like her mother, with no one to attend her funeral, her death barely noticed.

Then Elsa remembered the magazine. It was still in her bedroom, tucked into the drawer of the nightstand, filled with the stark portraits of sad-eyed Rwandan refugees. She pulled out the magazine and looked at the pictures that had riveted her so long ago, and she found that once again, she was consumed by the unremitting misery in the images. Surely, all these years later, these people were dead.

But what if a nurse had gone and helped?

She inhaled deeply, and as she did, a calmness settled over her, and she knew—she would go. Somehow she would help, she would make a difference; however small, in whatever small corner of the world that needed her, she would *help*. She sat straighter and exhaled slowly. These people *needed* her—and she needed them.

A few days later, she approached Maureen in the hospital cafeteria.

"Maureen, do you remember the conversation we had years ago, about the refugees from Rwanda? The ones in that magazine I told you about?"

"Of course, honey. That's what got you started on the road to nursing school." She paused for a moment, staring into space. "It seems as if there are always refugees in the news, doesn't it? One sad story after another. Today it's Sudan and the Balkans. Tomorrow it'll be someplace else. Yet most of us forget the tragedies as soon as the stories fade from our television screens. You have a good heart, Elsa, to still be thinking about them." Maureen sighed and gazed at her generous lunch. "Makes me feel guilty to have so much and do so little."

"I didn't mean to make you feel guilty, and you do a lot for people who come through the ER. Look at everything you've done for *me*. It's just that now seems like a good time for me to do something. With Mama gone, and no one waiting for me at home, I think I'd like to volunteer with one of the aid groups, if they'll have me." She paused for a moment, then continued. "I wanted to make sure it was okay with you. It'll take me away from the hospital, after all."

"Oh, honey, of course it's okay with me. You go right ahead, and let me know if there's anything I can do to help. I'd be so proud of you, doing something like that. Hell, we'd *all* be proud of you."

Elsa knew she'd need experience to apply, so with Maureen's guidance, she threw herself into her work with a renewed sense of purpose and saw patients and families much like her own, devastated by drugs and alcohol and tragedy. She focused on learning the ropes in the constantly bustling maze of the ER, and her days became a frenzied blur of misery, gunshot wounds, and overdoses. Yet she tackled it all with unbridled energy, more determined than ever to make a difference, treating every day as if it was a starting point for getting where she wanted to be.

Somehow, in the grim haze of that chaotic apprenticeship, Elsa learned how to save lives and how to recognize when someone *couldn't* be saved. Those were the hardest ones. They reminded her of Diana. But in order to do her job, she needed to learn to deal with her emotions and do what needed to be done.

Elsa soon settled into the routine of the ER, but even the *routine* wasn't so routine. There were new hazards every day, and though she learned to break into a sprint when she heard the overhead intercom buzz out, *"Arrest team to Trauma One,"* her heart quaked as she ran. The announcement usually meant that a gunshot or stab wound victim was arriving, and she was expected to assist. It wasn't long before she knew where to stand, and how to pass equipment when the surgeon decided to open someone's chest and perform heart surgery right then and there. Early on, the senior trauma surgeon had even directed her to hold a heart in her hands while he repaired a deadly wound. Terrified, she'd held it tenderly as though holding a fragile piece of glass, but the wounded heart was slippery, and she was sure it would slide from her hands. Her own heart beat faster, and beads of sweat collected under her face mask, clouding her vision. She could hear the chaos at the edges of the trauma room, people shouting about blood and the operating room, but there in the center, it was almost calm, except for her own hidden panic. *Oh, God,* she thought, *don't let me faint.*

"Squeeze the damn heart," the surgeon barked. "You're the pump! Squeeze harder!" Elsa held her breath and squeezed as the surgeon worked, willing herself to memorize every detail of the dramatic procedure. She exhaled only when the patient was rushed into the operating room. The following day, Elsa learned he'd survive.

She knew that she would too.

Slowly but surely, she found that she loved the adventure of the ER, the adrenaline rush of saving lives. Sometimes she'd run alongside the stretcher holding a flimsy piece of gauze over a gaping wound to staunch the flow of blood. She learned to insert intravenous lines as though she were gliding a piece of silk over someone's arm, and she learned to place nasogastric tubes as though she were dropping a fishing line. She learned to deliver screaming babies and to wrap the dead.

And the next time a chest needed to be opened, the surgeon had shouted, "Get Elsa! I need her next to me!" She'd pushed through the crowd and hurriedly tried to insert an intravenous line, but the patient's veins had collapsed. "Forget that," the surgeon said as he inserted the rib spreader into the incision and cracked the chest open. Blood sprayed everywhere. Elsa felt it drench her own scrubs, but she stood perfectly still, only her hands moving as she reached for a surgical drape.

"Here." The surgeon pointed to a small laceration in the heart. "Put your finger there. Don't move." Elsa reached out, her hands steady, and jammed her finger into the tiny hole.

She watched as he searched for the aorta; every vessel looked the same.

"There," he said. "Where's the clamp?" Out of the corner of her eye she watched as an intern handed the instrument to the surgeon. With steady hands, he clamped the vessel. Instinctively, Elsa called out. "Note the time," she heard herself shout, glancing up at the wall clock. "Start the timer." She inhaled deeply through her surgical mask. She felt as though she was watching someone else, someone calm who knew exactly what to do.

When the bags of universal donor replacement blood arrived, she placed them under her arms to warm them, just as Maureen had taught her.

"Let that intern warm that blood," the surgeon told her. "Now suction that out for me." She passed the blood and took the suction tube, placing it right into the chest cavity, vacuuming out the blood so the surgeon could see the heart. She watched as he placed a tiny suture into the young man's right ventricle.

"Get an atrial line in, Elsa," the surgeon said, directing her. Her hands trembled.

"Here?" she asked, glad for the face mask that muffled her shaky voice. When he nodded, she inserted the intravenous catheter into the man's heart and connected it to the blood tubing.

The flaccid heart had quivered before it began to beat—stronger and stronger—until Elsa could hear her own heart pounding in her chest. She covered the gaping wound with moist pads and the surgeon and his interns pulled at the stretcher, heading to the OR.

"You're at nine minutes," she said, placing the timer on the stretcher. "You have eleven minutes left to get that aorta unclamped."

"I knew you had it in you, Elsa," the surgeon said, patting her on the back as he hurried by.

Maureen had watched it all from the doorway. "Well done, Elsa. I'm so proud!"

"My God, I was so nervous. You couldn't tell?"

"No, honey. All I saw was an ER nurse. Now, back to work. You've got a line of patients waiting."

The floor was slick with the patient's blood as Elsa tossed her surgical gloves and mask on the floor, which was already littered with syringes, medical debris, and discarded latex gloves. She switched off the monitors and paused, looking around. It didn't look much different from the day Diana had died, but everything had changed. Everything. She was an ER nurse now. If she could do this, she could do *anything*.

She turned and flicked on the intercom. "Housekeeping to Trauma One," she said as she stepped over the debris and headed back to triage.

Before long, it was Elsa who was calling, "Arrest team to Trauma One." She almost couldn't believe how far she'd come, how her confidence and her skills had grown, and she knew, with each passing day, she was closer to her goal.

Elsa went back to the library where she'd spent so much time and began to research relief agencies. There was one agency she'd seen profiled on CNN—Aide du Monde—with headquarters in New York City. But when she contacted them, they politely informed her that she'd need at least a year of experience, preferably in an emergency room, before they would be able to consider her for a nursing position. She'd only been in the ER for six months, so she swallowed her disappointment and promised to call them when she'd reached that milestone.

The day her year was up—and not a minute later—Elsa called Aide du Monde, commonly known as ADM, to make an appointment to visit their New York office. This time, she got one.

With her lips colored a daring red for confidence, she arrived there one afternoon in the spring of 2001. Days of interviews followed.

"So please tell us why we should choose you. How can you help?" a tall, bespectacled man had asked.

She took a deep breath. She knew her answer had to be perfect. "It's all about making yourself try harder," she said, her voice calm as she told them about learning how to open chests and save lives in the ER. "I know I can help," she said, finishing. "I absolutely know I can." The two men who interviewed her smiled then and nodded— signaling approval, Elsa hoped.

She was asked to submit what seemed like a glut of references and had to write a personal essay explaining her reasons for wanting to become part of their team. It seemed more difficult to join ADM than to get into Harvard. But finally, she called Maureen with the news.

"I'm in," she said breathlessly into the phone. "They said they'd call when they have an assignment for me." There was a brief silence and Elsa wondered if they'd been cut off.

"That's wonderful, honey," Maureen said finally, and the connection made it seem as if there was something in her throat. "I'm so proud of you."

Elsa rang off and went to apply for a passport. Over the next few days, she got more vaccines than she'd received in her entire lifetime. Then she returned to Boston and waited for the call.

It took a long time, but her phone finally rang late one morning in early September. A man named Jean-Claude, his voice a lilting French accent, offered her a post in Afghanistan. Thrilled that ADM finally had a place for her, Elsa eagerly accepted, and Jean-Claude promised to call back soon with more details.

Hanging up the phone, she crawled back under the covers. She had one more night to go on the night shift, and, still exhausted, she hoped to get some more sleep.

But her mind was racing.

Make a list, decide what to pack . . . who to tell . . . bills to pay.

Maybe I should let go of the apartment, she thought. *Maybe I could sublet.*

Surrendering to the inevitable, she got out of bed and dragged herself to her desk. She tried to focus, to make a list of things she'd need, but fatigue overcame her and she could only think of one thing to take. At the top of the page, she wrote out *LIPSTICK* in capital letters and underlined it.

Pen and paper still in hand, Elsa fell asleep.

Elsa woke that evening with a feeling of lightness. She was almost giddy. Her life was about to change.

She worked through the night shift and kept her secret to herself. She wanted Maureen to be the first to know and planned to tell her on Tuesday morning at the change of shift, but the ER was too busy and Elsa was too exhausted to hang around until things quieted. So she dragged herself home, took a long, hot shower, and pulled on her nightgown, then settled in for a cup of tea and the morning news.

She clicked the television on, expecting to see the newscaster chatting about the weather or the morning traffic. Instead of the usual smiling faces, however, a somber reporter's voice was shaking.

"A plane has just crashed into the World Trade Center in New York City," he said. Stunned, Elsa sat back and watched the live report. Suddenly, there on the screen, a second plane appeared and flew into the second tower.

Elsa's hands flew to her mouth.

She stood and moved closer to the television.

Flames, horrific flames, burst from the gaping holes where the planes had pierced the buildings.

People inside were trapped, the reporter announced, and some—desperate to escape—had jumped from the highest floors. The cameras caught it all, the specks of bodies hurtling through the air to the concrete below.

Her hands trembling, Elsa was seized by a feeling of dread, but she couldn't pull herself away from the terrible images. She was still watching when the towers crumpled and collapsed, sending thousands of people to their deaths. Reporters said that it was a terrorist attack, and the planes had come from Boston.

The morning was sunny, and despite her closed shades, bright light was leaking in around the edges. Elsa ran to her front window and pulled the blinds open. People were still walking, cars were still moving, drivers were still yelling and honking their horns. It seemed like an ordinary day.

Except it wasn't.

Suddenly, she didn't want to be alone. If the world was ending, she needed to get out of there. She picked up the phone and called Maureen at the hospital.

"Have you seen it?"

"We're watching it now. It's just awful." Maureen sounded defeated somehow.

"Do you want me to come back? Do you know anything? God, it's terrible. And the planes came from Boston." Her words came out in a rush.

"I don't know, honey. A Phase One disaster has been called here and we're on alert, but no one knows what will happen. Stay home, get some sleep. I'll call if we need you."

But Elsa didn't sleep. She stayed in front of the television and watched as the details of the attack were revealed. In the evening, she called the telephone number mentioned in a news story and tried to volunteer at the World Trade Center site.

"I'm an emergency room nurse," she said. "I can help." A harried official took her name and telephone number and said they'd be in touch.

She dialed ADM but there was no answer.

Her world had suddenly turned as gray as the ash that covered Lower Manhattan. Elsa had never felt more isolated. She kept the television on all day and into the night, needing the hum of voices to lull her to sleep.

When her alarm clock buzzed, she was already up and showering.

Relieved to go to work and to be back on the day shift, Elsa heaved a sigh as she walked through the ER's doors. At least there were people there. The staff and the patients were gathered in the waiting room, glued to the television.

Maureen was still there; she'd stayed all night, just in case.

"How are you, honey?" she asked as she gave Elsa a hug. She turned back to the television. "I never thought I'd see anything like this, such evil. It gives me the chills."

She turned and looked at Elsa. "I hate to think of you all alone in that apartment," she said, continuing. "Do you want to stay with me and Jack till this is over? You know we'd love to have you."

"Thanks for the offer, but I'm okay. *You're* the one who should get some sleep. Go home to Jack. We'll call if we need you."

For the rest of the day, a crowd kept vigil in the waiting room and though the faces changed, the numbers in front of the television never diminished.

When the terrorists were connected to Afghanistan, Elsa wondered what the effect would be on her assignment. Sure enough, before the week was out, her mission was canceled and all international aid workers were evacuated.

Jean-Claude reassured her when he called with the news. "Not to worry. We will have another assignment for you soon," he said, and then he paused. "If we reopen our programs in Afghanistan, would you still go?"

Elsa answered without hesitation.

"Oh yes. I'll go. I'll go anywhere."

In early October, CNN reported that the U.S. and coalition forces had started bombing Afghanistan.

At work and on the streets, people cheered.

Elsa held her breath.

What next?

A persistent ringing jarred Elsa out of a sound sleep. She fumbled for the phone, her eyes still closed, as the bright sunlight seeped through her tightly shut blinds.

"Hello," she groaned into the receiver.

"Hello, hello, Elsa." A faintly familiar French accent greeted her. "It is Jean-Claude calling from Aide du Monde in New York."

"Oh, hello," she answered, suddenly awake. She hadn't heard from ADM in over five months.

"I am sorry we have taken so long," Jean-Claude continued, "but I am happy to say that, finally, we have a posting for you."

"That's wonderful," she said quickly. "Where is it?"

"We still need you in Afghanistan, in a place called Bamiyan," he replied. "The home of the famous Buddha statues. Well, there are no Buddhas now of course, thanks to the Taliban, but there in Bamiyan, we have a clinic and hospital. The mission will be for one year. You can go, yes?"

A year, she thought, pushing aside her fears.

"Yes, of course. When will I leave?" she asked.

"Probably in a few weeks. We just wanted to be sure you would accept the post. Thank you for saying yes. I will call you later this week with details. Until then, good-bye."

"Good-bye," Elsa replied. She hung up the phone with trembling fingers.

It was really going to happen—she was going to *Afghanistan*. She almost couldn't believe it.

It was a cold, gray morning in early March when Maureen drove her to the airport and said a tearful good-bye.

"I'm so proud of you, Elsa. Promise me you'll be careful," Maureen said, her voice straining with emotion. "Just come back to us safe."

Only later, when Elsa stood in the long line that led through the security maze at Logan airport, did she feel the first real threads of worry about Afghanistan. But the arrangements had all been made; it was too late to back out now, not that she wanted to anyway. This trip was everything she'd ever wanted. She tried to shake off her anxiety, but tears gathered in her eyes as she boarded the plane and sat peering out of the scratchy little window at the blurred runway. It would be her last look at Boston for a long time.

The first leg of her journey took her to the ADM offices in Paris to pick up medicines and some of the supplies she would need in Bamiyan. It was the first time she'd been outside of the United States, and she yearned to see some of the famous City of Lights, but there was no time.

There were no commercial flights into Afghanistan, so she was booked on a flight to Peshawar in northern Pakistan, the tribal, frontier city that was the point of entry for all the aid going into Afghanistan. Peshawar was a crumbling old city teeming with refugees, freedom fighters, aid workers, intrigue, and centuries of history.

Elsa landed in Peshawar in the late morning, and the instant she emerged from the plane, she was hit by the full sun and murky heat of the day. She stood in the plane's doorway at the top of the metal stairs and looked out, the scents and sounds full upon her, and paused.

"*You!*"

She jumped as a soldier barked at her and motioned brusquely with his machine gun. Her palms were sweating—along with just about every other part of her body—as she descended the staircase and stepped onto the cracked and steaming tarmac. The soldier frowned and pointed the way to the arrival terminal. Elsa fell in behind the other passengers.

The terminal, a squat two-story building, was teeming with activity. Turbaned men in oversized pajama suits and women in loose dresses and veils filled every available space. Elsa hesitated, looked at her own jeans and cotton shirt, and felt conspicuously out of place in the heaving, exotic crowd.

Suddenly she realized she'd lost sight of the line of passengers, who'd somehow blended into the crowd. She stood there alone and tried to read the signs. Panic began to grip her when she realized none of them were in English.

A flash of movement caught her eye and there, at what seemed to be the entrance to the terminal, she saw a young man waving a sign with her name on it. Relief flooded through her, and she hurried to his side.

"Come, come," he said. "My name is Ajmal, and I am here to help you with the rest of your travels. Follow me, please." He took her passport and visa and guided her through the long lines and confusing maze of Immigration and Customs, and then he collected her lone suitcase and a bulky carton of supplies she'd gathered in Paris. He lifted the carton onto one shoulder and lifted her suitcase with his free hand.

Finally, he paused.

"You are from Amrika, yes?"

"Yes, yes, I'm Elsa. Well, you know that, I guess," she said, grinning. "After all, you have the sign." As he smiled back, some of her nervousness melted away.

"I am from Afghanistan." He put his hand over his heart. "It is the place of my birth and where my heart resides. You are here to help my people?"

"Yes, well, I hope so, but I'm sure I still have a lot to learn."

"You have come here, a stranger, to help us." He paused and pointed out his car, a small, white sedan held together with duct tape and wire. "We are already grateful to you." Ajmal grinned broadly again, and Elsa noticed that he was missing almost half of his teeth.

"We do not have much time, mees." (He pronounced "miss" as

"mees.") "You cannot even see the old city. There is too much to do. These medical supplies will be sent on to your destination. *You* will need Afghan clothes and some additional supplies, and you will be on the United Nations flight to Afghanistan this afternoon."

Ajmal spoke in short, rapid bursts, and he drove the same way. As he pulled away from the airport, Elsa hung on tightly, certain the tires were about to fly off.

While he maneuvered the car through the dusty alleys and streets of Peshawar, she got a dizzying look at the city that Kipling had once described as "the Oldest Land." From the looks of it, not much had changed. The streets swarmed with starving children, crippled beggars, frail men, and skeletal horses. Veiled women hurried along, lugging babies and parcels.

Could Afghanistan be worse than this? she wondered.

Ajmal brought the car to a screeching halt outside a maze of stalls selling everything from clothes to rifles. He ushered Elsa inside a tiny shop where the dim light brought needed relief from the sun. He gestured to her as he spoke to the shopkeeper. After a few minutes, Ajmal turned to her.

"This man is a great tailor, and he supplies clothes for everyone that ADM sends into Afghanistan. He says it is an honor to meet you." The shopkeeper looked briefly at Elsa and laid his right hand over his heart and bowed slightly as Ajmal continued.

"He cannot touch you or measure you for clothes, so—from your appearance—he will guess your size and bring out dresses and pants that he has already sewn." Ajmal settled himself cross-legged on the carpet and motioned for Elsa to join him. She wasn't sure how to sit on the floor; she tried to cross her legs too, but it didn't seem right, so she knelt and sat back on her heels.

A young boy scurried into the shop from a back room. He balanced a silver tray that held a delicate teapot and several cups. He squatted and placed the tray on the carpet and in one swift movement, he poured a cup of steaming tea and pushed it to Elsa. Smiling, he passed her a bowl of sugar cubes and a small pitcher of cream. He stood and almost ran from the shop.

"Thank you," Elsa called after the fleeing figure. "Is he afraid of me?" she asked her guide.

"Perhaps. Though there are more and more foreigners here now, not many locals have a chance to meet one. He's probably running home to boast that he saw a foreign woman." Ajmal flashed his toothless grin and filled his little cup with spoon after spoon of sugar cubes.

Elsa grimaced as she watched. That explained the state of his teeth.

The shopkeeper appeared, laden with several long dresses and large, wide-legged pants. He held them up for Elsa's approval and laid them on the counter. He produced several large head-scarves and draped them alongside the dresses.

Elsa pulled herself up, glad to be off the floor and standing again, and leaned over the items.

"Oh," she said, "they're beautiful. Should I just hold them up to myself?" She held a dress in front of her and turned to Ajmal. "Does it look right?"

Ajmal nodded his approval, and she set aside the items she wanted to buy. He spoke again to the shopkeeper, who hurried to the back, returning with a full-body cloak called a *burqa*. It was enormous and intimidating with its accordion-like folds of fabric. Designed to slip over the wearer's head like a tent, it covered everything from her head to her toes.

"You will need this, mees," Ajmal said. "There are still places where women must stay covered. Better that you should get it now and keep it with you."

Elsa's final purchase was to be a pair of shoes, and Ajmal pointed out some cheap plastic sandals, the only footwear available at the little shop. Their shopping done, Ajmal signed the bill.

"ADM will pay for your clothes," he explained as he guided her back to the car.

Behind the wheel of the car, the polite Ajmal became a demon again, speeding through the narrow streets, beeping at donkeys and people alike. Elsa held on to her seat until they came to a stop in front of ADM's little local office. He looked at his watch and asked her to hurry. "You will need to change into your new clothes for the trip to Kabul. Please hurry, we don't have much time."

He showed Elsa to the bathroom and once she was alone she

pulled off her jeans and shirt. She'd been wearing them since she left Boston, and it was good to peel them away. She looked at her new clothes and chose a tan-colored dress and pants. She pulled the pants on, fastened them around her waist, and pulled the long dress over her head. She draped one of the scarves over her head and turned to look in the mirror. A woman from another time stared back at her. In the full-length dress, the puffy pants, and the scarf, she looked as though she might have stepped from a history book, a character from one of Kipling's stories. If it hadn't been for her familiar green eyes, thick chestnut hair, and full lips still toting a faded coat of cherry lipstick, she might not have recognized herself.

She smiled at her reflection and swiped a fresh layer of color over her lips. *Now* she was ready.

Ajmal knocked and again asked her to hurry. She picked up her things and joined him. In a flurry of instructions, he told her that the UN flight was early, and she would be flying to Kabul—Afghanistan's capital—within the hour. He packed Elsa, her lone suitcase, and her new purchases into the car and drove her to the UN booking office, where he said good-bye.

"*Khoda hafez,* good-bye," he said.

"Thank you so much, Ajmal." She gripped his hand and pumped it as she spoke. Uncomfortable with her effusive thanks, he slipped his hand from hers and hurried away, grinning nonetheless.

Pulling her bags and her suitcase behind her, Elsa found a seat in the lounge and waited. There were only three other passengers, Japanese aid workers heading to northern Afghanistan for a brief stay. They were loaded down with heavy boxes, filled—they said—with computers, radios, and satellite phones.

After a short wait, the small group was taken by van to the airport, but this time they were driven right past the crowds of travelers lugging bags of every size and shape. They were ushered to the UN terminal, a relatively quiet place, where they waited yet again. Finally, an hour later, they were led out to the runway to wait for their flight.

They stood with their luggage under a raggedy plastic tarpaulin held up by sticks, protecting them from the sun. They watched as a small plane with the UN logo on its wing taxied up to them. The pilot appeared in the plane's doorway and jumped down to greet them.

"Hello, hello," he said briskly. "Things are pretty calm right now, so I think we will have a good flight, but there's never a guarantee, so it's best to cover the procedures if we go down." His words sent a shiver through Elsa, who hadn't considered the possibility, and he continued, pointing as he spoke.

"Once we're on the ground, pull that lever by the front window, push open the door, jump onto the wing, jump down toward the back of the plane, and wait there for me." He paused and pointed away from the plane.

"But if I don't follow you, or if we're under direct fire, then run like hell for the best cover you can find."

Elsa marveled at the way he calmly described a situation she could hardly imagine, and she forced herself to listen carefully to the rest of his instructions.

A short time later, their seat belts clicked securely into place and they were off to Kabul. She could barely contain her excitement. Her fears had evaporated. Ajmal had been so kind and the pilot so skilled. Everyone, it seemed, knew just what to do. She settled into her seat. She was going to be fine.

Within the hour, the little plane descended into Kabul, and Elsa pressed her face against the window to watch as it was all but swallowed by the soaring mountain ranges that ringed the city. As they touched down, she saw that the airport was dotted with machine-gun-toting soldiers, tanks, antiaircraft turrets, sandbags, and military aircraft. The plane stopped in the middle of the runway and the pilot released the little door and staircase. The passengers descended and waited while he threw down their bags. To Elsa's surprise, he didn't follow them but turned to slip back into the plane.

"Good luck," he yelled as he pulled up the hatch.

Elsa picked her bag up and hesitated, not certain what to do, wondering if she'd missed something Ajmal had said.

Should she wait where she stood or somewhere else?

Was someone coming for her?

The little trio of Japanese men picked up their own bags and headed into the main terminal, glancing back to see if she was following. Deciding there was strength in numbers, Elsa picked up her things and shuffled after them into the terminal, and there in the crowd stood an ADM staff member waving another sign with her name on it.

She smiled, turned, and waved good-bye to her fellow travelers before joining him. He grabbed her suitcase and plunged into the hubbub, guiding her through Immigration. Once the necessary forms were signed and filled out, he led her to another decrepit sedan and drove her through Kabul's crowded streets to the Aide du Monde office.

He was silent as he drove. He was a bearded man with drooping eyes and a full head of bushy, black hair. Elsa smiled and tried to speak with him, but he never answered.

The city was bursting at the seams with people and animals and rubble, so there wasn't an inch of room left. Turbaned men, veiled women, and raggedy children hurried through the streets, competing with dogs, goats, donkeys, and automobiles for precious space.

The murky, sour smell of exotic foods, spices, and body odor filled the thick, lazy air. She surely wasn't in Dorchester anymore, but Dorchester had just as surely prepared her for this place. Misery was misery, and if there was one thing she knew, it was that.

Despite the chaos of the route, this driver—to Elsa's relief—was much less frenetic than Ajmal had been. After a short ride the driver stopped on a quiet street and yelled out. A large gate opened and the driver maneuvered the car inside, where it jerked to a halt alongside a beautiful, old stone and stucco home surrounded by surprising bursts of bright roses.

"Thank you," Elsa said to her driver as she stepped from the car and was greeted by a bearded, turbaned man. He wore thick glasses and a pleasant smile. He bowed his head and held his hand over his heart.

"Hello, hello, we are very happy to see you," he said in a deep, booming voice. "I am Qasim and you are Elsa, yes?"

Elsa nodded and bowed to the man.

"No, no, miss, do not bow to me. I bow because I cannot touch you in greeting; Islam forbids it. But you can say hello. That is enough."

Elsa smiled in return. "Good to meet you, Qasim. And thank you, I could use more lessons like that."

"It will come to you quickly enough," he replied, still smiling.

Qasim ushered her into the house, which, he explained, was empty save for the cook and a guard. He also told her that he was retained by ADM to maintain the house as a place for new volunteers to rest before the last leg of the journey.

"ADM has not enough staff these days," he said apologetically. "There is no one here but us," he added, and he pointed to a smiling, toothless man wearing a grimy apron. "This is Faizul. You are hungry, miss? He has cooked for you." Faizul bowed slightly and showed Elsa to the table.

"Please sit," he said.

Too tired to say no, she sat and watched as Faizul brought out the food. *He must be expecting a crowd,* she mused, because he carried out a platter of rice, one of greasy chicken, and a bowl of yogurt. To that he added large loaves of warm, flat bread and a glass of water.

"Please, will you join me?" she asked both men.

"No, no. This is for you," Qasim insisted.

"Please, it's too much for just me. Won't you sit?"

"Thank you, mees, for your kindness, but we cannot. You must eat and enjoy."

She inhaled the scent of the flat bread, realized that she was hungrier than she had expected, and broke off a piece. It was warm and soft and grainy. She bit into it and smiled. She ate the rice and chicken, and then finished the bowl of yogurt. Faizul had guessed correctly after all. He must have seen plenty of others like her, tired and famished more than they knew.

"Thank you. It was wonderful," she said. The cook grinned broadly.

"You should sleep now, mees," Qasim suggested. "You leave early."

She was shown to a small bedroom with an adjoining bathroom—a luxury, she guessed. From what she'd been told, this would be her last night with electricity and running water. She took a long hot shower and threw herself onto a lumpy, stale-smelling bed. But she didn't care; she fell asleep quickly and slept soundly on the stained sheets.

Elsa woke to an urgent rapping at her door.

"Mees, mees! Hurry, hurry."

She rose, splashed water on her face, pulled on the clothes she'd worn the day before, and headed to Qasim's office. She was given a carrying case of supplies and a manila envelope filled with papers outlining her job. Finally, he led her to a jeep with the bright red and yellow ADM logo painted on the side for the final leg of her trip to Bamiyan.

As he turned her over to the driver, Qasim held his hand over his heart, just as he had the day before.

"Good luck, mees. *Khoda hafez*."

Her driver, a bearded young man with greasy uncombed hair, held open the door and pointed to himself.

"Ismael," he said proudly.

Elsa echoed the motion and said, "Elsa." She climbed into the little jeep; Ismael followed suit and gunned the engine, and they headed off.

He turned to Elsa.

"No Inglisi. *Famidi?*"

Assuming he had told her he didn't speak English, Elsa nodded.

A short time later, they left the paved surface of Kabul's streets and turned onto the rough and rocky roads that led northwest through the countryside. Their route wound through village after village that had been pounded into dust from years of war. In one particularly devastated village, people ran alongside the jeep and yelled "thank you" in clear English.

She peered out through the dirty windshield. The road seemed endless, and the villages and their drab, one-story mud houses melted into one another. After a few hours, Ismael stopped the car at a small stand for a meal of beans and rice. Elsa and Ismael sat cross-legged on the ground to eat. Elsa had trouble eating the rice with her fingers as Ismael was doing, so she scooped it into the warm naan she'd been given and ate it off the bread. Once again, she'd been so wrapped up in the journey, she hadn't realized how hungry she was until she caught the scent of the food—mint, saffron, coriander, and God knew what else—and it stirred her appetite.

She ate until her plate was wiped clean, and Ismael nodded his approval.

Back in the jeep and on the rugged road, Elsa needed a bathroom break. She scoured her little book of Dari phrases in search of the right words.

"*Tashnob, lotfan.* Bathroom, please," she said. Ismael coasted the jeep to the side of the road and pointed to an abandoned mud house.

Elsa climbed out, clutching a small fold of toilet tissue she'd carried since Paris. She stepped carefully into the little house and looked around. In Paris, they'd told her that these old, crumbling buildings sometimes held hidden land mines, but her desire to empty her now full bladder outweighed her fears. When she noticed footprints and a pile of feces in a corner, she followed the prints, praying that if that route had been safe for someone else, it would be safe for her as well.

She tried to squat and pull up her dress as she pulled her pants away, but the urgency was too great and her new clothes too cumbersome, and before she could manage it all, she felt a gush of warm urine soaking her pant legs and pooling in her sandals.

"Shit," she murmured out loud, then glanced around self-consciously. She tried to mop up the urine, but her pants were soaked and she finally gave up and walked back to the jeep.

She climbed in, leaned back, closed her eyes, and fell into a restless sleep until Ismael's words woke her.

"Mees, *inja,* Bamiyan."

Elsa sat forward and looked outside.

While Kabul had been a devastated city packed with people, vehicles, and animals, it had boasted some of the services of a real city: occasional electricity, running water, large buildings, even paved streets. But Bamiyan seemed chiseled out of some long-forgotten age where it had remained frozen in time. While Peshawar had evoked Kipling, Bamiyan was almost biblical—an alien landscape peopled with veiled women astride donkeys led by bearded men. The homes, nestled amidst a harsh mountain backdrop, were squat, sand-colored buildings, each no bigger than a small garage. As far as she could see, there was no electricity or running water, and food—what there was of it—seemed to be cooked over open fires. She'd also heard that animals shared whatever small living space a family occupied.

This was an austere and unforgiving land and Elsa, who'd never even gone camping, was awed by the rugged countryside. She couldn't imagine how she'd ever be able to live like this, but she'd have to learn. This would be her home for the next year. She felt her stomach tighten.

Ismael continued on and finally stopped the jeep by the ADM gate. When Elsa climbed out, exhausted and dusty, a tall, thin man rushed out to meet her. He had long shiny hair drawn back and secured with an elastic band.

"Oh, it is so good that you have come," he said enthusiastically. His accent was heavy and French. "Welcome, welcome. I am Pierre Dubois." Elsa was comforted by his gracious welcome and she started to relax.

It's going to be okay, she told herself. *No need to worry—I got here.*

As he guided her into a small compound of short mud and plaster structures, one of which seemed to be an office, Pierre spoke quickly. "I am being sent to another office, out beyond Herat. The only reason I am still here is to make certain you are briefed. My bags are already packed. ADM, as I'm sure you know, does not have enough staff. We must all make sacrifices.

"So . . . ," he added, hesitating and watching her face as he spoke, "you will be in charge here for the time being."

The knot in Elsa's stomach grew larger.

"But I've never done this sort of work before," she protested. "I won't know what to do here by myself."

"It will be fine," Pierre said as he reached out and held her shoulder. "Not to worry. This is an easy post. The staff at the clinic will take good care of you."

Elsa took a deep breath. She didn't even know what to say.

"Come, sit. We have a lot to do. I must teach you about this post."

Elsa spent the rest of that day hunched over with Pierre, trying to ignore the buzzing flies and learning her responsibilities. The reports and order forms seemed endless, and she wondered how she'd ever get through it all on her own.

"You see," he said confidently when they had finished, "it is not so bad. Remember—protocols, procedures, and reports. While you are here to assist the staff in the clinic and the hospital as a nurse, you must also act as the administrative representative for our organization and manager of the clinic. Do not be afraid to ask for help."

Elsa chewed at her lower lip. *Who can I possibly ask for help if I'm here alone?* She didn't say it aloud; she didn't want to sound snippy.

Pierre showed her their little library, a single bookshelf filled with books on the diseases and injuries she'd encounter. He pulled a small, green, soft-covered book from the shelf.

"This is Aide du Monde's handbook for field staff. Keep this with you," he said. "This one reference book will tell you everything you need to know about the medical problems they suffer from here."

The book was small, not much thicker than a paperback novel. She flipped through the pages.

"Malaria? Is there malaria here?"

"No, no, not so much. Look through the pages. Do not worry." He smiled.

"One more thing." He paused, his expression turning serious. "We do have rules. You may have heard that there are U.S. soldiers here in Bamiyan, yes?"

Elsa smiled and shook her head. She hadn't heard, but it was welcome news, a relief even.

Pierre frowned.

"We at ADM disagree with their involvement here. So, first rule"—he paused again—"is that you must not, how you say . . . *fraternize*. Do you understand? We must not be confused with the soldiers. We take this very seriously."

Elsa nodded, hoping he didn't notice the disappointment she knew was etched on her face.

"Well, you may not see them anyway. I myself have seen very few of them." He turned and gathered his bags. "I am taking the satellite phone," he said. "Another will be sent to you. For now, Johann at the UN office will be happy to allow you to use his sat phone.

"The office in Paris will send help for you," he assured her as he headed for the exit. "Do not worry. You will do fine here." He opened the door and gestured to a clean-shaven young man. "Come, come. This is Hamid. He will be your interpreter, your assistant, your—how you say—your right hand." Pierre smiled. "I am sorry for the rush, but it is getting late, and I have to go. Ismael will drive me, but we must leave now so that we can be in Yakawlang by dark."

Gathering herself up, Elsa stood straight and held out her hand. "Thank you, Pierre."

He took her hand and shook it. *"Bon chance, mon amie,"* he said. And with that, he left.

Elsa swallowed her fear and smiled as she turned to Hamid. He had beautiful, coal-black eyes, but other than that, he had an average face with average features and was of average height. He looked like so many other young men Elsa had seen along the roads during the journey here except that he was perfectly shaved and coifed. It was obvious that he took great care with his hair, which was the deepest black she could have imagined and which he'd coaxed into a faultless back-sweep.

He reminded her of Elvis Presley.

"I am Hamid, as you heard." He sounded nervous, and somehow his anxiety calmed Elsa.

"Hamid," she said. "Do you have a last name?"

He nodded. "I am Hamid Naseer, eldest son of Afsar, of Kabul. I am known as Hamid. It is enough for us. You will see; most people call themselves by one name only."

She smiled and held out her hand before remembering what Qasim had said. She pulled it back.

"Well, you know that I'm Elsa Murphy, but just call me Elsa. That's enough for me as well. I'm to be the nurse here. I've never been in a foreign country so I'll need lots of help."

"Myself, I've never been out of Kabul. Well, there was a trip to Kandahar with my father, but even Kandahar is a city. This . . ." He looked around as he spoke. "This place, Bamiyan, is something else entirely. It is dusty and primitive. I will need help myself." He smiled, a broad grin that showed off his straight, white teeth. His was the first full set Elsa had seen since leaving Paris.

"What did you do in Kabul?"

"I was studying. I hoped to be an engineer but with all the interruptions in my education it will be many years before I will be an engineer. *Inshallah*—you know that means 'God willing'?" Elsa nodded; she had learned that much from her Dari phrase book. Hamid continued. "*Inshallah,* I will return to my studies in Kabul next year. There is nothing in Kabul just now. No jobs, only beggars. This job will help my family and will let me save again for school."

Since Hamid had arrived in Bamiyan before Elsa, he'd already learned the lay of the land, and since darkness had not yet fallen, he showed her around her new home. Located on the outskirts of the village, the Aide du Monde compound was located in an area of falling-down or bombed-out shells of former homes. Surrounded by a high metal wall, the compound housed four small mud-and-plaster rooms and a separate washroom.

"Your house," he announced as they began their tour, "was a Taliban house."

"Taliban? *Here?*" Elsa could barely contain the fear that name evoked. "One Taliban soldier? Many? What does that mean?"

" 'Taliban' is used to describe one man or a band of men. They probably stole this house, and when they left, the original owner wanted no part of it. When Aide du Monde came to town looking for an office, he sold it."

"That gives me the creeps," Elsa said.

"It is safe now. Though their bullet holes remain"—he pointed to a series of holes in the wall—"the Taliban are gone. Come. See for yourself." He ushered her from the office. "It is a fine house."

Just one more thing to worry about, she thought as she followed Hamid into her bathroom.

The bathroom was about the size of a closet and contained a small, plastic water tank and a heating urn. To bathe, Hamid said, Elsa would have to heat water in the urn and pour it into another bucket to wash.

"The water for the compound," he continued, "is supplied from a nearby well and brought by a donkey. We have hired a man who will spend his day bringing water to you. You are very lucky. Here in Bamiyan, the women and their children collect their own water from the streams."

The windowless rooms were lit by kerosene lantern or candles. The toilet was a mud latrine located in another closet-sized room built onto the roof. Elsa would have to climb a set of mud stairs to get there.

Hamid guided her to another tiny room. "Your room," he said.

She stood in the wood-framed doorway of her new living quarters and peered into the tiny space, though "tiny" seemed too generous a word. About eight feet by ten feet, the room looked like the inside of a cardboard box. The walls and the floor were made of dried mud, and everything was brown except for her bed—a foam pad covered in a splash of red fabric smack in the center of the drabness.

"Though the winter has all but passed, the nights and mornings are still cold," Hamid said, pointing to a pile of blankets. "They will keep you warm until spring."

Elsa wrapped her arms around herself to ward off the chill that was already settling in the air.

"Where is your room?" she asked.

Hamid looked shocked.

"Oh, Elsa, not here. I cannot live here with you. Islam forbids it."

"But we will work together, won't we?" For some reason, this made a great deal of difference to her. "I'll be allowed to be your friend, won't I?"

"We will work together, yes, but men and women cannot be friends." Then he fell silent, and he seemed to think about it for a minute. "But you can be my sister. Allah will allow that. Yes, you will be my sister." He smiled, looking pleased that he'd worked that out.

"Where do you stay then? Are you near?"

"I have rented a small room in the bazaar. It is not far. Tonight, a *chowkidor*—a doorman—is outside. He will not let anyone in. You will be safe. Rest up, and I will collect you tomorrow."

With that, he bid her good night.

Elsa glanced around the room, acquainting herself with her new surroundings in the fading light. It made her bedroom in Dorchester seem palatial.

Worn out from her long trip and overwhelmed by her new life, she was too exhausted to do anything more than throw herself onto her sleeping pad and pull up a blanket. In the pang of loneliness and worry that followed, she thought of her mother and wished she were still alive to see Elsa now, half a world away—in *Afghanistan*.

6

A loud wailing jolted Elsa awake, and she sat straight up on her sleeping pad. Though it was still dark, she knew it was morning, and the wailing was the traditional call to prayer. She'd heard it the day before, when she was working with Pierre, and he'd explained that she would hear it five times a day. She looked at her watch, but the room was still too dark and she couldn't make out the time. So she pulled the blanket up to her chin to stave off the night's lingering chill, lay back, and listened.

The melody was haunting, beautiful almost, but she was still tired, and though she tried to shut out the sounds, it was no use. She was wide-awake.

Jet-lagged and sleep-deprived, she sat up again and fumbled to find the tiny box of matches that Hamid had left. With the small box in hand, she struck a match and lit her kerosene lantern. The dim glow was a welcome change from the darkness.

She looked at her watch—four thirty.

Oh God, is every morning going to be like this?

With the lantern to guide her, she threw on a robe and made her way to her tiny washroom, where there was a dusty but work-able mirror, and in the soft glow of the lamp, she looked at herself. The mirror was nailed a bit high up on the mud wall, and since she was only five foot four, she had to stand on her toes to get a good look. Her usually bright eyes struggled to wakefulness as she swept her hair into a bun and secured it at her neck. She brushed her teeth without water since the man with the donkey had yet to arrive, and she ran a dry cloth over her face before swiping a bright red gloss over her lips. Red, she thought, would be a good color for her first day in Bamiyan. A vivid red always made her feel powerful, taller almost. Her lipstick supply—five tubes in all, a color for every mood—had been the first thing she'd packed for the trip. It was the one thing she knew she'd need, the one thing that would make her feel alive and whole. Smiling to herself, she remembered the first time that little tube of color had transformed not just her lips but her spirit as well. She might be without water and electricity over the next year, but she wouldn't be without lipstick.

Picking up the lantern, she went back to her room and pulled out the little green handbook Pierre had given her. By the soft glow, she looked it over again.

Finally, when she saw a sliver of sunlight through her doorway, she pulled on her new clothes—the long-sleeved, knee-length dress and the balloon-like pants with a heavy sweater over it. She draped her scarf over her head and slipped her feet into the plastic sandals. Except for the lipstick, she thought she could pass for an Afghan woman.

Hamid arrived with the sun.

"Good morning," he said, seeming oblivious to the chill. "You look well. I've brought warm *naan*. Shall I heat yesterday's water for coffee?"

"Oh, yes," Elsa replied gratefully. "I have the matches you left, but I have no idea how to start a fire for cooking."

"Here, let me show you."

Hamid gathered a handful of kindling and some paper from a pile by the door. He knelt and struck a match and lit a small fire under the small heating grate. He placed the kettle to boil and set out cups and instant coffee.

"You will light the fire for your bathwater this same way. *Famidi?* Understand?"

Elsa nodded and broke off a piece of the warm bread.

When they finished their modest breakfast, they headed to the hospital.

The March air was crisp, just as Hamid had warned her it would be, and Elsa could see her own frosty breath when she exhaled. She pulled her sweater close around her and strode through the gate. She and Hamid walked to the back of the ADM compound and crossed a shallow stream before they stepped onto a well-worn path that snaked through once lush fields, now brown with rot and neglect.

"What about the land mines? Is it safe to walk here?" Elsa asked, suddenly remembering the warnings she'd received in Paris.

"The mines have been cleared in Bamiyan proper. We are safe here," Hamid replied.

Elsa took a deep breath. *One less thing to worry about.*

They crossed a rickety wooden bridge and she inhaled the sharp smell of cooking fires. Tiny, colorless mud houses dotted the road. It seemed as bleak as any place could be, and only the brilliant blue sky offered the relief of color.

They emerged from the fields into the village center, a single main street with a semblance of hustle and bustle, boasting weathered stalls and shops offering everything from soap to teakettles. There were even hitching posts where a few donkeys were tied up.

"I live there," Hamid said, pointing to a crumbling building with an outside stairway that led up to a second floor.

"Nice," Elsa said. "Is your room upstairs?"

Hamid nodded in reply. "I have a view of the village's main road. I see everything," he said confidently.

Elsa peered around, fascinated by the village center. Though the marketplace was splashed with bombed-out buildings and the debris of war, there were tiny lights—Christmas lights almost—draped around some of the stalls. The center was busy, and becoming busier by the minute, as people milled about. Those who were nearby stopped all chatter and watched Elsa. She stared right back and after a moment of curiosity, they went back to their business.

Elsa continued to look.

With their slanted eyes and broad noses, the people had an

almost East Asian appearance. They were darker than she'd expected, but on closer scrutiny, she saw that their weathered skin was stained not just by the sun and the wind but with a coating of grime. She looked down at her own hands and saw that a layer of dirt had already worked itself under her nails. She wondered how long it would take for her own skin to take on the sooty stain.

Deep black kohl lined the eyes of most everyone she saw—women, children, even men. The women wore large metal earrings that danced from their earlobes and thin, shiny bracelets that jingled like tiny bells when they moved. Their dresses and head-scarves were bright reds and yellows, not like the drab hues she'd chosen for herself in Peshawar.

"Hazara," Hamid said as if reading her thoughts. "The people of Bamiyan are Hazara—wild peasants to some, brilliant warriors to others. You can see for yourself how colorful the women are, and though they wear the veil, they don't often wear the full cover of the *burqa*."

They were a beautiful sight, these Hazara, exotic and mysterious all at once.

"The Hazara," Hamid said, "are a fierce people. You can see for yourself how sturdy they look. It's been said that even the women here fought back against the Taliban invaders."

"The women?" Elsa asked.

"Ahh, that's a story for another time," Hamid said, pointing to something in the distance. "We are almost there."

She and Hamid continued on until they arrived at the hospital compound, and when they entered the gate, she got her first look at where she would work. The flat, one-story building had been whitewashed, setting it apart from the mud brown that dominated the village.

Hamid had already been here, and he told her what he'd learned.

"The hospital has eighteen beds and those are only for the very sick," he said. "Most people who come here for care are attended to by their own families."

As they walked down the hallway, Elsa peeked into the rooms. People in the throes of typhoid or meningitis lay drenched in sweat on the old, metal cots. The stench of disease and unwashed bodies mingled in the air. The rooms were crowded with family members since at least one—and often more—stayed with patients to wash and feed them.

The clinic was located next to the hospital, another squat, whitewashed mud building, and it had three large rooms. Two of them were examining rooms and one was a kind of makeshift emergency room. There was no X-ray equipment, no EKG machines, and no lab, but there were cabinets filled with intravenous fluids, sutures, and dressing kits—just enough to patch up an injured or ill patient.

Elsa looked around and drew a slow breath. The grounds of the clinic were mobbed; crowds of villagers, all clamoring for attention, milled about. She swallowed the lump in her throat and felt whatever confidence she'd had begin to slip away.

Hamid was nervous too. Elsa could hear it in his voice.

"Come, come," he said. "You should meet the staff. They are all Afghan but some, I think, speak a little English." He ushered her into a small office and stepped up to two people who appeared to be physicians.

One was a pretty young woman named Laila. She was tiny, with sparkly eyes, dark hair, a singsongy voice, and a persistent smile. She looked so happy, Elsa thought, unable to grasp why.

Laila's husband, Ezat—a dour-faced man with a full beard and what seemed to be a permanent frown—was the other physician. Elsa wondered if Laila's constant smile was meant to offset Ezat's expression of choice.

Ezat stood and spoke, his voice soft despite his scowl.

"Why have they sent a woman, a nurse, here? It is an insult to me. What can you possibly teach us?"

Elsa felt the color rise in her face and spread to her ears. Her voice sounded timid despite her frustration.

"Aide du Monde has sent me here to work with you, not to teach you. In fact, you can probably teach me a thing or two." She paused and took a deep breath. "But I want you to know—I am here to stay."

Ezat scowled again and strode away.

The rest of the introductions were a blur, and Elsa could barely remember the names, though the staff—two male nurses and a cleaner—had been welcoming. Still reeling from Ezat's anger, the sheer number of patients, and the dizzying array of situations, she announced her intent to look around. She wanted to become as familiar as she could with the setup.

Though the hospital compound was tiny compared to Boston, she could see immediately there was a lot to be done, yet somehow, she had forgotten everything Pierre had said. There was something about managing the hospital and clinic, and creating protocols and procedures, but beyond that, she was at a loss. Panic welled up inside of her again, and she went outside to find a place where she could be alone.

She sat on the low stone wall behind the hospital and pulled the medical handbook from her bag, hoping it might provide some answers. As she turned the first page, Laila appeared and joined her on the wall, pulling herself up to sit.

"I speak a little English, Elsa," she said tentatively. "I am sorry about Ezat. He is not always the most polite, but he is a good doctor. Are you all right? You seem so nervous."

"Oh God, Laila," Elsa said. "I'm terrified. Ezat may be right. Now that I'm here, I'm not sure what I can do." She closed the book with a thump and set it in her lap.

"Do not worry." She put her hand over Elsa's. "You are here to help us. We want to know how best to *really* help our people, and you can show us with what you know and with what is in there." She pointed to the green book. "One thing that would help would be to get more of those, so that Ezat and I can have one."

"There's a little library at the office. I'm sure I saw another copy. I'll bring it tomorrow."

"You see?" Laila smiled. "You have helped us already. We can study the book together." Then she jumped down from the wall. "I have to get back. There is much to do. Tomorrow, you can work with me." With that, she turned and walked back toward the clinic.

"Thank you, Laila," Elsa called after her. She felt better already.

Elsa opened the book again, to read through the table of contents and introduction. To her dismay, she'd never even heard of half the things that were listed there: filariasis, leishmaniasis . . .

Good God, what is this stuff?

She spent the morning on the wall, reading and memorizing the symptoms of malaria, typhoid, meningitis, goiters, worms, and dysentery, and then she read the treatments and doses of the medicines again and again.

She finally closed the book and sighed.

She couldn't imagine how these people survived at all.

She and Hamid ate a dinner of beans and rice, and once she was alone, she tried to work out her new daily routine. She used a large ladle to transfer water from the tank in the courtyard into a bucket. She half carried, half dragged the full bucket into the bathroom and poured the water into the heating urn. She took a handful of the kindling that Hamid had left and placed it under the urn, then struck a match and fanned her little flame to life.

One small victory.

She gathered her soap, shampoo, towel, nightgown, and kerosene lantern. Once her water was heated, she filled a large bucket and squatted down. She soaped herself up, scrubbed, and then rinsed off with some of the water. To wash her hair, she knelt over the bucket and dunked her head in. She poured shampoo over her head and dunked her head in again to rinse her hair.

There was no way she'd go through this every night, she decided. *At least tonight I'm clean,* she thought with relief. *That's something.*

Back in her own room, Elsa shivered and wrapped herself in a heavy sweater and a pair of thick socks before burrowing under two blankets for the night. She leaned over and blew out the flickering light on her lantern. Before she could think about how tired she was, she was asleep.

The following morning, she met Laila at the clinic and gave her the green handbook. Laila's smile grew even wider than it had been yesterday.

"*Besiar tashakore,* my friend. Ezat, come and see what Elsa has brought!"

Ezat poked his head out of the examining room. His brow wrinkled at the intrusion.

"*Che'ast? What is it?*" he asked impatiently. Unfazed, Laila answered in her singsong voice.

"A book, Ezat. Elsa brought a handbook for us to share."

Ezat strode from the room and took the book from Laila. He ran his finger over the cover and a faint smile crept onto his lips.

"*Tashakore*, Elsa, *tashakore*. Pierre could never remember to bring this." He held on to the book and disappeared back into the examining room.

Elsa followed Laila on her hospital rounds, and Hamid followed Elsa like a shadow. The little parade caught the attention of patients and visitors alike, and to each one Laila explained that Elsa was a nurse from Amrika, come to help.

A wizened old woman, who seemed too frail to even sit, pulled herself from her bed and leaned in to Elsa, running her fingers along Elsa's face. She smiled then, nodded, and took Elsa's hand and caressed it.

"You see," Laila said. "She likes you. Many people will feel the same way. You'll do fine."

Once rounds were complete, Laila headed to the clinic. "I am already behind. See the crowds. It is like this every day. There are too many and not enough of us. We will see the sickest first, maybe others if there is time."

Elsa watched as people were turned away. To be chosen from the line, the villagers seemed to have to prove their sickliness. Fights broke out, and desperate people became even more desperate.

"Too many patients for just the two of us," Laila said. "But there is nothing we can do."

"Isn't there something I can do to help?" Elsa asked.

"There are so many waiting, and many have simple problems—skin diseases, coughs. See those for us, Elsa, and choose patients whose problems are familiar to you. That would be a good way to help."

Armed with penicillin, ointments, painkillers, and her little green handbook, Elsa made her way through the crowds and tended to rotting leg ulcers and long-festering sores. She squatted down and gently cleaned away the dead tissue and pus from a bony old man's rancid leg before rubbing in ointment and covering it with gauze.

She was comfortable with this stuff. Back in the ER, she'd tended the same decaying ulcers on the homeless men who'd slept in the city's tunnels.

Another gnarled old man bent and watched her as she cleaned his wounds. When she'd finished wrapping the gauze and taping it all up, he held up his leg for a look. Satisfied, he gave her a wide grin, and holding his hand on his heart, he bowed to her before he limped away.

She doled out penicillin and pain pills to shriveled villagers with deep, wracking coughs, and she dispensed tiny pills to flush out worms from children's bloated bellies. Caught up in her work, she forgot her nervousness, and she smiled at them while she did what she could to make them feel better.

She noticed that the crowd watched her with interest, this young foreigner who'd come so far to wash an old man's foul-smelling sores. At the end of the day, Laila came out to watch, and she told Elsa that she'd heard one patient murmur, "She is sent from Allah."

A persistent knocking at the front gate roused Elsa from her routine the following morning. She pulled on her head-scarf and hurried to open the gate, expecting to see Hamid. Instead, a small, nervous European man stood before her. He pulled his wire spectacles from his nose and spoke.

"You are Elsa Murphy?" He wiped his sweating brow with his sleeve.

She nodded and wondered if he was from ADM.

"I am Johann, from the United Nations," he said as he turned and pointed out a nearby compound where a UN banner hung. "Pierre Dubois gave me your name. May I come in, please?" he asked, his voice quivering.

"Of course. Come in, come in. It's good to meet you," Elsa said as she stuck out her hand.

Johann took her hand with both of his and held it surprisingly tightly. She could feel the dampness in his palms. *He's more anxious than I am,* she thought with a smile.

"I . . ." He seemed to have trouble getting started. "I am sorry to be blunt, but I have come to give you bad news. Aide du Monde has contacted me and asked that I inform you—" He stopped, the words catching in his throat. He raised his hand to his eyes, and she was surprised to see tears there. After a moment, he continued.

"Pierre never made it to Yakawlang. His vehicle was stopped by bandits or maybe Taliban, and—" Johann wiped the tears from his eyes with his hand and cleared his throat. "He and the driver were killed."

Elsa felt the color drain from her face.

"*Dead?* Pierre and Ismael? Oh, God." She felt her knees go weak and she leaned against the wall.

"It is terrible news, I know. Pierre was my friend." Johann blinked his tears away. "But this is Afghanistan. It is a sad reminder to us all that this is a dangerous place."

Though she'd barely known them, Elsa felt a deep sadness envelop her. What had Pierre said? *We must all make sacrifices.*

Her eyes welled up, and she glanced at Johann.

"Did ADM say what they want me to do? Will the program close?"

"No, no, I think nothing will change for you. Of course, it will be some time before they can send another person, but you are needed here, and for now at least, Bamiyan is safe."

He sighed and turned to go, but he paused and glanced back.

"If I can help you, Elsa, please come and see me."

She thanked Johann, closed the gate, and stumbled back to her room.

Dear God, she thought, *what am I doing here? Alone in Afghanistan in a Taliban house.*

She almost wished they would send her home. Maybe she shouldn't have come after all. She closed her eyes and waited until Hamid arrived. When she shared the news with him, his eyes grew wide.

"It was almost dark when they left . . . too late, I think, to travel those roads. The bandits see a fancy foreign vehicle, and they know it carries men who possess money and radios. If Pierre had waited till morning, the roads might have been safe."

He shook his head sadly, and they set off for the clinic.

Elsa's day passed in a blur, a heaviness settling in her chest and worry tangling up her thoughts. She knew when she came to Afghanistan there'd be danger, but it hadn't seemed real until today. What could she really do? She wasn't ready to go home. She hadn't even been there a week; she had to give it time. She *couldn't* leave. She wouldn't abandon the clinic, and Pierre, after all, had been killed leaving. No, it was safer to stay put. She took a deep breath. ADM would send someone.

When she told Laila and Ezat about Pierre's death, she was sure that she saw something in Ezat's eyes—perhaps even tears—but he turned away quickly.

7

Elsa had been in Bamiyan less than a week when she'd seen the U.S. helicopters roaring overhead as she walked along the road. She'd stopped and watched, her head thrown back, her eyes open wide. The mere sight of them had enlivened her, and she'd known it was only a matter of time before she saw the soldiers. She looked for them each morning as she climbed the stairs to the roof. But wherever they were, they were well hidden from her view.

Elsa began most mornings there on the roof, sipping coffee and watching as the village came alive. She listened to the first crow of the roosters, the bray of the donkeys, and the sounds of people stirring as they echoed across the village.

One morning, as she and Hamid crossed the nearby stream and headed off to the clinic, a band of tiny boys and one little girl joined them and tagged along all the way to the hospital. They chattered and asked Elsa questions all the way, which Hamid translated with undisguised amusement.

"What's your name?"

"Elsa. What's yours?"

With laughter, the string of names filled the air all at once.

"Seema."

"Bouman."

"Noori."

"Hussein."

"Syed."

"Assadullah."

Then they resumed their interrogation.

"Do you have children?"

"No, not yet."

"Oh," they replied sadly, for to be childless was considered a tragedy in Bamiyan.

"Where's your husband?"

"I don't have one."

And their eyes searched her face and her hands for the deformities that surely must have prevented her from acquiring a husband.

Finding none, they sighed and chattered on.

"Can you read?"

"Can you count?"

"Are there schools where you come from?"

"*Balay*, yes," Elsa said, nodding, and she asked Hamid to tell them that *they* should be in school. But they just laughed again.

"There are no schools here. We can't go to school. We have work to do." And, as though they'd just reminded themselves of their chores, they were off, running back through the fields.

Childhood was short-lived in Afghanistan.

The band of children followed her every day. One bright morning, Elsa watched as they ran off, and there, just beyond the field, she spied a small U.S. Army convoy traveling the main road. Hidden from view by the field's shrubbery, she paused and stood on her toes to watch as the convoy stopped and a soldier jumped from his vehicle. Craning her neck to see what he was up to, she saw that tiny Syed had fallen and scraped his hands. He sat alone at the side of the road sniveling and crying. The soldier knelt by Syed's side and spoke quietly to him, then reached forward and lifted the small boy onto his shoulders. Syed shrieked with laughter and the soldier turned, and Elsa's breath caught in her throat. Even from this distance, she could see that his eyes were the deepest blue imaginable, and when he smiled, they sparkled. It was that easy smile that held her gaze. She exhaled slowly and watched as he gently set Syed on a heavy rock by the side of the road and examined his injuries. He spoke to the boy, who smiled and nodded, and with a wave, the soldier jumped back into his jeep and the convoy moved off.

"Come, let's go." Hamid's words pierced her trance and she turned.

"Sorry," she said. "I was daydreaming." She turned back to the path, her mind racing with thoughts of the handsome soldier.

Shortly after her arrival in Bamiyan, Hamid found a female neighbor to live with Elsa. Her name was Amina, and though she was about Elsa's age, she would act as her chaperone, the protector of her virtue and her reputation, as well as be her cook and companion. Amina had lived in the compound next door, and she had eagerly accepted the position when Hamid had offered it.

Amina had been born with an extra finger on her right hand, her "good" hand. In Amina's culture, Elsa was told, the left hand was considered dirty, used for cleaning oneself but never for eating or touching another person. To have the good hand somehow marked made it dirty as well, evil in the minds of the superstitious. More than one man had refused to marry her once he learned of her extra finger.

In spite of her affliction and the sentence it carried, Amina was possessed of a relentlessly cheerful nature and a strikingly serene face with clear brown eyes, flawless skin, and waist-length black hair. She smiled broadly when Hamid introduced her to Elsa, and though she spoke no English, she seemed to communicate well enough through gestures and nods.

Elsa led her around the small compound and when they arrived at Elsa's room, Amina scowled. Shaking her head, she walked right in and motioned for help as she propped Elsa's suitcase on end and showed how it could be used as a small table. There she arranged a flashlight, a lantern, and a few books. She smiled then and nodded.

Together they hammered hooks into the bare wall to hang clothes and trekked to the bazaar, where they bought a colorful floor mat woven of hard plastic, as well as small pillows decorated with intricate beads and tiny mirrors, all intended to cheer up Elsa's room.

Amina negotiated the price of every item Elsa purchased. She tucked her extra finger into the palm of her hand and held her sleeve over it, waving the covered hand widly, frowning and raising her voice until she deemed the price reasonable. As they left each shop, her sweet nature returned instantly, and she demurely lowered her gaze and almost whispered, *"Tashakore."*

At each stop Elsa watched, fascinated. It became clear that Amina was a force to be reckoned with.

At home, they developed a familiar routine. In the morning, Amina prepared tea and rice, and Hamid picked up the warm *naan* on his way to the house. After their shared breakfast, Hamid and Elsa headed off to the hospital and Amina remained behind to do the chores. She cleaned and prepared dinner.

But Amina was paid for her labors, a fact that separated her from most Afghan women. And Hamid revealed to Elsa that Amina had dreams now, not just because of the money but because she worked for a foreign nurse. She planned to ask Elsa to cut off her hated extra appendage, convinced that without it, she would find a husband.

I hope it never comes to that, Elsa thought. But she kept her silence.

Every morning, Elsa conducted her own nursing clinic, and with Hamid by her side, she saw countless villagers complaining of simple problems. She kept her green handbook in her pocket and she consulted it frequently. The first time she identified leishmaniasis on her own, she wanted to shout with joy. Instead, she smiled broadly as she painted the wound with gentian violet and sent the patient on his way. Each day brought more small victories, and before long, the endless line of patients had dwindled to a manageable length.

When the clinic was closed, she tried to work on her growing pile of paperwork. It was an exhausting routine, but she was adjusting to her ascetic lifestyle.

Living by candlelight and kerosene lantern limited what she could get done very early or very late, so she squeezed every minute she could out of the daylight. Fortunately, the days were growing longer, and she usually arrived home by dusk. After dinner, however, she and Amina lived in near darkness since they had a limited supply of kerosene.

As for washing, it involved so much preparation—stoking the

fire, filling the urn, and heating the water—that Elsa began to skip a day or two here and there. Other adjustments were more challenging. Sleeping on the floor pad was difficult since it was firm, and the floor was cold and hard. She missed sitting, too. Here she squatted for everything—to eat, to talk, to visit, even for the latrine. She longed for a seat or a bed or a toilet, and she quickly tired of the never-ending diet of beans and rice.

But she was careful not to complain. Hamid had told her more than once how well she was living. The food, the rooms, the donkey that delivered water—all were considered luxurious in Bamiyan.

In those rare moments of quiet, Hamid taught her Dari—the Afghan variation of the Persian language—and the basics of polite behavior. And he did his best to help her understand his culture.

"Like it or not," he said self-consciously, "it is often whispered that foreign women are prostitutes, and many believe they are here to steal good Afghan men."

Elsa smiled and wondered if she should tell him about the blue-eyed soldier before deciding to keep her secret crush just that. "Gimme a break, Hamid," she said in her best Boston accent, rolling her eyes. "Do I look like a prostitute?"

"This is not a city, Elsa," he said, glancing around nervously. "*I* know that it is not true but these are illiterate people." His voice dropped to a whisper. "They are peasants really. Many do not understand why anyone—a woman especially—would come so far for people she doesn't even know. Naturally, they suspect . . . how do you say it? Secret motives."

He paused to make certain that she was taking him seriously.

"You must take care. Look away from men and when you meet them, do not put out your hand. Instead, hold your hand over your heart. And remember, if the women feel they can trust you around their men, they will accept you."

Elsa shook her head and dropped the subject. The etiquette lesson over, they worked on Dari. Thankfully, Hamid was a patient teacher.

"*Che taklif?*" Elsa said, focusing carefully on the pronunciation.

"*Che taklif?* What's wrong?" She repeated it over and over until the words came almost naturally.

"*Mariz,* sick?"

"*As-salaam alaikum. Chetore asti? Khoob asti? Jona jurast?*" *That just might be the longest hello in the world,* she thought.

"What does it all mean?" she asked.

"May peace be upon you. How are you? You are well? How is your health?" Hamid replied. "It is long, but it is the formal and proper way to greet someone. Try it," he urged.

Elsa sighed and repeated the greeting.

Hamid leaned forward and tried to hold in his laughter.

"*Kh* is a guttural sound. You must say it from your throat. It doesn't sound like a hard K. Try it again."

Elsa struggled with the sounds, but she kept at it, determined to master them.

She was determined, as well, to find her niche, and she decided to spend more time in the clinic's emergency room. It felt like the one place where she could demonstrate her expertise and prove to Ezat that she *was* valuable. Yet the emergency room, Laila had told her, was Ezat's domain.

"I'm not certain this is a good idea, Elsa," Laila said, her brow furrowed. "Ezat doesn't even allow *me* in the emergency room and if you go in there, he will not be happy."

"Then it may be just what he needs to understand that I'm here to stay," Elsa replied.

Elsa and Hamid spent one long afternoon in the emergency room, cleaning, sorting, and figuring out exactly which supplies she had and what she might need. It was familiar work, and she felt more comfortable than she had since she arrived.

When they'd finished, she stood and stretched. Through the open window, she saw Ezat striding purposefully toward the ER.

"Uh-oh," she said, nodding toward the window.

Hamid spun just as Ezat pushed open the door. He froze and stood in the middle of the ER. His jaw was set; he was clearly angry.

"What are you doing to *my* emergency room?" Ezat boomed.

"*Our* emergency room." Elsa stood her ground. "I've made some adjustments so it will work better. I moved the suture trays and the dressing material here." She gestured to one side. "And I placed the intravenous fluids over there. Just small changes, but you'll see that this setup will make things go more smoothly." She smiled, hoping to ease the strain.

Ezat's nostrils flared and his scowl deepened, but he didn't speak. Disconcerted by his silence, she continued.

"Ezat, I worked in a big emergency room in Amrika." She cleared her throat. "This is the sort of thing *I* know. We treated gunshot wounds and accident victims and burn victims, and sometimes, we performed surgery right there in the ER. I'm not saying we can do all that here, but we can at least *try* to do better." She hoped her voice sounded firm.

He folded his arms across his chest. "And if it doesn't work?"

"Ezat, just give it a chance. Give *me* a chance. We *are* going to work together and this ER is a good place to start."

He raised his eyebrows, turned, and walked out the door.

A few days later, morning clinic was interrupted by a persistent blaring horn. Elsa stepped away from her line of patients to look and saw a white vehicle just outside the gate, its bright UN banner waving in the breeze. She could just make out Johann waving furiously at her. Excusing herself, she hurried to his side.

"Johann, it's good to see—"

He interrupted her before she could finish.

"We have an emergency here. He's bad, very bad. One of the mine clearers." Johann shook his head. "Right onto a mine, he . . . he just stepped and . . . please just help him." He pointed to the backseat of the jeep, and Elsa leaned in to look.

There, crumpled and bleeding, lay what remained of a young man. Where his legs should have been, only bloody stumps were visible; his right arm had been torn from its socket and someone had laid it across his chest. His face was covered with blood and one eye was open and staring.

She yelled for Hamid to bring a stretcher. Johann was speaking, but she heard only a loud roaring in her ears.

Hamid and Ezat, a gurney in tow, mercifully arrived and reached into the vehicle to move the young man. Frozen in place, Elsa stood and watched as they lifted him from the car. She was still watching when his shredded arm fell to the ground.

The bitter taste of her half-digested breakfast filled her mouth.

"Elsa," Ezat ordered. "Get the arm and put it here!" He pointed to the man's bloodied chest.

But she couldn't move. Her head was spinning, and she tried to gulp in fresh air, but the smell of the blood and the sight of the wounded man made her stomach heave instead. Her hand flew to her mouth as if she could hold the vomit back. She turned away and vomited the *naan* and tea she'd had for breakfast. Then she slumped against the UN vehicle, Johann at her side.

Ezat shot her a disgusted look, reached down, and lifted the bloody stump, placing it onto the gurney. "Let's go!" he said.

He shook his head as he pushed the gurney past her to the emergency room.

"Elsa, my dear," Johann cried, worry wrinkling his brow.

"Oh, God. I don't know what's wrong with me." She felt tears sting her eyes. "I *know* this stuff, Johann. I work in an ER. I know what to do."

She stood shakily, and he reached for her arm.

"Sit, just for a minute. It's hard to see them at first, the victims of these land mines."

"No, no, Johann." She moved away and took a deep breath. "I have to get to the ER or Ezat will never let me forget this."

She turned and walked as quickly as she could to the ER, but she hesitated for an instant before she pushed open the door and walked inside.

Ezat, an Afghan nurse, and Hamid stood around the gurney. The smell of blood and of death filled the small space, and Elsa held her breath.

Ezat turned, his eyes accusing. "He is dead. And you . . . what of you?"

"I froze. I'm sorry, but I *do* know what to do. Next time will be different."

Ezat fixed her with a steely gaze.

Elsa turned away, blinking back tears.

* * *

That night, she lay on her pad and reminded herself that she *did* know what to do. She'd learned it all in nursing school and then in the ER. *Next time,* she swore silently, *I will be prepared.*

She replayed the scene over and over in her mind, but this time, she reached into the vehicle and pulled the injured man out and worked over him, saving his life.

I know I can do this, she thought, until she fell into a fitful sleep.

PART
2

Parween

8

Bamiyan, 1988

"A husband, Mama? No." Parween groaned as dramatically as she dared.

"Now hush," her mother murmured firmly. "Your childhood is finished. We must look to your future." Rahima fixed a steely gaze on her daughter's dirt-stained face. "As long as you are quiet and respectful, and can cook and clean, *inshallah,* we should have little trouble."

But something in her eyes spoke of doubt.

Knowing it was an important topic, even if she didn't especially want to discuss it, ten-year-old Parween folded her grimy hands into her lap and sat cross-legged on the threadbare carpet, trying to listen to her mother. She tucked in her bare feet and rearranged her fraying dress and loose pants as she listened. Her veil, a shawl almost, was draped haphazardly across her head.

"This is how it must be," Rahima continued firmly. "So there's no use pouting. Just do as you are told, or you will find no husband at all."

That would be fine with me, Parween thought. But she kept silent.

She didn't want a husband, yet by age ten she had already learned that what she wanted would make no difference. The youngest of four children—cursed with the added misfortune of being a girl— Parween had spent her entire childhood answering to others.

And now this, this talk of marriage, just after moving from the only home she'd ever known! *How can life be so cruel?*

Parween Saleh had been just a year old when the monsters from the north, the "Russkis," had invaded her homeland, a dusty village called Onai deep in the mountains of central Afghanistan. She'd learned to crawl—and then walk—amidst the land mines that dotted the landscape. She'd learned to sleep through the buzz of attacking helicopters and to hide at the sound of the monstrous vehicles that rumbled past the squat, one-story mud houses and out into the distant countryside.

It often seemed the fighting was going badly, for more than one villager had returned limping or blind or without his legs.

War brought only misery.

And then, all at once, right before her tenth birthday, the foreign soldiers had disappeared from the outskirts of her village. *The fighting is done,* the villagers said. Parween was left with her mother and two brothers—her older sister had already married and left the house—plus three goats, four chickens, and a mangy, nameless dog.

Parween couldn't remember her father. He had disappeared early from her life when, as her mother told her, he was called to defend their country against the foreign invaders. Only later did they learn that he wasn't coming home, having been "martyred" for their country's cause.

She had lived all her life in Onai, with her family waiting for her father's return. But once his death had been confirmed, the small village offered little sustenance, and even less hope, to the fatherless family. Her mother was soon forced to sell their goats and abandon their dog. Though it was common practice for a dead man's brother to marry the widow, ensuring that the family was cared for, Parween's father had no brothers and no family to speak of, so Rahima had been forced to turn to her own relatives for help.

This meant uprooting her children and moving their scant belongings to Bamiyan village, where they would live among the large extended family of Parween's uncle Abdullah. A shepherd by trade,

Abdullah lived in a mud compound that boasted several large rooms, each housing an entire family.

The trip was long, so long Parween thought it would never end, but finally, after a full day of travel by rickety bus and weary foot, they arrived at their new home. The fertile green valley was nestled in the shadow of great sand-colored cliffs dotted with caves. The gravel and dirt road was crowded with people walking or sitting astride donkeys, the buzz of laughter and friendly conversation filling the air. Parween's eyes grew wide as she spotted two gigantic statues carved into the face of the mountain. Fascinated as she was, she caught only a glimpse before the family reached their destination and unloaded their things into their new home.

While her brothers explored every nook and cranny of the compound, Parween stood in the center of the family's room and looked around curiously. Each of the rooms opened onto a central courtyard that offered an open cooking area, a small well, and an open latrine off to the side. The dirt floor of the little room in which she stood was covered by a fading and fraying hand-woven carpet.

How beautiful it is, she thought with delight. *It's so soft on my feet.*

They hadn't owned a carpet in Onai, and she squatted to run her hands over the worn fabric, its smooth feel and hint of color a welcome change from her old floor.

Real window frames covered with plastic sheeting broke up the monotony of the mud-brown walls and offered her a murky glimpse out into the courtyard. The nearby well was a luxury, allowing them access to water without forcing Parween to trudge for hours balancing water jugs on poles across her back as she had in Onai. When the jugs were full, the poles—old sticks really—had gnawed at her bony shoulders, and she'd spent hours rubbing away the soreness. But with the well, all of that was finished, and she smiled in relief.

Life will be easy here.

Parween was tiny; her brothers even called her scrawny. As the youngest, she'd always been the last one fed. But what she lacked in size, she more than made up for in spirit. She had learned early on to look out for herself and she clung to that skill with fierce determination. Most often, her siblings were involved in their own chores and drudgeries and had little time for their youngest sister. Though she'd always had to spend part of each day trudging home with those heavy water buckets and performing other exhausting chores, Parween had still managed to find time for fun, as well.

She had run with the boys over the rolling hills around Onai, her veil flying out behind her. It was the boys who had taken the time to teach her to fight, to hold her fists just so and deliver punches that had sent more than one of them sprawling in the dirt. They had taught her how to recognize and sidestep the hidden land mines, which everyone knew could blow you right up to Allah, and to avoid the small explosives disguised as toys, which could tear off your arms. But they'd also taught her how to spit so far she could hit a tree, and how to whistle like the birds. *Nothing* would ever feel as good as spitting farther or whistling louder than the boys could.

Aside from what the boys taught her, there was little opportunity for schooling—and for girls, no school at all. Reading and writing were useless in the countryside; there was nothing to read, anyway. Counting your sheep or cows or even your money was important, so most boys could at least do that. The boys of Onai had shared with Parween the magic of numbers, and she took to practicing, pointing at roaming sheep and counting, *"Yak, do, say, char . . ."* Her talent with numbers made her proud; she didn't know any other girls who could add.

But according to her mother, her flair for numbers and fisticuffs would have to change now that they'd made the move to Bamiyan village.

While her brothers settled in, Parween sat and listened to her mother as everything that had ever made her happy slowly slipped away like dirt between her fingers. How could she live without running, without the wind rushing through her hair? How could she ever slow down and simply walk without letting her callused feet skip over Onai's rutted roads and grassy fields? How could she ever survive without spitting or fighting? And, worse still, how could she live without the genuine easy friendship of boys? She'd seen what happened. Once a girl grew up, she was hidden away with no friends, no fun, and nothing to look forward to.

Parween slumped as she sat. How could she ever bear this misery? She picked at a fresh scab on her hand. Was this to be her last battle scar? She heaved a sigh.

Once Rahima was done with the lecture, she dismissed her daughter with a wave. Parween stood, tugging to straighten the veil on her head, before shuffling out into the warm sunshine. If she was going to be stuck here, she might as well have a look.

Just across the way, she stopped and peered up to study the two soaring statues, which her mother had called Buddhas, sculpted right into the mountain. They were so tall she had to crane her neck to get a good look, and to see their heads, she had to lean back so far that she almost fell over backward. But there they stood, silent sentinels watching over the entire village.

One was larger than the other, and both were nestled in deep indents that cast dark shadows in the bright sunlight. Each figure was draped in carved robes, and they were worn smooth in places. The cliffs surrounding them were dotted with many small caves, some rounded and others square, and as she watched, Parween's attention was drawn by motion that seemed to be *everywhere*.

Her gaze followed hurrying villagers as they scrambled up the steep mountainside and vanished into its hidden recesses. Unable to contain her curiosity, she crossed the road and fell in behind a group of children as they climbed. She struggled to keep up with them and her feet were caught in several of the spiky crevices along the way, sharp stones nipping at her feet.

As she straightened, a little room built right into the mountain caught her attention and she stepped inside. The earthen floor was smooth and free of the irritating little rocks and pebbles that had so vexed her as she climbed. But it was the walls, covered in brightly painted designs, that held Parween's gaze. She reached out and passed her fingers over the colorful hues that decorated the cave's walls. Like the giants, these decorations were worn smooth in places, yet the beautiful reds, blues, golds, and other colors remained vivid.

Smiling and pleased with her discovery, she left the room and found a narrow, steep stairway carved into the cliffside that led upward, toward the top of the carved Buddha. There, just above the statue, a final room beckoned.

It held no paintings, but it opened onto the valley, and when Parween stepped inside, she could see the entire village, green and lush and teeming with homes and people and animals. She tried to make out Uncle Abdullah's compound but she was so high up that everything looked the same. In the distance, however, she saw Bamiyan's center. The little marketplace, lined with shops and bazaars, was crowded with people.

Determined to see as much as she could on her first day, Parween scrambled back down the stairway, then down the side of the mountain, and headed off in the direction of the bazaar.

Strands of matted hair peeked from underneath her veil. Every inch of her was crusted with old dirt. To wash in Onai had meant trekking the long distance to an icy cold stream where she'd had to lean into the biting waters and scrub with coarse soap. For Parween, it had been too much trouble; it was easier to just stay dirty, and besides, being clean wasn't important. It wasn't like being tall, tall enough to pluck the freshest apricots and the sweetest apples from the highest branches. It had been months since she'd had a proper wash.

Even here in Bamiyan, she was like most of the other kids, scrawny and hungry for entertainment, and for something to eat. The bazaar, filled with food and trinkets and who knew what else, offered endless temptations. She walked the short distance to the marketplace, and stepping from a dark and narrow road into the bright and open space, she froze, spellbound by the swirl of activity and excitement that surrounded her.

The scent of fresh *naan,* hot from the tandoor oven, drifted on the breeze and drew her to a baker's shop on the bazaar's main road. When she peeked inside, the heat of the ovens hit her full-on, and she blinked to clear the sting from her eyes. Tendrils of steam danced in the air, rising from an oven built right into the earthen floor of the little shop. It was open, and she could see a blazing fire at the bottom of the cavernous, cylindrical space; they

baked the bread by slapping fresh dough onto the sides. A man—
the baker, she supposed—did just that and then slid the cover back
into place.

The room was smoky and dark, and as she entered, Parween had
to blink again to get a better look. Two men, covered with grime
and soot, sat cross-legged in the center of the shop, arranging hot
loaves of *naan*. Another man stood off to the side mixing the flour
and water. He was the one who'd closed the oven, and he moved
again to the center of the bakery.

As the baker kneeled and lifted the cover, Parween ventured
farther in to get a closer look. In one fluid motion, the man slid out
two hot loaves of steaming bread and then slapped two new pieces
of dough onto the oven's side walls. Parween's empty stomach roared
to life at the sight of the warm bread, and finally the seated men
turned to her.

"*Naan?*" the older one asked.

"*Afghanis na doram,*" she replied sadly. *I have no money.* But the
older man broke off a large piece of the warm bread and handed it
to Parween. She hesitated, but he motioned for her to take it and
thrust it into her hands.

"*Tashakore,*" she whispered, thanking him, overwhelmed by his
generosity. She backed out of the little room, clutching her treasure,
and squatted on the ground outside to watch the townspeople as
she ate.

The bazaar was *filled* with people. The women, children in tow,
wore colorful dresses and pants and bright shiny jewelry as they
walked purposefully through the street. The men milled about, talking and laughing.

Parween leaned back against the baker's storefront and took slow
bites of her bread. *With all this smiling, things must be pretty good here,*
she supposed. Even the donkeys, hitched to posts outside of little
shops, seemed content.

The sound of sweet music filled the air. It was a sound that Parween had rarely heard in Onai, where people had no money for
luxuries like music. Yet in this marketplace, several merchants had
cassette players and were playing exotic Indian music. The melodies

of lutes and voices competed with the hum of generators—the more successful shopkeepers could afford to provide electricity for a few hours each day, it seemed.

The buildings, too, were sturdier than those she'd seen before. They were made of wood, and some were even two stories tall. Parween noticed the strings of colored lights wound around some of the shop openings. Once darkness fell, those little colored lights would surely create magic in the night.

What a grand place Bamiyan is.

Directly across the road from the bakery stood an open-air butcher shop. The butcher himself sat on a wooden chair, winding his faded turban around his head. Sides of beef, strung up to dry, were covered with flies, and dogs and mice darted about in search of the drippings. Parween was mesmerized watching them chase after the stray bits of meat. When the dogs got too close to the hanging beef, the butcher reached out and swatted at them.

Still squatting, Parween licked the last crumbs of bread from her fingers, stood, and headed off to explore.

The unmistakable aroma of grilling beef filled the air and she followed her nose to an alleyway where a turbaned, toothless man rotated kabobs on an outdoor fire. He turned and spat the gristle he'd been chewing onto the ground and then noticed Parween standing there. Studying her with gentle eyes, he wiped his greasy hands on his shirt and smiled.

"Besheneen, besheneen," he said as he motioned for her to sit on the little stool beside his fire. She sat, and he handed her a hot skewer strung with three blackened kabobs. This time, she did not hesitate. She greedily took the skewer and tore into the scorched meat. She hadn't eaten meat in several years, not since a girl from Onai had been married to her cousin, and the long-forgotten taste of charred beef filled her mouth.

Mmm . . . heavenly.

She chewed and chewed, and was loath to swallow. She wanted this moment to last. Who knew when she would taste beef again?

"Tashakore," she said after she had finished the last bite. In reply, the man slid a broom to her and motioned for her to sweep the dirt

and trash away from the ground around his fire. Parween happily took the broom and swept with new energy.

When she had swept every trace of loose dirt from the ground, she passed the broom back to the gentle-eyed man, murmured her thanks, and headed home. As she walked back through the bazaar, she passed a shop displaying glittery plastic sandals and stopped to admire them. The rows upon rows of delicate shoes entranced her. She looked down at her bare feet and longed to slip them into the ornate sandals. But she knew her mother wouldn't buy such a luxury for her youngest and most wayward child.

She continued on, stopping in the fields to watch a girl about her own age exchanging blows with a boy. Parween scrunched up her face and squinted. Surely, this was a hallucination or the work of the *jinn*—those mischievous spirits that lay in wait for the souls of innocent boys and girls. She rubbed at her eyes and opened them again. The two *were* fighting. The girl had gained the upper hand, holding the boy down with her knees while she delivered the final punch.

"Aha," the girl shouted as she stood triumphantly. "That'll teach you! Throw stones at me and you'll pay the price."

The boy stood, nose bloody and fists raw, and ran off. When he'd gone, the girl turned and saw Parween. Hands on her hips, with eyes big as figs, she glared and called out, "And you—do you want to fight?"

"No," Parween called back, breathless with the thrill of what she'd just seen. "*Khoob asti,* you are good."

"*Tashakore,* who are you?"

"I am Parween from Onai. We just moved here today."

"I am Mariam," the girl replied, retrieving her head-scarf from the ground.

Parween nodded. "Will I see you later?"

"Yes, why not?' Mariam said as she turned and raced back through the fields.

Parween heaved a sigh of relief. She'd never expected to meet another girl who could fight. *A girl!* Maybe things would be okay after all.

At dusk, after sharing a skimpy dinner of rice with her mother, Parween trudged back up to the Buddha's caves, climbed to the top room, and gazed out over the landscape. The nearby caves and terraced landscapes were punctuated with small patches of light from fires, kerosene lanterns, and wax candles. The strings of colored lights in the bazaar twinkled, just as she'd imagined. Music wafted from the village shops and Parween was captivated once more by the beauty of it all. She curled up against the wall and simply stared until she was nearly asleep for her first night in Bamiyan, nestled above the giant Buddha.

Within days of their arrival, Rahima was hired to sew small pieces for the village tailor. Parween's brothers, Abdul and Noori, also found work. Abdul tended to the village elder's herd of sheep, and Noori helped repair motors and engines on the few trucks that drove through Bamiyan.

The family had not counted on such good luck. With the promise of money flowing in, they allowed themselves some small luxuries. Parween received her coveted sandals, though not the glittery ones she had so longed for. Instead, her mother chose a serviceable and sturdy pair made of dark gray plastic. She also received a new veil, colored a deep pink and embroidered with tiny roses at the edges.

"*Baraye man?* For me?" she whispered as she took her gifts and held them close before hugging her mother and smiling. She'd never owned anything so beautiful, and for the first time in her life, she wanted to keep them like new. And for just a moment, she wanted to whistle as the boys had taught her, but she thought better of it.

Instead, she raced to the well, filled two buckets with cold water, and found her mother's small sliver of soap. She scrubbed her feet red and nearly raw before she slipped them into her first pair of new sandals. She washed her hair and scalp, as well, rubbing so hard that her skin burned under the ministrations of the caustic soap. Her hair and even her fingers shone from the scrubbing, and for days she smelled of lye.

Life settled into a routine. For weeks Parween's mother did not bring up the question of a husband and Parween allowed herself to hope that maybe, just maybe, the subject had been forgotten. *After all,* she thought, *with everyone working so hard, who has time to think of such things?*

And once the novelty of the new veil and sandals wore off, she prayed that Allah would rescue her from the life her mother had planned.

9

When Parween was twelve, disaster struck.

Parween was promised to a young man.

Though she would not marry for four more years, her entire life was suddenly laid out before her, a dreary repetition of babies, cooking, cleaning, and field work—the tasks that shaped the life of every Afghan woman.

Her childhood was effectively over. She was no longer allowed to walk to the bazaar alone or through the nearby fields. She would never again climb her beloved Buddha and gaze out over Bamiyan.

There would be no school for Parween, either. Though she'd asked her mother if she could enroll, Bamiyan's lone school had closed its doors. There had been a period of relative quiet after the Russkis had left but before long, the region's warlords were fighting one another. The country was thrown into turmoil once again. She'd heard her brothers discussing it with Uncle Abdullah. Both wanted to join the struggle, but Abdullah had forbidden it.

"There has been enough of this fighting," he'd said. "We must learn to live in peace." She'd watched as her brothers had stormed off, anger glinting in their eyes.

No good will come of this, she'd thought. Fighting always brought misery.

For Parween, the misery of her own fate was sealed, and she was expected to slide easily into the role of the promised young woman. Not even Allah had been able to rescue her from her destiny.

Parween's days began before the sun rose, while the compound still retained the chill of night. She raised herself from her sleeping pad and rolled it up so that it could be used for guests to lean against when sitting. She quietly snuck out of the family's room and gathered fuel for the fire, and then she stoked the ashes of the previous day's fire, coaxing it back into life.

She trudged to the well, filled her leaky plastic containers with water, and filled the family's small kettle to the brim. She prepared a breakfast of yesterday's *naan* and last night's rice, and when all was ready, she woke her brothers and mother.

Her older sister Shookria had long since married and moved into her husband's house, disappearing into the life and village of her new family. She rarely came back to visit, and it would likely be the same for Parween. She'd been so young when Shookria had married that she could scarcely remember her sister, though Parween did remember Shookria's wedding day. It had been an exhilarating event—a full day and night of celebration. Because the women celebrated apart from the men, they were able to laugh and dance and wear makeup applied with a heavy hand. A wedding was as much for them as it was for the bride. Parween had been caught up in the revelry. She had never known such bliss.

A cousin had applied makeup to Parween's eager face, and when she peered into the tiny fragment of a splintered looking glass, she smiled broadly at her own reflection. It was queer to be looking at—admiring—herself, but she couldn't help it. With her brown hair freshly washed and her bright green eyes lined in kohl, her reflection was quite pleasing. Then her cousin had pulled out an old tube of colored wax and applied it to Parween's lips, and when she glanced back into the mirror to see her mouth ringed with the red gloss, she could barely contain her joy. She was one of *them*. She was as beautiful and grown-up as the women who crowded around the bride, and she was fascinated with the alluring girl the makeup had created.

When her cousin left the tube behind to join in the dancing, Parween had pocketed it. It remained one of her prized possessions, and she took it out from its hiding place now and then to remind her of her sister and of how she'd felt that day she'd first worn the waxy color on her lips.

In Bamiyan, she shared it with her best friend, Mariam, and the two applied it reverently and sparingly in the privacy of Parween's home, gazing into an old mirror and dreaming wistfully of their futures.

Parween was consumed by her chores from dawn to dusk. After preparing breakfast, she tidied up the family's room and swept the dirt from the carpet. Then she piled clothes into a large basket, slipped a bar of soap into her pocket, placed her veil on her head, and trudged off to join the compound's women on their trip to the nearby washing stream. Along the way, others would join them, and by the time they made it to the stream, there would be a large group of women and girls, laughing as they plunged the clothes into the biting cold waters. After much scrubbing, the clothes would be strewn about on the ground and hung on low tree branches to dry.

The work was backbreaking. The icy water ate through bony fingers and settled into the skin of cracked and worn hands. Yet sitting back to allow the clothes time to dry offered the women the chance to share gossip and tell stories. They gathered along the stream's edge, with their feet dangling in the water and backs resting against the trees.

"You heard that Farouzan's husband thinks she is too ugly, didn't you?" asked one gossipy old hag, her gray hair peeking out from her head-scarf. "He has demanded that she leave his house!" The old woman sat uncomfortably, her hunched back unable to lay flat against the tree.

"No, no, it's the *jinn* that made him tell her to leave," another replied.

The old woman snorted and blew her nose into her scarf.

Mariam sat next to Parween on the ground, laughing, and dipped her clothes into the stream.

Mariam was as small as Parween. She had black hair that was shiny when it was clean—which wasn't very often—and large brown eyes that saw everything, or so she claimed. She lived near

Parween's family in a mud compound much like the one Parween called home. They were best friends with the same future laid out in front of them—marriage, children, and an endless cycle of cleaning and cooking. Until then, however, they met whenever possible, to giggle, gossip, and daydream.

"Ahh, did you know that Kandy-Gul gave birth to yet another daughter?" said a young woman not much older than Parween. "That's five in all. Daoud will be looking for another wife." That elicited a smattering of laughter from the women. Everyone here knew that a wife was only as good as the number of sons she gave to her husband. Daughters, though loved, were second-class citizens at best. But it was different in Uncle Abdullah's compound, where women were treated kindly, for which Parween and her mother were very grateful.

The women at the stream continued to chatter. Once the clothes were merely damp, Parween and Mariam gathered them into their baskets and headed home, saying their good-byes when Mariam reached her doorway. Just a short distance farther on, Parween entered her own compound, deposited the clothes, picked up a basket, and headed off in search of fuel for the fire.

She preferred to find scraps of wood, but so did every other woman and child in Bamiyan, so the supply was scarce. More often than not she had to settle for the steaming pieces of fresh dung left by cows and goats, even dogs, in nearby fields. Gathering them into her basket, she was glad she'd thought to bring it along. Frequently, she found herself tucking the stinking, moist dung into the folds of her dress. The stench of it remained in her clothes, a fragrant reminder of her duties.

At home, she shaped the dung into flat discs and laid them out to dry in the sun before placing them just outside the family's room. That done, Parween began preparing dinner. There was rice to clean and pick through; she had to remove the persistent mealy insects that often found their way into her food stores. Unless they were picked out before cooking, they provided a crunchy, foul-tasting accompaniment to the meal. And if her brothers were forced to spit out tainted rice, the fault would be Parween's alone.

It had happened only once and their ire had been enough that she had sworn never to let it happen again.

Once she'd washed the rice, she pounded down meager pieces of mutton or chicken, when they were lucky enough to have it. Otherwise she sifted through beans to add to the rice. The cooking took hours, requiring constant stirring and attention. Her brothers, or sometimes Rahima, who still worked for the tailor, would bring home the fresh warm *naan* that they ate with every meal.

Each evening, when her two brothers arrived, Parween served them a sweet green tea that was the mainstay of their diet. Each tiny cup was filled with steaming liquid and five or six generous spoonfuls of sugar.

Once the men had had their fill of the food, Parween and her mother would fill their own plates with whatever was left. When dinner was done, it was Parween's job to gather the dishes and tidy up the room.

She would pull out the sleeping pads and lay them around the room. If it was already dark outside, Parween would light a small lantern to help her find her way to the well. There she would draw up water to wash the metal dishes and pots. Only when her final chore had been completed could she make her way to her own sleeping pad and fall into a cherished slumber, where at last her time was her own.

With all of her responsibilities, Parween mercifully had little time to ponder her eventual marriage, yet she had caught a glimpse of her intended.

Raziq Khalid was actually her second cousin, and he lived with his family right in her own compound. He was young—maybe twenty-five, though Parween couldn't be sure—and he was handsome, with brown hair and intense eyes so dark that they looked like bits of coal.

He was smart as well, and he worked in the bazaar, helping a merchant arrange his accounts and orders. Parween learned that he could read and write, not only Persian, but English too. His family had lived in Kabul, where opportunities for education had been plentiful, and he had gone to school long enough to learn more than most Afghans would ever know. His family had moved to Bamiyan after the Soviets left, when Kabul had been beset with fierce fighting among the warlords vying for power.

They had arrived the year before, and Uncle Abdullah's cousin was Raziq's mother, so the match was approved quickly. The marriage, however, wouldn't actually take place until Parween reached the age of sixteen. At first she had been horrified at the idea of marriage, but once she actually saw Raziq she found herself curiously pleased.

Mariam was relentless in her teasing, however, and though Parween tried to maintain an indignant pose, more often than not, they collapsed together giggling as they wondered about her future husband.

In fact, Parween was reasonably certain that Mariam felt a twinge of envy, though she proclaimed loudly that she was happy for her friend. Mariam's own match had not yet been arranged, and she frequently commented that she hoped for one only half as good.

"Who do you think my husband will be?" she said one day as they sat by the stream waiting for the clothes to dry. "We may have already seen him, you know." She tugged at her veil.

"Perhaps you will marry the baker's son," Parween answered dreamily. "Maybe he has seen you buying *naan* and he is smitten with you."

Mariam giggled in reply.

"Or perhaps he is the boy you were fighting the day we met."

Mariam collapsed in laughter. "Ahh, that was quite a day. It was right after you came to Bamiyan, yes?"

"It was. And when I saw you on the road bashing the head of that surly boy, I knew I'd found a friend for life. As for your husband, whoever he may be, he will surely be handsome and brave, and he will love you as though he chose you himself."

Mariam sighed. *"Inshallah."*

Mariam was one of nine children and lived in a tiny house where there seemed never to be enough food, clothes, or money. She was never missed when she slipped off to Parween's, and that was where she'd spent much of her childhood, alongside her dearest friend, almost another daughter to Rahima. She dreaded the thought that marriage would separate them but prayed she'd still be close by.

Before long their guessing games came to an end, and a match was made for Mariam. She was promised to an old man in the distant village of Mashaal. The news left the girls devastated. They clung to each other, mourning for Mariam's future, crying and making promises of eternal friendship.

"Please don't forget me," Mariam wailed, tears running down her cheeks.

"Never, my friend," Parween swore.

They pledged to somehow get messages to each other, though they knew in their hearts it was a promise just waiting to be broken.

When the time came for Mariam to leave Bamiyan, Parween caught sight of her friend's betrothed as he arrived to collect her. Her heart sank and she ached for her dear friend, as her new husband—a wizened, toothless, filthy old man—stood in Mariam's home, scratching at his greasy beard while looking her over.

Mariam withered under his gaze.

She would be his third and youngest wife, and—if things turned out as everyone hoped—she would be the first to produce a son. Until then, she would be a veritable slave, a mother to his five daughters, one of whom was fifteen, just like Mariam. Only a son would raise her from her status as the lowliest woman in the house.

Because Mariam was to be the third wife, the wedding celebration consisted only of a small dinner for family. Parween, desperate to see her friend one last time, slipped unseen into the women's room where Mariam sat with her sisters. Though for once the women's food was plentiful, Mariam was unable to eat. She turned her tear-stained face to Parween.

"Have you seen him?" she cried, her brown eyes red.

Parween held her hand. "Yes," she replied, holding back her own tears. "But, *inshallah,* he is kind and will be good to you."

That didn't seem likely, she knew, but she didn't know what else she could say to ease her friend's fears. Instead, she held Mariam close and stroked her hair.

"*Tars na dori,*" she whispered. "Do not be afraid." She repeated it again and again until Mariam drifted off into a restless sleep, and Parween slipped away.

Early the next morning, Mariam was taken from the women's room and placed astride the old man's donkey for the journey to her new home. Parween ran to her and slipped something into her hand.

It was the old tube of lipstick she'd kept after her sister's wedding. They'd run the bright red wax over their lips so many times, there was only a small fragment of color left in the treasured tube.

"So you will remember me," Parween whispered.

Mariam gripped Parween's hand and held it to her damp cheek. "I will always carry you in my heart, my friend."

And with that, she was gone. Tears streaming down her face, Parween watched until her best friend's slight figure receded into the horizon.

10

$\mathcal{P}$arween was married shortly before her sixteenth birthday.

Uncle Abdullah, proud to have made such a good match for his niece, invited not just family but friends and even neighbors to the joyous celebration. Parween had tried to get a message to Mariam, but there had been no word in reply and no way to know if she could somehow get to Bamiyan for the wedding.

Still, more than a hundred people crowded into the small compound.

Parween's mother and aunt prepared her for the festivities. She sat regally but nervously on an embroidered pad—a bride pad. She was catered to and surrounded by all the female guests, who busied themselves applying her makeup in heavy colors and in a dramatic fashion. The kohl that lined her eyes was the deepest black, the lipstick as red as the brightest summer poppies, and the powder on her face was whiter than the snow that capped the Hindu Kush. When they were done, the women stepped back to admire their handiwork.

"Ahh," they murmured all at once. "You are a beautiful bride."

Parween let a smile settle on her colored lips as she peered at her reflection. She hadn't worn lipstick in the year since Mariam had left. Though her mother had a small tube, there'd been no joy in it without her dearest friend. *Oh, if only Mariam were here,* she thought, *to share my new lipstick and to see me in my gauzy white dress and white silk veil.* She closed her eyes and thought of her friend.

Finally, she was led from the women's room for the ceremony. She stood nervously by Raziq's side, surrounded by Uncle Abdullah and her brothers as the mullah read the prayers. Once the prayers and recitations were done, the Koran was passed over their bowed heads and a shawl was draped over them. A shiny mirror was held under the shawl, allowing the husband and wife their first married glimpse of each other. Raziq smiled broadly into the mirror; Parween, nervous still, covered her smile with her hand and looked away.

The Koran was passed to Raziq, who read a short verse. Then the shawl was pulled free, and Parween and Raziq were proclaimed husband and wife.

Parween turned to look at Raziq and there he stood, staring her full in the face. Stunned, she turned away. No man had ever looked straight at her before—at least not since she was a child—but he was her husband now.

Husband!

A thrill passed through her. She almost couldn't believe it. She let her gaze drift downward and felt a little giddy as her stomach leaped.

The meal began and she sat next to him, but despite all of the wonderful food that had been prepared, she couldn't bring herself to eat. Her stomach was still dancing with excitement.

"So, my beautiful wife," he said. "No appetite today, of all days?" He grinned broadly and touched her hand.

Parween's heart raced. He had called her beautiful. Was she? Did he really think so?

Today is what paradise must be like, she decided. She gazed at him again and this time her heart soared.

"You must eat, Parween," he said gently yet playfully. "I want a strong wife, not a helpless one." He smiled, and Parween dutifully picked at her food.

"My husband—" She hesitated, almost afraid to speak to this stranger with the gentle eyes. "I am strong, and even if I eat little today, I will not disappoint you." She looked away then, and Raziq caressed her hand.

"My dear Parween, I have no fear of that. I hope not to disappoint *you.* You see, I am a bit nervous today as well. I have never been this close to a woman, and though we are strangers to one another, we are now husband and wife." He took a slow breath. "In time, we will grow comfortable together. Today, let us just be happy."

Parween felt a smile creep across her face once again.

Once the bridal meal was finished, the women prepared to escort her back to the women's room, where the wedding celebration had already started. She turned and smiled shyly at Raziq before she let herself be led away.

To her chagrin, Parween discovered that she would be a silent observer at her own wedding and would not be allowed to celebrate. "I should be dancing, shouldn't I?" she asked, and this was met by shrieks of laughter. "Can't I join in?" Her mother lovingly chastised her for paying so little attention during their prepatory talks. A married woman, she explained, had to show her modesty and obedience.

Parween sighed. It had been more fun attending to the bride than *being* the bride.

The raucous party went on for hours and eventually Parween drifted off to sleep amidst the noise and the festivities. In the morning's first light, guests started to trickle away, and she was nudged awake to join her husband in his house, another small room in the compound. She knew this was extraordinarily lucky. While most women were torn from their families, the fact that he was a cousin meant that she would be able to stay within the same familiar walls.

Still, she found herself terrified at the thought of what was to come next.

Once they were alone, Raziq proved as kind and thoughtful as he was handsome. "You are trembling, but do not be afraid," he said as he lifted away her dress. "You are my wife, and this is the way of husbands and wives." He reached out and touched her bare skin. A rush of electricity flooded her body and her heart fluttered with his closeness and his touch.

He gently eased Parween into what had been described to her as the "marriage act," and after a moment of pain, he went slowly and she didn't feel the embarrassment she'd expected. After hearing so many bawdy stories describing the miseries of sex, she was unprepared for Raziq's tender caresses and murmurs of satisfaction.

Perhaps, she mused silently, if she became pregnant with a son, it would all be worth it.

As Parween and Raziq settled into married life, she was surprised to find that she actually had fewer chores than before. Until they had children, her responsibilities would be limited to Raziq and their animals—the lone donkey, two goats, and a few skeletal chickens. Life would be far simpler than what she was used to.

She found it easy to talk to Raziq, and when she finally shared with him that she knew her numbers and she could actually count, he smiled with pleasure.

"Uncle Abdullah told me that you were smart, and I'm pleased to see that he was right. Do you want to learn more?" He folded his arms over the book he held. "Then, someday, you will be able to teach our children."

Parween could hardly believe her ears. To *learn*—it was her dream.

"I speak some Inglisi," Raziq continued, "and I have no doubt that someday it will be useful in some way. Would you like to learn to speak Inglisi?"

Her jaw went slack; she was speechless. Without warning, she flung herself at Raziq and kissed his cheek.

"Oh yes, my dear husband, oh *yes!*"

That evening, their small house became a classroom. Raziq decided to start with numbers, since it had been years since Parween had counted anything besides her chickens or goats.

"Yak, do, say, char, pinge . . ." The numbers rolled easily from her tongue and once Raziq was confident that she knew them well, he translated them to English. This was far more difficult and they practiced over and over. For all of the difficulty, however, she was an eager student.

Once she'd mastered the numbers, Raziq guided her through common phrases, and before long, they were exchanging entire sentences. "I am from Bamiyan. My husband's name is Raziq." She always giggled when she said that.

"My wife is named Parween," he responded with a wink.

In the evenings, he taught her to read and write the elegant Persian script of Afghanistan. She struggled with the ornate letters as Raziq leaned over her shoulder, the smell of shaved pencils and worn erasers on his hands.

"Try again," he said gently whenever she faltered. His patience was matched by Parween's persistence and before long, she could identify letters, then whole words and sentences. To her delight, she discovered all the things there were to read. Raziq brought home books and newspapers and Parween devoured them, reading aloud so that Raziq could hear her pronunciation of the words.

Each day, Parween had plenty of opportunity to read as she made the solitary trek through the bazaar to deliver a warm lunch to Raziq. An entire world opened up for her as she read signs on storefronts and labels on packages. She especially liked the sign in the grimy front window of the bakery that proclaimed in scrolling Persian script BEST BREAD IN BAMIYAN. The scrolled lettering was so delicate, so appealing, that she couldn't resist going in. The fresh bread she purchased there was wrapped in old newspaper, which gave her something else to read.

Friday was Islam's holy day and Raziq's only day off, and they often hiked into the nearby mountains to picnic by a cool stream. They would pick the sweet mulberries that grew there and add those to their feast. After lunch, Raziq would lie against a towering tree and read to Parween. Sometimes, they would read together, practicing their lessons.

"Someday, I will have my own business," Raziq declared. "I could do numbers and accounts from a little office in the bazaar and have merchants come to me with their books. What do you think? Would you like to be married to a successful businessman?"

"You are successful already, and no matter your job, I am happy to be your wife." She sat closer to him, touched his arm, and smiled.

One afternoon, Parween brought Raziq to the Buddhas. She enjoyed his amazement as she scurried up the mountainside and disappeared into the highest room above the larger of the two statues. He struggled just to keep up with her, and her face shone as she pointed out the bazaar and their own home, and then the Hindu Kush mountain range in the distance. Since they were alone, looking out over Bamiyan, Raziq pulled Parween close.

"I love you, my dear wife," he whispered almost conspiratorially. "How lucky I am that Allah chose you for me." Parween never tired of hearing his words. Raziq was more than just her beloved husband, she realized. He was her beloved friend.

Almost exactly a year after their wedding, Parween discovered that she was pregnant. Her monthly bleeding stopped and she consulted her mother, who confirmed that it was a sure sign of pregnancy. That evening, Parween prepared a special dinner for Raziq, even slaughtering one of their scrawny chickens for the meal.

"What is this?" he said as he entered their room and smelled—and then saw—the special meal, a roasted chicken lying atop a bed of rice.

"Raziq," she said, blushing and unable to contain her excitement, "I am with child." She almost sang the words, she was so happy.

Raziq took her hands in his and kissed them. "Today, you have given me all I've ever hoped for. Is it a son? Can you tell?"

"No, no, I cannot know, but I am thinking that it will be a big, healthy boy."

As the pregnancy progressed, she felt the stirring low in her abdomen. She guided Raziq's fingers over the swelling, so that he could feel the flutters and kicks that were beginning. Together, they delighted at the growing life in her belly.

"It is surely a healthy boy, my dear," Raziq said.

One afternoon, not long after they'd felt those first flutters, she made her daily trek to the bazaar for lunch with Raziq.

On her way home, she felt a stabbing pain and nearly doubled over there in the lane, but she managed to stagger back home.

By the next morning, she lay on her sleeping pad, gripped by waves of throbbing agony.

Drenched in sweat, she sent Raziq away.

"Go to work," she begged, pulling herself erect and doing her best to hide what she felt. "There is nothing you can do. It will pass soon." Whatever was occurring, she didn't want him there.

Reluctantly, he agreed, but only after he'd fetched a doting Rahima, who sat by her side, rubbing her back.

Parween folded into herself and tried to rub away the cramps, but they only grew stronger. Though it was too early, her baby was coming.

Rahima summoned the midwife, but there was nothing to be done. Parween delivered a tiny baby—their wished-for boy—but he never breathed his first breath. She saw him, a tiny, perfectly formed baby tethered to her by a bloody cord. Parween asked to have him wrapped in a blanket, so that she might hold him for a moment. She held her baby tight and then handed him to Rahima.

"Take care with him, my mother; do not let the earth touch his tiny body." And she turned away and cried.

Raziq had been called home, and he stayed by Parween's side. "I have seen him and he was a fine baby. Do not cry, my wife. *Inshallah,* we will have another baby, a healthy one." They prayed together to Allah, asking for a healthy baby, and they swore that they didn't even mind if it was a girl.

Raziq was right, though it took three years and hundreds of prayers to Allah before Parween was delighted to finally announce that she was pregnant again.

"You see," Raziq said as if it had been only a day. "I knew we would be blessed."

This pregnancy continued long after she felt the baby quickening. In the end, Parween delivered a healthy baby girl who arrived with a lusty cry.

From the very first moment, Parween was in love with the perfect child they'd created, and they named her Zahra, for the little flower that she was.

Raziq took great joy in his baby girl. As soon as she could walk, she toddled about after him, and when he hoisted her onto his shoulders she shrieked with delight. It made no difference to Raziq that she was a daughter, and he proudly showed her off in the bazaar. He loved her as much as he would any son, and he said as much.

Parween had never known that married life could be so sweet, yet her own joy was tempered by the knowledge that marriage had not been kind to Mariam. Word had trickled back through visitors from Mashaal that Mariam had delivered two stillborn boys. Her inability to produce a son for her aging husband had made him a laughingstock in the village. Humiliated, he took out his anger on Mariam by beating her regularly.

Her status as the lowliest wife also meant that the older wives, jealous of her youth, would target her as well. She was already their servant and she became their easy prey. It was said that they kicked her as she bent to clean, threw out the water she'd trudged so far to collect, and tainted her rice with mealy bugs. Though covered in bruises that would last for days, she suffered in silence and prayed to Allah to give her a son.

Parween ached for her dear friend.

One night as they sat to supper, the baby sleeping at Parween's side, she spoke.

"You remember Mariam, my friend? She married the old man from Mashaal."

"Of course I remember her. She was like your shadow, or perhaps you were hers."

Parween's eyes filled with tears at the memory. "Well, her marriage did not go so well. She has been beaten and treated badly, by both her husband and his other wives. I want to help."

Raziq sighed.

"This is business between a husband and wife," he said softly. "We cannot interfere in their private matters."

Parween's tears came freely then.

"Please, Raziq, if what they say is true, he will kill her if this goes on. She is lower than a stray dog in his house. And I love her as a sister." She fell silent and forced herself to stop crying. "If you can't help, then I will do it alone."

Her voice was firm.

Raziq sat silently for a time, and then he leaned toward her. "Try to get word to her to come here. If we can hide her, we can find a way to arrange a divorce."

His words warmed her. She felt such love for him that she blushed.

"But you are not to go to Mashaal alone," he said, continuing, his voice firmer now. "Do you hear me?"

Parween nodded.

The next day, she sent out word through the village's women, begging Mariam to come back to Bamiyan, and then she waited for her friend to appear.

11

$\mathcal{W}$hile she waited for word from Mariam, Parween continued to trek to the baker's, eager to read the newspaper in which the *naan* was wrapped. These old newspapers, often from Kabul, offered her a glimpse at the changes that were taking place in Afghanistan. As soon as she delivered the warm bread to her mother, she hurried home to smooth out the paper and examine it for the latest news.

She read about the fierce fighting in the countryside among the warlords for control of the nation. Little of that fight had come to Bamiyan, but the villagers followed the events with keen interest. The outcome, they knew, would affect them all.

When the Taliban finally wrested control of Kabul from the Northern Alliance, it seemed as if peace might finally reign. But the longed-for peace would not last.

The Taliban, it turned out, were strict followers of Islam. It was reported that they had enforced *purdah,* an old practice designed to keep women out of sight and out of the way. Under their rule, women were banned from walking outside without a man, and when they *were* outside they had to be cloaked in the full covering of the *burqa*—no strands of hair or glimpse of skin would be tolerated. Even women's shoes had to be silent, no clicking heels or scuffing soles.

Parween's eyes grew wide as she read on.

Punishment for offenders would be swift and final, the Taliban had announced, and to demonstrate their absolute authority, they had shot dead a young woman on the streets of Kabul after she was found walking alone with her head uncovered, her hands outstretched as she begged for food. Parween wondered if she'd begged for her life as well.

But it would be Raziq, and not the newspapers, who brought home word of the latest and most ominous developments.

"It's happened—the Taliban have come," Raziq announced one night, his eyes downcast.

The news sent a shudder through Parween.

"They have taken two houses just up the road. And today, four of them—all carrying Kalashnikovs—patrolled the bazaar. You should have seen them, young men really, but filthy, with matted beards and greasy turbans and stained shirts. They mean to enforce the old ways." He reached out and gently touched Parween's arm, looking at her so intently that she felt a hint of fear.

"Things are not the same, my wife," he said, his expression grim. "You must wear the *burqa* if you expect to walk outside of these walls."

Parween pulled away, her face flushed with anger. "I will not wear the *burqa*, Raziq. I will not be hidden and ignored."

He shook his head sadly.

"That is your decision, and I will respect it, but it means that you won't be allowed to walk through the bazaar. Is it worth that to you?"

"It is," she said. She glowered at him. "I will not give in to the Taliban. They are like mad dogs." She folded her arms across her chest.

Raziq drew in his breath, a frown wrinkling his face.

"You must never speak like that beyond these walls. Do you understand? They would sooner kill us both than put up with a defiant woman."

"They are evil—"

"That may be so, but they are here, and there is nothing to be done. We must accept their rule . . . for now."

Parween saw sadness in his eyes now, and her anger faded.

Raziq reached his hand up and ran it over his chin. "Did you know that I will no longer be allowed to trim my beard? They have instructed us to let our beards grow long and matted. You see, we will all be forced to abide by their rules, even the children." He let his gaze rest on Zahra as she stumbled about the room, laughing and babbling. "The Taliban have banned the games and joy of childhood. No kites, no sports, no laughter, no music. They say it will take us from our prayers and we will forget that it is Allah alone we should worship."

Though she didn't press the matter, Parween knew in her heart that she could not yield to the new ways.

As the days passed, her resentment grew like a fist twisting and curling in her stomach. She watched as her mother, who'd been forced to leave her job with the tailor, grew quieter and somehow older. And with each day Parween spent in the isolation of their compound, she became more certain that something had to be done.

"We must fight back," she whispered one day to Raziq.

He took a deep breath and his expression said that he had dreaded this conversation.

"These are not matters for you, my wife," he said, pleading with her. "You must stay quiet; we don't want them to notice us, *any* of us."

Parween was disappointed at his response.

"But they *have* noticed us. They have stolen our lives and left us with only a shell of an existence. My mother and I are prisoners in our own home, and our daughter has no life ahead of her, save one of utter misery."

"But there is nothing we can do. They are everywhere, and none can stand against them." He paused, then continued. "You must not allow yourself to be concerned with this. Concern yourself with our home and our child. This is not your trouble."

Parween felt anger bubbling up inside her. She'd never really argued with Raziq, yet this time, she was certain he was wrong. She started to answer him with a caustic remark, but she caught herself.

He was her husband. He would know what to do.

"I am sorry, Raziq. I will trust your words."

Each day, Raziq reported another thing that the Taliban had destroyed. In the bazaar, the music had stopped and the little twinkling lights had been taken down. Once a bustling and joyous community, Bamiyan became a living ghost town. Villagers hurried out for their errands and then hurried home again.

Yet a hint of revolt remained, a trimmed beard here and a bit of music there.

And the Taliban noticed.

And so, on a sunny day in early October, they gathered up a handful of village men, some so old they had to be carried. Raziq was in the bazaar when the roundup occurred, and he watched as Parween's brother Noori was pulled away from the engine he was working on. He hurried to a nearby shop to ask what was happening. There he met his friend Wazir and two shopkeepers, who were as puzzled as he, and the little group followed the Taliban and their prisoners to the end of a barren dirt airstrip at the edge of town, in full view of Bamiyan's beloved Buddhas.

A crowd of villagers had gathered, and they watched as a senior Taliban screamed at the frightened men.

"Infidels! You have ridiculed Allah with your ways. Your women are not covered properly. Whores! Your mothers, your wives, your daughters, all whores!"

The spectators murmured as he spoke, and then rifles were cocked, and the crowd stilled.

Even the breeze seemed to quiet.

With a chorus of *"Allah u akbar"* ringing in the air, the Taliban steadied their rifles and executed each prisoner with a single gunshot to the head. A few cried out, and when the sounds of killing had ceased, the gunmen moved through the rows of bodies and shot any who still seemed to have signs of life.

Some of the onlookers were summoned and they were told to dig long trenches, then to push the dead into them.

Terrified, the villagers dug as they were ordered. With tears in their eyes and pleas to Allah asking him to forgive them, they pushed the bodies of their family members, friends, and neighbors into the long trench and shoveled dirt over the bodies, erasing all signs of the massacre.

Raziq, Wazir, and the others had watched it all in horror. Though he dared not speak, for fear of being overheard, Raziq knew that his wife had been right. Something had to be done to rescue Bamiyan from the misery the Taliban had brought.

He hurried home. He wanted to be the one to break the news of Noori's death and hoped he could find the words that might soften the blow. He ran the last few paces, and he was breathless as he opened the gate to Abdullah's compound and stepped inside.

There by the well, he saw Rahima and Parween, chatting and pulling up buckets of water. Zahra played at their feet, tipping the buckets and splashing the water.

Parween turned at the sound of the gate opening. "You are home early today," she said as she smiled. "Is the shop closed? Are you finished for the day?"

Raziq was silent. The expression he wore sent a chill through Parween.

"What is it?" she asked.

Rahima stood and turned toward Raziq.

"Che taklif?" she asked.

Zahra ran to her father, and he bent to kiss her.

"Go inside, my little one. I will follow in a minute." Zahra obeyed and toddled away.

Parween and Rahima stood perfectly still, their eyes pleading with him, and he finally spoke.

"It is Noori. He is dead. The Taliban killed him, and many others, today. They shot them." His voice broke.

Rahima moaned and sank to her knees. "My son," she cried as she covered her face with her hands.

Parween was confused.

"What do you mean, shot? Was it an accident?"

"It was no accident; it was an execution. They shot twenty men today, Noori among them."

"But what had they done? Why Noori?" She couldn't grasp what had occurred.

"They took Noori and the others for no reason that we know. They hadn't done anything. The old man Ali-Haq was among them. He couldn't even stand there by himself. He had to lean on the man next to him."

At that, Parween cried out, and she reached for Raziq.

"Oh, God, did Noori suffer? Where is he? Can we bury him?"

"No, no, we cannot." Raziq almost whispered his reply. "They have buried him with the others right where they were shot." He paused and added, "I do not think he suffered. His death was instant."

Parween knelt by her crying mother and wrapped her arms around her.

"Do not be sad, Mother. Noori is a martyr, as was Father, and they both reside in paradise now." She struggled to keep her own voice from cracking and held back her tears.

Raziq bent to whisper to Parween.

"I must return to the market now. There is still work to do." He stood and placed his hand on the gate's heavy latch.

Before he could open it, Parween appeared beside him.

"Please do not go. There is danger out there. Stay here. We need you."

Raziq steadied his trembling hand.

"I must go. I will be safe. I will return tonight. Perhaps there will be news. Perhaps it was just a terrible mistake."

Raziq strode quickly back to the bazaar, to the shop of Wazir, he of the twinkling lights and colorful veils. The lights had been dimmed, and the veils—too ornate these days—had been packed away. The men, six of them in all, sat in the back of the shop and talked, their voices low.

Wazir, the eldest, spoke up first.

"They have taken our freedoms, our property, our children's laughter, and now this. They will murder us all if we don't drive them away."

Faizir agreed.

"We cannot just sit back. We fought against the Russians. We must fight back against our own invaders, as well."

"How many of you have weapons?" Wazir asked, and every hand shot up.

Raziq stood.

"It is true that we must act, but we must be careful, take our time, and take them by surprise. They will be expecting us to respond to today's massacre. We must wait and act when they least expect it.

Let us all give it some thought and meet again in a week's time to discuss our options. Above all, we must take care not to arouse their suspicions."

There was a murmur of agreement, and the men elected to meet again in a week's time. Raziq hurried back to his little office in the bazaar, where he took out his prayer mat, knelt toward Mecca, and asked for Allah's guidance.

Whispers of revolt bubbled through the village and the group of six grew, so that in just four weeks' time there were more than twenty men crowded into Wazir's tiny back room. Each man had at least one weapon of his own. Though their guns were old and poorly maintained, they would have to do.

They met weekly, and their plans took shape slowly and secretly.

Meanwhile, the Taliban rolled their heavy artillery and tanks into Bamiyan and claimed homes and property for their own. They shot people and animals alike, set fire to the potato crops and fields of sprouting wheat.

The Taliban swaggered through the bazaar and pointed fingers at young men whose beards were trimmed. Many young men were snatched from the street without warning.

They simply disappeared.

By early winter of 2001, the men decided that they had to act soon. They risked discovery if they waited too long.

They chose a moonless night in late February and prayed that the deep black sky would offer them some protection. They would make their assault on a house in the village where a cluster of Taliban lived.

Raziq and a band of twenty men crept through the scorched fields and over the mud wall that hid the targeted house from view. Once over the wall, the men separated and waited for the signal, the flare of a match.

As the match was struck, they all shouted to Allah and rushed into the house, bursting through doors and diving through windows.

In the chaos that followed, every single one of them was killed.

Though the villagers had weapons, the Taliban were possessed of plentiful and superior arms and they had known this day would come. They had been ready to fight, and they were merciless.

Raziq was badly wounded but still conscious as the Taliban moved from man to man. Whether dead or dying, each man was hacked with a sword, and in his last moments it seemed to Raziq that the victors relished the task.

The next morning, the village buzzed with the news. Uncle Abdullah hurried to the Taliban house and there he saw Raziq, swinging from a tree, his body slashed until he was barely recognizable. Abdullah covered his mouth but the vomit came anyway.

He fell to his knees and cried to Allah. When he could finally rise, he pulled himself away and turned for home.

Once there, he hurried through the gate and into the room where Parween was singing softly to Zahra as she folded up their sleeping pads.

"Good morning, Uncle," she said, her face lighting at the sight of him. "Will you share tea with us? Raziq isn't here. I think he may be in the bazaar, but I would enjoy your company with my tea."

Abdullah sank to his knees and Zahra scurried behind him, out the door, and into the courtyard.

"No, my dear, not today." He paused and took a deep breath. "I have very bad news for you, for all of us." He hesitated and took another long breath. "Raziq and a group of brave men attacked the Taliban last night. There was a terrible fight and Raziq and the rest—"

But he couldn't speak. Sobs came instead of words. He couldn't even look at her.

"What, what, they all *what*?" Parween rushed to him. "Has Raziq been arrested?"

"They are all dead." Tears fell from Abdullah's eyes as he spoke, landing softly on his beard.

Parween's arms and legs went numb, and she fell to the floor in a heap.

Oh Allah, so that is where he went.

She couldn't breathe, and an ache settled in her heart.

No, no, let it not be true.

She was sinking, like a pebble thrown into a stream, falling deeper and deeper.

Uncle Abdullah wrapped his arms around her, and Parween buried her face in her hands and cried.

She stayed curled up on the floor that day and moved only when her mother laid out her sleeping pad and led her to it. Rahima covered her and slept beside her, whispering words of comfort that Parween never heard. The only words that resounded in her mind were those that Uncle Abdullah had spoken.

They are all dead.

Raziq was dead. The Taliban had killed him.

Word came that the men had all been buried in another mass grave. She would never have the chance to hold him one last time or to prepare his body for a proper burial. The Taliban had stolen that small act from her.

It was more than she could bear.

Parween sat alone each day, her knees drawn up, tears spilling quietly from her eyes, until one sunny morning weeks after Raziq's death.

Without warning, Zahra's shrieks filled the air. Her terror roused Parween and she lunged for her daughter. The little girl had toddled too close to the cooking fire, and she had scorched her arm, leaving a raw, blistering burn. Her howls were a mixture of fear, pain, and betrayal.

Parween held her, rocking them both until finally Zahra quieted, and then she rose, dried her eyes, and tended to her daughter's arm. It was as though she'd never been away.

But she *had* been away, and she had changed. A quiet anger simmered in her heart and she wanted vengeance. Someday she would get it. That single thought gave her purpose and allowed her to rise each day.

Thankfully, there was no talk of having her marry Raziq's brother. He had only one, and in those days of turmoil and chaos, no one knew if he was still alive. He had long since moved to Kabul, and there had been no word in months.

There had been no word either of Parween's brother Abdul, who had worked tending sheep. One day he had failed to return home after his work in the fields. It was assumed that he had either been killed or left to join the fight against the Taliban. Either way, the result was the same. Loved ones simply disappeared, and there was nothing to be done, no way to discover the truth.

Rahima moved into Parween's little home, and with the baby, they managed to subsist on the money and supplies that Raziq had hoarded. Zahra was safe, at least for the moment, and Parween intended to keep her that way. Raziq's foresight freed her from the day-to-day worries of survival, yet only vengeance would ease her heartache and dim her anger.

It might not happen today or even this month, but it *would* happen, and she could wait. She was a woman, after all. She was used to waiting.

12

By spring of 2001, the Taliban had occupied the village of Bami-yan for three years, and they announced that they would destroy Bamiyan's Buddhas. The announcement stunned the people of the village, who pleaded for them to reconsider. But the Taliban ignored the outcry and set explosive devices at the bases of the magnificent relics.

Parween watched from her compound as the centuries-old sculptures collapsed in endless clouds of dust and debris. Her beloved Buddhas, which she'd adored since she was a little girl, which had stood for generations, were destroyed in an instant.

The Taliban respected nothing—not women, nor children, nor anything of beauty. Parween's hatred for them grew.

Parween climbed to the roof of her small house, as she often did these days, to take a look at the surrounding countryside. Perched on an incline, the house's roof offered a clear view of the village center. This day, it was not the landscape that held Parween's gaze but the Taliban she could see strutting about as they planted what could only be land mines. She remembered the lessons from her childhood in Onai, and the shapes and sizes of the mines were unmistakable. The Taliban never saw her as she peered from the roof and watched them closely. She knew every inch of Bamiyan, its fields and trees, its valleys and streams, and she kept track as the strangers planted their seeds of destruction.

She watched them lay the mines in a distinct half moon pattern, working out from the center of the spot they'd chosen. They covered each mine with dirt or brush to hide it from view. She counted the paces as they walked between the mines and committed everything she saw to memory.

Once in her room, she bent to her writing paper, and by the glow of her candle, she sketched out little maps, perfect replicas of the patterns the Taliban had followed as they buried the mines. She gave the maps to Uncle Abdullah, who passed along the warnings— *stay away from this field or that stream, and if you cut through Arif's field, avoid the trees.*

The word was passed, and the grateful villagers wondered just who was the source of the vital information. No one—especially not the Taliban—could have imagined that the information came from a woman.

But Parween wasn't the only woman to defy them. Word traveled that a young widow had thrown off her veil, dressed in men's clothes, gathered a Kalashnikov, and ridden off to join a group of young rebels. She was quickly becoming a legend as stories of her exploits spread. They said she'd killed more Taliban than any of her male comrades. In a pitiful attempt to discredit her, the Taliban had branded her a traitor to Islam. But she was a heroine to the villagers who heard of her feats. Many claimed to have seen her as she rode through distant villages, her plaited hair flying out behind her, a bandolier strung across her chest. Her legend took on special meaning for the people of Bamiyan, who claimed her as their own.

Surely, they said, only a Hazara woman would rise up in such defiance.

Parween imagined that the revered young rebel was Mariam. She had heard that Mariam's husband, in a sinful effort to save his own life and endear himself to the vicious Taliban, had offered them his pretty young wife to enjoy while they were in Mashaal. This latest news had been carried back by Haleema, a gossipy old woman who had moved from Bamiyan to live with her son in Mashaal. When she'd returned for a visit, she'd hurried to the house of Uncle Abdullah to share what she knew with Parween.

"Ahh . . ." Haleema ran her tongue along her lower lip and glanced about the room with her narrow eyes. "It is best if no one else hears. What happened to your friend is very sad, I'm afraid."

She paused and wiped her sweating brow with the end of her long veil.

"What happened? Just say it!"

"The Taliban are not the pious men of religion that so many believe. In Mashaal, their immoral, wicked ways were well known, and they greedily accepted the old man's offer of his young wife. Poor Mariam was thrown at their feet and she was forced to open her legs to them all."

Parween gasped and covered her mouth with her hands.

Haleema's voice grew softer. "They beat her, as well, and covered her with burns and bruises."

Parween closed her eyes to the images and held her breath.

"It has been said that Mariam begged her captors for mercy but the Taliban do not listen to the rantings of dogs or women. Mariam was forced to live like an animal, and when the Taliban were finally finished with her, even her evil husband refused to accept her back. He said that now she was nothing more than a whore."

Parween felt hot tears sting her face. "Has no one helped her?"

"The whisperers have said that Mariam escaped to the caves along Mashaal's mountainside and that some of the village women are caring for her there, but I do not know for certain. She may be there in the caves; I just do not know. I am sorry, Parween."

"We must find her. Get word to her to come back. When will you return to Mashaal?"

Haleema thought for a moment. "In the coming weeks, *inshallah*, if all goes well for my son."

"Please, pass the word. Someone must know where she is. Tell her that she must come home to us. Please, Haleema. Promise me that you will do that."

Haleema nodded, and Parween kissed her cheeks.

* * *

Not long after she heard the news of Mariam's misery, three fierce-looking Taliban stormed into Parween's compound, demanding food and money. Uncle Abdullah was in the bazaar and Rahima's pleas for mercy were ignored. Parween, with Haleema's words fresh in her mind, went to her mother's side.

"What do you want?" She scowled, wondering how men so young could be so evil.

Cold, black eyes peered back at her over their bushy beards.

"We know you have money, whore! Give it to us." One of them prodded her with his rifle as they made their demands. He held a finger at the side of his nose and snorted heavily, snot bursting onto the ground.

The sight of them, the closeness of them, made her skin crawl, yet Parween replied calmly. "I have buried our money in the field. Of course, you may have it if Allah wishes. I will show you where it is."

Once she had donned her *burqa,* the greedy Taliban pushed her to the door and she led them to a nearby empty field. She walked tentatively at first, trying to recall where the mines here were planted, and looked about anxiously. Then she saw it—the crooked old apricot tree that had shaded the Taliban as they'd laid their mines in this field.

She stared at her feet to get her bearings and count her paces. The Taliban followed closely. Straightening, she stood tall and took several long strides through the field. Her sudden bravado angered one of the Taliban, who reached out to slap her. As he reached forward, he stepped right onto a mine and in an instant he was blown to bloody bits.

"Allah u akbar!" she yelled in surprise as she was thrown to one side by the explosion, and his remains rained down on her.

The two remaining Taliban—just boys really—stopped and glanced about, horror etched on their faces, beads of sweat collecting on their brows. *Where to step, what to do?* Parween could almost read their minds. The dead man had carried the only weapon, and his companions now stood as helpless as Parween. She saw the pleading in their young eyes, and she hesitated.

She almost wanted to say, *Stop! Don't step there!*

But she didn't. Instead, she turned and ran, and as she did, she heard the explosions.

Slipping into a narrow alleyway, she arranged her *burqa* so that the gore wouldn't show and tried to slow her breathing as she returned unseen to the compound. When Rahima found her, Parween had washed away the blood and recovered her composure.

"Oh, my child," Rahima cried. "I prayed to Allah to protect you."

"I am fine, Mother," Parween said, surprised at how calm she sounded. "They didn't really want any trouble."

Rahima wrinkled her brow and reached for her daughter. "You are shaking. Are you certain that you are unhurt?"

Parween pulled away. "I'm fine. They wanted only to frighten us. They won't bother us again."

The next day, word spread of the deaths, and it was assumed by everyone—including the Taliban—that the deaths were due to the stupidity of the three men.

Parween was never suspected.

She was, after all, only a foolish, useless woman.

In September, the Taliban left Bamiyan. Uncle Abdullah returned from the bazaar one night with the news.

"The Taliban *raft,* they have left," he said, a smile spreading on his face as he spoke. "Allah has answered our prayers. There is no sign of them."

"I do not trust them, Uncle," Parween replied doubtfully. "No one should. If it is true, then where have they gone?"

"Ahh, little one, be thankful at least for this. For now, they have left. I saw women in the village today, just walking. You should come with me tomorrow, get some air."

Parween felt dizzy.

"It is true? You are certain? It is not a trick?"

"See for yourself," he answered.

The following day, she and her mother walked to the bazaar, where Parween smelled the fresh bread and read the old newspapers for the first time in what seemed like forever.

But her joy was short-lived as October arrived and the bombs rained down. There had been whispers in the marketplace that the Taliban had attacked Amrika but that didn't make any sense; the Taliban were stupid, and they were cowards. No one with any sense at all would do such a thing.

But why else would Amrika send bombs and soldiers?

When the foreign soldiers moved in, the Taliban fought back, but only faintly. When their defeat was imminent, they trimmed their beards and tried to disappear into the countryside.

But the villagers did not forget. When the foreign soldiers came through in November, the people of Bamiyan pointed out the once-feared oppressors who tried, to no avail, to make themselves as invisible as the women they'd so tormented. The villagers showed the Taliban the same mercy they had granted their victims. In Bamiyan alone, the soldiers and locals rounded up some one hundred Taliban prisoners.

The people came out to cheer the American soldiers as they rode through Bamiyan in their tanks and jeeps and fell from the heavens, parachutes billowing out above them. It seemed as though Allah himself had sent them.

Parween stood on the side of the road and watched it all in wonder. She wished Raziq were there to see it with her.

PART
3

Friends

13

Elsa's first harrowing month in Bamiyan had finally come to an end, and with it much of her angst and timidity. Even the strange-sounding diseases—leishmaniasis, typhoid, malaria, and intestinal worms—problems that had been unimaginable on her first day, had grown less daunting once she'd actually seen them.

She'd developed routines to brace herself for the day, and each morning she climbed to the roof to have her coffee. There, she'd watch the village come to life, the cows and donkeys and children fanning out across the roads, chores already under way. But there were more than children and animals waking in the village one morning, and Elsa scrambled for a better look when she heard jeeps rumbling by. Certain it was the convoy of her blue-eyed soldier, she craned her neck and squinted, blinking away the sun. But when the jeeps came into focus, they were adorned not with the U.S. Army lettering but with the UN logo instead. Disappointed, she sat back down to finish her coffee. There'd been no sign of the soldiers since that morning she'd spied them on the road. Pierre was right. She might not see them again at all.

Then another morning, as she sat on the roof with her coffee, the unmistakable whir of a helicopter broke through the morning quiet. Elsa stood tall, her eyes scanning the sky, and there, fluttering down from hovering U.S. Army helicopters, were men held aloft by billowy white parachutes. They drifted off to land, hidden from view by the hilly terrain.

She wanted to jump with joy. Perhaps her soldier was among those men.

Within days, as if she'd willed it, a soldier arrived at the clinic and asked for Elsa. He was wearing camouflage pants, a tan T-shirt, and a baseball cap. A rifle hung from his shoulder and a pistol was strapped to his belt. She swallowed the tinge of disappointment she felt when she realized he was not the soldier she'd seen on the road. Still, he looked every bit a GI Joe—blond, handsome, tanned, and ready to fight.

He held out his hand and announced in a Southern drawl, "I'm Lieutenant Dave Martin, and the Chief sent me to find you. We're with the Fifth Special Forces Group out of Fort Bragg, North Carolina. We're stationed not far from here. We only recently found out you were here, and we'd like to offer to help you in any way we can."

Elsa shook his hand and, composing herself, replied.

"I'm Elsa Murphy, a nurse with Aide du Monde," she answered. It was wonderful to be in the company of another American, to think and speak in English, but she was anxious. "I'm not sure that it's safe for me to be seen with you," she said softly.

"I understand," Lieutenant Martin said reassuringly. "That's why I'm here. We'd like to talk with you, Miss Murphy, and the Chief would like to invite you to come to supper a week from Sunday. Are you available?"

Elsa hesitated. More than once the French-based ADM had warned her to avoid the soldiers—"the invaders," they'd called them. *You are forbidden to fraternize with them,* Pierre had said. *It is our first rule.* But unless she told the office in Paris, how would they know she'd *broken* their rule?

The lieutenant must have seen the doubt in her eyes.

"You'll be safe; we promise you that. We know where the ADM compound is, and we can pick you up at eighteen hundred hours." He paused and smiled. "Sorry. Six P.M., outside of your house. If you wait there, we'll collect you. No need to worry."

She forced a smile. "Then I'll be there," she said, wondering if her blue-eyed soldier would be too.

"See you then." He waved cheerfully as he headed out the gate. Elsa watched as he jumped into a jeep and drove off in a cloud of dust.

Elsa returned to the clinic and to ten Taliban prisoners who were waiting to be seen.

"Taliban?" she asked Hamid uneasily. "I thought they were all in jails around Kabul."

"There is a prison here in Bamiyan that now holds about one hundred Taliban," Hamid answered. "They were captured by villagers or the police or the U.S. soldiers, and they are here still. They have come today with medical complaints. The Bamiyan police are with them, and it is your decision whether or not they will be seen."

Elsa hesitated. "Why is it my decision?"

"You are the administrator of this clinic and it is your job, Elsa, to make these decisions."

"Hmm." She paused to think. "Well, we have a duty here to provide medical care. I suppose I should have a look. Where are they?"

Hamid led her behind the clinic to where the prisoners sat huddled on the ground with four police officers nearby. Elsa approached them slowly. They were a wretched bunch, not particularly vicious or frightening, just pathetic. They were filthy and their clothes were tattered and probably infested with lice. All of them were bearded, scrawny men who'd had any arrogance beaten out of them.

Through gritted teeth, Elsa asked each of them, in Dari, what was wrong.

"Mariz? Che taklif dori?"

Each had a minor complaint—a cough, red eyes, the terrible itch that comes with lice. There wasn't a really sick one among them. Elsa noticed that one of them sat trembling, tears running like little streams through the layers of dirt on his face.

"Che taklif?" she asked Hamid, nodding toward the little man.

Hamid spoke to the filthy man, who spoke softly as he condemned the Taliban and declared that he was not one of them.

"I was taken prisoner only because I was caught taking food for my starving family. I am not Taliban!" His tone was fierce and convincing, so much so that one of the police officers moved forward menacingly, only to be waved off by Elsa, who asked the man his name.

"I am Mohammed from Sattar," he replied politely. "I am but a simple farmer whose fields these infidels burned. I have a cough and am very tired." He placed a bony hand over his heart. "May God bless you for helping me this day."

Elsa wanted to know if his story was true, so she wrote his name and village down. Perhaps Hamid could help her confirm his claim.

Finally, with the rest of the prisoners looking on, Elsa nodded to Hamid. "If you move them all to the emergency room, I can see them quickly. We don't want them here for long."

Hamid grunted at the prisoners and guided them to the clinic.

Two days later, Elsa and Hamid stopped at the village prison and spoke with a representative of the provincial governor's police. Elsa saw Mohammed through the bars of his crowded cell, and he watched intently as she inquired about his crimes. He waved and put his hand over his heart.

"*Salaam alaikum, chetore asti? Khoob asti? Jona jurast?*" he said loudly.

The police were frank. "Oh no, no, he is not a Taliban soldier. He stole food and he must pay for it before he can be released," one policeman declared.

"But he has no money. How can he do that?" Elsa asked.

"That is his problem, not mine," the policeman replied. "It is the law."

"But—" Elsa felt Hamid's foot nudge her own.

"We must go," he said. "He is just doing his job."

Before they left the jail, she turned and raised her hand to Mohammed.

"*Alaikum salaam,*" she called out as she turned to the door.

On the walk home, she asked Hamid to find out how much money Mohammed would need to buy his way out of jail.

Hamid reported the following day. "It will take five hundred afghanis—ten U.S. dollars—to get him out of jail."

"Just ten?" Elsa turned and fished a ten-dollar bill from her bag. "Here," she said, handing it to Hamid. "I knew I'd need it one of these days. When you have a few minutes, will you go back?"

Hamid smiled. "You are a kind woman, Elsa."

When Mohammed was released, he returned to the clinic with Hamid to bestow endless blessings on Elsa.

"*Tashakore,* you are very kind to help me. Because of your kindness, I will return today to my family in Sattar. I hope that someday, *inshallah,* I will see you again."

"You are very welcome," she replied somewhat self-consciously. "I hope that someday, you'll come back and visit us."

Mohammed salaamed, bowed, and headed home.

Though Friday was Islam's holy day and most of the village and the clinic were closed, Elsa and Hamid continued to work most Fridays for at least part of the day. There was so much to do when the clinic was open that it was her only time to do paperwork and to figure out what supplies and medicines they needed. Besides, it wasn't as if there was much else for either of them to do in this tiny village, far from home.

So she threw herself into work. She started by organizing the pharmacy. Located in an old stable behind the clinic, it had never been properly cleaned before the medicines and supplies were moved in, and it still carried the unmistakable stench of animal waste. Containers of drugs were covered with bits of hay and other remnants of the stable.

She worked with the record keeper, Sidiq, a hunched-over, humpbacked young man who spoke excellent English in the whiniest voice Elsa had ever heard. He had nothing else to do on Fridays and he welcomed the chance to work. His face was etched in a permanent scowl, not from any bad intentions, but from the *jinn,* he said.

He had been arrested in Kabul for having a clean-shaven face in a time when only long, flowing beards were allowed. He had been thrown into the infamous Policharki prison for a full year and during that time the *jinn* had stolen into his mind. They had made him sad and crazy; he screamed and spit, and feigned seizures. Inexplicably the Taliban didn't kill him. Instead, they'd thrown him out of the jail.

"If the *jinn* want you, then they can have you," the Taliban had finally declared.

"And so I left Policharki, thinking the *jinn* would escape from my soul once I was released, but they didn't let go," Sidiq explained sadly. "They held on tighter to my mind and made me an unpleasant sort. Even my mother hated to be around me. I would suddenly start to spit and scream for no reason, and there was nothing I could do but let the *jinn* have their way.

"Finally, I mustered the strength I would need to pass ADM's interview for national staff, and I came here to Bamiyan. The *jinn* don't seem to like Bamiyan and I think they may have left me, though you can never be sure with the *jinn*."

Elsa learned then that he was looking for a wife. "I don't think I'll get one in Kabul, though. If people know the *jinn* have you, there's no way they'll let you near their daughter. I think that maybe here in Bamiyan, I can make a match."

Elsa immediately thought of dear Amina, who so desperately wanted a husband. She looked closely at Sidiq. Though homely and cursed with a voice that could cut through wood, he was sweet and intelligent. And after all, if the *jinn* had prevented each of them from finding a spouse, why not damn the *jinn* and introduce them to each other?

What could it hurt?

When he paused for a moment to catch his breath, she spoke up.

"I know it's not my place to make introductions, but my friend Amina is unfailingly kind and beautiful, and it is only an extra finger on her right hand—which she says was given to her by the *jinn*—which has prevented her from making a match of her own."

"Ahh," Sidiq replied. "When the *jinn* get hold of a girl, well, that's it, isn't it?"

"But surely you have to agree that it's silly," Elsa said, pleading with him. "Her only affliction is an extra finger, *nothing* else. We can even try to have it cut off. Would you consider meeting her?"

"Hmm." Sidiq seemed to consider it for a minute. "It's not our way here in Afghanistan, but, well . . . I guess it can't hurt, just to meet her."

"It's agreed then. Come home with me this afternoon and have tea with us."

At the news of Elsa's tea, Hamid's mouth wrinkled into a frown.

"Elsa, families arrange marriages here, not foreign women with teas and special afternoons. This is Afghanistan. I think that you are making a big mistake."

But she wouldn't be swayed.

"Oh, Hamid, both of these people want to be married and their families have had no success in finding them partners. What's the harm?"

Hamid shook his head and fell silent.

Sidiq confessed timidly that he agreed with Hamid.

"I'm not so sure that this is a good idea." His voice rose to a higher pitch as they headed up the road to Elsa's house. "Still, tea in the afternoon is always welcome."

When the three of them arrived at home, Amina, who'd had no warning, was so flustered at having two men in the house that she had to be coaxed from her room. Even then, she sat holding her veil over her face and across her extra finger, too nervous to speak or even drink her tea.

As for the usually chatty Sidiq, he was suddenly struck silent except for the loud slurping sound he made as he sipped his tea. If he even noticed Amina, he showed no sign. It was left to Elsa and Hamid to somehow fill the unexpected silence, and mercifully the afternoon tea was over almost as quickly as it had begun.

That evening, Elsa apologized to Amina.

"I'm sorry," she said. She repeated it several times. "It's just that he's looking for a wife, and he's really very nice, but I should have asked first. I hope you're not angry. I won't try anything like that again."

A smile crept across Amina's lips. She lowered her gaze and caressed her extra finger. Elsa noticed the smile and realization swept over her.

"Ohh, you liked him, didn't you?" she asked.

Amina remained silent, but her smile grew wider.

For all of his seeming indifference to Amina's hidden charms, Sidiq arrived at the clinic the following morning and presented Elsa with a cherished gift. It was a delicately beaded hand mirror held in a tiny, hand-sewn velvet pouch.

"Oh!" Elsa exclaimed. "It's beautiful. I can't accept it though; it wouldn't be right." She tried to give it back to Sidiq but he pushed it into her hands again.

"It is for you. You must take it. I made this and others when I was in Policharki. My mother brought the beads and mirrors, and I would work all day gluing and arranging the little beads to frame the small looking glass. My mother hoped that if the *jinn* caught sight of me and my reflection, they would become confused and take their leave of me.

"But it never happened, until yesterday, when I felt the *jinn* leave me forever as I sat to tea with you and your friends. I believe that I am going to speak with Amina's brother. Hamid has pointed out his house to me and has promised to accompany me there so that I may present myself and my intentions."

He finally stopped to take a deep breath, and he smiled.

"No rose is without thorns, and she *is* a rose, my dear Elsa. *Besiar tashakore,* many thanks to you, my sister."

Elsa murmured her own thanks and rushed off before Sidiq could see her tears. She clutched the little mirror and placed it gently into her pocket.

14

With her routine established, Elsa found time to write to Maureen, and though there was no postal service in Afghanistan yet, Johann had promised to slip the letter into his next UN pouch and have it mailed from Geneva. She'd knocked one morning at Johann's gate on the way to the clinic but there was no answer. She stuffed the letter back into her bag, and she and Hamid headed off.

When she arrived at the clinic, she made her way through the hospital ward in search of Laila for their morning rounds. There seemed to be an undercurrent rippling through the waiting crowd, but with her still limited grasp of the language, she wasn't able to put a finger on it. So she scanned the halls for Laila and as she did, she spotted Johann.

"Johann," she called, pulling the letter from her bag and marveling at this bit of unexpected luck.

Pushing his thick eyeglasses over his nose, Johann turned and almost ran into her. "Elsa, I've been looking for you. You are needed." In his already shaky voice, he explained that a local bus had exploded when it drove over an antitank mine in a nearby village.

"It is just terrible. There will be many dead and injured. When these mines explode, everything nearby is decimated. *Everything.*" His voice quivered as Laila joined them, listening intently. "We need you to help at the scene. Can you help, do you think?"

Elsa turned to Laila, who nodded her approval.

"Go, Elsa," she said quickly. "And take Ezat with you. I'll get ready for the injured."

Elsa turned to Johann. "I can help." Noticing the hesitation in her own voice, she repeated it. "I *know* I can help."

If he noticed her anxiety, he gave no sign.

"You can go in my jeep. I will send another soon."

Elsa quickly packed first aid supplies and other necessary items into a backpack. Ezat appeared beside her and worked silently, gathering equipment. Together, they found Hamid and the trio set off in the UN jeep.

Hamid sped over the rugged terrain and through dusty villages, but it still took more than thirty minutes to get to the scene. They had no way of getting more detailed information, of even knowing if anyone survived. Elsa sat in the jeep, clinging to her seat, checking and rechecking her supplies and glancing at her watch. Ezat sat quietly, looking out.

When they finally arrived, Elsa stepped quickly from the jeep. Twisted metal, charred body parts, and blood-soaked clothes lay strewn about as if they'd rained down from the sky. Everywhere she looked, a body or a body part lay in a pool of blood. Elsa felt her mouth go dry and her legs go weak; she fought the urge to look away.

Small pockets of fire still blazed and the smell of smoke and burning flesh filled the air, stinging her eyes and throat. Crying survivors, their clothes torn and bloodied, wandered through the wreckage and searched through the burned and crushed bodies that littered the ground. Even the road and the trees bordering it were charred and pockmarked from the blast.

A gray-haired woman, her veil in shreds and scattered like confetti in her loose hair, kneeled in the road as though praying. She held something tight in her hands, and as Elsa moved closer, she saw that it was a child's bloodied sandal.

Nearby, a young man whose head was laced with cuts and skin was scorched stood in the midst of the blast site, his arms outstretched and face turned to the sky. Though he seemed to be screaming, only a faint mewling sound came from his lips.

Clusters of people huddled together, some bleeding, some crying, some just watching. Suddenly, they stopped and turned, and Elsa felt their eyes come to rest on her. Her throat tightened. She looked around again and gulped a mouthful of air.

The devastation was unimaginable.

She turned and saw Hamid and Ezat nearby, standing perfectly still and just looking over the scene.

Oh God, she thought, *what do I do? If we were in Boston, what would I do?* And suddenly, she knew.

"Triage." She said it out loud. "I need to triage and then we can help." She hesitated, took a slow, steadying breath, and turned to Hamid and Ezat.

"Hamid, please ask the injured—those who are able to walk—to sit over there." Her hand trembled as she pointed to a crumbling stone wall by the side of the road. Then she gestured to a clear area closer to the wreckage. "See if the onlookers can move the badly injured here where Ezat and I can examine them."

Ezat nodded agreement, and Hamid rushed off to direct the movement of the injured.

As she stood in the road, Elsa saw that there were still people lying under the mutilated wreckage of the bus. She walked to the twisted metal frame and knelt down for a better look, but it was too dark. She hunched down farther and crawled through the pieces of wreckage. The metal and glass gnawed at her hands and knees as she made her way along the edge of the mangled wreck. She adjusted her eyes and looked again. She could just make out three lifeless bodies, two of them crushed by the weight of the bus. They lay in pools of blood, pieces of jagged metal piercing their lifeless frames. She scrunched down and reached out to touch the face of a tiny girl, but she could find no pulse and the little girl's skin was gray and scorched. She was dead. Elsa gently closed the child's eyes before briefly closing her own, praying for strength. She took a deep breath and reached in to feel two more bodies, both crushed beyond recognition. They were dead too.

Moving on, she searched for any signs of life—a pulse or a breath—but there was nothing, just silence. She crawled away from the wreck, tears blurring her vision.

She stood, wiped her eyes, brushed debris off her hands, and turned to the victims who were lying on the road. She could see Ezat tending to victims and Hamid standing nearby. He called to her.

"Here, Elsa, over here! These people are badly hurt. They need you."

She hurried over and went first to a woman who lay quietly with her eyes open, staring at something Elsa couldn't see. Her head was covered in blood. Her breathing was steady and she seemed stable, so Elsa simply covered her wounds.

While she moved from victim to victim, more vehicles began to arrive, some bearing the UN logo. Some of the onlookers were even helping now. A familiar hum, not unlike the sounds in Trauma One, filled the air, but Elsa stayed focused on triaging until a soft sniffling reached her ears. She turned and saw two small boys clinging to each other.

"Brothers," Hamid said over his shoulder. "Their parents are under the bus." Though their clothes were bloody and torn, they had no serious injuries that Elsa could see.

"Will you move them away, Hamid, so that they don't see this?" She motioned to the wreckage, and Hamid guided the two boys to the side of the road.

A groaning caught her attention, and she whipped around. A slender young man lay in the road with his left arm and leg bent at impossible angles. The front of his large shirt was soaked with blood. His breathing was labored and his eyes were glassy. His face was covered in blood, his features obscured by shards of glass and metal.

He had a terrible head wound; shrapnel from the explosion had probably pierced his skull. He would be unrecognizable to family and friends. Elsa bent over and gently unwrapped his turban. Cascades of black hair fell out.

She looked closer.

This was no man.

This was a *woman*.

Elsa listened to her patient's chest and heard a faint heartbeat. She noticed then that this tiny, bone-thin woman was pregnant.

"Oh, shit," she whispered. "Hold on. We're going to get you to our hospital as quickly as we can." The woman moaned.

Hamid helped and together they straightened out and splinted the woman's arm and leg with tape and pieces of wood. Elsa rummaged through her supplies and pulled out an intravenous set. If the woman received fluids, she might live until they could get her to the hospital, and there, just maybe, they could deliver her baby.

Elsa's hand was steady as she applied the tourniquet and found a suitable vein. She threaded the catheter in and hooked it to a bag of fluid. She motioned to Hamid, and they gently lifted the woman into the back of the jeep. As they lifted her, a tiny worn tube of lipstick rolled out of her pocket and tumbled to the ground. Elsa picked it up and rolled it in her hand.

Lipstick? *Here?*

"I'll hold this for you," she said softly as she tucked the tube into her pocket. Elsa wanted to leave for the hospital right then but there were several more victims for Elsa and Ezat to check before they could go.

Suddenly there was a faint cry, and she turned to see the villagers pull a tiny form from the belly of the bus. He was covered with blood, his legs were crushed, and one arm was gone—no doubt torn from his body in the instant of the explosion. One of the villagers passed him to Elsa.

She took the little body, but though he was still breathing, she could see that there was no hope. She cradled him in her arms as he heaved a final sigh and died. She stroked his hair and touched his cheek, then tenderly passed him to the crying man who'd held him.

"I'm sorry," she murmured before she turned away, tears pooling in her eyes.

Beads of perspiration ran down her face, mingling with her tears and clouding her vision. She wiped them away with her sleeve and tried to shake off the terrible sadness she felt.

Ezat and the arriving personnel were dealing with the rest of the victims in the wreckage, so she turned her attention to the remaining survivors sitting by the stone wall. Their injuries were relatively minor, and they could easily be transported to the hospital for further care. She and Hamid helped to load them into the jeeps sent by the UN. Before long, all of the survivors had been located.

"Hamid, let Ezat know that we're heading back. This second

vehicle can take him when he's ready." She watched as Hamid spoke to Ezat, who turned to her and nodded. *Was that an approving half smile?*

She nodded in return, and she and Hamid climbed into the vehicle with the badly wounded pregnant woman. Elsa held her hand during what seemed like an endless ride, and once at the hospital, she asked Hamid to stay with her while she went to find Laila.

"Laila, the explosion was terrible," she said quickly. "I can't even begin to describe it. Ezat will be back soon, and most of the people that we brought back can wait for treatment, but there's one, a young woman . . ." Elsa lowered her voice and continued. "She was dressed as a man. She has a terrible head injury and I think she's going to die. Actually, it's a miracle that she made it here."

"Well, if it's hopeless, let's see to the others then."

"No, Laila, the woman is pregnant." Elsa stopped to catch her breath. "Maybe we can save her baby."

Laila nodded, and Elsa motioned for Hamid to help them carry the woman into the treatment room, after which he quickly hurried out.

Laila leaned over the woman and examined her. She looked up, her eyes flashing.

"Feel her abdomen. Those are contractions. The baby is coming."

They pulled out the delivery tray and washed and gloved for the imminent birth. Elsa took a vial of Pitocin from the tray and drew it up into a syringe. It would hasten the contractions and the birth, but it soon became clear that it wasn't needed. Laila slipped a small gloved hand inside the woman and said she felt the baby's head as it descended the birth canal.

"It's coming. Get the scissors and ties and a blanket."

Elsa gathered the equipment and within minutes the baby was expelled in a rush of blood and fluid. It was a boy, scrawny and already malnourished. He took his first breath and gave a feeble cry just as his unknown mother breathed her last and died.

Laila handed the baby to Elsa and covered the woman.

"At least the baby is alive," she said, pausing sadly. Then she turned again. "If you're all right here, I'm going to see if Ezat is back and then we'll see the rest of the patients."

"Go, go. We're fine."

Elsa washed the tiny orphan and wrapped him in a hospital blanket. Then she foraged in the pharmacy for nutritional supplements, preparing some formula in a well-used baby bottle. She sat cradling the small bundle, urging him to suck, which he did eagerly. *How different from Diana,* she thought with a touch of sadness.

Once he had drunk his fill, he fell asleep in Elsa's arms, and she sat there rocking the infant as her fingers searched her pocket for the old worn tube of lipstick. It was the one clue the woman had left behind that might identify her.

Looking up, Elsa stood and went over to the baby's mother. "Your baby is okay," she said softly, smoothing the sheet that covered her.

She finished up late, staying to help Laila and Ezat care for and settle the other victims and their families. Reluctantly, she gave the baby to one of the hospital staff and, Hamid at her side for the trek, headed back to her own room for the night.

Early the following morning, Hamid knocked at the gate.

"Elsa, there are already people gathering at the clinic—people looking for family. I think you should come now."

Elsa grabbed her head-scarf and hurried through the gate after Hamid.

Word had spread about the explosion and villagers had gathered to see if any of their own had been among the injured or dead. The staff had set up an old tent to use as a small morgue, lining up the bodies and covering them with sheets.

Elsa walked through the tent and lingered by the body of the woman who'd delivered the tiny baby. No one had come to claim her.

Poor soul, to die alone like that.

She stepped outside and saw Johann, who hurried over. Pushing his glasses up on his nose, he took Elsa's hand. "Thank you, Elsa. Laila and Ezat told me what a wonderful job you did yesterday. Thank you so much. You have helped the people of Bamiyan greatly."

Uncomfortable with Johann's effusive comments, she just nodded and hurried away, running right into a grim-faced Ezat.

"*Taliban.*" He almost spat out the word. "The police said it was the Taliban who laid that mine."

Hamid's eyes grew wide with the news.

Elsa felt a shiver. "But I thought they were either in prison or gone?"

"No, they are not gone. They are still here, waiting, just waiting."

She didn't know what to say, so she turned to the crowd that had gathered. Many were speaking excitedly and even more just stood there waiting quietly. Those, she thought, were the saddest.

Elsa asked Hamid to interpret so that together they could help. They approached a tiny woman who was standing alone. Her face was hidden by the veil she held across it.

"Miss." Hamid spoke softly. "Are you looking for someone? Can we help you?"

Hamid's voice had startled the woman, and she hesitated before pushing her veil away to reveal her face. She was young, with a fresh-scrubbed face and sparkly green eyes. She wore a determined expression, and she looked right into Elsa's eyes.

Elsa hesitated. There was something about this woman. She felt almost as though perhaps they'd met before, but she would have remembered that intense gaze. She watched as the woman held her hand over her heart and spoke as Hamid interpreted.

"I am Parween, and I am looking for my friend. Her name is Mariam, and she may have been on the bus from Mashaal. I am not certain but I have been checking the buses recently. Have you seen her?"

"Do you have any other information that could help us? Any jewelry or special clothes she may have been wearing?" Elsa asked.

Parween smiled as if remembering her friend.

"She is small and beautiful with long black hair and deep dark eyes, and though I have not heard that she was on the bus from Mashaal, in my heart, I know she was." Her face darkened as she spoke.

Hamid relayed what she had said, and Elsa remembered the pregnant woman's long black hair spilling onto the road. She held her breath as her hand found the old lipstick still tucked into her pocket. She pulled it out slowly and rolled it into the palm of her hand.

"Does this belong to her?" she asked softly.

Parween covered her mouth, her fingers fluttering there.

"Oh, that is Mariam's," she said. "I gave that to her. I knew that she would be here. Where is she? Please bring me to her. *Allah u akbar.* I knew that Allah would keep her safe."

Elsa passed the tube of lipstick to Parween, who looked into Elsa's eyes and suddenly realized that there were tears there.

"Che taklif?" Parween asked.

Elsa took Parween's hands and sighed.

"Your friend did not make it. She died yesterday after delivering her baby. I am so sorry."

Parween seemed puzzled and pulled away.

"You are wrong," she said. "Mariam is not pregnant. Yet she is here. I know it. This is her lipstick. Please. Please, bring me to her."

"She is here; you are right," Elsa replied. "But she has died. I was with her when it happened. We can bring you to her, but you must know that she suffered terrible injuries. You may not recognize her."

Parween's confidence dissolved, and her face crumpled into grief.

"Please," she said through a cascade of tears. "Bring me to her."

Elsa took the young woman's hand and guided her to the tent where Mariam's body lay. They could hear the others' cries as they approached the makeshift morgue. Once inside, they walked to the rear of the tent, and there Elsa knelt to gently lift the sheet and reveal Mariam's bloodied face.

Parween gasped and fell to the ground.

"Oh no, no, no!" Her cry filled the tent. She bent to the lifeless form, lifted it into her arms, and sat there in the dirt, rocking Mariam and stroking her face. "Oh forgive me, Mariam. I should have come for you. Forgive me, dearest." Parween held the broken body close and cried until her tears ran dry.

Elsa kept a respectful distance and waited until Parween's sobs quieted. Then she reached out and gently touched her, whispering, "Mariam's baby is alive. Would you like to see him?"

Parween trembled.

"Sai'est?" A baby? Is it true?" she asked.

"Balay, balay, yes," Elsa replied. She led Parween from the tent into the glaring morning sun and into the hospital. The crib had

been rolled into the hallway and there lay the tiny infant still wrapped in the blanket from the previous night, asleep with his little hands scrunched into tight fists.

Parween gently picked the baby up.

"A boy, yes?" she asked, and Elsa nodded. Parween smiled and looked the baby over closely, checking everything, even counting fingers and toes. She held Mariam's child close, and when she finally looked up, she fought back her tears to speak.

"He will come with me." Parween gazed down at the baby. "Mariam escaped from Mashaal to have this baby. I know that she was coming here so that her baby could live."

Elsa was struck by Parween's decisiveness. She was the exact opposite of everything Elsa had seen and heard of traditional Afghan women. And she would get no argument from Elsa. Parween and the baby already seemed to have bonded. Awake now, the baby clung to her veil and dress.

"I will send my family to bring Mariam home. We will take care of her." Fresh tears stung Parween's eyes as she bundled the baby up and turned to leave. She hesitated, then spun around and took Elsa's hand, speaking haltingly in English.

"Thank you, thank you for help . . . from you."

And with that, she turned again and hurried off, her veil trailing behind her as she headed out of the gate and down the road.

15

Parween arrived home cradling Mariam's tiny son in her arms. She rushed through the gate and went in search of Uncle Abdullah. She wanted him to be the first to know.

"Uncle," she called when she spied him tending to his little patch of garden. "I must speak with you."

Abdullah turned and smiled when he saw Parween. He pushed himself up, and it was then that he saw the tiny baby in her arms and the tears in her eyes.

"Who is this?" He reached out and gently stroked the baby's face.

In a rush of words, Parween shared the news of Mariam's death in the bus explosion. She inhaled deeply.

"The baby is Mariam's, but his father, I think, was one of the Taliban who so tormented her. I am sure that Mariam was running from her husband and from Mashaal to protect her little one."

Abdullah sighed and sat heavily. "Ahh, you are right. Poor Mariam. Hers is another senseless death in a lifetime of so many."

Parween felt a familiar sadness grip her heart, and she handed the baby to Uncle Abdullah, who sat there gazing into the little bundle's face.

"There has been too much misery, Uncle, but this baby, *inshallah*, is a sign of happier times to come."

Abdullah rocked the infant. "Such innocence, such promise. May Allah grant him a long life free of the misery that so plagued his poor mother." He looked up at Parween. "He is sent from Allah. You must take him as your own; it will be safer for him if he is thought to be yours."

"Yes, Uncle, I think so too. Please keep him with you until I have decided what to say to my mother."

"The truth, Parween." He said it firmly. "The truth will be enough."

Abdullah arranged for two local men to bring Mariam's body home to be buried. Parween and the women would follow tradition and wash her, wrap her in white fabric, and lay her to rest in the small cemetery just outside the compound walls.

By the afternoon everything was ready, and Parween and the other women walked the short distance to bury Mariam. Once the box that held her had been covered over with earth, they gathered heavy stones to mark her resting place, and they prayed to Allah to watch over her. A river of tears flooded from Parween's eyes.

Will this misery never end?

When the service was finished, she dried her tears and collected the baby from Uncle Abdullah. She carried him to the courtyard where the women had gathered. They all sighed in sadness.

"Mariam had been lovely," they murmured. "What a terrible end."

Parween held the baby tight and looked into his eyes.

"This has been a sad day, but Allah has granted a wish of mine and my dear husband. Today I went to the clinic with pains low in my stomach, and there, I learned that I was not only with child, but that he was about to be born."

She smiled and held the baby out for all to see. "It is Raziq's final gift to me. All the more precious because he was so unexpected." She almost held her breath as she spoke, afraid that they might see through her false words.

But the women only sighed and cooed and gazed at the baby. "Allah has not forgotten you, Parween. He has given you a boy baby to dry your tears." They passed the baby around, exclaiming over the likeness to his parents.

"Why, he has your eyes," an old woman with thick spectacles proclaimed.

Another disagreed. "But I am certain that he has Raziq's chin."

Parween smiled. She saw only Mariam when she gazed into the baby's sweet face, with his pert nose and deep brown eyes—he was the image of his mother.

She was relieved though that the women accepted the baby as her own. She would have no difficulty claiming she had been pregnant. Women here, so thin and covered in voluminous layers, often hid pregnancies until a baby was delivered. No one would think to question the tiny widow; neither would they think to count the months since Raziq's death.

As fate would have it, most of them couldn't count anyway.

Rahima, though, knew her daughter well, and once they were alone, she asked where the baby had come from. Parween whispered her reply.

"Mama, he is Mariam's infant but it is best if I take him as my own. She delivered him before she died."

Rahima opened her mouth wide in surprise, and then a smile settled on her lips as she stroked Parween's hair. "You are a good girl. He is a gift from Allah." She planted a kiss on Parween's cheek and on the infant's head. "What name will you give to him?"

"Raziq, Mama. Don't you think it fits him?"

"I do," Rahima answered. "It is a good name."

Zahra watched her mother and grandmother with this new baby, and she eyed the infant warily. At just three years old, she was used to being the baby in the house, the center of attention. She toddled over and pinched Raziq until he howled, and Parween bent to her.

"He is your brother. Someday, he will decide your fate and arrange your marriage. You should be good to him."

Zahra shrieked in protest and ran off.

"Ahh." Rahima laughed. "She *is* your daughter."

16

Though it seemed an eternity had passed since the soldiers' invitation, Sunday had finally come. Elsa lingered over her lipsticks before choosing a soft plum tint, and just before six o'clock, she announced to Amina that she was going to the UN office for dinner and meetings with Johann. "I'll walk with you," Amina replied.

"No need. It's just around the corner. I won't be gone too long." In truth, she wanted to share the news of the soldiers with Amina, but she decided to wait—she wanted to be certain that the soldiers didn't mind if she told.

Amina hesitated, not sure how to respond, and before she could broach the subject again Elsa strode through the gate. She tucked herself unseen into the outside corner of her house and waited. Lieutenant Martin had been right; hers was the last house on a seldom-traveled road. No one would see her. Within minutes, she heard the approaching jeep come to a halt, and she peered out to see the front passenger door open. A hand motioned for her to get in. She jumped inside and heard the lieutenant's calm voice.

"Evening, Miss Murphy." He turned the jeep and headed back along the dusty lane.

"Oh, please call me Elsa."

"Well then, I hope you'll call me Dave." He stepped on the gas and maneuvered the jeep along the rocky lanes and over a wobbly bridge that quivered when they passed. She peered at the clusters of mud houses, smoke curling from small cooking fires, children shrieking and running about, a small neighborhood almost. Before long, they left behind the well-worn paths and small houses and came to what at first appeared to be a deep, impenetrable grove of trees. But as they got closer, Elsa saw that there was a small gap between the trees, big enough for a jeep but too small to be seen from a distance.

Elsa watched astonished as Dave deftly guided the jeep through. "I thought this was some sort of forest."

"That's precisely what the previous owner wanted people to think. A Hazara commander once owned this place, and he wanted it hidden and well protected. It's been so well concealed that most people in Bamiyan don't even know it's here."

The road narrowed and the jeep slowed as gates appeared through the heavy brush. They were clanked open and then shut loudly once they'd passed. After a few minutes, they passed through a second set of gates, and the jeep finally ground to a halt at the entrance to the soldiers' quarters. Nestled on a mountaintop, the house had a commanding view of the valley and the surrounding area. In the gathering dusk, she could just make out the Buddha hollows off in the distance.

Elsa got out of the jeep and waited as Dave took his flashlight and pointed the beam to light her way. Before her was a fortress, a castle-like building made of heavy stone and ringed by barbed wire and gun and rocket turrets. With Dave in the lead, she crossed a kind of moat, a ramp over a deep ditch, and stepped into a house ablaze with electric lights. A large American flag hung in the entryway and boxes of ammunition, sandbags, and rifles were scattered across the floor. She heard the unmistakable sounds of a television newscast, of water running, and of something sizzling on a stove.

She'd stepped back into the twenty-first century.

American voices filled the air, and Elsa was suddenly surrounded by camouflage-clad men. Dave made the introductions just as a tall, graying, distinguished-looking man made his way into the room, held out his hand and greeted her in a clear Boston accent.

"Miss Murphy, good to meet you," he said warmly. "I'm Major

Doyle, but more commonly, I'm called the Chief. Please"—he motioned toward a chair—"have a seat."

"Please call me Elsa."

The Chief directed another soldier to get her a drink, and she was served an ice-cold Diet Coke and ushered to a soft chair. She sank into the plush cushions and curled her fingers around the smooth, wet glass.

She sighed. *Heaven.*

The Chief said that he had only recently learned that she was there.

"To tell you the truth, I was goddamn pissed off that my intel had failed. I shoulda known an American was here. It's our job to know this stuff and for—what was it, more than a month?—that information didn't get to me." He shook his head. "Somebody's going to answer for that."

She'd only just met him, but already she didn't want to be that person.

"I assume you've heard about Pierre Dubois and the Taliban, or maybe they were bandits—we'll probably never know for sure. But his death underlines that this is a dangerous place, no doubt about it. That's why it was so important for me to know you were here, in case you got into any trouble."

The Chief paused, and it seemed to Elsa as if he was letting his words take hold.

"I thought his replacement would be another Frenchman," he continued.

"It was terrible about Pierre," Elsa replied sadly. "But if the soldiers never noticed me, that's a good thing. It must mean I'm fitting in now and hardly worth a second glance."

The Chief scowled. "Not likely. The soldier who reported you to me said he saw a woman wearing sunglasses and lipstick, said she screamed foreigner. Do you have a bodyguard? A weapon?"

Elsa shook her head. "No, no, nothing like that."

This time he grunted his disapproval. "You should be protected, Miss Murphy—Elsa. You're an American, a soft target here."

"But I'm an aid worker," she said. "I *was* nervous when I first arrived." She tried to downplay the almost overwhelming fear she'd felt after Pierre's death. "But I'm here to help. People know that now, and *that's* what will keep me safe."

"Oh, Jesus." The Chief rolled his eyes. "That won't keep you safe, not a bit. There is real danger here, and always where you least expect it. Bamiyan may *seem* safe but there is trouble even here. Understand?"

Trouble? Here in Bamiyan? she thought, but she nodded.

"You have to be on the alert, Elsa, but know that we'll take care of you too. I wanted you to come tonight so that everyone here could get to know you in case we need to extract you quickly."

"What does that mean?" Elsa asked. *"Extract?"*

"Well, you're an American, and this is an active war zone. Obviously, I can't share any details with you but we are here for a reason and we have not sat idle. We have reason to believe that there are active Taliban and al-Qaeda forces about, and there is always the possibility that they might set their sights on you. I wanted my men to get a good look at you, and if the situation warrants a hasty rescue, we'll know you, and we'll get you out quickly."

"It's hard to think of Bamiyan as a war zone." Her mouth grew dry, and she sipped from the glass.

The Chief's brow wrinkled. "If you need to get word to us for any reason, you can leave a message for us at our drop site. There's a small music store in the bazaar. The glass front is covered with cassette labels and pictures of tape players. There's usually some Indian music playing inside. You can't miss it. Just ask for Majid and tell him that you have a message for Dave. Majid will hold it for us."

"I'll remember that, though I hope I won't need it."

"Well, we hope so too, but we have to be prepared. And we'd like to be sure that you're prepared, as well."

With that, the somber mood lifted, and Elsa sat down and joined them for spaghetti with meatballs, warm crusty bread, and more Diet Coke. Life's ordinary pleasures had never seemed as extraordinary as they did here.

She glanced around and was disappointed to see that her mystery soldier was nowhere to be found. *Perhaps he's been assigned somewhere else,* she thought sadly before joining the conversation. She told the soldiers about her own living conditions and they sniggered at the description of her mud room, her latrine, and her bath. They'd rigged up real hot-water showers, toilets, a washing machine, and a kitchen, and they'd built real beds. They had the benefit of a generator that allowed them to create this little oasis.

After dinner, she joined them in front of the television, where they watched the news. *The news.* It was surreal to be sitting there surrounded by American soldiers watching television.

Elsa looked at her watch; it was almost ten o'clock.

"It's late. I have to get back." Her voice hinted at the disappointment she felt. After hasty "good nights," Dave spirited her back home.

"See you soon, Elsa," he said.

"Thanks, Dave."

She jumped out of the jeep and walked quickly into her own compound. Amina was nowhere to be seen; Elsa thought she must have gone to bed already.

She felt a little like Cinderella after the ball, and she definitely didn't feel like heating water for a bath, so she pulled on her nightgown and curled up on her sleeping pad to read by her lantern. But her head was spinning.

She thought of the soldiers' luxuries, and though she'd enjoyed her evening, she was comfortable now in her little house and little room. She still wished for a bed and a real bath sometimes, but it had been long enough since she'd had either that her longing for them had diminished. As she lay thinking of how accustomed she'd grown to her life there, a determined scorpion scurried toward her. She took her book and brought it down hard on the deadly pest. She smiled as she blew out her lantern and lay back to sleep.

Ꙩn the weeks since his arrival, Raziq had been a sweet baby, cooing and smiling, and despite Zahra's protests, he brought joy into Uncle Abdullah's compound.

But he needed care and attention, and Parween rose at his first cry to feed him. The family's goat provided his milk and Parween mixed it with the fancy foreign formula she found in the bazaar. Whether it was the goat or the formula Parween couldn't say, but as the days passed the baby seemed to thrive.

Zahra, glum at the baby's arrival, was coaxed into helping her mother care for him. "Be my little helper, sweet one, and sit by him while I heat the water for his formula."

Zahra sat by him and stroked his face till he smiled. "Mama, look, I made him smile." And she giggled with her power over this tiny thing.

While she was feeding the baby, Parween stoked yesterday's fire to life and prepared tea. "Zahra, help Mama. Get the dishes and set them out." She sighed when Zahra scrambled to follow her orders.

Parween watched her sadly. Though she was barely three years old, her life was already laid out before her—marriage, babies, cleaning.

The cycle would continue after all.

*   *   *

Though Rahima was no longer young, she had returned to work for the tailor one or two days a week and still helped Parween with the babies and chores. With the addition of baby Raziq, life seemed to be steadying for the little family until Parween took a good look at Uncle Abdullah, the family's revered patriarch and protector. They lived in a place where men didn't often live beyond age forty, and Abdullah was elderly at fifty-five. There was no denying that his endless energy had been sapped by war, by the Taliban, and by his family's heartbreaks. He remained a kind and truly gentle man despite his misfortunes.

Yet with all of his family responsibilities, Abdullah had long neglected his own health. He'd been coughing for as long as Parween could remember, but they'd overlooked it until the morning Parween saw that he'd been coughing up blood.

"Uncle, what is this?" She pointed to the blood. "You are sick. What is wrong with you?" Her stomach clenched at the words, at the possibility that he might be ill, really ill.

"I am fine, little one. I've been coughing like that for years. Do not worry about me. I have many years left."

"Uncle, you are sick. You have to go to the clinic. Please. I'll go with you." But Abdullah was reluctant, and only after a full afternoon of coaxing did he finally agree to go to the clinic the following day. Rahima stayed home with the children.

"Now, Mama," Parween instructed her mother that evening, "the goat's milk must be mixed with this powder and warm water. He likes to take his time eating and I let Zahra help." She took a breath as if she was planning to continue, but Rahima interrupted.

"Parween, I have raised four children. I can do this."

The following morning, Parween and Abdullah made the short trek to the hospital, where they joined hundreds of others waiting to be seen. People were hollering in the hopes of being noticed and taken from the line.

Uncle Abdullah, appalled at the ruckus required to be chosen, turned to Parween. "Ah, there are so many waiting, I won't get in. We'll come back another time." And he turned to leave.

She knew full well that if he left, he would never return. "Uncle Abdullah, please stay. Let me look for help. Don't go yet."

Just then, she saw the nurse who had helped Mariam. The woman was hurrying through the gate, headed for the hospital. Parween rushed after her and in clear, soft English, said, "Miss, sorry, miss. I am thanking you for Mariam, for the help. You remember me and my friend Mariam?"

Elsa smiled when she saw Parween and stuck out her hand.

"Salaam alaikum, chetore asti? Khoob asti? Jona jurast?"

"Miss, please to speak Inglisi. It will help me." Parween smiled.

"Please, call me Elsa. How is the baby?" Elsa asked her. "How are you managing? Is there anything I can do?"

"I am here today with my uncle, a very good man," Parween replied, choosing her words carefully. "He is sick, coughing blood, but there are too many people waiting and I fear he will not be seen." Parween went on to describe Uncle Abdullah's weakness and persistent bloody cough, and Elsa nodded in understanding.

"Please, bring him in here," she said, and she pointed to the emergency room. "I can see him there."

After much coaxing from Parween, Abdullah's once impressive figure graced the entrance of the emergency room. Elsa motioned for him to sit and introduced herself.

Parween introduced Uncle Abdullah and offered to interpret. Through Elsa's probing questions, Parween learned that her uncle had been told long ago that he had tuberculosis and had even been treated, but when he'd returned to Bamiyan, there had been no treatment available. Since he'd felt well, he never thought of it again until Elsa asked.

Elsa took out her stethoscope and listened intently to Abdullah's heart and lungs, and when she was finished, she sighed and sat back.

"Without an X-ray, which we can't do here, I can't be absolutely certain, but your uncle's symptoms—his bloody cough, his fatigue—are classic signs of TB. It seems likely that it never went away, and since there is still no treatment here in Bamiyan, he will have to go to Kabul for the medicine. Even then, I suspect that it has advanced and has eaten away at his lungs. I'm sorry I don't have better news."

Parween felt weak and her shoulders sagged with this new worry. "It is bad then? There is no mistake?"

"Well, I can't do an X-ray, but his symptoms and his history suggest that it may be very serious."

She paused, seeing the horror on Parween's face.

"I'm sorry to use that word but he *is* very ill. I know that you suffered at the loss of your friend. I don't want to see you lose your uncle as well. He really needs treatment."

Parween closed her eyes and took a long, slow breath. She turned to Abdullah and told him that he still had TB, and it was very bad. He seemed to shrink a little with the news, but he quickly pulled himself up and spoke animatedly to Parween. She turned to Elsa.

"He says he cannot leave us to go to Kabul. He is very grateful for your help and would like you to come to dinner at our home."

Elsa hesitated. "Does he understand that the TB will only worsen if it is not treated?"

Parween spoke to Abdullah again and turned to Elsa. "He says that Allah has always taken care of him and, *inshallah,* God willing, he shall again. He also wants to know when you will come for dinner."

Elsa smiled. "I would like to come, but I don't know where you live."

"Do not worry," Parween replied. "I will come for you next week, and in the meantime, I will speak to my uncle. Perhaps I can convince him to go to Kabul."

She and her uncle departed with copious thanks, endless blessings, and a renewed promise of dinner.

Throughout the week that followed, though her days were consumed by work, Elsa often found herself wondering about Parween and her uncle and hoping that he would make the decision to travel to Kabul for treatment. She hoped too that they'd remember the dinner invitation, but with all of their worries, she wasn't counting on it.

When she told Hamid about it, he frowned.

"Do not expect them to come for you. Under the Taliban, it was illegal to share tea with a foreigner, and though the Taliban no longer rule, old habits stay on. People still fear the Taliban, more so since the bus explosion, and they may be afraid, too, of your foreign ways, Elsa. Remember, this is Bamiyan, not Kabul."

Even though she'd had the same thoughts, Elsa was disappointed. She wanted to get to know the people here, yet maybe he was right. Maybe they just weren't ready for her.

But only a week after she'd been to the clinic, true to her word, Parween arrived at the clinic and announced that dinner would be served that evening once Elsa was finished with her work. When she left, Elsa rushed to find Hamid.

"She has come, Hamid. I'm invited to dinner tonight. Will you go to my house and tell Amina that I'll be home later?"

Once his surprise had passed, Hamid smiled. "I'm glad for you, Elsa. Have a good night. I will tell Amina, and I will see you in the morning."

Elsa finished up her duties at the clinic and joined Parween, who'd been sitting just beyond the gate. "I'm ready," Elsa announced, and the two headed up the dusty old road to Parween's home.

Uncle Abdullah's compound, though home to many, was small. Similar to Elsa's, it was hidden by a large outer wall and contained several small rooms off the main courtyard. Each family shared one small room and the courtyard. They also shared a well and latrine, which Elsa noticed were precariously close to each other. She reminded herself not to drink the water as she was ushered to Uncle Abdullah's home, accepting the plentiful greetings of neighbors and family, shaking hands, salaaming, bowing, and finally entering the room.

A bright red vinyl tablecloth had been placed on the floor over the rug. It reminded her of the one her mother had kept on their kitchen table.

Parween made the introductions.

"This lady is Uncle Abdullah's wife, Noorem." A small lady smiled shyly before hurrying off. She returned with dishes and another woman.

"This is my mother, Rahima." Parween nudged Rahima, who smiled broadly and took Elsa's hands.

"Well-kum." She stretched out the sounds and spoke slowly.

"She's been practicing all day." Parween laughed and ushered Elsa to a pad that had been pulled out for seating.

Uncle Abdullah entered the room and bowed his head to Elsa. *"Salaam alaikum, chetore asti? Khoob asti? Jona jurast?"*

She smiled and returned the greeting. He whispered to Parween and she turned to Elsa.

"He says he is very happy that you have come to share dinner with us."

"Tell him, please, that I am very happy to be here. It is my first visit to a home here in Bamiyan." When Parween translated, Abdullah beamed.

They sat around the tablecloth, and Rahima and Noorem brought out full platters of food and placed them before Elsa.

"Please, please," Parween said, pointing to the food. "Eat."

Elsa leaned forward and dipped her fingers and bread into the bowls of rice, goat, beans, and yogurt. There was little conversation; her hosts were busy watching her. Elsa ate heartily with her fingers until finally, she'd eaten her fill. She leaned forward and waved her hand.

"*Bas,* enough for me." She tried to push her plate away but Uncle Abdullah slid it back and spoke to her.

"No, no, you must eat more," Parween translated.

Elsa ate a little more and tried again to say she'd had enough, but still Abdullah insisted.

"You must eat," Parween urged her. "It is impolite to turn it away."

Elsa took smaller and smaller bites and finally, she sat back and patted her stomach to emphasize her words. "*Bas,* enough," she said through a mouthful of rice.

Her host laughed. "You eat like a bird," Uncle Abdullah said.

Elsa tried to broach the subject of Abdullah's illness but he would have none of it.

"*Inshallah,* I will recover," he said.

Parween sat forward. "He is a stubborn man. *Inshallah,* he will change his mind."

Inshallah, God willing. Everyone here left *everything* up to God. It made Elsa crazy. *God wants you to help yourselves,* she wanted to shout. But there was no use. They believed it would all work out as God willed and there was no use in thinking otherwise. She decided not to try to sway Abdullah; it was his decision after all.

As they sat back, satisfied with the meal, Parween leaned forward and, pointing to Elsa's mouth, said, "Leepstik of you is beautiful. From Amrika?"

Elsa smiled and remembered the little tube of lipstick that had identified Mariam for her friend. She wondered if Parween had the same craving for the glossy colored wax that had claimed her own attention since childhood. She reached into her pocket and produced a shiny new tube of lipstick and handed it to Parween.

"Try it." Parween took the tube excitedly and ran the soft plum tint across her lips. She jumped up and took Elsa's hand and they ran to Parween's little room, where she took out her tiny looking glass and admired her reflection.

"Ohh," Parween exclaimed. "It is beautiful." And she rolled the glossy tube in her hand.

Elsa reached out and curled Parween's fingers over the tube.

"For you," she said, smiling.

"No, no," Parween replied, but at Elsa's insistence she finally dropped the tube into her own pocket. "I have not worn lipstick since my own wedding. Thank you," she said, and for the first time since Elsa had met her, she smiled with what seemed to be genuine happiness.

Parween's mother arrived in the doorway with Parween's two babies. The girl held back shyly for a moment but then toddled forward cheerfully on her chubby little legs. Parween took Mariam's baby into her arms. Pushing her daughter forward, she announced, "This is my first, Zahra." As if on cue, Zahra giggled and fell to the floor in a heap.

Parween held her arms out to Elsa and uncovered the baby's face. "This is my baby Raziq, named for his father," she said, smiling coyly.

"Ohh, is this—" Elsa hesitated, realizing others might hear her.

Parween nodded. "He is my son."

"May I hold him?" she asked, and Parween gently passed her the little form swaddled in old veils and pieces of fabric. Elsa cooed and cuddled the baby.

"So you are married?" she asked.

"I was married for almost seven years. My husband, Raziq, was a good man, a hero." She paused. "The Taliban murdered him." Tears appeared in her eyes, ready to fall, but she used her veil to wipe them away and collected herself.

"It was Raziq who taught me to speak Inglisi and to read and write. I miss him every day but he taught me much and he will live forever in his children—and perhaps in other children, as well. Someday, I hope to teach the children of Bamiyan."

She paused and pointed to a little pile of books in the corner. "Those are mine. I have borrowed them so that I may learn more."

Elsa stared at the pile of books. "Do you know whether the UN plans to open schools in Afghanistan?"

"We have heard rumors but they are only that. The people are still too afraid of the Taliban to build a school here."

Elsa looked down at the tiny, sleeping baby she still held in her arms. "He looks so well. It's hard to believe now how he came into the world." She paused. "So the girl . . . Mariam . . . she was your friend?"

Parween sighed and her eyes welled up again. "Mariam was like my sister. There was no one like her in the world. We grew up together in Bamiyan, and we dreamed that one day we would marry and live close to each other. But it was not to be."

Elsa sat forward. "You don't have to tell me if it's too hard."

"No, it is better that Mariam's story be told, for if you know her story and pass it on, she will not be dead. She will live in the hearts of those who speak of her."

Parween shared the haunting story of Mariam's short life.

"I was not certain that Mariam would come home. There had been no word but I hoped that she was coming, and I checked the bus from Mashaal every day for any sign of her."

"Oh, Parween, I don't even know what to say. I am so sorry. You and your friend have endured so much."

Parween heaved a sigh. Then she seemed to brighten.

"Tell me about yourself, about your life in Amrika. You have a husband?"

Elsa laughed. "No, no husband, not yet. *Inshallah,* someday. No real family either." She told Parween about Diana and Margaret. She hadn't spoken of Diana in years and just sharing those memories felt like releasing her own ghosts.

"Diana," Elsa explained, "was a beautiful and delicate baby, too delicate, my mom said once, for this world." She blinked away her own tears. "My mother worked every single day of her life. She was unselfish and unfailingly kind, but I almost feel as though I never really knew her. She worked so much, she just wasn't around."

"She sounds like a good woman, as though she could be the sister of my own mother," Parween said. "I think that Allah meant for us to be sisters."

Elsa smiled. They both lingered long after dinner, reluctant to break the unexpected bond of friendship they'd forged there in the little mud house.

Finally, as the last of the day's light started to fade, Parween walked Elsa home. They walked just beyond Elsa's house and Parween paused at a desolate patch of land. "There." She pointed to the end of the UN airstrip. "That is where the Taliban executed the villagers and where they buried them. That is the place where my beloved Raziq was buried; others too are buried there." Parween dropped her gaze and paused, remembering.

"When your soldiers fluttered down from the sky, they fell right there as well." Parween recalled the sight fondly. "With their white robes billowing out above them, we were sure that they were angels of light sent from Allah." She smiled and looked at the sky. "Some of us believe that still."

18

$\mathcal{A}$ few days later, as Elsa sorted supplies at the hospital, several rugged-looking Special Forces soldiers pulled up in their jeeps, walked purposefully into the hospital in their heavily booted feet, and politely asked to speak with her. An Afghan nurse summoned Elsa and pointed toward the soldiers.

Wondering what might be wrong, she hurried outside, but she could see that Lieutenant Martin—Dave—was smiling. He took off his cap as she approached.

"The other evening, you missed seeing someone I wanted you to meet," he said. "He's seen you cutting through the fields, and he's been hoping for an introduction ever since. We all caught hell for having you to dinner when he was in Bagram." Dave grinned and moved slightly, and a smiling soldier—her mystery soldier—stepped into her view. Elsa held her breath.

"This crummy-looking fella's Mike, Lieutenant Michael Young, our tactician." Mike gave her an embarrassed grin.

"Like Lieutenant Martin said, I been wanting to meet you," Mike said. He was another Southerner and had a thick drawl not unlike his friend's. His sparkling, deep-blue eyes were even more alluring up close, and Elsa found herself paralyzed by his gaze.

Mike stood six feet tall and his coffee-colored hair was tangled and windswept. He sported a growth of scruffy beard and wore army-issue camouflage pants and a tan T-shirt. He had a pistol strapped to his thigh, his boots were dusty from his recent trip, and he exuded an easy self-confidence that mesmerized her. She could have stared at him all day.

Suddenly, she realized she was doing just that, and as she glanced away, she realized he'd been staring at her too.

When she got hold of herself, she stuck out her hand and stammered, "I–I'm Elsa Murphy. It's good to meet you." She was so nervous she couldn't believe she'd actually spoken.

"I'm sorry that I couldn't meet you when you came to dinner," Mike said, seeming anxious to fill the awkward silence and very aware of the watching soldiers. "I know that we can't talk right now, what with you being at work and all, but can we meet later? This evening maybe?"

She was flustered by his question. His voice was so unexpectedly soft that she wavered for an instant.

"I . . . I managed to get out last week, but I'm afraid I can't do it again, at least not this soon. It would look odd." As it was, she thought, people were probably wondering what she was doing out here for so long. She needed to get back.

"You're right, you're right," he said in a voice tinged with disappointment. "I'll be in touch later this week, then?"

"It's a deal." Elsa paused and reached out to shake his hand again. She realized then that her own palms were clammy and her heart was pounding.

"It's a pleasure to finally meet you, Miss Murphy." Mike smiled as he turned to leave.

"Please call me Elsa," she said in a voice that had more of a squeak than she would have liked.

"I'll do that, Elsa," he said. "And call me Mike." He waved as he joined the others, jumping into his jeep and driving off. She stood in the grimy dust cloud but didn't notice it. She wiped her damp hands over her dress, took a deep satisfying breath, and headed back to the hospital.

An hour afterward, her heart was still pounding.

* * *

Several days later, as Elsa was walking through the clinic gate, she heard someone calling her name.

She turned and saw Mike Young standing there, and she almost fainted with surprise. He stepped to her side and spoke, looking vaguely uncomfortable.

"Dave and I were wondering if maybe you could come over for supper tonight," he said. "He's gonna fry some chicken."

Elsa's heart fluttered, and she could feel the color rising in her face.

"Oh, I'd love to," she said as calmly as she could. "Should I wait at the same place?"

Mike grinned broadly. "I don't know where that is but I'll ask Dave, and we'll see you at six."

"That would be nice," she said. Once he'd gone, she sighed and went back to work, having to force herself to concentrate. Fortunately, the workload was relatively light, and she rushed through the rest of her day. Then she hurried home to take a bath even though it had been only three days since her last one.

She hadn't been this clean since she'd arrived in Bamiyan.

As she walked through her little house, she found Amina cooking.

"Oh, that won't be necessary tonight. I'm sorry, Amina." Struck by a combination of guilt and conspiratorial excitement, she decided to tell her about the soldiers. It didn't seem right to deceive her again.

Despite the time she'd spent preparing dinner, Amina smiled happily at the news.

"He is handsome?" she asked. They'd learned to communicate in bits of Dari, English, and when all else failed, simple sign language.

"*Balay,* he is the most handsome man I have ever seen."

Amina nodded her approval and helped Elsa to heat her bathwater and choose a clean dress. When she was washed and dressed, Elsa drew a soft pink gloss across her lips and smiled at her reflection in the mirror.

"Don't wait up for me," she said as she opened the heavy gate and hurried to the outside corner to wait.

Within minutes, the jeep pulled up, the door opened, and Elsa slipped in. They sped away.

"I can't tell you how happy I am to have dinner with you tonight," Mike said, and she noticed with interest that his uniform was spotlessly clean and newly ironed. "I saw you last month," he said, "and I knew you were not an Afghan."

"Oh no." Elsa laughed. "Did my lipstick give me away?"

"Well," he said, "that and the sunglasses. When I heard you speak, I knew you were an American." His voice dripped with an easy Southern charm. They sped along the now familiar road over the wobbly old bridge and slipped once again into the small gap between the trees. When the jeep stopped, Mike jumped out, quickly opened her door, and leaned in to help her out. He held her hand as they stepped into the safe house, where Elsa heard music and caught the scent of dinner.

Dave walked from the kitchen wiping his hands on the towel tucked into his belt. He reached out and kissed Elsa's cheek and announced that dinner was ready when they were.

"I'm not joining y'all," he said. "I got letters to read and one important one to write."

"Letters?" Elsa asked.

"Yeah, to my wife, Lisa. We've got a satellite dish set up here but she's not crazy about the Internet. She likes getting letters and photos in the mail, something she can hold and touch. I take as many pictures as I can, and I make sure to write her at least once a week."

"That's really sweet," Elsa said.

"Dave will do *anything* for his wife," Mike joked. "Hell, she almost wouldn't let him come here till I promised her I'd take care of him and send him home safely."

"Aww," Dave said. "Mike just doesn't know what it's like to be madly in love—yet. He's still a lonely bachelor."

Relishing the awkward moment his comment had created, Dave grinned and pulled the towel from his belt. "Enjoy dinner. I'm sure I'll see y'all soon." With that, he disappeared into one of the rooms.

There was another awkward silence. *Oh God, am I nervous. I don't have much experience with dating. Mike, on the other hand, with his easy confidence, is surely more experienced.*

She took a deep breath and finally spoke. "So the safe house isn't really like an army base then?" she asked.

Mike smiled in reply. "It sure isn't," he answered as they walked to the kitchen. "The Special Forces do things a little bit differently. Even this safe house is really just a house. No barracks here—we share rooms, and we take turns cooking and cleaning. We live together sort of like a family and tonight, most of the family is out, which leaves you and me." He paused and looked at her, as if wondering how she would react.

Elsa laughed, let herself relax, and decided to change the subject. "So have you and Dave known each other for a long time?"

"Seems like it. It's been a few years at least. We met in the reserves, and then we both reenlisted in September. Felt like we had to *do* something after 9/11. Know what I mean?"

"Yeah, I do. I tried to volunteer in New York on 9/11. I called the number that they flashed on TV, but no one ever called me back. I just wanted to do something too."

"Have you seen it? Ground Zero, I mean?"

"Only on television, and that was awful enough."

"Dave and I went up to New York before heading here. We just wanted to see what we were fighting for." He looked away, then focused again and continued. "Television just doesn't capture the scope of it. Thousands of people dead and buried right there, lost forever. It's powerful to see it up close, to feel the immense horror of that day." He shivered at the memory and busied himself gathering up forks, knives, and plates to set the table.

"You should go there, Elsa. See it for yourself before they put up another high-rise to make people forget what happened there."

Elsa nodded.

Mike turned and motioned for to her to sit as he took Dave's carefully prepared meal from the oven.

"But for now, eat up," he said with a smile.

She smiled back and picked up a piece of chicken, eating it slowly and licking her fingers clean. Both of them were hungry, and they tore into the delicious food.

"How long have you been here in Bamiyan?" Elsa asked.

"Let's see, we got here in late September, but we were up north.

We saw our fair share of fighting there and when things quieted down, we were deployed here to Bamiyan. Boy, I'll tell you, the day we arrived, the villagers lined the road and cheered. Wasn't what we'd been expecting, but it sure was nice." Mike paused to take another bite. "Dave even took pictures of them that day, to show the folks back home. He hasn't stopped taking pictures since. His camera's gonna die."

Elsa laughed. "At least he brought a camera. I didn't even think of it."

"So," Mike said after they had made short work of the food, "tell me about yourself. I already know that you're a nurse, but not much more."

"You first," she said, too self-conscious to talk about herself.

"All right, well, I'm the oldest in my family—four of us, all boys. I grew up in North Carolina in a little place called Chatham, where my dad was a bus driver and my mom chased us around." Mike paused, lost in some long-ago memory.

"She died when I was about nine. Cancer. It musta been tough for Dad, but he never showed it. Anyway, he raised me and my brothers on his own. He's a good man, even coached my Little League teams. He was convinced that baseball would take me through life. I was a good player, but there were a thousand other kids out there just like me, and when no college scholarships or minor league offers came, I knew I had to find something else."

Mike stood to clean up, and Elsa rose to help.

"Not tonight," he said. "You're my guest. Besides, I was the oldest in a house of boys. If there's one thing I can do it's clean, so just have a seat."

She sat back down. "So what was the something else?" she asked.

"Well, I wanted to go to college. I wanted to be an engineer and design roads and bridges, but my dad couldn't afford the tuition. Bus drivers just don't make much. Anyway, I joined the army for two years, and once my time was up, I used the tuition assistance program to attend Duke. Got myself an engineering degree, a job offer too good to pass up, and I headed to Dallas to work."

Once he'd finished clearing the table, he sat next to her.

"I don't get back to North Carolina much. My dad's still there, still driving a bus and trying to make ends meet. My youngest brother, Adam, is still at home, but John's in Florida and Matt's in school in New York."

"You're lucky to have a big family."

"Yeah, I guess I am. So what about you? What brought you to Afghanistan? Did you want to save the world?" he asked, his voice soft and his gaze intent.

"Yeah, actually, something like that." Elsa nodded, thinking of the newsmagazine she'd held on to for so long. "The Rwandan genocide," she said. "I saw pictures in a news magazine that just tore me up, and I knew that someday I'd help."

Mike seemed to sit straighter. "I remember that. I may have even seen the same pictures—babies and families dead on the roads and in the fields. I remember being riveted by the horror of it." He shook his head. "I was in college and I just figured they needed soldiers to protect them, more than I could give them anyway, but you . . . you saw a chance to help, to really *do* something."

He leaned toward Elsa and suddenly her shyness slipped away, and before she knew it, she was telling Mike about her life, about Diana and Margaret and then even about her brother and sister.

"They're still in Boston, I think," she finished, "but Tommy's got a problem with alcohol and Janice is on drugs, so I'm not even sure if they're still alive."

"Oh, jeez." He grimaced. "That must be tough."

Elsa nodded. She could hardly believe how much she'd told him. It must have been this place, she thought, the intensity here that gave her the courage. At home, she never would have revealed so much— *Dirty laundry,* her mother would have said, *don't air it in public.* But here, it wasn't dirty laundry, it was just part of who she was.

Mike leaned forward and brushed back a silky stray hair from her face, his touch soft and fleeting like a summer breeze. The feel of him shot right through her and her heart raced.

"I'm glad you're comfortable enough to talk." Mike looked down at his hands. "I like you, Elsa. I hope it's okay to say that."

"Yeah, it is. I feel the same." She could feel her cheeks turn red.

He pulled her closer and kissed her full on the lips. Then he put his arms around her and just held her.

Elsa sighed. She could feel the heat of his body seeping through his shirt and she nestled closer and whispered, "I'm so glad to have met you, Mike."

"I'm glad too, Elsa. I'm glad too."

She snuggled into him and inhaled his clean, soapy scent; he had taken a bath too. They might just have been the cleanest people in all of Bamiyan.

At that moment she heard heavy footsteps approaching the house, and she looked at her watch.

"Oh no," she said. "It's almost ten already. I have to go."

Mike kissed her again and, not wanting her to have to deal with the returning soldiers, led her out a side door and back to the jeep for the ride home.

"I'll see you soon, Elsa," he whispered as they pulled up by her gate, his hand lingering on hers.

They kissed one more time and she got out, slipping quietly through the gate. She hurriedly got ready for bed and replayed the evening over and over in her head before she finally drifted off to sleep.

19

Mike Young—even his name is perfect, she thought as she lay in her room the following Friday. Elsa was hopelessly infatuated, but she just couldn't help herself. She wondered if Amina felt that way about Sidiq. Though he'd told Elsa he planned to speak with her brother, there'd been no more talk from either of them. She reminded herself to ask Hamid if he knew anything.

She'd decided to give in to Bamiyan's customs and take Fridays off. She took her time before she rose for her morning cup of coffee on the roof.

Parween was prodded out of sleep that same morning by the urgent cries of baby Raziq. He was an early riser and he bellowed loudly to announce his needs. She slept alongside him on her little pad, so she reached out and whispered to him, then cuddled closer and planted a kiss on the sweet softness of his face. Raziq reached for Parween's hair and pulled at it.

"That's enough for you, little one," Parween said as she rose from the pad to collect the goat's milk for the baby. She perched him on her hip and headed outside into the early morning.

Rahima, already outside and stoking the morning fire, reached out with a tin of milk for the baby. Parween squatted and sank her feet into the soft ground, offering the milk to Raziq, who devoured it quickly before falling back into the deep, rich sleep that only babies know. Parween smiled and hoped that someday soon she and the children could go on picnics and walks as she and her beloved husband had done.

As if she sensed her daughter's longing, Rahima spoke up. "Your friend Elsa is a stranger here. I am certain that she would enjoy spending a day with you."

Parween wrapped the baby and tucked him into the clothes basket. "She is probably busy. The clinic is always filled with patients."

"It is surely closed today. And if she labors as hard as you say, she'd probably like to do something besides work."

"It's true. I could show her the Buddhas' caves. I haven't been there since . . ." Her voice trailed off and her gaze fell on the sleeping baby. So much had changed since she'd been there with her dear husband.

Rahima cleared her throat.

"I am here to watch the little ones. Go, go!" And she shooed Parween out the door.

Amina called up to the roof, where Elsa sat with her coffee.

"You have a visitor," she announced. Elsa scurried down the old ladder and was pleased to find her new friend waiting. She kissed Parween on each cheek and launched into the copious Afghan greeting.

Parween smiled. "I am well," she replied. "If you are not occupied with work this day, I would like to invite you to come with me to see the Buddhas' caves. They lie above the empty holes where the Buddhas once watched over Bamiyan." With that last statement, Elsa thought she detected a hint of sadness in her friend's voice.

She had seen the caves on the road to the clinic, the great gaping hollows in the mountain fronts that had once housed the revered Buddhas.

Amina turned and spoke to Elsa.

"Ahh, you must go. The views are like nothing else you will ever see."

Elsa was intrigued.

"I'd love to go." She asked Amina if she'd like to accompany them, but the young woman shook her head.

"I will spend the day at my brother's house. It is past time for me to visit."

Elsa reached into her pocket for her lipstick and held it out to Parween.

"Oh no, not today. I cannot wear it in public where men might see it, only behind my own walls."

"Not even just a bit of color?"

Parween shook her head. "No, no. Here we can only use it on special days or hidden at home. But it is your custom to wear it. For you, lipstick is as ordinary as a veil is to us. You must wear it."

Elsa smiled, self-conscious now. "Well, then I'll wear it for both of us." She swiped a bright swath of cherry red across her lips.

Waving their good-byes, Elsa and Parween set off down the dusty road leading to the Buddha's mountains. Once there, Elsa gazed up at the magnificent hollows, now just deep, yawning holes in the mountains. Before she'd come to Afghanistan, Elsa had spent hours on the Internet researching Bamiyan, and she'd seen pictures of the great Buddhas on her computer.

"You can almost see them there, you know?" Elsa said as she looked upward.

Parween nodded. In her mind's eye, she *could* still see the soaring Buddhas that had greeted her on her first day in Bamiyan. She sighed and hurried on.

"Follow me," she said. They trudged up the mountain, Elsa struggling to find footholds as she went. The ragged face of the mountain tore at her hands as she pulled herself along, and she strained to keep up. She followed slowly, and it was then that she noticed the sturdy caves that had been carved into the sheets of rock that clung to the mountain. Those caves and hidden crevices had resisted the dynamite and explosions that had made dust of the once magnificent statues.

They climbed through the cracks and gaps in the side of the mountain and finally stepped onto a narrow, sandy staircase and entered one of the small rooms that had flanked a Buddha.

Elsa stood in the dusty room, and once her eyes adjusted to the darkness she saw the colored scrolls and intricate designs painted on the walls. Though faded, the gentle blues and once vibrant reds brought life to the sand-colored rocks. She reached out to touch the painted walls but caught herself; this place was a kind of museum, all the more precious for its location and survival, despite the cruel weather and even crueler explosions.

Parween grew quiet as she gazed at the brilliant art. "You see," she said, "the Taliban weren't able to destroy everything."

Eventually they both pulled themselves away from the unexpected designs and stood to look out on the parched countryside, framed by the sloping valleys and softly rolling peaks of the Hindu Kush mountain range.

"This is beautiful, no?" Parween whispered.

Elsa held her breath. The countryside, though beautiful, was littered with the remnants of decades of war.

"What about all of that?" Elsa pointed to a row of bombed and burned-out tanks, pieces of shrapnel, and discarded rocket launchers scattered about the landscape.

Her friend thought for a moment. "They remind me that we are finished with war. *Inshallah,* we are finished with it forever."

Elsa nodded. *"Inshallah,"* she said in agreement as she turned and scanned the countryside, searching for any sign of the soldiers' house, but wherever it was, it was well hidden.

"Come." Parween's voice interrupted her thoughts and Elsa scurried to follow as her friend left the cave and headed back into the sunshine, then farther up the mountainside. Elsa blinked to adjust to the light and saw that many of the caves seemed to be inhabited. People were scrambling up with water and food and disappearing into the mountain's crevices. It was like a stone-age apartment house. She turned a questioning glance to Parween.

"Yes, people live in these caves. Hundreds, maybe even thousands of villagers fled here when the Taliban attacked their villages. Those who have nowhere to go live here still."

She explained that the government had recently announced that they did not want people living in these caves, and anyone caught would be thrown in jail—or worse.

"But these people don't care what the government says," Parween explained. "When officials come through Bamiyan, they disappear, become invisible. Only a close inspection would reveal that the caves are still occupied." She laughed. "The government men will never make the climb to inspect the caves. They are soft men and the climb is hard."

"Could I maybe see inside a cave? See what it's like?" Elsa asked, fascinated with this almost prehistoric way of living.

Parween searched the landscape for a friend who lived there with her small daughter.

"Her name," Parween said, "is Bas-Bibi. She lived beyond Garganatu with her husband and children in a poor village. The village did not care what the Taliban said; they lived as they pleased. Their women never covered their faces and their hair was always spilling from their veils. They dared the Taliban to force them to adhere to the strict rules, and last winter the Taliban arrived to make an example of them."

Parween paused, a strange look crossing her face. She took a breath and continued.

"Just as in Bamiyan, the Taliban wanted only to crush resistance and strike fear into the hearts of the villagers. They marched into the village, set fire to the old homes, burned up the little crops, and killed the livestock. The villagers were afraid that they would be murdered just as their goats had been, and many—including Bas-Bibi, her husband, and their two children—fled to the mountains with only the clothes on their backs. Though they found safety here, they had no protection from the bitter cold and the falling snow, and so they huddled together at the edge of a small cave for warmth.

"One morning, when Bas-Bibi woke, her husband and youngest child, a tiny girl of four, lay dead next to her. They had frozen to death." She shook her head.

"Bas-Bibi and her daughter buried them there in the snow and trudged back to Garganatu, where they stayed only until they could arrange transportation here to Bamiyan. And now they live here," Parween said as she turned to look at the caves.

They climbed up higher in search of Bas-Bibi and before long, Parween called out a greeting.

"*As-salaam alaikum,* Bas-Bibi. *Chetore asti? Khoob asti? Jona ju-rast?*"

A smiling woman poked her head out of one of the mountain's small openings and invited Parween and her companion into her little cave. Even with her delight at seeing a friend, Elsa thought Bas-Bibi looked older than she must have been. Her face, covered in the grime and soot that coated the cave, was streaked with lines of worry and defeat. Stray pieces of greasy hair peeked out from her veil, and her threadbare clothes had long since faded. She and Parween greeted one another effusively with kisses and smiles and when they were done, Parween turned and introduced Elsa.

"Elsa," Parween said proudly, "comes from Amrika. She is a nurse, helping here in the clinic."

Bas-Bibi smiled again, kissed her cheeks, and asked Allah to bless her. Elsa, discomfited by all the attention that was being lavished on her, could only smile in return.

"This is Sabia," Parween said as a thin little girl bowed to her. She was covered in a fine layer of dust. "She is, I think, about eight years now."

Elsa smiled and a wide grin spread on Sabia's grimy face.

Bas-Bibi insisted that they stay for tea, and she sent Sabia to collect water from a nearby mountain stream. While they waited for her return, Elsa had a look around the cave, which was about the size of her own room. Although there were no courtyards, no wells, and no latrines nearby, it was surprisingly cozy.

"This is nice, isn't it?" she asked Parween, her voice tinged with surprise.

"Yes, yes, Bas-Bibi has made it a pleasant home." Parween explained that Bas-Bibi had been given some essentials from the UN. Sleeping pads, blankets, and cooking utensils lined the wall. A scrap of heavy plastic sheeting covered the dirt floor and a larger scrap covered the entrance to the cave. A small cooking area was set up by the entrance. It was as bare-bones as any stone-age existence had surely been, but in many ways, it was as homey as Parween's own little dwelling.

Sabia reappeared with the water, and Bas-Bibi started a small fire at the edge of the cave. Much of the smoke wafted back inside, burning Elsa's eyes and covering all of them with a layer of soot. *That explains the layers of perpetual grime,* Elsa thought.

Bas-Bibi brought the little metal pot of tea to a boil and poured it into sturdy aluminum mugs, and the women sat cross-legged on the cave's plastic-covered floor, sipping the sweet tea and chatting.

Once they'd finished their tea, they said their good-byes, Elsa offering to return with medical help if ever Bas-Bibi or her daughter needed it. As she and Parween climbed back down the mountainside, Elsa struggled to maintain her footing and wondered how Sabia, with her stick-thin legs, could possibly manage the daily scramble up and down the mountain over this pockmarked terrain.

"Parween," she said, "I meant what I said about helping."

Parween smiled in reply. "I know."

20

One morning, not long after bringing Elsa to the caves, Parween sat by the washing stream with a group of friends. They'd just strung up their clothes to dry and had gathered along the craggy rocks to gossip. She had left her two sleeping children at home with Rahima, and now she drew in her knees and looked around.

"*As-salaam alaikum,*" Parween called out to old friends.

Soraya, a young woman who lived just to the north of the caves, greeted her and squatted beside her. Parween kissed her and returned the greeting.

"It is good to see you, Soraya. It has been a long while."

"Parween, I was so sorry to hear the news about Mariam. I know that she was your true sister, and my heart broke for your sadness."

Parween kissed Soraya's cheeks. "Thank you. I miss her smile, especially here at the stream."

"I have heard that Allah has blessed you with a son. May he bring blessings and peace into your home."

At the thought of her sweet baby, Parween said, "You must come soon and see him. He is a handsome babe."

"I will, Parween, I will. But today, I have come not to do my wash, but to speak with you." She paused. "About a private matter," she whispered.

"What is it?" Parween leaned forward.

"Could we speak over there by the apricot tree? I don't want eavesdroppers today."

"Of course, of course," Parween said as she rose and moved to the shade of the tree. There, Soraya took a slow, deep breath and began.

"It is about my cousin, a little girl named Meena. She needs help and my family has asked me to speak with you. I know that if anyone can help us, it is you."

"You know I will help if I can."

"Meena is just eight years old. She is the youngest child and the only girl in a family of five. They live just west of Herat. You know those small villages, yes?" Soraya spoke softly and looked around to make sure no one was listening, then continued.

"Meena's oldest brother, a stupid boy of sixteen, took up with a bad group in their village, and they preyed on others in nearby villages, stealing and vandalizing. He made the mistake of robbing the house of Noor Mohammed, an underling to the powerful and feared warlord Rashid-Najaf, who rules that area beyond Herat. Surely you have heard of him?"

Parween nodded. Everyone had heard of Rashid-Najaf. He was said to be ruthless and vile, pillaging and robbing his way through the region without fear of retribution. He was the undisputed law in that part of Afghanistan.

"Noor Mohammed," Soraya continued, "felt important because of his attachment to Rashid, and he saw the robbery as an assault, not just on his home but on his reputation. He ordered payment for the debt that the robbery incurred, but my uncle's family is penniless. Noor Mohammed didn't care. He demanded that they hand over either their son for punishment or their small daughter—Meena—as payment. The son is a whimpering dog and he begged to be saved. He would surely be killed, he cried, if given over to Noor Mohammed. He promised to be a good son if only they would protect him."

Parween knew that though it was illegal, it was not so unusual in Afghanistan's farthest regions for destitute families to give daughters away to pay off debts, and she could almost guess what had happened.

"My uncle is a poor man, and he reluctantly gave his only daughter to Noor Mohammed so that his son's debt would be wiped clean. He believed that Meena would be safe, but when the day came to hand her over, he wasn't so sure."

Parween's gaze grew solemn as she listened.

"My uncle is not a bad man," Soraya said, "but he is desperate and was afraid for his whole family. He hurried back to his own village that day and prayed that Noor would treat her well." Soraya cleared her throat. "It is difficult for me to share this sad story." She closed her eyes for a minute before starting again.

"Noor Mohammed was not a kind man. In Noor's house, Meena was beaten and burned and was starved for days at a time. When she was fed, she was given scraps of barely edible food. The family even pulled out clumps of her hair just to hear her screams. Her only companion was the family's goat, who was treated better than she."

A knot grew in Parween's stomach and she swallowed to push it away.

"After weeks and weeks of hearing Meena's forlorn screams, the people in the surrounding homes finally had the courage to act. When Noor's family had all left for their weekly trip to the mosque and bazaar, the men from nearby homes broke into Noor's house and rescued Meena. They found her chained to the goat and cowering. She didn't understand that she was being rescued."

Her eyes filled with tears as she spoke.

"The decision had been made to take her immediately from the village, for the men were certain that Noor would be furious when he discovered that she had been rescued. Though they had gladly saved her, none of them wanted to be identified as her rescuer, for Noor would surely turn on them. Meena was brought first to the house of my grandfather, where she was kept hidden while the women tended to her wounds. She is but a little girl . . ." Soraya's words trailed off into quiet tears.

Parween reached out and rubbed Soraya's shoulder. "I know it is hard, but you must finish."

Soraya swallowed her tears. "The warlord, Rashid, learned of Noor's cruelty and was enraged. He ordered Noor beaten and evicted from his home. Now, we've heard that both Noor and Rashid are searching for Meena, Noor to silence her forever, and Rashid, reportedly, to save her. My grandfather decided to bring her here to us, and that is why I am here today. She is here in Bamiyan, but we need your help. Bas-Bibi told me that you are a friend of the American nurse and that she has offered help if it is needed. My family hopes that you and your friend will help Meena."

When Soraya had finished with her story, Parween sat back and took a slow deep breath. She reached over and patted Soraya's hands.

"I will help. I believe that Elsa will help too. I will speak with her today and we will decide what to do. I will come to your house once I have spoken with her."

Parween's whispered words belied the storm building within her, and when she rose to collect her clothes from the tree branches, her hands shook. She ripped the garments from the trees and piled them into her basket. She walked back to her own house to drop off her laundry, and then, still shaking, she strode to the clinic.

When Elsa spied her friend through the clinic's window, she went out to greet her.

"*As-salaam alaikum,* Parween. Good to see you." As she got closer, however, she could see that Parween was troubled. "*Che taklif?* What is wrong?"

Parween asked Elsa to sit while she shared Meena's story, staring at the ground much of the time, as if to control her emotions. When she was finished, she turned to Elsa.

"I remembered how you offered to help Bas-Bibi, and I said that you would help this little girl. Can you? *Will you?*"

Elsa was stunned by the story Parween told. She sat forward and sighed, then responded in a rush of words.

"Of course I will help. She can stay at my house. No one will have any reason to suspect that I have a little girl hidden there. Amina and I will take care of her. But what of her wounds? She must need medical help. I'll get some supplies together."

She paused, and Parween filled the silence.

"You must not tell anyone of the little girl. *Famidi?* She must be our secret if she is to be safe, if we are *all* to be safe."

"Shall I come with you?"

"No, no," Parween answered. "It will invite less notice if I quietly slip her into your house. I will bring her on the back of my donkey." She touched Elsa's hand. "*Besiar tashakore,* many thanks, my dear friend."

They set off in different directions. Elsa went through the hospital's supply room and quickly gathered vitamins, nutritional supplements, antibiotics, and bandages and tucked them all into a large bag. She found Laila and told her that she was going home to catch up on paperwork. She found Hamid and told him the same. She hated to lie, but if the little girl was to be safe, she couldn't tell them the truth.

She left the clinic and walked through the fields alone, arriving home in minutes. She told Amina about their soon-to-be houseguest and, to Elsa's surprise, the quiet young woman embraced the plan. They hurriedly set up the extra room for Meena.

Elsa and Amina waited all afternoon before they heard the knock at the gate. Parween and Soraya had finally arrived, and they quickly unloaded a small bundle from the back of the donkey and hurried inside. With the gate shut securely behind them, Parween made introductions and unwrapped tiny Meena.

Elsa stepped back and waited as the child was uncovered. Soraya squatted and held Meena, a shriveled, doe-eyed little girl with a deep frown etched onto her bony face.

Elsa reached for her and lifted away the remaining covers to get a closer look. Wounds and burns in various stages of healing—some draining purulent material—riddled her body. Her scalp, covered only in scattered wisps of hair, was smeared with oozing, crusting, stinking sores.

Elsa swallowed back the bile that rose in her throat.

How could anyone do this to a child? She took a deep breath and tried to smile as she examined the tiny form before her.

A shrill cry pierced the stillness, startling Elsa. It came from Meena.

"*Tars na dori,* do not be afraid, little one." Elsa's voice faltered as she murmured, and Parween tried to sound soothing as she translated. "You are safe." She attempted to gather Meena into her arms, but the little girl pulled away and cried out again in protest.

"Sorry, little one; *tars na dori*."

Soraya stepped in and explained to Meena that Elsa was a nurse who would take care of her until she was well.

"*Famidi*, understand?" Soraya asked softly.

Meena, her eyes wide and watching Elsa's every move, nodded and whispered, "*Balay*." But her voice was filled with fear.

Elsa's hands trembled as she gently bathed Meena, who was so frail Elsa feared the tiny arms and legs would snap with her efforts. Once the bandaging was done, she poured out three vitamins and one antibiotic pill for Meena. Amina appeared with a glass of sugary, milky tea and Meena washed down the pills before draining the glass.

"She must be exhausted. She should sleep," Elsa said. She led them to the small room that she and Amina had prepared. Soraya covered Meena with a soft blanket and lay beside her, humming softly as the others watched from the doorway. It wasn't long before the girl was asleep, and the four women slipped out of her room and sat together in the courtyard to make their plans.

Parween wondered aloud how she could ever bear it if something were to happen to Zahra or baby Raziq.

"If it were my own child, my life would be ended." She glanced to the room where Meena slept.

Elsa swallowed the lump in her throat. "I don't think I have ever seen a sadder child or heard a sadder story. Does this happen often?"

"More in the old days than now," Parween answered. "But with the misery that runs through the countryside, it will happen more often unless we fight back."

The women murmured their agreement.

"What of her own family in the village?" Parween asked sadly. "Do they know that she is safe?"

"Yes." Soraya sighed. "Her father's heart is broken, but his only wish is that she be safe. Someday, *inshallah*, she will see them again." She paused. "I must say this to each of you . . . thank you, thank you for your help. My family will never forget this."

There was yet another cousin in Kabul, she told them, married but childless, who would claim Meena as her own child.

"Though we have a place for her, the trip to Kabul by bus is long for a little one with such injuries. We are not sure yet how we will get her there."

Elsa thought for a moment. "What about the soldiers?" she said, thinking of Mike. "Maybe we can ask them for help."

"No," Soraya said. "It is best if they do not know. They may not be able to help, and we don't want to invite their prying eyes. They are foreign after all. They won't understand."

"But—" Elsa started to speak, but Parween took her hand and piped up.

"Soraya means only that they are men. No matter how good, they are men. We must do this together."

Elsa smiled wanly. "Well, the UN has the little airstrip not far from here, and they often have flights to Kabul. Once Meena is ready, that would be the safest and quickest way for her to travel. I know Johann, the UN officer here; I will ask him if it is possible to get Meena on a plane to Kabul. I am certain he will help once he has heard this story."

Soraya's eyes widened. "But you must not tell him that she is the child the warlord seeks. It is best if *no one* knows that."

Elsa nodded. "I will keep the secret. Will you travel with her, Soraya?"

"Yes, yes. I will stay with her until she is safe. And while we speak of that, may I also stay with her here in your house?"

Amina smiled broadly. "It will be good to have another woman in the house," she said. "I am often alone."

The four sat and shared tea until Parween stood. "My mother will wonder what has kept me. I must get home."

Soraya stood and embraced her friend. "*Tashakore,* dear Parween, *tashakore.* Please give your mother my blessings."

Elsa said good night and settled into her own room, wondering what else they might do to help Meena.

That first morning, Elsa rose early and left the house before Meena ventured from her room. It would be better, she told Amina, if there were fewer new faces for Meena to deal with, and she wanted to catch Hamid before he arrived at the gate.

She planned to tell him that she had women guests and that he wouldn't be allowed in for a while. She knew he wouldn't question her, and he didn't. Instead, he looked pleased.

"Ahh, Elsa, guests! Good, that is good."

Parween arrived at the house early. "How is she?" she asked.

Amina frowned. "Not eating, not speaking." She shook her head.

But Soraya smiled. "She is safe, and though she did not eat so much, at least she ate something. *Inshallah,* tomorrow she will do better."

Yet they seemed unable to convince Meena that she was safe. She spent the day hiding behind Soraya, peeking out at Parween and Amina, but otherwise it was as if she wasn't there. She didn't make a sound.

In late afternoon, Parween said good-bye.

"Tomorrow, Meena. I will see you tomorrow."

Meena didn't reply.

When Elsa arrived home, they all sat together in the kitchen to share supper. Meena only picked at the food on her plate, but she did gulp down three large glasses of the sugary tea. Elsa was relieved.

"At least it's something."

That night, Meena's sad eyes filled with tears when Elsa poked at her wounds and bandages, but even her cries were silent.

"I'm so sorry to hurt you, but I have to clean your wounds." Elsa tried to smile, hoping that might comfort Meena.

"It will take time," Elsa said, trying to reassure herself and the others. "She was locked away for weeks; she's only been safe for a few days. We have to give her the time and space to trust us."

The second and third days were replays of the first. Meena spoke little and barely ate, and Amina, worried, picked absently at her extra finger.

"She will starve, Elsa, yes?"

"No, no, not yet. She'll eat. We just have to be patient and let her take her time."

On the fourth morning, Meena ate a little of the warm *naan* and rice and pushed the rest away. She spoke only when asked a question, and even then her answers were simple—a whispered *balay* or *nay,* nothing else. She kept her head down and stayed close to Soraya.

Parween arrived in the late morning, and Meena buried herself in the folds of Soraya's skirts.

"I think she needs children around her. Let me bring my two and see if it helps." She hurried home and returned with Raziq, bundled in her arms, and Zahra in tow.

Zahra scurried in, and she searched the rooms and courtyard as though she were moving in. When she spied Meena, she ran to her and chattered as though she'd always known her. She reached out and gently touched the bandage on Meena's scalp.

"Dard mekona," she asked softly. *Does it hurt?* Meena nodded in reply.

"Ohh," Zahra muttered as she took Meena's hand and led her outside. The women watched through the doorway as she encouraged Meena to play pretend. She took a handful of dirt and sifted it through her stubby fingers.

"This is rice. See." She giggled, and Meena *smiled*.

The women could hardly contain themselves, but they remained silent for fear of ruining the moment.

Meena sat and watched Zahra as she played in the dirt. She didn't join in, but she didn't race back to the safety of Soraya's skirts either.

At lunch, the two girls sat together. Meena ate a full serving of rice and bread, and Amina relaxed. After lunch, they sat outside again until Meena fell asleep in the dirt.

On the fifth day, with Meena's budding recovery fresh in her mind, Elsa arrived at the clinic to the news that two strangers had appeared in search of a little girl. Laila's eyes flashed with fear when she described them.

"They carried guns, Elsa, and asked for the doctor in charge. Ezat was angry to be interrupted, and he snapped at them, asking what they wanted. They told him they were looking for a kidnapped child, a small girl," she said, motioning with her hand to indicate the size.

"They came here because they said she has injuries and might need medical care. But Ezat told them to leave, no such child has been here. Have you seen her?"

"No, no, I have seen only the usual village children." Elsa held her breath, afraid that Laila would see through her words. "Have the men gone?"

Laila frowned. "I think so, but with men like that who can know?"

Elsa wanted to race home to sound the alarm, but that would only rouse suspicion. She forced herself to stay, to work as though it were a day like any other, but her hands trembled when she cleaned the rancid, ulcered skin of an old man, and she lost count when she tried to dispense pills for a young woman with a cough.

Her stomach was in knots, her eyes darting as she looked again and again for any sign of the strange men. But there was nothing. Still, she worried. Could they be watching? Did they suspect she harbored the child? When the clinic was finally closed, Elsa rushed to get her things and headed for home.

When she entered her gate, the house was quiet, and she went in search of the women.

She found them gathered in the courtyard sipping tea.

"There is trouble," Elsa announced, her voice soft. "There were men at the clinic looking for a kidnapped girl."

A chill settled in the air.

Amina put down her cup. "Who were they?" she asked. "Do you know?"

"No," Elsa answered, "but Ezat thinks they have gone. He told them she wasn't here."

The women looked at one another and then at the napping Meena.

Elsa sighed heavily and wished she knew what to do. "Should I tell Hamid? Have him stay so there is a man here?"

"No, no," Parween answered quickly. "We must tell no one. That is the safest way."

Soraya bit her lip. "We will have to move more quickly," she said. "Get her to Kabul sooner than we had planned."

The women nodded in agreement.

"I will speak to Johann in the morning," Elsa said.

That night, Meena tucked her hand into Elsa's as they walked to the bathroom for her bath and bandage change. She barely winced when her wounds, which seemed to be scabbing over already, were cleaned.

Elsa took a closer look. Did she wish it or was there really a sparkle in Meena's eye, a shine to her wispy hair, and a rosy hue to her cheeks when she laughed?

Ahh, Elsa thought, *she is surely better.*

But that thought was not enough to ease Elsa's fears. She lay awake that night, her muscles taut, her senses alert for any sound that might signal danger.

But there was nothing, and Elsa felt herself drifting off to sleep. It was then that the sudden early morning call to prayer broke through the silence, sending a momentary shiver down her spine.

In the morning Elsa knocked at the UN office, and Johann invited her inside. Squinting, he pushed his eyeglasses back into place and spoke.

"Hello, hello, Elsa. What a pleasant surprise."

"I have a favor to ask, Johann," she said, hoping he wouldn't notice the quiver in her voice.

"Come, come, have a seat." He guided her into his little office and pointed to a chair by his desk.

Taking a deep breath, she told Johann the story of a wounded, starving child who needed care in Kabul.

"I hope that it is not an imposition to ask if she could ride along on the next scheduled plane to Kabul. Of course, her cousin will accompany her, and the UN will have no responsibility for her once she is in Kabul." Elsa picked nervously at her fingers as she waited for his answer.

In heavily accented English, Johann replied.

"But of course, my dear, we will help. As it happens, a flight leaves in two days. Can she make that one?"

Relief flooded through Elsa. "I'm sure she'll be ready then." She stood and reached out to take his hand. "Thank you so much, Johann, you are always so kind. Thank you."

She raced home to share the news.

* * *

Meena wailed at the news that she would be moving yet again.

"I want to stay here," she cried. "Don't make me go." She sobbed, dropping to the floor and hugging her legs. She buried her head in her knees.

"Meena, you must go," Soraya pleaded. "Your cousin is waiting for you. She's been waiting for a long time. You don't want to make her sad, do you?" She touched Meena's shoulder but the little girl jerked away.

"I don't care if she's sad. I don't want to go!" Meena wept and refused to be consoled. Each of the women took a turn speaking to her but she remained firm.

Elsa smiled at Meena's determination. It was just a week since she'd arrived, a shriveled, pitiful little thing, and now here she was, defiant and angry. She wished that Meena could stay; she'd brought so much life into the house. But she had to go. It was the only way she'd be safe, that they'd *all* be safe.

The women continued their attempts to convince her. No one wanted to force Meena. She'd had enough of that already, but with only two days before the plane was scheduled, Soraya was firm.

"Enough of this. You are going to Kabul, do you understand?" Meena dropped her head and nodded through her tears. Soraya's tone turned soft. "Little one, you must go. I will be with you, understand?" Meena flung herself into Soraya's arms and cried herself to sleep.

On the appointed day, Johann sent a message that the small plane had arrived and was waiting for them. The little group walked together to the airstrip to see Meena and Soraya off. Few people in Afghanistan had traveled by plane, but they'd seen planes flying overhead, and even Meena was excited to board the plane and soar through the sky, so much so that it silenced her protests.

She and Soraya shared kisses and tearful good-byes with Elsa, Parween, and Amina, and the women watched as the two climbed on board. Meena turned and gave them a last sweet smile and wave before she was swallowed up in the belly of the plane.

Tears stung Elsa's eyes as she blew a kiss. The three stood and watched as the engine roared to life and the plane sped along the strip of dirt before it took to the air and disappeared over the mountains.

Elsa breathed a deep sigh of relief. "She's safe. We *did* it!"

Parween turned to her. "Thanks to you, my friend."

She kissed Elsa's cheeks and smiled.

"I am thinking you are an Afghan woman, for sure."

Elsa smiled. "But the lipstick," she said, pointing to her red lips, "stays."

21

Spring came suddenly to Bamiyan. The days seemed to grow longer, the sun brighter, and the air warmer almost overnight. Elsa folded up her blankets and packed away her sweaters, eager for the change of season.

Mike must have felt it too. One afternoon, he arrived unexpectedly at the clinic and suggested a picnic.

Butterflies filled her stomach at the very sight of him.

"A picnic," she said, her words almost a sigh. "I've never been on a picnic."

"Really? Then let's do it," he said. "Tomorrow's Friday, and at the very least, it'll keep you out of trouble," he said with a wink.

"What can I bring?"

"Just yourself, Elsa, just yourself. I'll pack some sandwiches and we'll have us an old-fashioned picnic."

A broad smile crept along her lips and her cheeks grew warm.

The following morning, Elsa rose early and went through the long process of taking a bath. Amina watched with an amused smile as she heated the water.

"Soldier?" she asked.

Elsa nodded. *Everything happens in its own time,* she thought. If she'd met Mike a year ago, she wouldn't have been ready. She'd have been too timid, too unsure of herself. But here in Afghanistan all that had changed, and the threads of unease that had knotted her up for so long had finally started to unravel. She smiled as she applied a second coat of cherry-red gloss to her lips.

It was late morning when Mike arrived in his jeep, and he and Elsa set off for their outing. "Where are we headed?" she asked, arranging her head-scarf as she settled into her seat.

"A beautiful little spot not more than ten minutes away. Ramatullah, our interpreter, took me there. It's got everything—fruit trees, wildflowers, and a stream that runs right through it all. Wait till you see it." He turned and smiled. The enthusiasm in his voice made Elsa's heart race all the more.

Mike guided the jeep beyond the village, past the last of the small houses, and onto a rugged road that ran alongside a rippling stream. They drove through groves of lush trees and fragrant flowers, and Elsa inhaled deeply.

Spring is here.

Mike eased the jeep into a small opening at the water's edge. "We're here," he said, reaching back for a small duffel bag. "In place of a picnic basket," he said as he grabbed a blanket.

They got out of the jeep and spread the blanket out by the stream. "Pretty spot, huh?"

"Oh, Mike, it's beautiful, a little slice of paradise."

They settled themselves onto the blanket, and Mike handed Elsa a Diet Coke.

"I sure never thought I'd be on a picnic in Afghanistan," he said, smiling, his hand resting on his sidearm. "But I won't be removing this. Regulations and all. Besides, I'd rather be safe than sorry. And though I know *you* haven't seen any real trouble, it is here."

He paused and looked up at the brilliant and cloudless sky. "Right now, we're just going to enjoy this beautiful spring day."

Elsa squinted against the sun. "It's so peaceful today. It's hard to believe that so much misery has taken place here."

"That's for sure. Hard to imagine having to live like this—no electricity, no running water, no school or toys for the kids, and one group or another always at someone's throat." He shook his head sadly. "These people sure have had a lousy time."

"I know," Elsa said, her brow wrinkled. "From the outside, they seem to lead such terrible lives. But then you get here, and it's suddenly not so terrible."

"I came here as a soldier," Mike said. "I expected to spend my days in fierce battle, and though we've had our share of firefights, some right here in Bamiyan, the people had been through hell and were happy to see us. Well, not everyone, but enough. Hell, an old man even stopped us to give us a map of land mine locations. There's still bad guys lurking, make no mistake, but there's definitely good here too."

Elsa nodded. "I came here thinking I was going to rescue desperate people, but the truth of it is they rescued *me*. They took me in as though I belonged. I've seen some desperate tragedies." She paused, remembering the bus explosion. "But mostly it's the Afghan people who've taught me how to deal with them.

"And then there's Parween," she said, smiling broadly. "She's become such a good friend, and I found her *here*."

"She lost her husband to the Taliban, right?"

"She did, and her best friend too. She hates the Taliban with a passion that I hadn't expected to see in a woman, at least not here."

"The people of Bamiyan are no fans of the Taliban, and they've had a tough time. I suppose because of that, they've welcomed us. I think that as bad as suffering is, maybe it's what gives people their strength. I mean, I think that when you suffer loss, it does *something*—good or bad."

He rubbed his chin and looked into Elsa's eyes. "Losing my mom had a big effect on me. It made me want to hold on tight to things and to people . . ." His words trailed off, his expression wistful.

Elsa nodded and picked at a stray thread on her dress. "I was so young when my father died, I don't have any real memories of him. My mom was my family. She worked so hard for all of us, but my sister and brother were beyond help. I thought when I graduated from nursing school that my mom and I could really make a life, you know, and have an easier time of it." She paused. "But that was before . . . before I found her. She'd died in her sleep, and that last morning, she looked more peaceful than I'd ever seen her."

She felt her eyes well up, and she looked away, embarrassed.

Mike reached out and tilted her face to his. "I know it's not like what happened to you, but after my mom died, I just felt so lost. It took me a long time to get over that sadness." He took in a slow deep breath. "I know how you feel, Elsa. I know what it's like to be alone. I hope you'll remember that."

Elsa felt her own sadness ease. "I will, Mike."

Mike laced her fingers through his. "It seems as though we were destined to meet here. At least it sure seems like it to me."

"But what if Aide du Monde had sent me somewhere else? I might never have met you. As it is, I was warned not to *fraternize* with the soldiers."

He kissed her gently and traced the outline of her smile with his fingertip.

A jolt of happiness ran through Elsa, and she could hardly breathe. She wanted to freeze this moment, to make this day last forever.

Mike inhaled deeply. "How about lunch?" he asked. "I have peanut butter and jelly. I wish it were chicken salad but we're late for a food drop."

"Peanut butter and jelly is a wonderful change from rice and beans," she said as Mike handed her a sandwich.

It wasn't long before she wanted to take back her words. The peanut butter was thick and gooey and stuck to her teeth and her mouth, and before long, Elsa put her sandwich down.

"That's it for me," she said, taking a sip of Diet Coke.

"Yeah, me too," Mike said as he reached out and drew Elsa close, encircling her in his arms.

He kissed her then, a deep, slow kiss that took her breath away. She felt it all the way down to her toes, and she wriggled free of her plastic sandals.

She smiled self-consciously. "ADM would definitely call this *fraternizing,* wouldn't you say?"

Mike laughed and pulled her closer. "Yes, they would."

She heard him sigh, and she nestled into his chest.

Is that his heart pounding or mine?

He rested his hand on her thigh and the sheer pleasure of his touch burned through her. She could hardly believe this was happening. This man who made her heart race and her hands tremble *liked her,* and she wanted to pinch herself to make sure it was real.

"When I met you, Elsa, you just about knocked me out. I can't believe I came to fight a war and found *you*."

"I felt the same thing. I was so nervous when I saw you, I thought I'd faint." She smiled at the memory. "My palms were sweating, my heart was racing. God, I was a mess."

Mike laughed. "You were beautiful. And it was *my* palms that were sweaty, and *my* heart that I thought would jump right out of my chest. Believe me, I got plenty of grief from the guys."

He kissed her forehead. "But it was all worth it."

It was then that a flash of movement in the trees caught his eye, and he stiffened. Reaching for his gun, he rose slowly.

"Shh, stay down," he whispered to Elsa.

She watched as he fixed his gaze on the trees and drew the pistol. He scanned the trees and the landscape, but there was nothing to see. He seemed to hold his breath while he listened.

An almost overwhelming fear washed over Elsa as she watched Mike search the area. *Everything he said was true,* she thought.

There is *danger here.*

Suddenly, with a cacophony of bleats, a runaway goat careened from the trees and raced for safety somewhere beyond them.

Mike watched, surveying the scene warily. But there was nothing more—no movement, no sound, even the bees were quiet. After a few moments of tense observation, he pointed his gun upward and released a shot into the air. He listened again, and still there was nothing. He exhaled slowly, replacing his weapon in his holster.

"Jesus, Elsa, I'm sorry. We need to get back. This is too big a risk, out here without backup. There really are dangers everywhere. Hell, there could be Taliban out there," he said motioning to the trees.

Elsa hugged herself and nodded, glad she wasn't alone.

Mike sat back on his heels and folded her into his arms. "That damn goat reminded me to stay alert. I'm a soldier first. I probably shouldn't even be on a picnic. I don't know what I was thinking." He smiled then. "Well, that's not entirely true. I *do* know what I was thinking."

He pulled her closer, and she *knew* she was safe. A small rush of joy chased away the last of her worry until a crackling sound filled the air. She looked questioningly at Mike.

"My radio," he muttered, pulling it from his bag. "Base, this is Bravo Two. Over." A voice, broken by interference, filled the silence, and Mike listened intently.

"Roger," he said into the receiver. "On our way."

He turned to Elsa and ran his fingers through her hair. "That was Dave telling us what we already knew—it's time to head back."

They quickly packed up their picnic and loaded the jeep for the trip back to Bamiyan.

Mike reached for Elsa's hand. "Let's do this again," he said, smiling. "But next time, we'll find a spot in Bamiyan."

His eyes shimmered when he smiled, and Elsa was drawn into them.

She reached out and touched his face.

"Mike . . ." She whispered his name as she leaned in and kissed him full on the mouth. "Next time, no peanut butter."

$\mathcal{O}$n the days following their picnic, Elsa raced through her time at the clinic, hoping for another visit from Mike. When he stopped by to tell her he'd be away in another village for a few days, her heart sank. He was a soldier first; there would always be real danger for him, not just runaway goats. She wasn't sure she could reconcile herself to the idea that something could happen to him. Maybe it would be best, she thought, if she held back, if they were just friends for now.

"Will you be safe?" Elsa asked.

"I'll sure as hell try to be, 'cause I'm hoping we can see each other again soon," he said, turning to leave. "I'd like to pick up where we left off." He winked, and her disappointment, along with her resolve to slow down, vanished.

"Why don't you and Dave come to dinner when you get back this Friday? I want you to meet Parween, and Hamid and Amina too. It will be my first dinner party."

"Now *that's* something to look forward to. We'll see you then."

Elsa, unable to hide her excitement from her new friend any longer, rushed to Parween's house to share her news and the invitation to dinner.

"The soldiers came to visit me at the clinic again!" she told her friend, the words tumbling out. "They are all so nice, and there is one . . ." Her voice drifted off; she didn't know how to describe Mike. She told Parween about their dinner together and the picnic.

"Your cheeks are red as poppies!" Parween said, her voice filled with delight. "Has this special soldier put the color there?"

Elsa's hands flew to her face.

"I guess he has," she confessed. "I'd like you to meet him. You can see for yourself."

Parween laughed. "Perhaps this is the man you will marry. Will your family arrange the marriage?"

"Good heavens, I just met him!" Elsa protested. "But no, we don't arrange marriages in Amrika. We wait until we fall in love. *Famidi?* Love?"

Parween nodded. "I know that feeling, for I loved my Raziq, and I would have chosen him for myself had my family not chosen him for me."

"I'm sorry, Parween." Elsa touched Parween's back. "You must miss him terribly."

"I do. I think of him every day, and I think how pleased he would be with the children. You would have liked him, Elsa, and he would have liked you."

Elsa wrapped her arms around her friend as Zahra toddled in and asked, "*Che'ast,* Mama?"

Elsa and Parween collapsed into waves of welcome laughter until Elsa pulled herself away.

"I have a question—I'll be seeing more of Mike, but do you think it's all right? That I'm seen with a soldier? Will people wonder?"

"I think it is fine," Parween answered. "People know who you are. They know you are from Amrika, as are the soldiers, and they understand that your traditions are different from ours. It is no problem for you to be seen with them. Even my uncle has spoken with them."

"Really? And it was okay?"

"Yes, Elsa. The people of Bamiyan see the soldiers as their liberators. You need not worry so much."

"But he's a soldier first; he made sure to tell me that much. I worry that maybe this isn't the right time to get involved with him."

"Whenever it happens," Parween said, "it is the right time. Do not worry so much."

Elsa resolved to take her friend's advice.

Only days later, Parween revealed her plans to travel to Mashaal by bus.

"I know that it has been almost three months since the bus explosion, but I must be free of worry that Mariam's cursed husband will come here to claim the baby. If he knows there is a boy child, he could make trouble for me. I want to be ready."

"But how can you get to Mashaal alone?" Elsa asked. Though women could now walk unescorted through their own villages, it still was not acceptable for them to travel any distance, certainly not on a bus, and certainly not alone.

"I will travel just as Mariam did, dressed as a boy. No one will notice me. Don't worry, I'll be safe," Parween declared.

"When will you go?"

"I've already made the arrangements. I go tomorrow. My mother will watch the children, and travel on Friday is easier since more people move about. I will invite less suspicion then."

But Elsa wasn't so sure. "Johann told me that he'd heard of increasing numbers of Taliban beyond Bamiyan." She'd secretly wondered if Johann's news had something to do with why Mike and the other soldiers went away so often lately.

"No, no," Parween answered. "There is no danger in Mashaal."

"Well then, since I have the day off, can I go to Mashaal with you?" Elsa asked. "I can wear the *burqa* I got in Peshawar, and no one will know who I am. I'll simply seem to be your mother or sister. It gives me a chance to see more of the countryside, and it gives you a traveling companion. What do you say?"

Parween smiled, glad for the offer.

"Tomorrow," she said. "It will be good to have you with me."

Elsa glanced at her watch. "What time shall I meet you?"

Parween showed her bare wrist in reply. "I have no timepiece. Be here when the full sun is just over the horizon. We will board the bus in the bazaar, and we will be in Mashaal before midday. I won't need much time there, and I expect that we will be back in Bamiyan in the late afternoon."

Elsa was excited at the prospect of traveling. It would be her first real trip beyond Bamiyan. Though she'd thought of Pierre and the warnings of both the Chief and Johann, she decided there wouldn't be any danger. She'd be traveling in daylight and under the full cloak of the *burqa*. Only Parween would know that an American was under it.

She considered leaving a note for Mike, but he probably wouldn't even get it until after they'd returned. She expected him and Dave for dinner the next evening, and she would tell him about it then.

Elsa rose the following morning, drank a quick cup of tea, and explained to Amina that she was traveling to Mashaal with Parween and would be back by dusk.

She rifled through her suitcase and pulled out the *burqa*. Shaking it out, Elsa wondered how it would feel. She'd looked forward to donning the mysterious garment, but when she pulled it on, she discovered that it was like being enveloped in a tent. She had to tug to get the head covering in place. It was tight and pulled at her hair. The woven grille-like opening for her eyes was hard to adjust to also, and it only allowed her to see straight ahead—all of her peripheral vision was lost.

It was hard, as well, to keep her pale hands hidden in the folds of the voluminous, pleated fabric as she'd seen so many women do. It was, she decided, an awkward garment, and Elsa walked slowly and clumsily once she had it on.

Parween's disguise, the loose *shalwar kamiz* that all men and boys wore, allowed her to move more freely. The baggy pants and shirt would hide all evidence of her femininity. She'd pinned her hair on top of her head, slipped on a prayer cap, and wound a turban over the cap, tucking away any stray wisps of hair. Elsa was astounded. Just as with Mariam, Parween had been transformed into a boy. Only close inspection would reveal the truth, and they didn't plan on any close inspections.

"Keep your head down and your words few like a good Afghan

woman, and we will be safe," Parween advised Elsa as she tucked a penknife into her shirt pocket. She turned to see the questioning look in Elsa's eyes.

"For courage," Parween said softly. She was already practicing speaking in a low murmur.

They strode to the village center and purchased two tickets. Elsa stayed quietly at Parween's side as they boarded the bus, and she kept her head down as Parween pushed through the crowd to seats at the back, as she had seen the men do.

Once they were settled, they had a clear view of the goings-on around them. Within minutes, the seats filled and the bus teemed with people lugging boxes and bags and chickens, and one angry goat who bleated in protest. The bus sputtered and groaned as the engine roared to noisy life with bursts of smoke and backfires. The air inside the packed vehicle was heavy with the stench of mangy animals and unwashed people, and Elsa, caught in the thick of it, pushed herself farther into her seat, uncomfortable with the closeness and grateful for the filter the *burqa* offered.

The road to Mashaal was a ragged unpaved stretch of dirt and rocks. It had been rugged in the best of times, but now with the added insult of land mines and burned-out tanks, it was downright treacherous. With her head turned full to the grimy window, Elsa watched as the driver maneuvered the bus perilously close to the marked mine sites at the sides of the road. It was only three months since the bus explosion, and she tried to push away her memories of the twisted heap of metal and the bloodied survivors.

"Ohhh," she groaned. Parween turned to the window and saw the source of her concern.

"*Inshallah,* we shall be safe."

Elsa shook her head and wished, again, that Afghans wouldn't leave so much up to God.

They settled in for the long bumpy ride through look-alike villages and parched fields. Occasionally, they passed a little patch of farmed land where stalks of wheat or rows of potatoes poked through the ground.

After traveling for almost an hour, the bus ground to a sudden halt and the driver announced that the road ahead was blocked. A large tree had fallen and several wagons and another bus were stopped, their passengers and drivers standing about discussing the dilemma. They had already tried—and failed—to move the enormous trunk. The passengers spilled out of the bus, most settling along the road to pass the time in prayer or conversation.

Parween and Elsa strode off to sit under some nearby trees.

Within the hour, a truck laden with UN supplies stopped at the roadblock. A burly driver and a scrawny assistant got out to survey the obstacle. They studied the scene, bent to feel the weight of the tree, and decided to try moving it with their truck. They motioned for the other vehicles to move out of the way, climbed onto their rig, revved the engine, and drove the truck until it was only inches from the obstruction.

The driver backed up slightly and then pressed heavily on the gas pedal as he shifted gears. The vehicle plunged forward, knocking the tree out of its way as though it were mere kindling.

The driver pulled on his rig's horn as he continued down the road. The onlookers cheered as they scurried back to their vehicles, ready to get on with their travels. Elsa and Parween scrambled to rejoin their bus and reclaim their seats as the bus set off for Mashaal.

In less than an hour, the bus lurched up a steep incline and onto another tortuous road framed by crumbling houses and abandoned tanks. Children dressed in rags scampered through the debris. Villagers were busy rebuilding their homes, patting down mud and fitting dried straw into cracks and gaps. Many of them stopped their labors and turned to watch as the bus passed by.

It rounded a corner, squeezed between rows of barely standing mud houses, and finally came to a stop under a towering tree. This was Mashaal. The driver heaved a weary sigh, pushed the lever to open his doors, slid from his seat, and announced that if anyone wanted to return to Bamiyan, he would be leaving in two hours.

The passengers—all in a hurry now—jostled to get off quickly. Elsa and Parween sat and waited for everyone to get off before they rose and climbed down from the bus.

Smaller than Bamiyan, Mashaal was another Hazara village, and the women there were even less hidden behind veils. Elsa adjusted the hood of her *burqa* so that she could finally see without hindrance, and she rearranged her veil to cover her hair, though she noticed that many of the women wore veils and scarves that allowed their own hair to spill out. Adorned with heavy pieces of pewter jewelry, these weren't typical cowering Afghan women. Their dresses and head garments were brightly colored, and, despite the warmth of the day, they wore heavy, multicolored vests embroidered with vivid beads and tiny mirrors. They walked about, almost strutting, graceful in their swaying skirts.

Many of them balanced heavy sacks on their heads and children on their hips. A small group that was shooing a donkey home stopped to watch Elsa and Parween.

"Parween, those women," Elsa said, shrugging in their direction, "they're watching us."

"We are strangers here. That is why they look," Parween replied as she approached the little group. *"As-salaam alaikum, chetore asti? Khoob asti? Jona jurast?"* she called, and they smiled and returned the greeting. "My sister has been sick; she has lost her voice." The women all nodded their concern as they smiled at Elsa.

"My name," Parween said, "is Walid, and my sister is Samyah. We are here looking for our cousin. She came to Mashaal some years ago to marry an elder. We have had no word of her since the trouble."

"Ahh, who would that be? Your cousin, what is her name?"

"Her name is Mariam, and she came from Bamiyan." Parween couldn't help herself, and her words came out draped in sadness. The women cocked their heads in unison and conferred with whispers before replying.

"Ahh," they murmured together, and the eldest—a small woman with weathered skin and gentle eyes—stepped forward to speak.

"We do not know where Mariam is now," she said. "She had a very bad time here, first with her old goat of a husband and his wives, and then with the Taliban." The women shook their heads in agreement.

"She was a sweet girl saddled with a miserable old man," one of them said.

"Did no one help her?" Parween asked.

They looked about for eavesdroppers and, seeing none, said that they had stepped forward once the Taliban were done with her. "They threw her onto the road and rode off on their fine horses. They were animals and she was nothing to them, not worth killing, and certainly not worth a kind word."

"The Taliban, may Allah crush them all." The oldest woman crinkled her nose and spat.

Parween smiled. Here was a kindred spirit.

"The old Omar-Saeed, her husband who had given her to the Taliban to protect his fat old behind, refused to take her back," the old woman said. "He had taken another wife and wanted nothing to do with Mariam. But his first two wives, disgusted at the old goat and sorry for their own bad behavior toward Mariam, rescued her from the road and brought her to my sister's house. Her husband was off in Yakawlang on business and we hid Mariam there for a few days."

The woman paused and looked away.

"She was in a bad way. She had been beaten and burned and those animals"—she spat again for emphasis—"had had their way with her. We washed her wounds and her poor bruised and burned skin and we fed her sweet tea and rice and prayed for her to get well. When my sister's husband was due home, we took Mariam up there." She pointed to the small caves jutting out from the sturdy overhead rock cliffs.

Tears stung Parween's eyes. She wanted to block out the words, the story of Mariam's suffering, and she dropped her face into her hands and cried softly.

Elsa drew her friend to her in a comforting embrace.

"Shh, don't cry," she whispered.

The strange encounter caught the attention of the little circle of women and they leaned forward to look more closely at the strangers from Bamiyan. Parween saw their questioning glances, and she swept the turban and prayer cap from her head long enough to reveal that she was a woman. She quickly pulled her hair back onto her head and replaced the little cap before winding the turban again.

The astonished women stared, and then, as understanding took them one by one, they smiled and each kissed Parween's cheeks.

"Mariam was my dearest friend," she said conspiratorially, "and I have come today to see if there is any word of her or her husband." She peered at each of them in turn.

The women shook their heads sadly.

"She just disappeared," the youngest one said, piping up. "I went one morning to bring her water and *naan*, but her clothes were strewn around the cave, and she was gone. We have had no word. We fear that she is dead. Do you know anything?"

Before Parween answered, she wanted to be sure that Omar-Saeed was no longer interested in Mariam. "What of her husband?" she asked. "Has he looked for her?"

The old woman finally smiled—a toothless, gummy grin—and answered. "Allah took care of him. An American rocket fell onto his house and killed him. He is now the dust that you grind under your feet."

Parween, relieved of the worry that he would come searching one day, burst into tears.

"Mariam . . . she has died." She cried as she told the women of Mariam's return to Bamiyan and her death in the bus explosion. She did not say that Mariam had been with child. It was best if the baby remained her secret.

The women sighed in collective sadness.

"It is better that way, for she couldn't live with what the Taliban had done to her. She is in Allah's hands now. Poor Mariam," the old woman said.

"Come," the eldest said. "Sit with us for tea in the cave where Mariam lived. You can see for yourself where she spent her last days."

Parween nodded, and the group turned to climb the rock cliffs above. The eldest woman scrambled ahead with the energy of a young man and turned to urge her younger companions to move with haste.

"Hurry," she said. "We don't want any prying eyes to find our cave."

The little group clambered up the rocks and into an opening, and Elsa and Parween stepped in and gasped in astonishment. The tiny hidden entrance concealed a well-stocked, carpeted room strewn with pillows, sleeping pads, and clothes. The old woman held out her arms and welcomed them inside.

"*Besheneen,* sit, my friends, we shall get tea." She struck a match to a small pile of kindling and a tiny fire flared into life. While the small pot of tea boiled, she handed a small pile of clothes to Parween.

"These," she said, "belonged to Mariam. They are the clothes we found here when we discovered she had gone."

Parween held the pile close and caught the faintest hint of Mariam's once familiar scent. She buried her face there and let the memories wash over her.

The old woman leaned to her and in a gentle tone said, "Do not be sad. In her last days here in the cave, Mariam was happy. Now we know why. She had planned all along to escape this place and return home. Those plans made her smile and gave her happiness. I hope that thought brings you peace."

Parween fell into the old woman's comforting embrace and sobbed as the woman stroked her back.

When her tears had subsided, Parween sat up and took the old woman's hand.

"Thank you, all of you, for helping Mariam." She wiped her sleeve across her eyes and rested her hand on Elsa's arm.

"This is Elsa, a nurse come from Amrika to help the people of Afghanistan. She is my friend, and yours as well." Elsa shed the *burqa,* and the women gasped in astonishment.

"Amrika," they said in unison. "May Allah bless you for your goodness." Elsa sat quietly as they each took her hands and kissed her cheeks.

Parween fidgeted with her turban.

"Tell me about Mariam's life here before the Taliban came."

"It wasn't all bad," the old woman said. "Though Mariam worked hard, she spent time at the washing stream, even when she had no wash, and she told funny stories that made us all laugh. She told us about her childhood friend who could count and fight the boys, and who one day threw a young boy right into the washing stream in Bamiyan!"

Parween laughed out loud.

"I had forgotten all about that. Ahh, he deserved it. I'd do it again."

The women grinned. "Mariam was a good girl. Even Omar-

Saeed's first wives began to understand that after a while. Right before the Taliban came, things were a little better for her."

The youngest woman, her cheeks red with the heat of the fire, spoke up.

"Mariam was always so kind to me. I hated the bite of the cold water in the washing stream, and Mariam helped me with my washing. She never complained, never told me to just do it, as others did." She looked at the old woman. "She was very kind."

"She was," Parween said. "No one hated the sting of that cold water more than Mariam did. She must have liked you very much."

The young woman's cheeks burned redder, and she looked away.

A weight of worry lifted from Parween as she sat with the women in the little cave and listened to their stories. Finally, Elsa looked at her watch and announced that they had to go.

"The bus will be leaving soon."

The old woman wound a piece of twine around Mariam's clothes and passed the bundle to Parween, who hugged her.

"*Besiar tashakore*. May Allah the Most Merciful bless all of you for your kindness."

Elsa donned the *burqa* once again, and they set off back down the rocky hillside and into an unexpected gust of wind. The surrounding trees rustled in response. Parween hesitated, a sudden knot of fear bursting through her brief moment of joy. She looked around. Just ahead, Elsa had stopped and was rearranging her *burqa*. Parween reached for her front pocket, her fingers searching for the knife she carried. Satisfied that it was there, she moved along, urging Elsa to hurry, uneasy until they reached the safety of the bus.

Once they'd boarded and taken their seats, Parween breathed a sigh of relief.

Elsa, who had been stunned into near silence by the day's events, took her hand. "Thank you for letting me come here and share this day with you." Her eyes filled up and she continued. "I wish I'd known her."

"Oh, Elsa, she would have liked you," Parween said, her fear all but forgotten. "And she would have loved your lipstick." She gazed out at Mashaal as the bus pulled away from the village. "I never thought I would have another friend like her." She paused and looked at Elsa. "Until I met you. Thank you for coming with me today."

Quiet tears spilled from Elsa's eyes, unseen through the *burqa*'s grille. "Thank you, Parween." She reached out and squeezed her friend's hand.

Parween sat back and let relief sweep over her. Her baby was safe.

Once she arrived back in Bamiyan, Elsa, still clad in the *burqa*, headed to the clinic, where she hoped to attend to an hour or two of long-neglected paperwork before dusk. As she neared the entrance, she noticed Mike's jeep. Dave sat inside, cradling his rifle. Mike was nowhere to be seen. Dave looked somber, and Elsa moved closer, forgetting that he would have no idea it was her under the *burqa*.

She hesitated before drawing up the garment.

"Dave, it's me, Elsa."

Dave looked stunned.

"Elsa! Where've you been? Mike's been frantic with worry." And with that, he raised his radio and spoke into it. "Mike, that item you been missing is here with me."

The radio crackled with the reply.

"You sure? I'll be right out."

Moments later, she heard Mike's questioning voice behind her.

"What the hell?"

She turned, and Mike breathed a sigh of relief, though his voice still trembled.

"Jesus, you scared me. Where *were* you? Never mind that, you're okay then?"

"I'm fine. I went to Mashaal with Parween. You're going to meet her tonight at dinner. Anyway, she had to go there on a family matter, and I went with her."

"You went to Mashaal?"

Elsa nodded, smiling.

"We're in a war zone, Elsa. I carry all of these weapons for a reason. You cannot run around like you're at home. Jesus, do you know how *dangerous* this place is?"

Elsa took a step back, surprised by his anger.

"But I was disguised. No one could tell I wasn't an Afghan,

and besides, I had a great day. I met some wonderful women and I just . . . I just had a great day." She stared at him questioningly.

"You cannot forget, even for an instant, where we are. We aren't playing dress-up."

"I *do* know where we are, Mike. I don't carry a gun, I carry a stethoscope, but I sure as *hell* know where I am."

Mike's expression softened.

"Do you know how easy it would have been for someone to recognize that you're not an Afghan and just grab you? Do you know how quickly you could have been captured or killed? I didn't even know you were gone till I went to the house and Amina tried to explain. We've been looking for you all day."

"You have to trust that I can take care of myself. I'm not going to put myself in risky situations. *Believe* me."

Mike reached out and touched her face. "Everything here is risky—*everything*. This is a dangerous place, and I was worried as hell. Just promise you won't go off like that again."

The flush of anger that had welled up so quickly in Elsa began to ease. "I won't. If you're still coming to dinner tonight—and I hope you are—you'll see *my* Afghanistan. Good friends and gentle people."

A smile crept onto his lips. "I wouldn't miss it for anything, but I *am* bringing my gun."

Oh God, Elsa thought, *he is a soldier first. But he'll see—I'll show him the Afghanistan I know.*

The evening was warm, and they dined in the courtyard, sitting cross-legged on the ground. They ate with their fingers, sharing bowls of rice and a plate of beef kabobs. The *naan* was warm, and they dipped it into the freshly churned bitter yogurt that Amina had prepared for their special visitors.

Elsa had wanted to invite Sidiq too, but Hamid warned her against it.

"Just wait, Elsa. He intends to speak with Amina's brother. It is best that they not be together again until then. Her brother might not understand."

The dinner was a success, everyone chattering at once. Hamid was especially pleased to meet the soldiers, and Mike in particular.

"I think that I would like to be an engineer like you. Is it a very difficult course?"

"Hamid, it's like anything. You gotta put some work into it, but it gets easier and easier and—maybe more important—it's fun. I think you'd like it. As long as I'm here, I'll be glad to help you with your studies."

Elsa felt such affection for Mike as she watched him that her cheeks flushed. He glanced at her just then and winked, and her face turned hotter still.

Dave shared stories of his Texas home; his wife, Lisa; and his two children, who were still so young that he worried they might not remember him when he finally returned home. When he spoke of them, his perpetually animated voice slowed and cracked.

"My wife's a nurse like Elsa here, and I hope y'all get to meet her someday. God, I miss her and the kids." He was lonely for all things home, and they urged him to talk.

"Well, my life's exciting to me, but I can't much see how y'all would find it interesting."

"But Mike says you're a detective; tell us about that." Elsa encouraged him.

"Well, I guess I do have some funny stories. I caught this burglar once only 'cause he stayed to eat." He laughed at the memory. "The guy broke into a house, cleared out all the jewelry and money he could find, and instead of making a quick getaway, he stopped to eat a plate of warm brownies on the kitchen table! A neighbor saw him in the house and called us. We walked in on him while he was sitting there chewing. He would have gotten away if it weren't for those brownies."

Elsa looked at Mike, who wore a bemused expression.

"I wish I had something interesting to tell you, but I don't. At home, I'm an engineer, and while it's exciting to me to see a bridge or road built, especially one that I designed, that's not near as exciting as detective work."

He paused and looked straight at Elsa.

"But seeing the good that Elsa does has made me think that maybe after I'm done with soldiering, I could build those roads in a place like this. Maybe even work with her someday."

His eyes locked onto Elsa's, and she could hardly contain the smile that swept over her face. It wasn't just the working together but the *done with soldiering* that made her smile. It felt for a moment as if they were alone.

Parween nudged her and Elsa, still smiling, composed herself and changed the subject.

"Parween has two children, even younger than yours, Dave. A boy and a girl."

"You got any pictures?" Dave asked as he reached into his shirt pocket and pulled out a worn photo. He passed it to Parween, who ran her fingers over it.

"It is beautiful. I wish I had a likeness of my husband and my children to carry with me."

"Hey, I got a camera with me—well, not *with* me, back at the house," Mike said. "I'll give it to Elsa and she can take your pictures."

Parween grinned excitedly. "*Tashakore,* Mike, *tashakore.*"

Long after the sun had set, Amina finally stood to announce that the evening was over. Elsa rose and walked Dave and Mike to the gate. Dave kissed her cheek.

"Good night, darlin'. I had one hell of a good time tonight." And he headed off to start up the jeep, leaving Mike and Elsa with a rare private moment.

Mike took Elsa's hands and caressed them as he planted a kiss on her open mouth. "I'm sorry for being such a jerk earlier, but you did give me a scare. I've been expecting that we'd have plenty of time to be together. But for that to happen, you have to stay safe. You can't forget where you are. Promise me—no more trips."

Elsa nodded. *No arguments tonight,* she thought. "I promise," she said, and she kissed him again.

Mike got into the jeep, and Elsa watched as it made a U-turn in the tiny road and headed toward the safe house.

She stood against the gate until the jeep had vanished into the night. She folded her arms across her chest and wondered what Parween would say to a man's warnings not to travel.

PART
4

Choices

23

Commotion outside the clinic interrupted Elsa's work one after-noon, and she looked through the doorway searching for the source. A frantic voice filled the air and she stopped to listen. It was Mike, of that much she was certain.

"Get Elsa!" he yelled again as she hurried toward the clinic gate. *Oh God, what is it?* she wondered. It was then that she saw him—covered in blood and dust, and carrying a small package. Her heart pounded as she ran, and it wasn't until she reached him that she saw the bundle he held was a bleeding, crying child.

"Take him, Elsa. Help him. We shot him."

Elsa reached for the small boy and looked questioningly at Mike. "What happened? Are you hurt too?"

"No, just him. He was in the line of fire. We'll talk later, just help him. Please."

Elsa could see the worry etched on Mike's face, and clutching the wailing child close, she turned and raced for the emergency room, yelling for someone to get Ezat. He appeared just as Elsa laid the small boy on the stretcher.

"He's been shot," she said as she cut the boy's clothes away to search for the wound.

Ezat shook his head. "How?"

"The soldiers. I don't know anything else. Let's just help him."

Elsa reached for an intravenous set and held the boy's arm tightly as she guided the needle into his vein.

The child's cries grew louder as Ezat poked and prodded the bullet hole.

Elsa stroked the boy's forehead. "*Tars na dori,* do not be afraid."

But *she* was afraid. Mike had shot a *child*?

The boy grabbed Elsa's hand and squeezed as Ezat continued to examine his leg.

Finally, Ezat looked up and smiled. "It's only a thigh wound. It looks as though the bullet went right through. We can sew this up and have him home in an hour."

A flood of relief washed over Elsa as she turned and reached for a small suture tray.

Just then Hamid, his breathing heavy, burst through the door. "What is it?"

"A gunshot wound," Ezat replied, pointing to the boy's leg.

"Shot himself, hmm?" Hamid glowered at the boy. "That will teach him."

"No," Elsa said. "The soldiers accidentally shot him."

Hamid looked at Elsa. "Mike? Is that why he's here?"

"I don't know," she answered. "I don't know what happened."

"Go, Elsa," Ezat said. "I'll sew him up. Tell your soldier the boy will be fine. He must be worried to have stayed."

Elsa nodded and hurried out to Mike. She saw him by the gate as he spoke into his radio, the boy's blood staining his shirt and his hand hovering protectively over his holster. When he saw Elsa, he put the radio down and turned to her.

"Is he okay?" His voice cracked as he spoke.

"It's just a small wound," Elsa said. "What about you? What happened?"

"A firefight due north. The kid ran right into the line of fire. Jesus, when he went down, I almost lost it. I ran out and scooped him up. Chief's gonna chew me up for that."

"Are *you* okay?" Elsa touched his arm.

"Yeah. I just never shot a kid before. I mean, I'd shoot a bad guy in a heartbeat, but a kid—" He shook his head.

"He's fine. You probably saved him."

"I guess. It's just that . . . well, I know that's why I'm here, to get the bad guys. It's just that sometimes it's a tough call. Hell, Elsa, I'd shoot your friend Hamid if I thought he was a bad guy, but a kid, well, that's tough."

Elsa froze. She couldn't have heard that right. "You'd shoot Hamid?"

"We're talking hypothetically here, but if he were a bad guy, you bet I would."

"You wouldn't hesitate?" She clenched and unclenched her fists, holding them tight at her sides.

"Elsa, I'm a soldier. There's no room for hesitation."

She felt herself stiffen, her heart pounding. "But maybe there should be."

Mike shook his head, his eyes heavy. "Elsa, you don't understand." She looked away.

He gripped her shoulder tightly for an instant before turning and pulling himself into his jeep. "The boy's dad will be here soon. Chief wouldn't let me take him in the jeep, but he'll be along shortly. I gotta go. We have a debriefing, and then Dave and I are heading out on patrol. We'll be gone a few days."

He paused as if waiting for her to say something, but Elsa was silent. The only sound was the rumble of the jeep as it pulled away.

Elsa turned and watched him go. "Be careful," she whispered.

Elsa could barely look at Hamid the rest of that day. He was like her brother, and Mike had just said he would shoot him. Now she felt as though she'd somehow betrayed Hamid.

When the clinic closed, she walked home in silence alongside Hamid.

"Why are you so quiet? Is it the shooting?" he asked.

"I guess," she answered, picking up her pace. She was eager to get home and just be alone.

At her house, she brooded, barely speaking until Amina finally asked, *"Che'ast?"*

Elsa just shook her head in reply. Of all the things she'd worried about with Mike, this hadn't been one of them. How could she tell her friends that Mike would shoot Hamid? *God,* she thought, *he'd probably shoot all of them.*

She kept to herself for days, mulling over Mike's words, trying to understand. But, try as she might, understanding wouldn't come. An aching disappointment settled in her bones, and with no word from Mike, it festered and grew. She swept and reswept her dirt floors, rearranged the books in her office, and started working on overdue reports, but nothing eased her mood. At the clinic, she was quiet. Even Ezat had stopped to ask if she was all right. "I'm just tired," she'd replied, not wanting to tell anyone about Mike's comment.

Where was he anyway? Surely, he was back by now. Didn't he want to explain himself? Talk to her? *Where was he?* His absence only served to increase her misery, her conviction that he was not the man she thought he was.

After endless days and nights of solitary discontent, she thought she'd explode. She had to speak to someone. So almost a week after she'd last seen Mike, Elsa hurried to Parween's house. Once she told Parween what had happened, she paused and took a deep breath.

"I haven't seen him since, and maybe the decision's already made for me, but I just don't know about him, about us. If he would shoot Hamid, would he shoot me?"

Parween shook her head. "What nonsense you speak, Elsa! Your words are foolish. Mike is a *soldier.* I understand that, and so should you. If Hamid was Taliban and threatened my family, I'd shoot him myself!"

"You don't mean that."

"I do. You've been lucky, Elsa. You don't know war or misery."

"But I *do.* I'm from a really poor section in Boston. I know it's not as bad as it is here, but there is trouble."

Parween rolled her eyes. "And there is gunfire?"

"Sometimes."

"And you've lost people you love to this war?"

"Well, in a way. My sister and my brother. It's a different kind of war, but it still brings misery."

"So, in your war, you eat, you go to school, you live in warm homes." She shook her head. "I think you do not know war, not *real* war. If you did, you'd understand Mike. He's trying to rescue us, to save us, and for that he carries a gun. I appreciate that. Why can't *you?*"

"Things aren't always as simple as you make them out to be." Elsa sighed, rolling Parween's words around in her mind.

"Things are not always as complicated as *you* make them, Elsa. You are like a tree—strong, yes, but rigid. Too rigid I think. If someone doesn't fit into your perfect idea of how things should be, you turn away. You should see this from Mike's point of view. He angered his superior by bringing the child to you. And you *question* him?" She shook her head. "*Na famidam,* I do not understand you."

Elsa felt her eyes well up. Maybe Parween was right. She was rigid. She did see everything in black and white. She'd done it with her sister and brother. They'd fallen from grace and she'd never forgiven them. She should have been more understanding of them, and of Mike. Instead, she'd pushed them all away.

Parween's voice softened. "When you see Mike—and you will—ask him if he'd *save* Hamid. That is the only thing you need to know."

24

Almost two weeks had passed since Elsa had seen Mike, and she was beginning to wonder if she would ever see him again. *If only he weren't a soldier,* she thought sadly. *If only*—She caught herself. If he weren't a soldier, she wouldn't have met him, and if he weren't a soldier, she wouldn't be missing him now, she wouldn't be praying that he was safe. Now the only "if" was if she would see him again. She picked up her pace on the lonely road.

Despite her earlier promise to Mike about taking risks, there were still times when Elsa walked to the clinic or to Parween's alone. She understood his concern—at least she told herself she did—but she was convinced it wasn't justified. This was Bamiyan, after all, and there was no war *here.* There were just friendly people who recognized her now, often waving or calling out as she passed.

She'd become more confident in her duties as the ADM nurse-administrator too, sometimes dealing with the paperwork early in the morning so she could finish up the day in the clinic. But at each month's end, with messages from Paris to read and detailed reports expected, the workload piled up. On those days, she sent Hamid ahead, and frequently it wasn't until early afternoon that she set off alone along the sparsely traveled road to the clinic.

Among her messages this afternoon, she'd learned that the UN was sending a European orthopedic surgeon from Kabul to see if any of the patients needed surgery. Johann had asked Elsa to draw up a list of potential patients, and as she walked along, she was preoccupied with the surgeon's upcoming visit, mentally reviewing the list she had begun to compile.

At least the surgeon's visit had given her something besides Mike to think about. She needed to talk with Laila and Ezat about the list. Easily twenty patients came to mind, many with limbs half-destroyed by land mines, others with long-neglected bone injuries. Her first thought, though, had been of Amina, and she hoped the surgeon would be able to attend to her. She knew the young woman would be overjoyed to be rid of her extra finger.

Elsa was lost in thought as a snorting and rusty pickup truck passed by. She paused to let the dust clear, and as she stopped, so did the truck, its engine dying with a growl. It was loaded with unkempt, disheveled young men who watched her from the bed of the truck. Dressed in traditional clothes and veil, she might have easily passed for just another Afghan woman, but as usual she donned her sunglasses and bright lipstick.

There was no mistaking it; she looked like a foreigner.

Several of the men stood up and leered at her. One of them climbed from the truck and stood in the road.

Elsa pulled her head-scarf a little closer and stood perfectly still, not sure what to do. The air was heavy, and the only sound she heard was the throbbing of her heartbeat pulsing in her ears. Her breath came in shallow puffs, and her mouth felt like cotton.

A second man stepped from the truck onto the road.

The hair on the back of Elsa's neck stood straight up. They were too close; if she ran, they'd catch her in seconds. She carried no weapons and nothing that she could turn against them. If she screamed, no one would hear. She was truly alone.

She held her breath.

The seconds ticked away like hours and the sudden braying of an errant donkey filled the air, breaking the silence.

"Elsa, wait!"

The glorious sound of Parween's voice broke through the pall of terror that hung in the air, and Elsa finally breathed and turned away from the truck.

From her house, Parween had seen the truck pass. The men were cloaked in the black turbans of the Taliban; the sight of them made her stomach turn, and she had hurried after them to investigate. When she saw Elsa, she had picked up her pace.

Parween darted to her friend's side and, seeing the surly group gawking rudely, pushed her veil away from her face. With all the ferocity she could muster, she spat right in their direction. She sneered at the men and shouted, *"Burro! Go!"*

Then she steered Elsa onto a nearby path that curved between trees and irrigation fields, offering them an escape route. As they made their way, they heard the loud rumble of the truck again as it started with a cough and drove into the distance.

"Oh, Parween, thank God you came along. I was so scared. Who were they?"

"Taliban." Parween spat out the word, her hate evident in every syllable.

"Weren't you *afraid*?" Elsa asked.

"I am tired of being afraid," Parween answered with an intensity that Elsa hadn't heard before.

"Were those some of the Taliban that were released recently?"

"Maybe . . . probably." Parween sighed. "They should never have released them. There will only be trouble."

"Why are they still here? This is Bamiyan. The soldiers will see them."

"The soldiers cannot be everywhere. And the Taliban are stupid. They don't care."

When they were both calm again, Parween peered out to make sure the truck and the men were truly gone. The empty road held only welcome silence.

Elsa took a few minutes to compose herself and turned to Parween. "Mike was right, and you were too. The Taliban are *everywhere*. Even Bamiyan is changing." She shivered at the thought.

"But for now, they are gone," Parween said. "You saw those *cowards*. They ran off at the approach of a shouting woman!" She chuckled, and Elsa let herself relax, and think about the day ahead.

*   *   *

Elsa sat with Laila and they began to formulate the list of surgical patients.

"What would Ezat think?" Elsa asked. "Shouldn't we ask him?"

"He'll be happy with the ones we choose. He trusts us *both*."

Elsa smiled at the words and bent over the list.

The number of possible candidates was endless, and they decided to choose only those who had lost limbs to the ever-present land mines for now. Other injuries—even birth defects—would have to wait.

"But"—Elsa paused—"I would like to include Amina on the list. What do you think?"

Laila looked over the list again. "We can include her and let the surgeon decide."

Two days later, the surgeon arrived. "This is Doctor Hans Deiter," Johann said. The surgeon, a small, thin man with tufts of gray hair peeking from his nose, turned to Elsa, who stretched her hand out in greeting.

"Please move the patients through quickly," Deiter snapped. "I have no intention of staying in Bamiyan any longer than necessary."

Elsa pulled her hand away. "Why is that?"

"There is no electricity, no showers. Primitive!" He practically grimaced. "I don't know how you can stand it, but I don't have any intention of finding out." He turned on his heel and hurried off.

Elsa saw Laila in the clinic doorway and called to her.

"Laila, the surgeon is here. Have you met him?" When Laila shook her head, she added, "He's awfully grumpy, but maybe it was just the trip. Are you ready for tomorrow?"

Laila looked away, and Elsa could see that there was a problem.

"Ezat," she said almost apologetically, "will not allow me to be with you when the surgeon is here. He says it is not right for me to be so near a foreign man. He is nervous and has forbidden it."

"Oh, Laila, can't we speak to him?"

"No, Elsa. He doesn't want me near. There's no use trying to talk him out of it. It's almost as if he is afraid that I will forget that I am an Afghan."

Elsa opened her mouth to reply but Laila spoke again.

"It is all right; it is his way. Please, you must not take offense. He will be there to help."

Elsa sighed. *Ezat isn't so different from Mike,* she thought, suspicious of people and customs he didn't understand. Well, she couldn't change any of that right now. "I'll miss you tomorrow. I'll ask Parween if she can come in to help interpret for the women. I'm not sure my Dari is good enough for our guest."

The following morning, Elsa set up the ER as a consult room for Deiter, who arrived and perched himself haughtily on a stool.

Elsa ushered in the first patient, a young man whose left arm had been mangled by a land mine. Hamid translated Deiter's questions for the man, who stood nervously as Deiter examined his deformed arm. Finally, the surgeon pulled away.

"He will be the first on the list, Elsa."

Elsa asked Hamid to bring in the second patient, a boy who'd lost his right leg to another mine. Ezat, who'd just arrived, accompanied the boy inside.

He mumbled something and nodded to Deiter, who turned to Elsa with a questioning look.

"This is Doctor Ezat. Although he speaks some English, Hamid will interpret so that he can present the male patients."

Each time Ezat spoke, he did it so softly that Elsa could barely hear him, but Hamid did, and he turned to Deiter to translate. The small boy stood and cried silently as Deiter poked and prodded his blistered stump. The doctor added the boy's name to his list and motioned for them to bring in the next person. Before the day was finished, he'd seen nine surgical candidates and had accepted them all.

"You've done an excellent job, Miss Murphy, Doctor Ezat. Good referrals all." He bade them good day and was whisked off in a fancy SUV to the UN office for the night. Ezat watched as the vehicle sped away, and then he turned to Elsa and *smiled*.

Burying her surprise, Elsa smiled back.

Relieved that they were halfway through the list, Elsa looked forward to the next day, when Amina would be seen. When she told

Amina that she'd included her name on the consult list, the young woman started to cry.

She couldn't stop her tears or her countless words of thanks and blessings, but Elsa had to offer a word of caution.

"Amina, your extra finger may not meet his criteria for surgery, but it's worth a try, don't you think?" Through her sniffles and cries, she took Elsa's hands and kissed them.

The next morning, Amina happily accompanied Elsa to the clinic, where she joined the group of four other patients already waiting.

Deiter arrived and settled himself on the stool. "I will choose only two or three more, Elsa." Ezat had not yet arrived but the surgeon was in no mood to wait. "You can send the first one in."

The remaining patients entered, one by one. He added only one of those to his list; the last he declared too old for surgery and the man, who was perhaps forty, was sent away without even an exam.

Ezat had arrived late, and his eyes shone with anger when Hamid told him of the surgeon's rejection of the old man. Without uttering a word, he turned and left.

Amina was the final candidate, and knowing there might be one more open slot on the list, Elsa had to hide her enthusiasm as she escorted her in to see Deiter. Amina, so nervous she was trembling, had to be pushed gently into the room.

Parween entered as well and spoke up.

"This woman has extra finger on her right hand. Very bad here, very bad. It can ruin her life."

Amina looked pleadingly at Deiter as she held her blighted finger up. He motioned her forward so he could examine her affliction without rising from his stool. He pulled at her useless extra finger and stood, a look of disgust on his face.

"*You*"—he turned to Elsa—"have wasted my time with this foolishness. An extra finger is not worth our time in Kabul. What nonsense. *This* is my list." He thrust the paper at Elsa and walked out of the room.

Her shock turned quickly to anger. With Amina's sobs behind her, she chased after him.

"Wait," she called out, waving the list in her hand. When she caught up, she swallowed an almost overwhelming urge to tell him off and instead asked when they could send the first patients to Kabul.

"Look at the list," he said. "Send the two young boys in ten days and we will decide then when their surgery will be." He hesitated and turned back. "I am sorry to be so abrupt, but I am busy and the last patient—" He shook his head. "What nonsense."

"But not to her. That extra finger has ruined her life."

"Nothing I can do about that. Nothing you can do either, I would guess." He waved his hand and hurried to the waiting UN vehicle that would take him to Bamiyan's makeshift airfield. There, a small plane waited to whisk the self-absorbed surgeon back to Kabul, where at least there would be electricity and some semblance of civilization.

Elsa returned to the consultation room, where Parween had already calmed down Amina.

"The doctor," Parween said, "would like to help you but he cannot, not this time at least. He was told to take only those with terrible afflictions and you are lucky in that yours is not as bad as the crippled woman who was carried in earlier." She paused and looked at Amina, who stood stoically.

"*Famidam,*" she whispered, picking at her extra finger. "Those who have real troubles should go first. *Inshallah,* someday my turn will come."

25

$\mathcal{W}$hile Elsa wrestled with her doubts about Mike, Sidiq had known from the moment he met Amina that he would marry her, and finally, some three months after their first meeting, he approached her brother, Rashid. Sidiq had wanted time, he said, to improve his appearance in the hopes it might improve his prospects.

He had also been practicing what to say with Hamid. They lived in the same small rooming house in the village, and Hamid had been tutoring him.

"Stand tall, breathe quietly, and close your mouth when you are not speaking," Hamid had told him. When Sidiq was ready, he'd sent Hamid ahead to speak with Amina's brother because Sidiq had no family in Bamiyan. Rashid already knew Hamid, and when he learned that a young man was interested in asking for Amina's hand, his mouth fell open. When he could speak again, he had many questions.

"*Sai'est?* But who is he?"

"He is Sidiq. He works at the clinic keeping records and files. He is a good man, and he has seen Amina."

"How do you mean?" Rashid asked, his voice rising. "Where has he seen her?"

Hamid paused. It wasn't proper for single men to see single women; he had to explain it so Rashid would understand.

"Well, you know that Elsa is very busy and sometimes, she works at her house. Sidiq has seen Amina there." He held his hand over his heart. "It was not improper, let me assure you. But he has seen her and knows of her extra finger. It matters not to him. He would like to ask your permission to marry her."

Rashid folded his arms across his chest.

"Bring him here, then. Let me meet him."

The following morning, Sidiq and Hamid knocked at Rashid's heavy gate. Sidiq's hair was clean, cut, and combed; the *shalwar kamiz* he wore was new; and he wore a genuine though anxious smile.

Rashid bade them enter and after suitable introductions and the obligatory two cups of tea, Sidiq announced his intentions.

"I am here to ask for your blessing and your permission." He paused and breathed noisily. "I know that this is not the custom, but as Hamid told you, my family is in Kabul. I can pay only the small sum of one hundred U.S. dollars. I hope that you will excuse my boldness, accept my offer, and allow me to marry your sister."

He sat back anxiously, wheezing, and waited for Rashid's reply.

To his delight, Rashid smiled broadly.

"*Balay,* yes, of course," he shouted almost gleefully. He rose and took Sidiq into his arms, planting a kiss on each side of his face.

Sidiq breathed a heavy sigh and his voice rose.

"*Besiar tashakore,* brother, *besiar tashakore.*"

Rashid rushed to tell his sister of her betrothal.

"My dear, the young man Sidiq from the hospital has asked to marry you and I have said yes," he announced happily. "You are excited, yes?"

"*Balay,* brother, *balay!*" She clapped her hands, and Rashid spoke again.

"I have set the date for three weeks from today so that Sidiq's family might have time to travel from Kabul."

The preparations were elaborate. Sidiq would pay for the marriage feast and arranged for a goat to be slaughtered the night before the celebrations. Half would be given away to penniless villagers, and the rest would be roasted over an open fire for the guests.

Rashid purchased the remaining food, rice with carrots and raisins and beans, all of which would be cooked at his house before the feast. Rashid's wife and female neighbors would also prepare fresh yogurt, and the Bamiyan bakery would bake the *naan* and special cakes.

Sidiq, flush with his own good fortune and hoping to impress his family, rented a small generator from the cassette store as well as a string of twinkling lights. A tape player and cassettes were borrowed for the event, and the village buzzed at the prospect of such a celebration.

Everyone hoped to be invited to the festivities, and most would be. Elsa, Parween, Hamid, Laila, Ezat, and the entire clinic staff would be there.

"I would like to invite your friends the soldiers," Sidiq announced. "Do you think they will come?"

"Well, if I get a chance, I'll ask them," Elsa responded. She wasn't sure if Mike would come; she hadn't seen him in over two weeks, since the day he'd brought the child to the clinic. She wasn't sure if he was off in another firefight or if he just didn't want to see her.

Unable to concentrate on her work, Elsa breathed a sigh of relief the morning she heard a jeep pull into the clinic drive. She knew without looking who it was, and she hurried to the gate.

Mike was covered in dust and dirt, his hair unkempt and a new beard sprouted along his jawline. Fatigue was evident in the slump of his shoulders, but the sparkle in his blue eyes was as bright as the day she'd seen him lift young Syed onto his shoulder. Her heart quickened at the sight of him.

"Oh, Mike, it's so good to see you. I was worried." She tugged nervously at her head-scarf.

Mike's face brightened. "I thought you might not want to see me so I stayed away. I even volunteered for another assignment."

Elsa felt her own shoulders sag. "I was worried that *you* might not want to see *me*." She looked around and then took his hand. "Come sit on the wall with me. I need to tell you something."

"Elsa." His eyes darkened as she spoke. "If you want to tell me it's over, just say it here."

"No, Mike, that's not it at all." She pulled herself onto the wall and patted the place beside her.

Mike leaned warily against the heavy stones, his feet kicking at loose gravel. "Just so we're straight on one thing, Elsa, I'm a soldier—at least for now. I won't be apologizing for that."

"Oh, Mike, I don't want *you* to apologize. I need to. I . . . I'm sorry, really sorry. I know you're a good man, a good *soldier*. I was so damn mad that day when you said you'd shoot Hamid if you had to, I couldn't get past those words. I didn't take the time to try to understand what it must be like for you." She adjusted her head-scarf and looked into his eyes. "I should have asked if you'd *save* Hamid, if you'd *protect* him from the Taliban, as well."

"You know I would, Elsa. I'm a soldier. I'm here to get the bad guys but I'm also here to protect the good guys."

She sighed, relief washing over her. Deep down, she'd known that would be his answer.

"But," he said, "I *am* still a soldier. Can you live with that? For now?"

She wanted to kiss him, but there were people around, so she kissed her own fingertip and drew it across his lips. "I can learn," she answered, "I can learn."

Mike smiled broadly. "I have to tell you, I was afraid to come here. Dave made me, told me to get off my sorry ass and just see you. I'm going to have to buy that man a beer one day."

"Well, you can't buy beer here, but would he settle for tea? Amina is getting married, and we're all invited. I hope you'll come—you and Dave."

"I wouldn't miss it. I gotta go back and clean up, but I'll see you real soon, Elsa."

She felt as though she were floating. She knew *he* was still in danger, that he still saw everyone and everything here differently than she did, and she also knew he would shoot if he had to. But after her run-in with the men on the road, she kind of understood why he saw things differently. Somehow, she'd learn to live with the rest.

With wedding plans in motion, Rashid's little house underwent a startling transformation. Separate rooms were set up for men and women, who would celebrate apart from one another. The house was swept and dusted, sleeping pads were washed, chickens and goats were shooed outside, and special plates and cups were rubbed till they shone.

The day before the wedding, Elsa and Parween washed Amina's flowing hair and prepared a warm bath for her. She sat in Elsa's little washroom and scrubbed off the years of grime that she had worn like an extra layer of skin. She slathered Elsa's creams and lotions over her body and then generously sprayed herself with perfume.

Elsa and Parween stood just outside the washroom and were overpowered by the scents that wafted out. Parween shouted, "Enough, *bas,* they can smell you in Mashaal!"

The three women were joined by Amina's sister-in-law and two cousins, who set about painting the traditional henna design on her hands and feet. They stained her skin in delicate orange-brown scrolls that would remain there for weeks, marking her as a newly-wed.

The women sat and shared tea, laughter, bawdy stories, and jokes about the marriage act.

"If his member is as big as that nose of his, you're in for a long night!" Parween declared, and they all howled with delight. Finally, Amina was ready for the next day's ceremonies and when the moon was high, she said good night, kissed her friends and family, and retired to her room for her last night alone.

At the first hint of morning, even before the call to prayer, Amina rose to prepare tea, but Elsa had gotten there first.

"Go back to bed! Today you are my guest!" she said, shooing Amina from the room. Not long after, Parween and the women of the family arrived to help with the final preparations. They surrounded the bride and brushed and wove her hair into a magical mix of bun and braid. They added plastic flowers and glittery barrettes to hold it in place, and when they stepped back, Amina carefully touched the creation. For the first time in her life, she seemed unaware of her extra finger.

Elsa and Parween, who were allowed to apply the bride's makeup, stepped up for their turn. Each woman took her time applying the powders, colors, and creams that would transform Amina. They saved the best for last and everyone in the room leaned in to watch as the lipstick was applied.

Elsa wiped the bride's lips clean and Parween dusted them with a hint of powder. Elsa took a tube of shiny red lipstick and applied the first coat of color. Amina was instructed to press her lips together to spread the color, and then Parween applied the second coat. They stood back and—pleased with themselves—let the color set before Parween took a tube of clear gloss and swiped it over Amina's lips, creating a sheer, glassy film over her now perfectly colored mouth.

They stood back; every woman in the room muttered "ahh," and they all rushed to put on the remaining colors. Many of the women lined up so that Parween and Elsa could work their lipstick magic. Elsa glanced at Parween, who was busily swiping color over an old woman's thin lips. The woman peered at her own reflection and grinned broadly. Elsa turned to the next woman and began to apply a bright swath of pink. The young woman giggled and held her hand over her mouth.

"Ohh, we are all so beautiful," she exclaimed. "Even Allah must be smiling today." A ripple of laughter erupted in the room.

"Allah is surely smiling," Elsa replied, "seeing us here, new friends and old, sharing lipstick."

The women busied themselves with the lipstick and when the bridal dress arrived, they exclaimed again. Although the dress was old and well-worn, it was exquisite, and today it belonged to Amina. She stepped into the delicate white fabric, dotted with beads and sparkles, and ran her hands slowly along the garment.

Sidiq's mother, Farah, arrived and kissed Amina repeatedly.

"You are an angel, a beauty. I am happy to have you as my daughter." She spoke in the same whiny, raspy voice that Sidiq had and smiled in the same gentle way.

Amina, whose own mother had died when she was a child, smiled at her new mother-in-law. When Farah stepped forward to lay the gossamer white veil on her head, Amina's eyes filled with tears. Rashid's wife stepped in and knelt to slip the bride's feet into the shiny, white patent-leather high heels that so many other brides in Bamiyan had worn. The shoes didn't always fit, but on Amina they were perfect, and she wiggled her toes happily.

Elsa took out her mirror and held it so the bride could see herself. Surely, there had never been a prettier bride in all of Bamiyan. A smile spread across Amina's bright lips and she held the mirror closer as if searching for some hint of her former self. But there was none. The bride who looked back was an image of pure loveliness.

There were tears in her eyes when she looked at Elsa and Parween. "Thank you," she said in perfect English. Elsa and Parween each kissed the bride and stepped back.

Elsa walked to Rashid's compound to see if all was set for the wedding. As a foreign woman, she was allowed to mix with the Afghan men, and she would be the only guest who could join in both the men's and women's festivities. She saw Mike and Dave standing just inside the compound, speaking with Hamid, and she warmed at the image of the two uniformed soldiers, sidearms in full view, drinking tea and talking.

Mike noticed Elsa and raised his tiny cup in greeting. Not allowed to touch each other in public, today they would be content with smiles and nods. Even dancing would be women with women and men with men. Elsa had laughed when she'd seen Mike and Dave's expressions when she told them they might have to dance together.

"Not me," Mike had declared. "I'm saving *all* of my dances for you."

Dave piped up as well. "I may love him like a brother, but I sure as hell won't be doin' the fox-trot with him any time soon."

Elsa winked at Mike as she passed by. She strode around a group of men rotating the blackened goat over a blazing fire, the pungent smell low in the air. Another group of men tended the enormous platters of rice. A table filled with large loaves of *naan* and plates of cookies and cakes drew her eye. Another smaller table displayed plates filled with fresh yogurt and slices of sweet melon.

Elsa spied Rashid and hurried to let him know that his sister was ready. He asked Elsa to escort Amina and the lady guests to the central women's room so that the celebration could begin. Elsa heard the first strains of the gay Afghan wedding music as she headed back out through the gate.

She returned to her house and announced that it was time. A large swath of fabric was thrown over the bride so that no one would see her as she made her way.

Once they arrived in the women's room, Amina's covering was removed and she was ushered to a seat of honor, high on several velvet pillows. There, she would watch the festivities, and the women would take turns sitting by her side, offering her food and drink and marital advice. Though she'd attended many weddings in her lifetime, Amina told Elsa she'd never been allowed to sit too near the bride for fear of somehow tainting the celebration with the sight of her loathsome extra finger.

Today, the seat of honor was hers alone. Elsa and Parween sat by her side and whispered soothing words.

"Sidiq will be a good husband to you, Amina," Elsa said softly.

Parween chimed in with her own good wishes for many sons. Amina sat in wide-eyed silence. After a while, Elsa patted Amina's hand and excused herself so that she could check on the men's party.

Music and laughter blared from the men's room as Elsa knocked and slipped in. There was much guffawing and slapping of the groom's back while the married men shared their own conjugal bed secrets.

"If her hair falls to her waist, then your pleasures will be endless. Shorter hair means shorter pleasures." They all laughed in reply.

Elsa arrived and stood at Mike's elbow and asked how they were doing.

"Well, if you got the beer, I think I'm just about ready." She longed to kiss him, but that would have to wait. Instead, she turned to scan the crowd for Sidiq.

She spotted him surrounded by the men of the family, and they quickly parted to let her through. Standing there with family and friends, he almost looked handsome. His hair was cut, washed, and coaxed into place; his new white *shalwar kamiz* was spotless; and in the elevated shoes he'd borrowed, he was noticeably taller. He exuded self-confidence—and the strong scent of cheap cologne. He smiled when he saw Elsa.

"My dear friend," he gushed. "Blessings on you for your hand in this glorious day. I will always remember your kindness to my wife and me."

Elsa held her hand over her heart and wished him many sons and a long life. She nodded and salaamed and backed away from the group, returning to Dave and Mike.

"Well, what do you think?" she asked. "Not like weddings at home, huh?"

Dave smiled wryly.

"I don't know, I think my wedding might have been like this, except we all drank more liquor than we needed! Wish they had some today."

Mike just laughed and raised his cup of tea in a toast.

For Mike and Dave, the wedding was more than a social occasion. It was an opportunity to mingle with the villagers and pick up bits of information. Just by listening patiently, they'd learned of more villages used as hideaways for the enemy—Ghazni to the south, Fardeen and Sattar to the north.

"If this information is reliable—" Mike held his hand up to Dave's questioning glance.

"I know what you're going to say. I know it came from one old man, and I know half our intel is bad—hell, more than half. And I know everything we've heard today is likely just old-man gossip, but maybe it's not. It's worth checking out anyway. And if it's good, we could team up with Bagram and attack these guys where they live. Really take them out. It could be the fight we've been looking for." Dave nudged Mike in warning, and Mike turned to see Elsa. Mike forced a nervous smile, clearly hoping she hadn't heard. God knows she had enough problems with their work there, and the less she knew the better off they'd all be. She stood beside Mike, and he inhaled her clean, soapy scent.

God, she's just beautiful, he thought.

Elsa clapped to the music as the men danced, each trying to outdo the other with fancy footwork and elaborate twirls. The excitement was contagious and soon, everyone was dancing or clapping.

When it seemed to Mike as if the dancing would go on forever, there was an announcement that it was time for the marriage ceremony, and Sidiq, Rashid, and the male family members left the room.

Elsa, Mike, and Dave were invited to witness the ceremony, in which Rashid would stand beside his sister as she married Sidiq. The words of prayer were spoken softly—too softly to make anything out—and once they were muttered, the Koran was passed over their heads.

Then a veil was held over the couple's heads as a mirror was passed in.

"What's going on?" Mike asked Elsa.

"They're having their first married look at one another," she whispered, still watching.

Within minutes the veil was removed, and Amina and Sidiq were pronounced husband and wife. Sidiq took his wife's hand and led her to the dining room.

Elsa brought the news to the women's room, and once she'd announced that Amina was now a bride, the women trilled their delight.

Rahima had already arrived with the two children, and Elsa greeted them all.

"Essa, Essa," Zahra shouted as she ran to Elsa, her arms outstretched. Elsa scooped her up and danced around the room. Zahra screeched in pleasure and reached for her mother, who joined them in the dance. Rahima and baby Raziq joined the festivities as well, and they all danced together before sitting for the sumptuous meal.

The platters of food were laid out and the women were encouraged to eat their fill. The female guests swarmed the food table where, for some of them, years of hunger would be sated this night.

In the bride's dining room, Amina sat by Sidiq and they were served by their guests. Elsa returned there and filled a plate high with the bride's favorites, roasted goat and rice and piles of the sweet cookies and cakes. Amina smiled, enjoying every morsel and every bit of attention. Once the celebration ended, Elsa knew Amina would add

Sidiq to her list of responsibilities. But the celebration would thankfully go on for hours.

Elsa looked around for Mike, and when she saw him heading to the gate, he waved her over.

"Elsa, we're leaving."

"I'm so glad you came," she said, taking his hand.

"I wish I could kiss you right here," Mike whispered, "but we'll just have to settle for a rain check." He winked. "I'll see you soon though."

Elsa felt weak at the knees and said good-bye. Not long after they'd left, she found Parween.

"Have you seen Amina? She's positively glowing," Elsa gushed.

"Yes, I was in the courtyard when Sidiq took her hand and caressed her extra finger. Amina's eyes teared and she smiled so, I thought she'd burst with joy." With that, Parween lifted her sleeping baby and held him closer. "You are glowing as well. Mike?"

Elsa's hand flew to her face. "Yes, thanks to you."

Parween kissed her friend's cheek. "It is time for us to be going also," she announced.

"Good night, my friend," Elsa said.

"Shab bokhai, rafiq è man," Parween replied.

26

With Amina in her husband's house, Elsa would live alone again, and while she wasn't worried, others were. Hamid planned to rehire the *chowkidor,* but he hadn't been able to locate the old doorman just yet. And Mike also wanted to provide some security.

Because of the myriad social taboos in Afghanistan, however, he couldn't be seen entering Elsa's house alone and remaining for any length of time, for fear that she would be dangerously branded a whore—or worse, targeted as a spy.

The morning after the wedding, Elsa rose and went into the little kitchen that had always been Amina's domain. She gathered her cup and jar of instant coffee and searched for a box of matches to light her morning cooking fire.

She looked about, searching in all the corners, and then her eyes fell on a piece of blue fabric. Hanging on a hook banged into the mud wall was Amina's indigo-colored *burqa,* seldom worn and now abandoned.

Elsa remembered how her own *burqa* had provided her safety when she'd worn it to Mashaal. *Invisible,* she thought; it had made her invisible.

She wondered if it might not do the same for Mike, and she held the fabric out for closer inspection. Amina was taller than both Elsa and Parween, and her abandoned cloak just might be the solution to their dilemma. If she could convince him to take off his boots and shroud himself in the folds of the *burqa,* he might be mistaken—at least at a distance at night—for a woman.

Hamid appeared early that morning, and they set off through the irrigation fields. Elsa, hoping she'd see Mike, carried the *burqa,* which she'd wrapped securely in paper. Along the way, they shared stories from the wedding celebration.

"Sidiq and Amina make a fine couple, yes?" Hamid smiled proudly. As the one who'd brokered the marriage, he felt invested in their future—almost like a brother to Sidiq.

They arrived at the clinic and there, idling just outside, was Mike's jeep. Dave sat in the passenger seat, his blond hair glistening in the sun. His pistol was strapped securely to his belt, and another handgun, fastened to his ankle, peeked out from under his pant leg. The sight of the weapons reminded her once again that their mission here—the details of which they never shared—was far more dangerous than she'd ever imagined.

Dave smiled as she approached the jeep. "Hey there," he drawled. "Late night, huh? You look beat."

"Thanks, that's what every girl wants to hear," she replied. "It *was* a late night but it was fun. I'm so glad I had the chance to see a wedding here, aren't you?"

Dave smiled wanly. "It reminded me of how much I miss Lisa and the kids. It's been almost a year since I've seen them."

He shook his head and pulled out their pictures, always in the pocket nearest his heart and long faded from handling.

She reached out and touched his sleeve. "Soon," she said. "You have only, what, two months left?"

Dave grinned broadly and replied, "You got it, doll, just two months and I am Bagram bound."

She smiled and asked if Mike was with him.

"Mike's *always* with me. Jeez, I spend more time with him than I ever spent with Lisa."

"Lucky you," Elsa said. "I wish I had more time with him."

"You're pretty much alone in that house right now. I'm sure you two can work something out. I know for a fact that Mike is hoping for some time with you," Dave said with a wink.

Glancing around to make certain no one was near, Elsa told Dave about her idea.

"Could work," he said. "Could work."

At that moment, Mike strode toward them and from their expressions, he knew they were up to something.

"What's up?" he inquired. "You two look like you're scheming."

He listened as Elsa told him about the *burqa*.

"Lord knows I done crazier things than that," he said, and chuckled. "You got this *burqa* with you?"

Elsa handed him the small package. "I'll see you tonight then?" she asked.

"Most definitely. I'll be there at seven sharp. Make sure that you're at the gate so I don't have to talk. There's not a woman anywhere who ever sounded like me—at least I hope not!"

At that, he leaped into the jeep and drove off in another cloud of dust.

Elsa rushed through her day, sending Sidiq home early to be with his new wife.

"Burro, burro," she commanded the smiling groom. "Enjoy some time with Amina." Then she rushed home as well, stopping only long enough to let Parween know she wouldn't be coming for dinner.

Parween smiled and nodded her understanding.

"I wish you a happy evening," she said with a knowing smile.

Elsa arrived home before four o'clock and threw herself onto her sleeping pad to take a nap before Mike arrived. She woke after an hour and stepped into her washroom to prepare for the evening, bathing and then rubbing her skin with the cream she'd loaned Amina for her wedding.

Elsa stood in front of her mirror and combed her hair, letting it hang loose at her shoulders. Daydreaming about the evening ahead, she took out her lipstick and lazily drew the soft pink color across her lips. Pulling on a bright green dress that she'd had made in the bazaar, she next donned the oversize pants that were now a part of every outfit she wore.

Draping her veil across her shoulders, she headed to the kitchen.

Rashid had sent over some of the leftover wedding food, so she gathered it up and set the floor for dinner. She had two forks and knives so at least they could eat with utensils. She wished she were serving steak and wine, but tonight they would settle for goat with rice and beans. She hoped that Mike's mind—like hers—wasn't on food.

She checked her watch. It was almost seven. She went to the main gate and opened it slightly. Within minutes, she heard the now familiar sound of an army jeep as it approached and then quickly sped away. She poked her head out and saw a tall figure, hunched over, clad in the indigo *burqa,* coming her way.

She pulled the tall gate open and Mike scurried in. Neither could hold back their laughter and they fell giggling into each other's arms.

Mike stepped back and pulled the *burqa* over his head, and it was then that Elsa noticed that he still had his boots on. He saw the concerned look on her face and piped up.

"I just couldn't wear sandals. I need my boots, honey. No one's around and I know that no one saw me."

Smiling warily, she led him to their little feast. They sat cross-legged on the floor and picked at the food before deciding they weren't really hungry after all. Their impatience hung in the air; they'd waited so long to be alone, and now they could only stare at each other.

Elsa sighed and gazed at Mike, who finally took a deep breath and pulled her to him.

"Oh, sorry, wait a minute," Mike said as he pulled away, unholstered his gun, and laid it beside him on the floor. Then he reached down and unstrapped a smaller pistol from his ankle. He sat back up and smiled.

Elsa felt a surge of relief to see him remove his weapons, a soldier no more—at least not tonight.

"Now I'm ready," he said as she led him to her room.

They fumbled with belts and buckles and buttons, and once they were both free of their clothes, they fell into a deep embrace. At Mike's touch, Elsa's body came alive. Her skin burned, her nerves on fire. The feel of his skin, as coarse as it was, rubbing against her own smoothness was almost too much to bear.

His tongue probed her lips and mouth and then down to explore her hidden parts. She thought she would burst with pleasure. She stroked his thighs and arms and when he lifted himself on top of her, the weight of him was as welcome as a blanket in winter.

Could this be happening to me? She was almost afraid to let herself trust Mike completely and let this moment take her where it would. When she finally gave herself up to him, the thrill of their coming together dissolved all of her doubts, and she knew this was meant to be. She wished the night would go on forever.

Immersed in passion as they were, Elsa had no idea how long their lovemaking lasted, but eventually they lay back and she let the happiness play over her. Though sated, they weren't sleepy, so they stayed up and—in between moments of renewed passion—talked about their dreams for the future.

"Now that I've met you, I'm not letting you go. So . . . what do you say? Maybe, when we get home, we spend some time together, and then, once I'm out of the army, we look into working somewhere as a team." Mike ran his fingers along Elsa's bare shoulder, and her skin tingled.

"Ohh, Mike, that sounds wonderful. Maybe we could go to Rwanda, or, well . . . anywhere they need us."

"I'll follow you anywhere, Elsa. Absolutely anywhere." His voice melted to a whisper, and pulling her close, he kissed her.

They lay together and finally, as light filtered into the room and the haunting sounds of the call to prayer rippled through the morning air, they fell asleep in each other's arms. By the time Elsa woke, Mike had slipped out and taken the *burqa* with him. She turned and ran her hand over the spot where he had lain. His scent still lingered in the air, and reluctantly, she rose and heated water for her coffee.

She could barely think as she absentmindedly poured the coffee and watched it spill over the brim of her cup. Smiling at her sudden ineptness, she climbed up to the roof to watch the village come to life. There, in the pale light of morning, the village seemed different somehow. It was softer, more peaceful. But then again, maybe it was her and not the village after all.

Her doubts had faded away. She loved this man.

27

While Elsa's life was filled with moments of pure bliss, Parween's was filled with worry.

Her beloved uncle Abdullah was dying.

Although he'd suffered from TB for many years, Elsa's diagnosis seemed to send his disease into overdrive. His once-hardy frame shriveled with each passing day, and his skin hung in loose folds. Four months after hearing the news, he was almost bedridden and in constant pain from the blood-spewing coughs that wracked his bony chest. He spent his days curled up on his sleeping pad.

His wife hovered over him, and his son Hussein was summoned from a nearby village. Only Parween seemed intent on fighting the disease.

"Uncle, please don't just give up," she'd begged. "We can try to get to Kabul as Elsa advised. Please, Uncle, please." There were tears in her eyes. She didn't know how she would manage without him.

Abdullah pulled himself up to a sitting position and hacked a cough that filled the room. He wiped his mouth with his scarf and sat back.

"Oh, my little Parween, it seems that only yesterday you were the tiny girl who arrived from Onai." He smiled at the memory. "Come, little one." He wrapped her in his skeletal arms. "You remember how angry you were then?" His breathing, heavy and slow, demanded great effort, and his words came out in short bursts. "You wanted adventure, not the veil, but you did as you were told, and Allah has taken care of you."

He paused again to cough, a cough that seemed to tear out his insides. He fell back onto the cushions.

"Little one, it is up to Allah. I am in his hands now."

Abdullah closed his eyes and Parween felt tears sting her own. She was glad of his nap, for he wouldn't see her sadness. This great bear of a man had been reduced to a fading shadow, and for Parween—and those who loved him so—these days were filled with unrelenting sadness.

She sent word to Elsa to come to the house as soon as possible.

Elsa had seen Abdullah several times over the last few months and had witnessed his rapid decline. Though she'd known his disease was in its late stages, she'd worried over its swift progression.

When Elsa arrived at the door, Parween collapsed into tears of grief.

"Oh, Elsa, please *do* something. Don't let him die, not yet. Please."

Elsa asked where he was and, with Parween by her side, walked softly into his room. The rattle in Abdullah's chest made such a racket it roused him from sleep.

"Oh, my dear Elsa," he whispered with difficulty as she examined him.

"Don't speak, Uncle," Elsa said as she sat by his side. She took out her stethoscope and listened to his heart and lungs. When she was finished, she sighed heavily and sat back, patting Abdullah's hand.

"The TB has progressed, and his heart seems to be affected now as well. It's not pumping as well as it should, and that's why he's swollen and short of breath. I think we can give him some medicine to strengthen his heartbeat at the hospital and take out the extra fluid. With less swelling his breathing will likely be easier. It's worth a try."

Elsa paused and turned to Parween. "Did he understand my Dari? Will he go?"

Parween whispered to Abdullah, who took Elsa's hand and muttered, "*Balay,* yes. Of course, I will go with you."

His son hooked up a little cart to the family's donkey and they all helped settle Abdullah there as comfortably as possible. Elsa and Parween walked next to the cart as it traveled the dusty road to the hospital. When they arrived, Elsa went to find a staff member and arrange for a bed. Abdullah refused to go in unless he could walk unaided.

"I'm not dead yet," he said stubbornly as he walked slowly to the entrance.

Elsa found Ezat, and with Parween's help, she explained about Abdullah, his disease, and the medicines she thought he'd need.

Ezat nodded as he listened. "I'll have a look at him. There's a bed in the far room; he can go there."

While Ezat and the staff made Abdullah comfortable, Elsa went back to work. By nightfall, Abdullah's breathing had eased considerably. With some of the extra fluid removed by the medicine, he was able to rest easily. Parween left him with his son by his side and went home to her babies.

Elsa stopped in to see him before she left for the day. He smiled broadly and sat up to greet her. "I believe that Allah sent you to us, Elsa." He took her hand and smiled. "*Inshallah,* I will see you tomorrow."

"You *will* see me tomorrow, Uncle."

Elsa was staying with Parween that night and when she arrived, she passed on the news that he was better. "He's doing so well, Ezat may release him tomorrow."

Parween smiled bravely. "Thank you, dear friend."

She sat to a supper of rice and beans with Parween, Rahima, and the children. Zahra curled herself up by Elsa and swiftly fell asleep. Once supper was finished, Elsa pulled out her own sleeping pad. She was tired; she just wanted to sleep.

"Wake me when the rooster crows, Parween, and we can go to check on Uncle Abdullah."

"*Shab bokhai,* good night, Elsa," Parween whispered.

The next morning, Ezat declared Abdullah well enough to leave the hospital. "The fluid will return, but for now he is well enough to go home. He can take his pills there."

Abdullah shook Ezat's hand and walked out of the hospital. With help, he pulled himself onto the donkey, where he sat for the trip home.

Within days of his homecoming, Abdullah was as short of breath as ever. Despite the medicines, the tuberculosis continued to gnaw at his lungs and swallow his life. He took again to his bed, but he remained calm, calling family members to his side for a final good-bye.

Parween cried and refused to say good-bye, so Abdullah spoke.

"Elsa is your true friend, little one. Take care of her, keep her safe. It is Allah's wish." Once Abdullah had dispensed with his good-byes, he lay back peacefully.

Parween stayed by his side. When his breathing slowed or rattled, she rubbed his chest and whispered, "Breathe deeply, Uncle, breathe deeply." And when she spoke, his breathing seemed to ease, and he would rest for a bit until the fluid in his lungs swelled up and caused him to choke again and again.

It went on like that for another day until finally, Parween's whispers and gentle touches were not enough. He slipped away quietly in the deep of a moonlit night while Parween and the family slept.

When Parween woke and went to check on him, she thought at first that the quiet meant his breathing had improved.

"Uncle," she called, "are you feeling better?"

But there was no reply and when she reached him, she saw that his skin was gray and it was cool to her touch. He was dead—there was no mistaking it.

Parween felt her heart grow heavy. She cried softly and kissed his hands and face before she summoned the rest of the family.

His wife and son washed him and prepared him for burial. Hussein went to the family cemetery and dug out a place next to Mariam's plot for Abdullah. The family wrapped him in his favorite gray *patou,* a blanket that he'd worn almost every day of his life, to carry him aloft to his resting place.

Elsa and Hamid arrived in time for the prayers and final good-byes. Parween and Rahima held each other tight and cried.

Elsa stood next to Parween and took her hand.

"He is free of pain and suffering. Surely, he is happy now in heaven."

Parween rested her head on Elsa's shoulder.

Hussein announced that he would move back to Bamiyan and take his father's place as head of the household. He sent for his wife and small son, and they traveled from the nearby village where he'd herded sheep for a wealthy landowner. Here in Bamiyan, he would manage the small sheep-tending business his father had developed, and he would manage the family's life, as well.

Although he was a good man, he was not nearly as open-minded as Abdullah had been about the family's women. It rankled Hussein that Parween, widowed then for more than a year, had not been claimed by Raziq's brother. He said it was not right for a woman to stay a widow; it was unseemly and improper.

He summoned Rahima to tell her of his decision.

"We must accept that in these difficult times, Raziq's brother may be dead, but even that does not change the fact that Parween is a young woman and must be married," he stated flatly. "I am a reasonable man, Rahima. Still, I believe that we must follow the custom." He paused and crossed his arms.

"And so," he said, continuing, "I have decided that I will take Parween as my second wife. You know me, Rahima, and you may rest assured that I will care for her as if she were my only wife. It is for the best, and it keeps the family together. I am sure she will agree. Please tell her of my decision."

Rahima stammered her reply.

"I . . . I don't know that Raziq's brother is dead. I don't know what has been arranged." She clasped her shaking hands together. "I will speak to Parween."

Rahima found Parween gathering eggs from their scraggly hen.

"I must speak with you, daughter. Come." She guided Parween to their room, where they could speak privately. She quickly told Parween of Hussein's intent.

Parween felt as though she'd been hit in the chest; she couldn't breathe, she couldn't think. Only one thought swirled in her mind, and she was firm when she spoke it.

"I will *not* be his second wife, or anyone's wife for that matter. How *dare* he?" Her voice dripped with anger. "We are fine. I do not need a man. Mother, you forced me once and I made a wonderful match, but I will not be forced a second time—and to be his second wife. *Aagh!* Tell him I would sooner marry a goat!"

"Calm yourself, Parween. Anger is not the answer," Rahima replied. "I have thought about it. I can tell him that you have had word from Raziq's brother and that he will be coming to claim you as his own wife, but when we do not know. You can say that you hadn't told anyone yet because of Uncle Abdullah's sickness. No one need know that the information is false."

Parween stared at her mother with astonishment.

"You would protect me from this?"

Rahima reached out and stroked Parween's hair. "Yes, child. I remember well the angry little girl who protested her role as a useless female. You did as you were told once. There is no need to force you again." She pulled Parween to her and held her close. "I will tell him. Do not worry. I will keep you safe, my child."

28

Though she was a wife now, Amina still worked for Elsa three or four days a week. She cooked, cleaned, washed clothes, and chatted about her new life. She exuded happiness, cherished all the more, she said, because she had never expected Allah to bless her like this.

She giggled when she spoke of Sidiq, his large nose and his high-pitched voice.

"Oh, Elsa, sometimes I cannot help myself, and I laugh when his voice rises so that I almost think it is a rooster speaking." She paused and put her hand to her mouth. "But I should not speak like that. He is so good, and in spite of my shortcomings, Sidiq is very kind to me. He has told me that he loves me. Can you imagine that, Elsa? He *loves* me."

Amina bent smiling as she worked. Elsa couldn't remember the last time her friend had fidgeted with her extra finger. What the surgeon wouldn't do, Sidiq's love had done instead, and the digit fluttered freely about as she cooked or cleaned or sat to share tea.

Amina did not keep to a set schedule, and she came and went to Elsa's house as she pleased. When she failed to show up for several days, Elsa wasn't worried; she assumed the new bride was still enjoying her time with her husband.

But when Amina finally appeared early one morning after an

absence of several days, she looked gray and wan. Elsa touched her friend's cheek.

"*Che' ast?* What is it?" she asked.

"*Mariz,*" Amina moaned as she fanned herself with a piece of fresh *naan*. The scent of the bread wafted into her nostrils and she suddenly covered her mouth and raced outside to vomit. She wiped her mouth on her sleeve and started to cry.

"*Che taklif?* What is wrong, Elsa? Why am I so sick?"

Elsa smiled and asked Amina when she'd last had her period. It was a few moments before she replied.

"Well, not for a while. Not since I married anyway."

"My friend, you have the classic signs. We won't be certain for perhaps another month or so, but I think you're pregnant."

"*Sai'est?*" Amina asked incredulously. "I might be with child?" She looked toward the heavens. "Allah, the Most Merciful, thank you for your kindness." And she retched again, but this time she smiled between heaves. Elsa waited quietly until she was done, and then she spoke.

"I think that you should tell Sidiq this evening. And take care of yourself. No need to work so hard here. Go home and rest. I'll see you when your retching has stopped."

Amina held up the laundry. "But I have washing to do, Elsa. I cannot go."

"You *must*. I had planned to go with Parween to the washing stream today. I've wanted to go for a while. Now at least I have laundry to bring. Go *home*." She tried to sound firm.

Amina placed the laundry back into Elsa's basket and put her veil back on her head.

"Thank you, Elsa." Amina's smile lit up her whole face.

Elsa piled her remaining laundry into the basket and set off for Parween's house. It was Friday, and she'd finally learned to enjoy her free time in Bamiyan. But there'd be no picnic today. Mike was in Bagram, and she planned to spend the day with Parween. The day was warm, the sky clear, the fields lush with sprouting wheat and potatoes as she walked with a spring to her step. It was September. It was hard to believe she'd already been there for six months.

The neighborhood children saw Elsa and followed. Seema, Bouman, Noori, Hussein, Syed, and Assadullah shouted all at once.

"Salaam alaikum. Chetore asti? Khoob asti? Jona jurast?" They giggled and ran to keep up. "Elsa, Amina is married, yes?" She smiled and nodded. The children giggled. "Then, you are next?"

Elsa laughed. "*Mumkin,* maybe," she replied. They ran off through the fields, pocketing dung as they went.

The compound was quiet when Elsa arrived at her friend's house. Parween greeted her and held her finger to her lips.

"The children and my mother are sleeping, so it is just you and I today," she said. She gathered up her own laundry, and they headed up the dirt road to the stream.

"I think Amina is with child," Elsa said, almost whispering. "She has the signs, at least."

"It is true? How wonderful for her. I remember how happy I was each time that I was pregnant. These are good days for Amina."

They turned from the road through a cluster of trees, and there Elsa saw women scattered about the bank of a swiftly moving stream. She walked to the water's edge and squatted down, placing her basket on the ground. Parween bent next to her and pulled out her own laundry. There was a smattering of greetings as they joined the women.

"Salaam alaikum," Parween called out. "This is my friend Elsa, the nurse at the clinic."

The women turned and smiled, some looking curiously at Elsa, while others recognized her and greeted her warmly.

"Salaam alaikum." Elsa smiled as she looked at the women in turn.

"She does her own laundry?" a weathered old woman asked Parween.

"*Balay,* she is like us." Parween raised her brows and looked directly at the woman who had asked the question.

"Tell her we are happy to meet her." The words from a smiling young woman broke through the sudden chill in the air.

"Ask her if she'll do my wash," the old woman cackled as she patted Elsa's hand and smiled.

Elsa, chuckling, bent to the icy water and removed the small bar of soap from her pocket. She pulled out her first bit of laundry and splashed it into the frigid current, scrubbing as she moved it up and down. It wasn't long before her fingers ached from the cold and the wet, and she leaned back on her feet and sighed.

"This is hard work, *really* hard. My fingers are frostbitten." She shook the water from her hands and dried them on her dress.

The old woman nudged her and motioned with her own hands, blowing on them and rubbing them together. Elsa followed suit and then plunged them right back into the stream, shivering at the cold.

Before long, Parween laughed. "You are almost finished. So little laundry you have you are lucky not to have to do washing for an entire family. Just hang it on the trees to dry, and then we will sit."

Elsa hurried, and when she was done with her own clothes, she helped Parween finish as well. This was why she had come, after all, to spend the day with the women, to listen to their stories and their gossip. She squeezed the water from the last of the laundry and draped it through the trees. Rubbing the warmth back into her hands, she sat down with her friend.

The warm sun shone on Elsa's dress and seeped straight through to her skin.

"Do you ever just fall asleep here?" she asked Parween lazily.

"Ahh, yes. You will see more than one of the women today with her eyes closed. This is the place where we find friendship and laughter and sometimes rest."

But Elsa didn't want to sleep; she wanted to hear the gossip. She sat up straight as the chatter began.

"Noma gave birth to a three-eyed baby," a sweet-faced young woman sitting nearby declared. The women chuckled in disbelief and her eyes shone with anger. "It's true," she said petulantly as she folded her arms and pouted.

Elsa reached out and touched her hand and she smiled.

Another young woman, with a tiny baby wiggling in her arms, giggled. "My cousin just gave birth to her twelfth child—another girl! Can you imagine? She would take a three-eyed one if it were a boy!"

A ripple of laughter passed through the women—even the one who had been pouting. Another tiny woman, bent and withered from years at the stream, almost crowed as she spoke.

"Waleed's wife ran off with the tinker. She's selling his wares and her own now."

They all laughed to think that anyone would run away with a tinker, the shriveled old men who sold trinkets from great metal trunks they lugged on their backs from village to village.

"Ah well," Parween added, "maybe she's looking for adventure."

They hooted in reply.

The bent old woman, determined to have their attention, spoke again. "My son has seen the lady rebel. She was riding across that mountaintop." She pointed to the distant Hindu Kush range. "Even now she fights against the Taliban who remain in hiding."

"*Sai'est?* It is true?" Parween asked with rapt attention. They'd all heard the stories, legends really, of the lady rebel, and they all believed that she was a Hazara. "What does she look like?"

"Why, she looks like you, Parween," the old woman replied, her eyes twinkling. "My son says that her dark hair was flying free and her eyes shone like bright emeralds. Her bandolier was strung across her chest and she outrode the men in her little band. He said he never believed in beauty until he saw her ride."

They all sighed and sat back.

"How lucky he was to have seen her," Parween said.

"Lady rebel?" Elsa asked. "Tell me about her."

Parween parted her lips to speak but just then, Soraya appeared, and she jumped to her feet to greet her, kissing her friend's cheeks.

Elsa turned and exclaimed, "Soraya, *salaam alaikum*. We have missed you. How is Meena? She is well?"

"Meena is very well, in school even, and her wounds are healed. She is a little girl again. My family and I are so grateful to you both for your kindness."

Soraya squatted down to embrace her friends. She rested her arms across her chest and heaved a sigh. "But even that happy news does not hide the sadness I feel for you, Parween. I have heard about your beloved uncle Abdullah. I am sorry for your loss, my friend."

Parween, a tinge of sadness in her eyes, sighed and gazed up at the bright blue sky. "Uncle's death is a cloud, a cloud filled with tears and sadness, but behind every cloud, the sun still waits. Today we have had a glimpse of that sun. Meena is safe, and Amina is with child. That happy news reminds me that though a cloud hides the sun, it does not dim its glow."

Elsa smiled and patted Parween's hand. Then she closed her eyes and leaned back, soaking up the sun.

29

"No, Mama, no!"

Zahra shrieked and squirmed and tried to wriggle free of her mother's arms, but she was no match for Parween's determination. Elsa approached with the injection.

"Be still, little one. I'll be quick."

Parween held Zahra tightly as Elsa vaccinated her.

"Hush, child, this will keep you healthy." Parween's voice grew soft.

Zahra's sobs faded as Elsa withdrew the needle. She rubbed her arm and buried her face in her mother's veil. Parween stroked her daughter's forehead and rocked her as they sat in the clinic.

Elsa disposed of the syringe and cleaned the room as she spoke.

"I forgot to tell you, Mike gave me his camera. We can get your pictures done."

"Oh, yes." Parween could hardly contain herself. "A picture like Dave's to carry with me."

Elsa stopped cleaning and turned to Parween.

"Have you seen the signs that the UN has posted?" she asked. "There are finally plans to open a school here."

Parween smiled, and she felt a rush of excitement.

"I did. I wanted to ask you about it. They are looking for teachers. Do you think that I might be able to teach?"

"*Inshallah,*" Elsa said. Parween marveled at how easily that word slipped from her friend's lips these days. "I think that we should speak to Johann. It will surely be his decision. I can ask, if you'd like."

Parween felt the first stirrings of joy at the possibility of her own children attending school.

School. The very word was magical.

That afternoon, a beautiful late September day, Elsa visited Johann at the UN office. She'd asked him more than once about opening a school, and she'd told him about Parween's desire to teach. She rapped her knuckles against the UN's metal gate and heard Johann's footsteps as he hurried to open it.

"Hello, hello, Elsa. How are you? Come in, come in." He pushed his eyeglasses up and squinted through them.

"Johann, it's good to see you. I was excited to hear the news and had to come ask about it." She waved one of the notices at him to emphasize her words.

"Ahh, the school. It is good, yes?"

"It is *wonderful!* Just what the children need. Do you still need teachers? Have you hired any yet?"

She followed him into his office, where he pulled out his ledger and searched the pages.

"Ahh, there was one young man, but he is no longer available, so yes, I need teachers."

"That's why I've come today. I've told you about my friend Parween—I'm sure you've seen her with me—she can count and read and write. She even speaks English. She would be an ideal candidate, and she would love to teach the children." Elsa paused to catch her breath. "Do you think there might be a place for her? Do you want to meet her? I could bring her tomorrow."

"Yes, yes, of course, bring her here." Johann scribbled something in his book and closed it. "Please ask her to come tomorrow."

"I'll tell her to come in the afternoon then. Thank you, Johann. You won't be sorry." Elsa waved to him as she passed through the gate and hurried to share the news with her best friend.

* * *

"It is true? He wants to speak with *me*?"

"Yes, tomorrow. I'll go with you if you'd like."

Gratitude glimmered in Parween's eyes. "Oh yes, please." She was full of excited energy and didn't know what to do next. "Tomorrow, then. I'll wait for you at the hospital in the afternoon."

But she'd still have to be hired by the man from the UN, she knew, and eager to make a good impression, Parween set out for the bazaar to purchase a new veil. She chose a drab brown one, a color that would surely prove she was serious, the type of woman who would be a good teacher. At least that was what she hoped it would say.

"Ooh, beautiful," Rahima said when Parween returned home.

Parween held up one of the UN flyers. "They're going to open schools here, Mama. *Schools!* Elsa has arranged it so that I can apply for a teaching position, and tomorrow, I have an appointment to speak with the UN. The *UN,* Mama. Can you believe it?"

"A *teacher.*" Rahima smiled and kissed Parween's cheek.

The following day, with her new veil covering her hair and Elsa at her side, Parween presented herself at the UN office. Elsa knocked at the gate, and once they were inside, she made the introductions.

Johann reached out his hand absentmindedly, before he remembered that tradition and custom prevented him from touching Parween.

"Oh, miss, I'm sorry," he said as he held his right hand over his heart.

Parween smiled. The man seemed more nervous than she was.

"Not to worry, sir," she said in her best English. "It is good to meet you."

"Your English is very good," Johann said, looking pleased. He invited them into his office and pulled out his ledger, writing as he spoke.

"Do you have a second name?" he asked, his pen poised over a page.

Parween hesitated. She'd never really used her own second name,

Saleh—she could hardly remember it. But she wanted Raziq to be with her and so she said softly, "Khalid. Khalid, my husband's second name."

"Well, Miss Parween Khalid, can you read and write?"

Parween nodded and then asked for a pen and paper. Johann passed her his ledger book and a pen.

"Write your full name there, if you will be so kind."

Parween's fingers drew the pen along the paper and scrolled out her name in Persian script, and then again in English letters.

"Shall I write your name?" she asked.

"Yes, please." When she had done so, he looked at the results appreciatively. "Can you do numbers?"

Parween wrote numbers in both English and Persian. "Shall I add them for you?"

"No, there's no need." Johann removed his eyeglasses and wiped them on his shirt. After a moment, he asked her the question she hadn't dared to hope for.

"Would you like to teach for us?"

"Oh, yes!" Parween clasped her hands together, and Johann wrote her name in his ledger. Her heart started to beat faster. A *teacher,* she would be a teacher.

Oh, if only Raziq were here.

"Very good, very good. But, well . . ." He paused and pushed his eyeglasses back on his nose. "You know how these things go; there is a small delay."

Parween's heart sank.

Johann continued. "I was just informed this morning that we shan't be opening the school just yet, but perhaps you can help us in the meantime. We will also be opening a school in Sattar, just north of Bamiyan. Perhaps you know it?" he asked.

Parween shook her head. It was a familiar name, but she didn't think she had ever been there. Johann continued.

"We need someone to have a look around, see if there is a place for a school. Would you be interested in having a look for us?"

"Of course," Parween replied. She *would* be a teacher; she had to be optimistic.

"But"—Johann's voice dropped—"I must check first with Kabul.

There is a monthly report that tells me if there are any problems. I don't think that Sattar has been listed on that report, but I can't be sure. So, I don't need you to go just yet, but perhaps in the next week or so, once I've had a chance to check the information. Could you go then?"

Parween tried to hide her disappointment. "I can go anytime," she said softly.

"Ahh, good. Then it is settled. I will see you next week, then. I should know by then when you should go."

Elsa and Parween left Johann's office and walked in silence, not knowing what to say. Parween stopped at Elsa's house for tea, and Elsa reassured her.

"Don't be disappointed. These things happen. You *are* going to be a teacher."

Parween wrinkled her brow. "I know, and I know he said to wait, but tomorrow's Friday. I could go to Sattar tomorrow. Perhaps then he will see how hard I will work for him. Would you come with me? We could ask Hamid, as well, so that we will have a man with us. I think that if I come back to Johann in a week and show that I have gone ahead and looked at Sattar, he will see that I am a serious person and that I will be a good teacher. What do you think?"

"I think that we should wait as Johann asked. There is no rush, Parween."

"But," Parween replied, "I am *tired* of waiting for men to tell me what to do. Johann said he *thought* it was safe. We don't need a report; we've been to Mashaal and we were fine. And as long as you wear the *burqa,* no one will know you are anything other than a quiet Afghan woman."

Parween paused to glance at Elsa. "We'll be safer still if Hamid will come. We're not staying long—just having a look. I *know* we'll be safe. Please, Elsa, say you'll come."

Elsa sighed. "If you really want to go tomorrow, I'll go with you," she said. "But I think Johann already considers you a serious woman."

But Parween wasn't listening; she was already making plans. "I must disguise myself again. I think it will be easier to ask questions and have a look around Sattar if I am thought to be a young man. And you will wear the *burqa* again. Yes?"

"Yes, I'll do it again—for you." The prospect of a full day in the *burqa* wasn't as exotic now that she knew just how confining it was. But for Parween's sake, and for safety, she would put up with the discomfort for a day.

They decided it would be best to leave from Elsa's house. Parween wanted to avoid the watchful eye of Hussein, who would surely object to her choice of clothing and balk at allowing her to make the trip altogether.

"I think we must leave early, as we did when we traveled to Mashaal. The bus to Sattar will surely depart in the morning. Oh, Elsa, I am so excited. Can you tell?"

Elsa laughed. "I can tell. Right now, though, I'm going to the clinic to find Hamid. I'll see you tomorrow."

These days when she found herself without a companion, she stayed to the main road, where she often ran into people she knew. Today, it was Hamid she saw as she walked along.

"I was just coming to see you, Elsa, to give you the clinic's weekly reports."

"I was looking for you too," she said. "Parween and I are going to Sattar tomorrow to have a look at school sites for the UN. We'd like you to come. Will you?"

Hamid looked intrigued. "Sattar?" he asked. He seemed to be mulling it over. "Sattar? Weren't the Taliban there?"

Elsa's pulse quickened at the mention of the Taliban, but she pushed her uneasiness aside. "I don't think so, and I don't think the UN would be considering a school where Taliban still lurk, do you? Besides, Parween thinks we'll be fine—we traveled together to Mashaal. And if you join us, we'll have the benefit of a man with us."

Hamid relented. "You're probably right. The soldiers have pushed the Taliban farther and farther away. But you *will* need a man to accompany you. Tomorrow's Friday, a good day for a trip, I guess. What time shall we leave?"

"*Tashakore,* Hamid. Be at my house at seven A.M. and we'll catch the early bus. You should know that I'll be wearing the *burqa,* and Parween will be traveling as a boy."

Hamid's brow furrowed. "Why?"

"It will keep all of us safer. We don't want to attract attention. That was how we traveled to Mashaal, and I am certain that no one noticed us. As for Parween, it will be easier for her to ask questions if she is disguised."

"Hmm," he said, as if thinking it over before replying. "See you tomorrow then."

"Yes, we'll see you then," Elsa said. She walked on, but instead of going to the clinic she turned toward the bazaar.

Mike was off somewhere on yet another mission in the countryside, which was just as well since Elsa had no plans to ask him about the trip, but she *did* want to let him know that she'd gone. She squatted by the side of the road and retrieved a pen and piece of paper from her pocket. She scribbled out a note and then folded the paper so many times, it disappeared into its own folds. She buried the paper in her pocket and stopped at a little shop that sold envelopes.

"*Yak,*" she said, pointing to the envelopes in the glass case. She passed the shopkeeper a coin and took the envelope, then reached into her pocket for the note. She scrawled on the envelope—*Mike*— and stuffed the little note inside. She sealed the envelope and started toward the cassette shop. She stood outside and looked around. She wasn't sure what to do next, and she approached the entrance warily. This would be her first "drop," after all, and she wanted to do it right.

Elsa entered the shop, looked around the tiny room full of cassette tapes, and stepped up to the lone clerk. He was a clean-shaven young Afghan wearing headphones, and he sat on a rickety old stool tapping his fingers and feet in time to his music. He quickly rose and removed the earpieces when he noticed Elsa.

"Please, please, may I help?" he inquired.

Elsa hesitated. "Is Majid here?"

"Ahhh," the clerk replied. "It is I, and you must want Dave. Well, as you can see, he is not here, but I expect him tomorrow. Do you have something for him?"

Sensing her uncertainty, he moved closer.

"*Tars na dori,* do not be afraid. You are safe here. I will be sure that only he gets your message." He smiled a warm, comforting smile.

Elsa relaxed and passed the envelope to Majid.

"Thank you, *besiar tashakore*," she said. "I was so nervous. Thank you." And she backed out of the little shop onto the main street of the bazaar.

She could almost imagine Mike walking through this same doorway and picking up her note when he returned to Bamiyan. She pictured him smiling, relieved that she'd used the drop site.

Hurrying from the bazaar, she headed home for a bath and early supper.

30

Early the following morning, Hamid and Parween arrived at Elsa's house.

Clad again in the confining *burqa,* Elsa pulled at the headpiece and complained.

"I thought it would stretch out, but it feels tight as ever. We could make some money if we could change the damn design."

Parween, dressed in the loose and comfortable clothes of a boy, was sympathetic, yet also amused at her friend's plight.

"Now you have a taste of what *we* have endured for generations," she said.

Hamid, unfamiliar with women's clothes and complaints, looked uncomfortable with the talk and went outside to wait. When they were ready, the three friends headed down the road to Bamiyan's center and purchased their tickets, then stood while they waited to board the bus. Once they finally climbed on board, they took seats at the back.

Parween fidgeted with the trailing ends of her turban, then realized her nervousness was showing.

"If I can get a good look around Sattar and maybe even write a report—like you do, Elsa—Johann is sure to be pleased."

Hamid leaned forward and spoke softly.

"I think we should look for Mohammed—you remember him,

Elsa. He's the farmer who was imprisoned with the Taliban, and you paid his ten-dollar debt."

"I do remember him." Elsa smiled. "He was a nice man, and you're right, he was from Sattar. At least he can tell us about the village."

Not wanting to talk on a bus full of strangers, they fell silent. The road was clear of debris, and within the hour, the bus pulled into Sattar. They all gazed out at the unexpectedly bleak landscape.

Parched fields lined the road. Many homes had been reduced to piles of rubble, and the carcasses of dead and rotting animals remained where they had fallen by the side of the road. Unlike in Bamiyan, there hadn't been much in the way of rebuilding the town or replanting the abandoned fields. It was a ghost town. Except there were still people living there. Those people—shopkeepers and villagers alike—watched the visitors warily.

Parween was disappointed. Sattar was a desolate village and not at all what she'd expected.

"It may be too soon for a school here," she said sadly. "They need homes first." Then she steeled herself, looking up one road and down another. "Still, I suppose it's worth a look around and a talk with Mohammed. And besides, I'd like to write a report, at least. I want Johann to have proof that I'm serious."

"You are surely the most serious applicant he's ever had," Elsa replied reassuringly.

Before asking for Mohammed, they decided to investigate a cluster of partially destroyed old buildings they had noticed on the outskirts of town. Hamid approached a shopkeeper in the bazaar.

"Those buildings," he asked, "the ones at the edge of the village, what were they before they were crushed?"

"The large pile of rubble?" The young shopkeeper paused. "Why, I believe that was a school, but the Taliban took a tank to it last year."

Hamid frowned, but Parween was intrigued with what she heard.

The trio stepped into the road and looked around. Parween spoke. "I think we should stop for tea first, perhaps introduce ourselves to people we meet, and see if there's anything to be learned about Sattar." Tea was a means of diplomacy. It was often said that one cup of tea was necessary to introduce yourself, the second for doing business, and the third for friendship.

Hamid nodded his agreement.

A ramshackle tea shop by the bus station was open and beckoning. They went inside and sat cross-legged on a worn carpet. The shopkeeper—a tiny, wrinkled man with a greasy, fraying turban—approached them where they sat.

"My name is Rasoul," he said as he looked them over.

To preserve their deception, they'd agreed that Hamid would do most of the talking. He spoke up and introduced Parween as his young brother and, pointing to Elsa, said that she was his eldest sister.

Rasoul nodded but didn't seem inclined to chat. Shriveled from so many years of service, he padded away to set a kettle to boil, filled with fragrant green tea leaves.

He returned with four china cups and a plate of cookies balanced on a silver tray. He retrieved the kettle with his gnarled hands and poured steaming tea into each of their cups, passing around sugar and milk. His duties performed, he stopped moving and sat to talk. But his manner wasn't welcoming.

"What is your business here?" he asked brusquely. His brow arched as he spoke.

Elsa remained silent and fidgeted with her teacup. Though she cradled it in her hands, she couldn't lift her *burqa,* so she never drank the sweet tea.

Hamid spoke up.

"We have come from Bamiyan. The UN asked us to—" But the sentence hung there, unfinished, as he received a warning nudge from Parween, and suddenly he was nervous, as if afraid that he might give something away.

Parween had been watching Rasoul; there was something unsettling about him. His right eye twitched and watered as he stared intently at each of them in turn. He seemed nervous, rising again and again and looking out through the door of his little shop even as he chatted.

Is he expecting someone? Parween wondered. *Oh, Allah, rid me of my suspicions. This poor old soul is but a simple shopkeeper and here I sit, enjoying his tea and worrying.*

She spoke up. "Our mother has heard that the UN would be coming here to distribute blankets and maybe food. She sent us to see

if perhaps we could be included. We haven't received anything yet."
To demonstrate their neediness, she held out her hands, palms up.

Hamid nodded and spoke.

"I think that we will just look around before we return to Bamiyan and our mother's inevitable questions."

"Such a long way—all for nothing. No, the UN is not here." Rasoul's expression didn't change and his right eye twitched furiously,
fueling Parween's increasing discomfort.

"Well, then," the shopkeeper said as he wiped his hands along
his shirt, "I'm sure you are eager to be on your way. Have a safe trip
home."

His eyes were filmy, and he wiped at them with his grimy hand
before he stepped to the rear of the shop.

He never offered a second cup of tea.

Hamid's questioning glance at Parween was met with a shrug of
her shoulders and a whispered reply.

"I didn't want to say that the UN sent us. It makes us sound
more important than we are." She didn't want to share her uneasy
feelings about Rasoul. There was no real explanation for her con-
cerns about the old man. After a few more moments, when it became clear that there would be no more tea, she stood.

"Let's have a look around."

Old Rasoul watched them. Hamid fished some coins from his
pocket and left them by the tea.

"Thank you, sir, for your kindness," he said as they left the shop,
but his words were met by only a nod and a grunt. They turned and
headed back through the town in search of the old school site.

As they walked, they saw that the outskirts of Sattar were deserted; there were no signs of everyday life. *It is quiet,* Parween
thought, *too quiet.*

"This isn't like Mashaal, is it?" Elsa whispered through the *burqa,*
unease settling in her thoughts.

"No, it surely is not," Parween answered, looking about at the
bleakness of the place.

As they walked back out through the village, a young man with
a matted beard passed by going the other way. Parween glanced at
him, and her blood ran cold.

His eyes seemed to linger on them, yet he never said hello or even nodded in greeting. She felt her skin crawl. Though he wasn't the only unkempt young man around these days, there was something about him.

Why am I so suspicious today? Parween chided herself silently.

Elsa and Hamid seemed not to have even noticed him.

The trio continued to the outskirts and tramped through the ashes, dust, and debris that had once been a school. Parween looked around trying to picture a school sprouting here from the dirt, then spoke excitedly in a mixture of English and Dari.

"It is a good spot, don't you think?" she asked her friends. "The UN could start here with a tent or build a school right where the Taliban destroyed one. That would make a tremendous impression on the people of this village."

Hamid and Elsa agreed, and as they stood and chatted—unprotected by walls or trees—Elsa noticed a lone form striding toward them.

"Someone's coming," she said, pointing to the solitary man.

Parween tensed as the figure approached. Beads of sweat collected on her scalp, and she rubbed at her turban.

Hamid turned and cast a questioning glance to the stranger.

"*Salaam alaikum. Chetore asti? Khoob asti? Jona jurast?*" The stranger raised his hand in greeting, and Hamid recognized Mohammed.

"Mohammed," he called out. "We were going to ask for you. How are you?"

Relief flooded over Parween.

Elsa pulled back the veil of her *burqa* to greet him. "*Salaam alaikum—*" She had only started her greeting when Mohammed reached them and stopped her.

"No, no, cover your face, miss. Take great care. You are surely being watched. There is talk that strangers are here, and that is why I have come. The Taliban are here. If they know that you are a foreigner, then you are all in danger. It is not safe. What were you thinking, coming here to Sattar?"

Elsa's delight at seeing Mohammed paled and her pulse raced. She hurriedly did as he said and pulled the folds of her *burqa* down over her face.

"Taliban? *Here?*" She looked at the others. "What should we do?"

Hamid just stood there, as if unable to speak. Aside from the Taliban prisoners at the clinic, he had never encountered one.

Parween felt a familiar anger burn through her skin. Instinctively, her hand tightened around the knife she'd tucked into her pocket.

"Where are they? They won't show themselves," she hissed. "The cowards."

"Shh, please do not anger them," Mohammed said. He glanced around, fear mirrored in his expression. "I will help you. Just walk with me and as we walk, we can think what to do." He turned to go. His hands and even his voice trembled as he spoke. "Word has passed quickly that there are strangers among us and that they traveled on the bus from Bamiyan. Because everyone knows that the soldiers are in Bamiyan, it will be assumed that the travelers only mean trouble."

"No, no," Parween protested. "We are only here to look for a site for a United Nations school. We don't bring trouble."

"But you *do*," Mohammed insisted. "You know how the Taliban hate education, and they hate foreigners even more. If they know that you are here to teach, they will surely kill all of you." Mohammed was firm.

"Sattar is a dangerous place these days," he continued, his voice so low Parween had difficulty hearing what he said. "I am surprised that you risked your safety to come here. But, *inshallah,* we will get you back to Bamiyan."

Elsa and Hamid fell into step as he guided them along the path. Parween hesitated and, fingering the folding knife hidden in her shirt, looked carefully around. But there was nothing to see. Reluctantly, she stepped in behind Elsa and the four tramped through the rubble in the direction Mohammed led them.

But she didn't *want* to follow. She didn't want to be fearful and skittish like an old woman. Without warning, she stopped.

"Wait," she said urgently. "We don't even know for certain that there is trouble. We can't just give up our plans. Perhaps we should just head back to the bazaar and wait there. At least there are people there, and we can learn if there truly is danger. Maybe we are frightened for nothing."

"No, no," Mohammed replied, his voice shaking. "There will be no help there. This is a Taliban village. You must protect yourselves. Come with me. If we can get to my house, I have a pistol and a wagon. *Inshallah,* I can get you out of here."

Just then, a rustle of movement sounded behind them. Now afraid of everything, Mohammed and the others turned cautiously, but there was nothing to see. The little group turned back to the path and continued along in silence until Mohammed stopped again.

"Shh, do you hear it?" His voice was almost a whisper.

Another rustle of movement reached Parween's ears. Elsa and the others looked back, but she saw only their trembling shadows.

Suddenly, a chill ran along Parween's spine and she held her breath, but this time she heard nothing. Not far away, she saw three figures darting through the trees. One held a Kalashnikov.

A tangled knot of fear exploded in Parween's mind.

The Taliban!

"Run!" someone shouted.

But as the others dashed ahead, Parween hesitated, slowed, and then darted behind the heavy trunk of a tree, her heart racing.

Taliban be damned.

And as quickly as it had appeared, her knot of fear began to unravel.

She was done being afraid. The Taliban had taken enough from her, from her family, from her beloved Afghanistan. She pulled herself up into the tree and settled among the leafy branches. And as she reached for the knife she'd hidden in her front pocket, her fear faded, and she took a long, slow, deep breath.

31

Dave and Mike arrived back in Bamiyan after forty-eight long hours on patrol. They stopped at the drop site to check for messages before heading to the safe house for sleep and a shower.

"This one's for you, Mike," Dave said as he handed over an envelope. He recognized Elsa's handwriting and smiled.

Mike tore open the envelope and unfolded the paper Elsa had so carefully folded up. The grin fell from Dave's face when he saw Mike's expression.

"What is it? What happened?"

Mike read him the short, simple message: *"Gone to Sattar with Parween and Hamid. Back later."* His voice cracked as he spoke.

"Oh sweet Jesus, what was she thinking?" Dave said. "We gotta get out there. She can't be too far ahead of us. The bus just left not an hour ago. Let's go," he said as he led Mike out the door, leaving a confused Majid behind.

Mike pulled himself into the jeep and reached for their radio while Dave revved the engine and drove away. The radio sputtered and crackled. Mike held his breath as he tried again and again to radio the Chief. Both men knew they'd need backup.

"God*damn* it!"

"Just relax, will you?" Dave said. "They're probably fine."

"Oh God, I should've told her about Sattar. She has no idea what she's walking into." Mike checked his pistol and then Dave's as their jeep sped across the barren countryside. He tried once more to radio the Chief but still couldn't get through. They knew the rules—they had no business going off like this. But they had no choice.

They arrived at the outskirts of Sattar in less than an hour. They stopped to get their bearings, and as they looked around, a young boy peeked out at them from a grove of trees. Mike motioned to him, and he ran, smiling nervously, to the jeep. Through a halting combination of English and Dari, they learned that the boy had seen the strangers, including the foreign woman under the *burqa* and the Taliban who stalked them.

"*Feringi,*" he whispered, and pointed through the trees to a group of small mud houses.

"Taliban?" Mike asked.

"Yes, yes, *balay. Khoob n'ast,* no good."

The boy pulled on Mike's sleeve and pointed.

"*Anja,* there," he said. Mike put his finger to his lips and motioned for the boy to be still.

They climbed back into the jeep, and Mike tried to contact the Chief one last time as Dave turned toward the houses. When they reached the point where they would make better progress on foot, Dave killed the engine and they unholstered their weapons as their feet hit the ground.

Parween watched as Elsa and the others raced for the house, the little band of Taliban weaving in and out of the tree line to follow. God, how she hated them. They were like stray dogs. No—they were lower than rats. Her face burned with the anger that had simmered for so long in her heart.

The scurrying Taliban passed around a rifle until it finally rested in the hands of the dirtiest one. She held her breath as they walked beneath her.

After what seemed an eternity, Elsa and the others reached the house. Just inside the entrance, she turned and stopped dead in her tracks. A growing sense of panic washed over her.

Parween.

Her eyes swept the horizon, but there was no sign of her friend.

Elsa's throat burned as she tried to catch her breath, and she felt as though her heart would explode in her chest.

She buried her face in her hands.

How had it all gone so wrong? What were they doing here?

What was *she* doing here?

A nurse from Boston in *fucking Afghanistan,* for Christ's sake.

Hot tears stung her eyes. With trembling hands, she tried to wipe them away.

"Oh, God," she whispered. "Where *are* you, Parween?"

She watched as Mohammed retrieved a pistol from under a sleeping pad. His house was modest, without even plastic to cover the windows, and he ordered Elsa and Hamid to stay down. Without a compound wall to protect them, they were easy prey for the Taliban and their rifle.

As Mohammed loaded his pistol, Elsa saw that he had only three bullets. He gripped the gun so tightly it left an imprint in his hand. He handed a knife to Hamid, and the three crouched, frozen in place, peering over the edge of the window to watch the Taliban approach, the Kalashnikov occasionally glinting in the sun.

"Can you see Parween?" asked Elsa, panic creeping into her voice. "Can you see her?"

Mike and Dave ran through the fields, their footfalls silent in the deep woods. Up ahead, they saw three Taliban hiding in a grove of trees facing a small house in the distance. In unison, Mike and Dave stopped, knelt, and searched for cover to make a final check of their handguns.

Mike's heart was pounding as he looked for any sign of Elsa. He motioned to Dave, and the two men stepped behind a small cluster of hedges.

"Do you see her?" Mike whispered. Dave shook his head, his eyes locked on the Taliban ahead,

Mike took a long, slow breath and checked his clip, silently laying a round in the chamber of his gun.

* * *

Parween calculated her distance from the house—probably half a kilometer away, maybe less. The Taliban were just at the midpoint between her position in the tree and Mohammed's house.

She watched as, suddenly—perhaps sensing that something was amiss—they ran for the house.

"Burro, Burro!" one of them yelled as they sprinted toward the unprotected structure.

Out of the corner of her eye, Parween noticed other movement, but there was no time to turn and look. She had to get down from her perch and join the race for the house. If she could get there quickly, she would be behind the Taliban and they would be surrounded—Mohammed and the others in the house, Parween at the rear. If she could surprise the Taliban, she could defeat them at their own game.

With her eyes and ears focused on the running men, she hung on to her knife, took a deep breath, and jumped stealthily from the tree, landing softly on the ground.

She was almost bowled over by two running newcomers.

Their decision made for them, Mike and Dave raced after the bearded men.

As they neared the house, they were startled by the boy who fell into their path, holding a knife. They yelled out and raised their weapons.

The Taliban heard the commotion and spun around. Seeing the soldiers, they let off a volley of shots. Mike and Dave found cover behind the trees and returned fire.

A searing pain burst in Parween's chest, her hand searching blindly for the source of the agony. She rolled on the ground, and it was then that she saw the blood—her blood—spilling from a small hole in her shirt. She couldn't catch her breath, and she struggled to get up, still clutching her knife.

The taste of blood filled her mouth. Her turban was tangled and she pulled it away, exposing her long, lustrous hair.

Dave knew then that the boy who'd fallen from the tree was actually Parween.

"Oh Jesus," he said as he and Mike leaped from their cover to pull her to safety.

In that instant of exposure, bullets flew again and Dave felt a hot poker burn into his head. He couldn't stand, he couldn't hold his gun, and he couldn't speak, though he wanted to scream. An explosion of lights stung his eyes and he sank to the ground, his hand hovering protectively over the pocket where his precious picture lay.

His head was on fire, pain tearing through him, and he tried to rub it away but he couldn't move.

Strong hands grabbed him and dragged him along. The fire in his head burst again, and he felt himself sink deeper and deeper into unconsciousness. He tried to fight, to speak, but the bullet had stolen his words. Dizziness overwhelmed him, and as he lay helpless in the dirt, the blackness enveloped him.

Parween heard the crack of the rifle and a sickening thud as Dave fell to the ground. His pistol dropped within her reach, and she stretched her arm out to grasp it. With her blood spilling out around her, she grabbed hold of it and summoned her last bit of strength. Raising herself up, she placed her fingers on the trigger as she'd seen so many soldiers do, and with the instincts of a natural marksman, she steadied her shaking hands, took meticulous aim, and fired at one of the Taliban.

She watched as the bullet tore into his shoulder, blood gushing from the wound. Clutching the pistol, she took aim once again, but with her shirt saturated now and her energy fading, she collapsed into the dirt. Her mouth filled with blood and she tried to spit it out but she didn't have the strength. She couldn't catch her breath, and she struggled against the crushing exhaustion that had overtaken her.

She lay back to rest for a minute, clinging to Dave's gun, and the final emptiness engulfed her.

With both Parween and Dave out of the line of fire, Mike jumped up and shot unrelentingly at the murderers. He watched as a bullet tore into the neck of the already wounded man. His eyes flew back in his head, and Mike knew the man was dead before he hit the ground. One of his companions, the one with the rifle, fired back, hitting the crackling radio tucked into Mike's breast pocket. The plastic exploded through his shirt.

He'd been in firefights before, but he'd never felt the fury he felt now.

He fired again, and a second man fell, blood pouring from his chest wound.

He's gotta be dead, Mike thought.

The last rebel standing shot back, and Mike stood straight up and took careful aim with his pistol, his finger poised on the trigger. He focused on his target until an excruciating fire exploded in his abdomen and the pistol fell from his hands.

He teetered and fell, and it was then that he saw a gaping hole in his shirt and stomach. His own blood and guts seemed to have exploded around him. He tried to hold in his insides with his hands, but he didn't have the strength, and he slipped quickly into nothingness.

There was an eerie silence in the little grove of trees as the lone Taliban turned toward the house.

32

Elsa held her breath as the frenzied shoot-out raged outside the house. Who was shooting? It wasn't Mohammed, not yet at least. He and Hamid were huddled on the floor next to her.

Are the Taliban shooting at one another?

Oh, God, at Parween?

Has someone come to rescue us? Are we safe?

Elsa held her head in her hands and prayed.

When the gunfire stopped, the sudden silence took her by surprise. Hamid rose from his crouched position, and in that instant, he became a perfect target for the last Taliban, who fired a round. She watched as he clutched his arm tightly and fell back to the floor.

"Allah, the Most Merciful, save me," he yelled as he held the wound.

Mohammed jumped to the window, and with a clear line of sight, he steadied his arm, aimed, and fired at the gunman.

With that final shot, a deep, bone-chilling silence settled around them. Even the birds were still. Elsa dared not breathe for fear of provoking more gunfire.

She crawled to Hamid, and after a quick check, she determined that his arm wound was superficial. She reassured him, helped him to sit, and then she stood to look out the window at the scene outside.

In the harsh sunlight, it took a moment for her eyes to focus, and when she blinked away her confusion, she could only stare in horror. Nearby, she saw the three Taliban, lying motionless on the ground, and farther on she saw a scene of utter bloodshed. She made out the camouflage-clad bodies of two soldiers and the body of someone very small, a boy maybe.

A suffocating wave of dread swept over her.

Oh, God, the boy is Parween, and the soldiers—oh Jesus, the soldiers . . .

She put a hand over her mouth to hold back her screams. She raced for the door. Mohammed tried to hold her back, but she shook him off and ran for her motionless friends.

She sprinted past the Taliban sprawled on the ground, her sandals tracking through their blood as she ran. Sweating, gasping for air, and crying, she reached the bloody scene.

"Parween!" she shrieked as she reached her friend, who lay on her side in a pool of blood. Her eyes were closed as if in sleep, her bloodied lips carried the trace of a smile, and her hand still gripped a pistol. Elsa knelt down to her friend and shook her, called her name again, and finally rested her ear over Parween's heart, but just as in the quiet grove, there was only silence.

She put her mouth over Parween's and tried to breathe life back into her friend, but Parween's mouth was filled with blood and her lungs were unyielding. Elsa pulled at her friend's shirt to find the wound, and she knew.

Parween was dead.

The panic that Elsa had held back tore out of her then and the scream she released startled even the birds, which rose up and away in fear.

With tears clouding her vision, Elsa cradled her friend in her arms, rocking back and forth on her heels. All around her was bloodshed. She held tightly to Parween, afraid to let go—afraid to look around—and then out of the corner of her eye, she saw the soldiers.

Oh God, Mike and Dave.

They lay motionless and bloody in the dirt. Her sobs caught in her throat as she gently laid Parween down. Turning, she reached for Mike, and she saw his wound, gaping and ugly. She held her hands over his shirt and tried desperately to hold back the blood that oozed from his body. Her hands came back warm and sticky, covered with blood and bits of body tissue.

Paralyzed by the disastrous turn of events, Elsa sank into the dirt. "Oh Jesus," she whispered, resting her head on Mike's chest. "Help me. I don't know what to do."

"Elsa, check Dave," a voice murmured. "He's really hurt. Help him, Elsa."

Mike's words, proof that he was at least alive, soothed her, and she touched his face. She turned, searching for Dave. He lay on his back, one hand held over his shirt pocket, his eyes open and looking to the skies. A gunshot wound in the side of his head told her everything she needed to know.

She wanted to scream, to take his gun and shoot wildly into the air, but she didn't. Instead, she kissed his forehead and gently closed his eyes.

A wrenching sorrow tore through Elsa, and she turned back to Mike and tried to think. *Be a nurse,* she told herself, *just do what you know.* With trembling hands, she tore away his shirt to inspect his wounds. There was shrapnel in his chest, but his larger wound, the one that bled most heavily and could kill him fastest, was the one to his abdomen. She pulled off her scarf to craft a pressure dressing. Once the flimsy bandage was applied, Elsa sat back on her heels to figure out what to do next but the chaotic scene threatened to overwhelm her. She pushed her hair back from her face and saw Mohammed and Hamid running toward her. The sight of them gave her a small measure of courage, and steadying her hands, she turned to Mike again.

"Mike," she commanded, her voice cracking, "do as I say. Don't move. We're going to get everyone out of here, and then we'll take care of you."

Mohammed approached with a cart, and Hamid followed, still clutching his wound. "We must get them in here—quickly, now—before we are seen," he ordered. They lifted Dave and Parween gently to the back and then carefully lifted Mike into the cart as well.

Elsa turned and retrieved both pistols, as well as the remnants of Mike's radio. Something shiny caught her eye, and she bent to have a closer look. There, on the ground where Parween had fallen, lay a glistening tube of lipstick, the same one Elsa had given her the night they'd first had dinner. Elsa dropped to her knees and clutched it to her chest.

A fresh flood of tears overtook her and the shock of what had happened started to creep in. Mohammed gently, but firmly, tapped her back. "Miss, we must hurry."

Nodding through her grief, Elsa stood up shakily and slipped the small tube into her pocket.

"We must go to the house of my sister," Mohammed said urgently as he steered the cart along a winding road. "The Taliban lying there will be found soon and there will surely be a search for the strangers who came to Sattar this day." He hastily guided the cart through the streets, eyes alert, scanning the few people they passed. Soon they turned toward a small compound.

"Fariba," he called. "Are you here?"

"Mohammed," a smiling woman answered. *"Salaam alaikum—"*

"Fariba," he interrupted, "there is trouble. I have come here with my friends." He turned and pointed. "This is Elsa and Hamid."

Fariba started to greet the strangers and then, seeing the blood that stained all of their clothes, she quickly covered her mouth with her hand. *"Che'ast? Che taklif? Mariz?"*

Mohammed took a deep breath and explained.

"There has been trouble, and we need your help."

He guided her to the back of his cart and showed her Mike and the others.

"Inside, quickly," she said as she opened the gate.

Elsa and Hamid helped to pull the cart into Fariba's courtyard.

With the gate shut tightly behind them, Elsa leaned against the cart and turned to Mohammed. "Is there anyone else here?" she asked. "Are we safe?"

"Yes, yes," Mohammed answered. "My sister is a widow, and she lives here alone. No one will think to bother her."

Mohammed and Hamid carried Mike into the little house, and Elsa bent over him to tend to his wounds. His paleness was ghostly.

"He needs surgery—soon. We cannot stay here, Mohammed. We must get him back to Bamiyan." Her voice was filled with the undeniable fear that Mike could still die.

Mohammed nodded. "Yes, you are right. But if we all go at once, we will attract too much attention. The Taliban are looking for you and Hamid, and probably the soldiers. We cannot go together."

She turned and looked at Mike, whose eyes were closed. Panic threatened to engulf her again, and she fought to hold it back.

"Help me, Mohammed," she pleaded. "Tell me what to do."

Mohammed paused, wiping the sweat from his brow. "I think that you, the soldier, and I should go first. We can pretend to be a family going to bury a brother. I have a box that we can hide him in," Mohammed said. "It is a wooden coffin that was intended to hold my body when my family thought I would die in Bamiyan's prison. My sister has kept it here." He pointed to what had appeared to be a long table, covered with a piece of cloth. Then he spoke rapidly to his sister, and she nodded.

"She agrees that we should leave quickly. She says that you will be safe, Hamid. No one ever comes here."

A momentary relief washed over Elsa and she turned to Hamid. "If you stay here, the soldiers will be back for you today. I know that they will come for you."

"You will be safe here," Fariba said softly. "But if by chance there is trouble, I have a weapon," she added. She pulled a large handgun from under her sleeping pad. "My husband's."

She opened the cylinder and checked her bullets. "Do not worry."

Through twinges of pain, Hamid nodded at Fariba.

"I must trust you, Fariba, and I thank you for your help."

"Please," Elsa asked, her voice so soft Fariba had to lean forward to hear, "do you have a blanket?" She looked back at the cart that still held Parween and Dave. "So I can cover them," she said, her voice breaking.

Fariba touched Elsa's arm and reached for a nearby blanket. Nodding to the cart, she handed it to Elsa. "Go," she said.

Elsa clutched the blanket and approached the cart. Parween and Dave lay side by side, their eyes closed, blood still seeping from their wounds. Instinctively, she reached out and checked for signs of life. But there were none.

Her friends were dead.

She wanted to fall apart, to let the grief swallow her, but there was no time. Not yet. Not until Mike was safe.

She gently covered Dave and Parween with the blanket, and she offered a silent prayer.

Elsa wiped her face on her sleeve and turned back to the house, where Mohammed was scurrying about preparing for their journey. She knelt by Mike's side and whispered their plans to him.

He nodded in painful agreement, then moaned and said, "Tell me about Dave. Is he hurt bad?"

Elsa hesitated and pushed down the dread she felt at sharing the news. "He's here, Mike, but . . . he was badly injured." She choked back her own tears and continued. "I'm sorry," she cried, "but he didn't make it. Neither did Parween—they're both dead." A choking sob tore from her throat.

Mike's body jerked with the news, and he struggled to push himself up, but Elsa wrestled him back down and held on to him.

"Mike," she whispered, but he seemed not to hear.

He closed his eyes and moaned so low and with such sorrow that Elsa thought he would die as well. His moan grew until an animal's growl of agony poured from the deepest part of him. He cried then with such raw force that Elsa thought his insides would spill from his wound.

She applied pressure to his gaping injury and begged.

"Please, Mike, you're still bleeding. You've got to stop."

"Oh God," he groaned. "Why Dave?" His grief-stricken wails faded and he lay quietly, tears spilling from his eyes.

Elsa explained that they were going to get him ready for the trip to Bamiyan.

"Just do as I say, Mike." She took a deep breath, steeled herself, and applied a heavy pressure dressing to Mike's abdomen. She tore a piece of fabric from the hem of her dress and wound it around him, tying it tightly to secure the dressing.

Mike lay quietly as Mohammed swathed him in a white martyr's shroud and placed him in the coffin. His blood seeped only faintly through the fabric, and Mohammed paused.

"Fariba," he called, "where is the small goat that I killed yesterday? I need him."

Fariba hurried outside and returned, pulling a headless carcass. Grimacing at the smell, Mohammed lifted it and packed it alongside Mike under the shroud.

"If someone opens this coffin, the terrible stink of the goat and the amount of blood will be evidence enough that only a dead body lies herein." He smiled grimly as he packed the shroud around the goat and Mike.

Mike gagged at the stench and Elsa told him to breathe through his mouth. She spoke softly and told him not to throw up or he'd start the bleeding again.

Mohammed held Mike's pistol up to Elsa. He put his hand on the trigger to demonstrate its proper use, and once he'd checked the bullets, he passed it to her.

"Famidi?"

Elsa nodded and wrapped her hand around the gun. Mohammed checked his own pistol then and hid it as best he could in his shirt.

Elsa turned to Fariba and pointed to the blood that saturated the front of Elsa's own dress. "I need a burqa, please. Do you have one I can use?"

Fariba lifted one from a hook and pulled it on over Elsa's head. Elsa kissed Fariba on both cheeks and with tears in her eyes, she knelt beside Hamid.

"You have been my true brother. I will see you later today, Hamid. May Allah watch over you."

"And over you," Hamid said as he reached to squeeze Elsa's hand.

Elsa pulled the *burqa* over her face, and she and Mohammed hurried outside. They struggled to load Mike's coffin into the rickety old hay wagon, and then Mohammed quickly harnessed his sister's two weary donkeys to the front of the wagon.

Hidden in the folds of the *burqa,* Elsa climbed into the back and sat by the coffin; she would play the role of distraught widow. As the emaciated donkeys set off at a painfully slow trot, Mohammed spoke.

"We will surely be watched. The Taliban are looking for the foreigner and the soldiers. Stay quiet and alert."

Elsa nodded, and caressed the side of the coffin. The stench of the rotting goat already oozed out into the air. Part of her hoped

Mike had already passed out so that he wouldn't have to endure the putrid odor.

"Mike," she whispered, not knowing if he could hear her, "stay strong. As soon as we are safe, I'll get you out of this damn box."

The road back to Bamiyan was tortuous, winding through the loneliest recesses of the valley. There were countless hidden groves from which Taliban or others could observe passersby.

"There are surely suspicious eyes following us," Mohammed said.

Before long his instincts were confirmed. A lone Taliban emerged from a line of trees and, waving his Kalashnikov in the air, let off a shot, demanding that Mohammed stop.

Mohammed pulled the reins on his tired donkeys and they stopped, looking glad for the unexpected rest.

"*Che' ast?* What is this?" the man demanded.

Mohammed remained calm and sadly explained that the man in the coffin was his dear brother and this woman was his widow.

Elsa's heart was racing but she kept her head down as Parween had taught her. Her hands trembled, and she folded them in her lap.

"Open it," the rebel demanded.

Mohammed stepped to the rear of the wagon and opened the lid, unleashing the hideous stench of the dead goat.

Elsa held her breath and tried to remain calm as she unfolded her hands and felt for Mike's pistol. She placed her hands firmly around the handle, the cold, hard feel of the metal fueling her resolve. She would shoot the man if she had to. She had no doubt.

"Aghh!" the disgusted Taliban cried. "Shut it and go. Bury him quickly. He is already rotting!"

Mohammed complied, murmuring his thanks to the Taliban and to Allah, and he whipped the scrawny donkeys to get them moving. Once they were out of earshot of the Taliban, he screamed, *"Allah u akbar!"*

Elsa crawled to the coffin and lifted the lid. She unwound the stinking shroud from Mike's face and started to cry.

"Are you okay? Can you make it to Bamiyan? Please speak to me."

Mike winced and nodded, though obviously in great pain.

"I'm okay," he said faintly.

"We'll be there soon. Just hold on."

Elsa replaced the shroud and pulled the cover of the coffin back down.

The donkeys finally seemed to sense the imminent danger and picked up their pace. Elsa and Mohammed watched every shadow, every bird that took flight, every rustle of leaves, for any hint that the Taliban were near. But somehow, against the odds, they made it.

They wended their way to Bamiyan's clinic. Laila and Ezat came outside, confused by the strange sight, and when Elsa pulled off the hood of her *burqa,* they jumped in surprise. She quickly explained what had happened, and together, they moved Mike to the small ER.

Ezat promptly tended to Mike's wounds, and when Elsa moved in to help, Laila shook her head and steered her from the room.

"No, you must take care of yourself. Ezat will look after your friend."

"I should be with him," she said. After protesting weakly, Elsa sent a message to the Chief.

It seemed only minutes before a pair of soldiers arrived at the clinic. One was a medic and he took charge of Mike, moving him to a clean stretcher for transfer to the safe house.

The Chief—red faced with anger—arrived in a second vehicle.

"What the fuck, Elsa? What happened?"

Through tears and sobs, Elsa relayed the events of the day.

"Dave's dead. Parween too," she said, tears spilling from her eyes.

The Chief slumped for an instant before he turned to his interpreter and began barking orders.

"Ramatullah, get this man, Mohammed, to explain where Dave and the others are and write it out so we can send in our men. Take him with you if he'll go."

The Chief turned and saw that Elsa was trembling. Despite what he must have been feeling, he softened his voice.

"Oh, shit, I didn't even ask—are you okay, honey?"

But Elsa couldn't answer. Sobs were her only reply, and she collapsed into a chair. He crouched beside her.

"We have to get Mike to the safe house. Do you want to come with us? We can get you out today."

She couldn't speak. She had to see Rahima, to wait for Hamid.

She couldn't go, not yet. She shook her head and rose to say good-bye to Mike, who lay on the stretcher they were preparing to place on the back of the jeep. The soldiers parted and let her through.

She took his hand and kissed him full on the mouth.

"I'll see you soon."

Mike's words were a whisper.

"Elsa, you can't stay. Promise me . . . you'll leave."

She nodded, and the soldiers returned, lifting the stretcher and moving it quickly to the waiting jeep.

Laila and Ezat had stood back as soon as the soldiers arrived, but now they stepped up next to Elsa where she sat. Laila crouched down next to her.

"Elsa, are you all right?" she asked, her voice filled with concern. Ezat stood next to her with his brow wrinkled.

Elsa cried and told them in more detail what had happened.

"Dave and Parween—" Their names caught in her throat. *How could they be gone? God, make it not true.*

"Oh, Parween," she cried, and her shoulders sagged.

Laila reached out and wrapped her arms around her.

"Come, we'll walk you home."

"I have to see Rahima."

"Yes, but you must clean up first. You don't want her to see all this." She pointed to the blood that covered Elsa's dress and hands.

Ezat and Laila escorted her to her house, and along the way even Ezat tried to comfort her in his limited English. When they arrived, Elsa turned to them.

"Thank you," she said, "but I need to take care of things myself now. Will you go back to the clinic and let everyone know what happened?"

They both nodded, and once Laila was convinced that Elsa would be all right, they set off again across the little stream.

When Elsa entered her bedroom, she saw Mike's camera sitting on her upended suitcase. It had been there for at least a month—it had almost become a part of the furniture—but she hadn't used it. She'd meant to take pictures for Parween, but she'd forgotten again and again.

Cradling the small camera, she remembered Mike's words. *Dave's used most of that film taking pictures of himself.* Fresh tears spilled from her eyes. Though there was nothing of Parween in the camera, at least Dave's wife would have something.

She poured water for a bath and cried still more. She washed quickly and donned a clean dress before she heard the unmistakable whir of helicopter blades. She climbed to the roof and watched as a U.S. Army helicopter landed in the distance, amidst swirls of dust and dirt.

It was the chopper that would take Mike to a proper hospital.

All was quiet for a while, then she heard the engine roar again and the helicopter rose. It hesitated for only an instant before it banked sharply, made a complete turn, and headed straight for Elsa's roof.

She stood and started to wave her arms. She screamed out, "Mike!" But the chopper didn't slow. "I love you!" she shouted, trying to carry her words over the screeching of the blades. She knew he couldn't hear her, but it didn't matter.

33

As soon as the helicopter was out of sight, Elsa climbed down from the roof and set off to see Rahima.

How could she ever explain what happened? She didn't even understand it herself.

The familiar walk seemed to take forever and only an instant. She knocked at the outer gate and was quickly admitted to dear Uncle Abdullah's compound.

She hesitated; it had been just hours since Parween had left this house for her journey to Sattar, and in that short time, the world had fallen apart.

Elsa choked back her grief and went in search of Rahima.

She found Parween's mother holding baby Raziq and chasing after Zahra, who ran straight into Elsa's arms, shouting, "Essa, Essa!"

The sound of her little-girl laughter filled the air. Elsa held Zahra tight as the tears started to fall. Her tears and her anguish and her unquenchable grief finally seized her, and she sank to the floor, consumed by large, gulping sobs.

Zahra pulled free and backed away, suddenly frightened.

"*Che taklif?* What is it?" Rahima said as she knelt to touch Elsa's shoulder. Then a thought seemed to strike her, and she looked around to see if there was anyone else with Elsa. A glint of fear appeared in her eyes.

The words caught in Elsa's throat.

"Parween, our beautiful Parween, has died," she sobbed.

Rahima seemed to stop breathing, and she sank to the floor.

Zahra started to cry.

Elsa and Rahima wrapped themselves around one another and gave way to their sorrow. They sat in a tight embrace until their tears were spent, and then they sat in mournful silence, holding Parween's babies close.

Elsa spent the next few hours with Rahima, and when the soldiers finally brought Parween home, she and Rahima washed the blood from her wounded body and tenderly dressed and prepared her for her final journey.

Parween's body was frail in death, and Elsa noticed for the first time how thin her friend was. Why hadn't she seen it before? Parween was not the sturdy woman she'd pretended to be.

Elsa left Rahima's side and walked outside for some fresh air. There, she saw Zahra playing in the dirt.

"Mama *mariz*?" she asked.

Nodding, Elsa drew the little girl into her arms and sat on the ground holding her.

Hussein, stunned into silence by the tragic turn of events, went quietly to the little plot of ground that held Abdullah, Mariam, and Parween's stillborn baby. He broke up the earth there once again so that Parween might be buried alongside those she'd loved so dearly. When he was finished, he hastily arranged for a small wooden coffin.

Word of Parween's death traveled quickly through Bamiyan and rumors began that Parween was surely the famed lady rebel whose exploits they'd all followed and admired. Though she'd fought them for years, the gossips said, the Taliban had finally caught her unawares.

There was unmistakable proof—Parween, dressed as a boy, had been killed in a shoot-out with their hated oppressors. Witnesses stepped forward with their own accounts of her heroic feats and though the stories were fictional, it no longer mattered. Her death elevated her status and she was declared *shaheed,* a martyr for all that was good in Afghanistan.

Later, Hamid, his wounds freshly bandaged, arrived at Parween's house and confirmed that Parween had saved them all.

"I have never seen such bravery, and Parween is surely the true lady rebel," he said proudly. "She fought alongside the soldiers and she saved us." He nodded to Elsa.

Rahima was overwhelmed by the stories of Parween's courage, and she remembered the plucky little girl who had so loved to fight and so wanted to run with the boys.

"It must be so," Rahima declared through her tears. "My own Parween, a true *shaheed*."

By the time they left to take Parween to her resting place, a crowd had gathered in the compound, and even more mourners lined the road beyond. The group grew until it seemed the whole village was there, and they fell into line and marched to the burial site just beyond the gate. Elsa and Rahima walked together, each holding one of Parween's children. Zahra wriggled herself from Elsa's grip and resolutely toddled beside the donkey cart that carried her mother's shrouded body.

A low hum followed the procession as people swapped their own accounts of Parween's adventures. With every step, her legend was swelling, and with each retelling of her exploits and the manner of her death, she became more and more important in the lives of those who had known her—and even those who hadn't.

The shriveled old woman from the stream, whose son had seen the lady rebel, declared that it had to have been Parween, and she marveled at the fact that Parween had kept silent when they'd talked of her that day at the stream.

Elsa shared how Parween had rescued her from the surly young Taliban by yelling at them and spitting in their direction. She had been a fierce warrior.

The gathering stopped at the burial site, and Elsa stepped forward to bid her dear friend a final *Khoda hafez*. Hussein lifted the coffin from the cart, and Elsa leaned over it and whispered.

"*Man shumura dost doram*. I love you, my dear friend."

When the coffin had been lowered into the ground and the prayers finished, Rahima reached for Elsa's hand.

"Come," she said, "it is time to go."

Elsa could only shake her head. "Not yet. I'll be along later." Her voice cracked, and she fell to the ground and buried her face in her hands. She lingered there after the mourners had left, and she curled up on the ground to be close to her friend one last time.

She lay there alone for a long time, and as the sun sank, she placed a gleaming tube of lipstick among the stones that marked Parween's resting place.

34

$\mathcal{I}$t didn't take long for word of the trouble—and Elsa's role in it—to trickle back to Kabul, and from there to Paris. So she wasn't surprised when the French administrator arrived in Bamiyan two days after the shoot-out.

"What were you thinking?" the Frenchman spat out. "We *never* collaborate with the invaders."

Elsa sat silently as she waited for him to finish his angry harangue.

"As soon as we find a replacement, you must leave," he announced. "You have compromised our clinic and our organization."

After a long pause, Elsa responded. "I am truly sorry. I only wanted to help, but it all went terribly wrong."

He held his hand up as if to stop her words. "*You* went terribly wrong," he said.

A sudden burst of anger washed over Elsa. "The villagers and staff will tell you that I *have* helped, but I'm not going to argue with you." She was surprised at her own boldness. It seemed only yesterday she'd been a timid new aid worker and yet here she was, shrugging off the French administrator's surly comments. She didn't care what he thought, and eventually she just stopped listening to him, though she sat politely.

He folded his arms across his chest. "Of course, we accept some responsibility," he said finally. "We should not have left you alone here, and it is true that you performed admirably. But still, we must replace you. You understand? We will replace you as soon as possible."

That same day, she spoke with the Chief, and he told her that Mike had done well enough in Germany that he was being transferred to Washington, D.C. "And you, Elsa, you have to leave. I've assigned soldiers to watch over you, but I can't guarantee your safety."

She'd seen them, always in the background watching, weapons at the ready. "I know," she said. "I'm making my arrangements."

"I can put you on a helicopter," he said. "Get you out today."

"Not yet," she said.

The Chief sighed but nodded. Then he blushed as he gave her the message that Mike had insisted he pass along.

"Mike says to tell you that he loves you and that he expects you to come home soon." The Chief leaned in and planted a soft kiss on Elsa's cheek. "He asked me to give you that, too, and I hate to deny my men what they ask." Despite his obvious embarrassment, he grinned.

It was all Elsa could do to hold back the tears.

"Oh, Chief, tell him that I love him too." Finally, she lost the battle, and her tears began to fall.

The Chief wrapped Elsa in his big, burly arms and held her.

"I'm afraid you'll have to give him that message yourself, young lady."

She fished in her pocket and passed him a roll of film.

"For Dave's wife," she said. "His pictures are in there."

The Chief took the film and blinked away the tears that lined his eyes.

Hamid left Bamiyan. Considering everything that had happened, he'd decided to take Mike's advice and return to Kabul, where he planned to enroll at the university.

With tears in his eyes, he took Elsa's hands in his. "You are my one true sister—" His voice broke. "I will never forget you. *Inshallah,* we will meet again in a safer place." He released Elsa's hands and wiped his eyes with his shirtsleeve. "*Tashakore,* my sister, *tashakore.*"

Elsa felt her own eyes well up. "Hamid, you are my true brother.

I don't know how I could have survived without you." A sob caught in her throat and she paused. "We will be connected forever, and I *know* that we will meet again."

Before their last good-bye, she asked him to write out one final translation.

"For Rahima," she said.

The following day, Elsa received word that a replacement had been located and she should be on her way as soon as she could arrange a UN flight. She spoke with Johann, who had been devastated by the turn of events in Sattar. Each time he saw her, he said the same thing.

"Oh, Elsa, whyever did you go? I wanted you to wait. I wanted you to wait." And he dropped his head into his hands.

Elsa rested her hand on his shoulder.

"I wish we'd listened. We shouldn't have gone. But Parween wanted to prove to you that she was serious, someone who would be a good teacher. You asked us to wait, and we should have. I am so sorry."

"Ahh," he said softly. "I should have insisted. I'm afraid I wasn't firm enough."

"Oh, Johann, it's not your fault. Parween was determined to go and I was determined to help her." She closed her eyes, remembering Parween's contagious smile, but today it brought only tears.

Johann reached out and covered Elsa's hand with his own.

When they'd both recovered their composure, Elsa asked about the next UN flight to Kabul.

"Why, my dear, there will be another flight in just two days. I wish for once that there would be a delay, so that we might keep you with us just a little longer."

Elsa smiled and thanked him for his help. He walked her to the gate and spoke again.

"Bamiyan will miss you, Elsa. If you are ever in need of work, I hope that you will consider joining us at the UN." He passed her his business card. "So you can reach me."

Elsa ran her fingers over the embossed lettering. "The last time I took someone's card," she said, slipping the card into her pocket, "it changed my life."

She kissed him on both cheeks, turned, and strode back to her own compound.

Her final days were lost in a blur of writing reports, tying up loose ends, and saying good-byes. That was the hardest part—the good-byes. There were Amina and Sidiq, who would soon be parents and who would stay in the little house with her until she flew to Kabul. There was Soraya, and then Laila and Ezat, the clinic staff, and the neighborhood children.

And there was Rahima, the most important good-bye of all.

She dreaded that final good-bye, but she had to do it. Each farewell was more painful than the one before, and she saved Rahima for last.

She approached Uncle Abdullah's compound and knocked softly at the gate. Hussein answered and ushered her into Parween's room. Rahima, crouched there on the floor and surrounded by Parween's sleeping babies, rose from her sewing.

She took Elsa into her arms. They hugged and cried, and Elsa promised to return.

"It's what Parween would have wanted. I will come back here someday, and if ever you or the babies need anything—*anything*—please let me know." She carefully explained how they could contact her and left a piece of paper with the instructions Hamid had translated before he left. Elsa's eyes filled with tears again as she reached into her pocket and withdrew a shiny tube of lipstick, the last of the tubes she'd packed so long ago.

"For Zahra," she said as she folded the tube into Rahima's hand. "Parween would want her to have a lipstick of her very own."

Rahima cradled the little tube and smiled. She turned then and gathered Parween's new brown veil and passed it to Elsa. "So you will have a piece of Parween," she said, tears collecting in her eyes.

Elsa's shoulders heaved with the cry that escaped her and she held the veil to her face.

"*Tashakore,* Rahima," she cried, folding Rahima into her arms.

They hugged one last time, and Elsa, clutching Parween's veil, reluctantly left the small compound she'd come to know so well. She stood outside for a final look around. Her heart was filled with memories of this place, these people, and how they'd changed her life.

She made the short journey from Parween's house to her own with tears falling from her eyes.

She arrived home to find that Amina and Sidiq had arranged a surprise farewell dinner. The hospital staff and neighbor children all crowded in and they sat, alternately laughing and crying as they shared memories of Elsa's stay in Bamiyan.

"She chased the *jinn* from my mind," Sidiq proudly proclaimed. "And she found me a wife." He smiled broadly at Amina, who gazed demurely at her husband.

"I think you would have found each other no matter what," Elsa said, trying to steer the conversation to her guests. "But I am glad to have attended your beautiful wedding."

Amina took her hand. "You will marry soon, yes?"

The children all giggled. Surely, now Elsa could find a husband. She felt a half smile spread across her face.

"*Mumkin,* maybe," she said.

When the evening was almost over, Ezat and Laila arrived to say good-bye.

Laila sniffled frequently.

"Please come back, dear friend," she said.

"*Inshallah,* Laila, *inshallah.*" Elsa blinked back her own tears.

"Yes, please come back," Ezat said slowly in perfect though halting English. "We will miss you here in Bamiyan."

Elsa's tears broke through, and she buried her face in her hands.

The guests trickled out one by one, leaving Elsa with Sidiq and Amina, who had finally begun to glow with her pregnancy.

Amina took Elsa's hands.

"If a girl, the name of my baby will be Parween."

Elsa kissed Amina and wrapped her in a warm embrace.

"*Tashakore,* my friend, *tashakore.*"

Elsa stayed up to pack, and when dawn came, she was ready for the journey home.

35

The next morning, Elsa shared a tearful good-bye with Amina and Sidiq, and then left on the first leg of her trip.

When she left her compound, she was surrounded by the children who had befriended her from the start, and she realized that they really didn't understand a good-bye like this.

Then she picked up her bag and walked alone to the little landing strip to wait for her UN flight. She stood in the dirt under a blazing sun and squinted into the horizon, hoping for a glimpse of the plane. A turbaned official stood nearby, but because she was a woman, he did not acknowledge her.

Finally, the plane appeared, slipping through the mountaintops and flying in low to land. Just then, an errant cow wandered onto the runway and the small plane was forced back into the sky. Villagers ran to the cow and coaxed him back off the dirt landing strip. Several minutes later, the plane finally landed, and the irate pilot jumped out to scream at the villagers about the cow.

Elsa stood on the edge of the field, waiting to board the tiny plane.

From a distance, Elsa heard the unmistakable sound of familiar voices calling her name. She turned; five of the neighborhood boys and girls were running to her for a last good-bye. Tears streamed down her face as she met them and tried to hold them all in her outstretched arms. They chattered all at once, a mixture of Dari and English.

"Will you miss me?"

"Don't go."

"Will you marry now?"

"Take me with you!"

"Promise you'll be back."

"I love you!"

Finally, in a haze of sadness, Elsa pulled herself away and boarded the plane. As it lifted above Afghanistan's mountains, she looked down to see, for one last time, the children running after her, waving and crying.

She held them tight in her vision until the plane lifted into the mountains and the children's tiny forms disappeared from view.

epilogue

Elsa's footfalls were silent as she slipped into Mike's hospital room. The sight of him lying quietly under crisp white sheets, surrounded by humming monitors and pumps, made her heart soar. He was *alive*. It would take some time, the doctors had said, but he was going to be fine.

She sat on the side of his bed and held his hand, stroking it gently before she leaned in and kissed him full on the lips. He opened his eyes and smiled drowsily before drifting back into sleep.

Elsa lifted herself onto his bed and curled herself around him, feeling the gentle rhythm of his breathing against her chest. "I love you, Mike," she whispered. He stirred for a moment and Elsa pulled him closer. She hadn't known until this moment how blissful holding him again would be. She pulled him closer still, melting into him.

This time, she'd never let him go.

AUTHOR'S NOTE

Since the horrific events of September 11, 2001, and the subsequent invasion, life in Afghanistan has certainly improved on some levels. There is better access to health care for everyone, including women, although there is still a long way to go. The UN has reported that an Afghan woman dies of complications from childbirth or pregnancy every twenty minutes, and one of every four babies born will not live to see his fifth birthday.

Tragedy and danger still linger. Land mines continue to threaten the lives of women and children on a daily basis. Latest estimates indicate that between one hundred fifty and three hundred people are killed or injured by land mines every month in Afghanistan. Many of them are children.

There are, however, hopeful signs. According to UNICEF, an estimated 5.4 million children now attend some form of school, most at the primary level; and the long drought has finally ended. Though wracked by poverty, misery, and war, Afghanistan is populated by some of the kindest, gentlest people imaginable. Despite decades of turbulence, its citizens remain unfailingly caring and polite.

In 2002, I spent six months providing health care to the villagers in Bamiyan and beyond as a nurse and humanitarian aid worker. There, I worked with the Hazaras, a long-reviled ethnic tribe in central Afghanistan.

The Hazaras were especially despised by the Taliban, and consequently, they were subjected to relentless punishment intended to break their proud spirit. But instead, the ruthless punishment empowered them, and they emerged as some of Afghanistan's most graceful and generous people. As if to emphasize their independence, in 2005, a woman was appointed provincial governor of Bamiyan Province.

Despite the recent progress and their own determination, there are worrisome signs as well. By all accounts, the Taliban have regrouped, and in 2009, the BBC reported that they have encircled Bamiyan.

But the people of Bamiyan are nothing if not resilient. There truly is a long-rumored lady rebel in Afghanistan—a warrior for goodness, they say—and her exploits are legendary, her reputation for courage boundless. To hear the stories of this remarkable warrior is to believe. Even now, I can almost see her as she flies on horseback across the top of a distant mountain range, saving her countrymen from one calamity or another.

It is that lady rebel who is the true inspiration for this story, and for the people of Bamiyan, because despite its persistent miseries, Afghanistan is a place where even in the darkest hours, hope lives.

For information on how to help the people of Afghanistan or some of the more than 42 million refugees and displaced around the world, please visit the International Rescue Committee at www.theirc.org.

READERS GROUP GUIDE

Lipstick in Afghanistan
Roberta Gately

Elsa Murphy is a serious, sweet Boston girl whose tough childhood made her want nothing more than to truly help people. After working tirelessly to finish nursing school and sweating through long hours in the ER, she decides to volunteer with Aide du Monde, a world relief organization. Elsa feels it's the best way to put her nursing skills to use, and she secretly longs to leave Boston and add some color to her life. But she has no idea what to expect when she is posted to a rural clinic in Afghanistan, just after 9/11.

From the moment she sets foot in Bamiyan, Elsa knows her life will forever be changed by what she sees and who she befriends. There's spirited Parween, a young mother who's been forced to silently accept the horrors the Taliban inflicted on her family and friends, but who longs to throw off her veil and fight back. And there's Mike, a handsome engineer in the U.S. Special Forces who teaches Elsa what it truly means to love. But when an innocent venture to a nearby town puts them in grave danger from a Taliban guerrilla unit, Elsa and her friends must fight for their lives—and Elsa discovers the real power that comes from friendship, and the strength she never knew she had.

QUESTIONS AND TOPICS FOR DISCUSSION

1. Throughout the novel, Elsa is somewhat naïve in her motivations and expectations. Do you see this as a positive or negative quality? Do you think that her naïveté is what really allowed her to embrace Bamiyan and be less of an "outsider," or do you think it has blinded her to the constant danger of her situation, making her reckless when she ought to have been careful?

2. Elsa says to Mike, "If you're still coming to dinner tonight—and I hope you are—you'll see *my* Afghanistan. Good friends and gentle people" (p. 194). Do you agree that even under such volatile circumstances, there can be such a dichotomy of views? That a soldier could never look at the place and people around him the same way a nurse or aid worker could, and that even though they're physically in the same location, their experiences are vastly different?

3. The story is narrated in third-person limited: that is, we see through the experiences of Elsa, and at times, through the experiences of Parween. Why do you think the author chose to write it this way? Was there another character that you wished to see at the center of the narration?

4. What did you think about Elsa's relationship with Mike? Do you think it would have progressed so quickly had they met under different circumstances? Do you think that being in Bamiyan gives Elsa a kind of courage that the Boston Elsa would never have had? Do you think the fact that they both sought familiarity in a foreign land (and found it in each other) made for a deeper relationship, or is that a superficial (albeit

passionate) connection that might not last in a place like Boston?

5. Before the encounter with the Taliban guerrillas, Elsa tells Mike of her plans to go "to Rwanda, or, well . . . anywhere they need us" (p. 226). Do you think she will follow through on that plan after all that has happened, perhaps by joining the UN? Do you think she feels she owes it to Parween to continue to help people? Do you feel Aide du Monde's decision to have her replaced was warranted?

6. *Lipstick in Afghanistan* has many strong female characters. Think about all the different women who impact on Elsa's life: Margaret, Maureen, Parween, Amina, Rahima, and Laila. What does Elsa learn from each of these women at various points of the novel? What do you think they learn from her? Think about the women who play a significant role in your life. What can you learn from them?

7. To a great extent, the male characters in the novel are quite clearly good (Uncle Abdullah, Mike, Hamid, Raziq) or evil (Mariam's husband, the members of the Taliban, Noor Mohammed). How did you feel about the portrayal of men? Did you find it accurate, or too simple? What about the fact that men were shown as both victims and perpetrators of crimes, while women were almost solely victims?

8. When Elsa tells Parween that she is angry at Mike for saying that he'd shoot Hamid if he had to, Parween's reaction surprises her. Parween says, "Things are not always as complicated as *you* make them, Elsa. You are like a tree—strong, yes—but rigid. Too rigid. . . . When you see Mike—and you will—ask him if he'd *save* Hamid. That is the only thing you need to know" (p. 203). Do you agree with Parween's and Mike's point of view? Or do you feel that Elsa is right to try and see the complexity of the situation—to want to always judge people on an individual basis, as impossible as it may be?

9. Parween willingly risks everything when she jumps from the tree and attempts to surprise the Taliban members from behind. What do you think of her decision? Do you think it was selfish—that she should have considered her mother and her daughter and the life they'd have without her before risking her life? Or do you think it was selfless—that her risk was a way to try and ensure a better future for her daughter, and for all women?

10. The story of the lady rebel is very significant throughout the novel. What do you think the legend symbolizes? What did you think about the fact that Parween, through her death, becomes the embodiment of the legend? How else does the idea of rebellion manifest through the book?

11. Do you think karma and/or fate play significant roles in the story? Support your answer with examples from the text.

12. Were you left with a sense of hope at the end of the novel— that things would be better for the women in Bamiyan (and also Elsa), or was there a lingering feeling of futility? Do the themes in this fictional account relate at all to your real world perspectives on war and change?

13. The title of the book is *Lipstick in Afghanistan*. Discuss the significance of lipstick to the women in the novel. What does it mean to Elsa? To Parween and Mariam? If you had to pick one overarching idea or theme for it to symbolize, what would it be?

Enhance Your Book Club

1. Do you have an item that is to you what lipstick is for Elsa? Something you could never travel to a foreign country without? Have each member bring her "lipstick" to the book club and discuss.

2. The Hazaras are a real tribe in Afghanistan. Do some research on their culture and way of life, and have each member present an interesting fact.

3. Visit the International Rescue Committee's website at www.theirc.org to see how you can help the people of Afghanistan or the millions of other refugees around the world.

A Conversation with Roberta Gately

What inspired you to write *Lipstick in Afghanistan*? Did you pull from many of your real-life experiences? What made you decide to write a work of fiction as opposed to a nonfiction account or memoir?

My inspiration came from the people of Afghanistan, whose stories and struggles, though the stuff of legend, often stay hidden in dusty villages and timeworn towns. I wanted to share the stories of the bent old woman who was likely starving, but who gave me a handful of chickpeas so that I might know that Afghans were generous; of the tiny girl who pummeled every boy in the village just because she could; and of the shy young woman who dreamed of going to Kabul as a legislator. Their stories are endless, their courage infinite despite Afghanistan's seemingly unending history of tragedy heaped upon tragedy. And ultimately, it is the women I hoped to unveil so that the reader might get an authentic glimpse into the lives and struggles of the women and girls and even the men of Afghanistan.

Although I chose fiction for this story, I have written a memoir—*From Africa to Afghanistan: A Nurse's Story*—and hope someday to publish it as well.

You really transport the reader to the remote climes of Bamiyan, evoking the village atmosphere in rich detail. How much time did you spend in Afghanistan? What did you take away from your time there?

I've been involved in aid work on and off for several years, and long before 9/11 I'd made several aid trips to Afghanistan and its environs. In 2002, I spent six months in Bamiyan providing aid both in the village and beyond. My work has provided me a glimpse into their lives, their everyday struggles and their triumphs and failures. I've gained a profound respect for the citizens of Afghanistan and a deep appreciation for their traditions and family values. Though on the surface they might seem very dissimilar to us, I found that there was more that connected us than separated us.

Many authors find that their characters are extensions of themselves, in one way or another. Do you find that to be true? Do you have a character you identify with most? Are any of the characters in *Lipstick* based on the people you encountered while in Bamiyan?

This story grew from the fascinating legend of the lady rebel. Is she real or a mythic figure? It's hard to say with certainty, but much like the people of Bamiyan, I was captivated by the tale. As for my main characters, they are all based, in some measure, on people I've met on one or another of my missions to Afghanistan and other spots around the world. Once I created the characters, I felt as though they almost wrote their own stories. Parween's courage dictated what she would and wouldn't do, what roads she would choose. Elsa's shyness hindered her until she gained her professional footing—and a firm friend in Parween. Mike was always a soldier—it just took Elsa time to see that.

You write about some truly horrific situations—for example, Mariam's exploitative marriage and eventual rape at the hands of the Taliban, and Meena's abuse at the hands of a village lord. What made you choose to include these topics? Are they based on true events, perhaps even ones you encountered firsthand?

Although not based on actual situations I witnessed, they are drawn from bits and pieces of stories I've heard. Though terribly disturbing, they serve to illustrate the incredible resilience of Afghanistan's women, who rise above adversity again and again. In both Meena's and Mariam's stories, it is the women who band together and defy not just their traditional roles but the potential explosive wrath of their society. These stories screamed to be told—so that women everywhere might understand the heartbreaking decisions that the women of Afghanistan face on a regular basis.

A point of contention in Mike and Elsa's relationship is that they have somewhat opposing views of the place they're in, because their roles and expectations are so different. Is that something you have found to be true in your experience?

Although I've met soldiers in many of the war-torn places I've been, I can't really answer that—expectations are based on perceptions, and with soldiers and aid workers alike the diversity of viewpoints is almost never what I expect.

As an aid worker, do you think Elsa behaves somewhat recklessly while in Afghanistan, especially when agreeing to go with Parween to Sattar? Or do you think it's difficult to judge such a situation until you've actually been there?

By the time Elsa accompanies Parween to Mashaal, she has been in-country for six months. She has already skirted danger by banding with the women to offer refuge to Meena and traveled secretly to Mashaal, both acts fueling her fledgling sense of self-esteem. Despite the confrontation on the clinic road with the surly young group of Taliban, she is confident that she can handle herself. She has grown accustomed to Bamiyan and has been accepted into the village. Elsa's decision to accompany Parween was only reckless in hindsight.

How do you see the story playing out? Do you think Elsa and Mike are meant to be together? Do you see Elsa joining the UN and continuing on in her aid work?

I am not sure how it will play out. Perhaps that is best left for the reader to decide.

Do you have plans to write another novel? Would you return to Elsa and this cast of characters, or focus on something entirely new?

I am working on a second novel. Based in Africa and tentatively titled *The Bracelet,* it is the story of a young aid worker who may have witnessed or perhaps only dreamed that she witnessed a murder in Geneva while en route to her posting in Africa. I would definitely write a sequel to *Lipstick.* I too am curious to see how Elsa and Mike play out!

Who are your writing influences and what are you currently reading?

Almost impossible to pinpoint all the writers who have influenced me, and they are an eclectic group. Early on it was Harper Lee, D. H. Lawrence, and Marge Piercy; and lately it's Ann Patchett, Elizabeth George, and Philippa Gregory—all brilliant writers whose novels make me swoon with reader's delight.

Reading: I just finished *The Help* by Kathryn Stockett and *Those Who Save Us* by Jenna Blum—both were spellbinding stories that absorbed me from the first page. The characters and stories were so beautifully written, I still mull over my favorite passages.

I've just started *A Reliable Wife* by Robert Goolrick.

What advice do you have for readers working on their first novels?

Write what you know, an oft-used phrase but the best advice I've received. If you know your story, you'll write from your heart. Beyond that—persistence, persistence, persistence, and as in everything that matters—hard work.

Does lipstick mean the same thing to you that it does to Elsa?

Oh my, maybe more. I have graduated from lipstick that melted in the heat on my very first aid mission to industrial-strength, all-day lipstick that has taken me through sandstorms, roadblocks, and countless dicey situations. When I am away and find that I cannot wash properly or that my sleeping mat is filled with bedbugs, a swipe of lipstick restores my dignity and soothes my soul. And at home, a tube of lipstick really is magical. It holds more than a waxy bit of color—it holds the promise of a brilliant smile, a brilliant day, both literally and figuratively.